SAFFRON

Titles available in this series

Yannis
Anna
Giovanni
Joseph
Christabelle
Saffron

SAFFRON

Beryl Darby

JACH

ISBN 978-0-9554278-5-5

Printed and bound in Great Britain by
MPG Books Group, Bodmin and King's Lynn

First published in the UK in 2010 by

JACH Publishing
92 Upper North Street, Brighton, East Sussex, England BN1 3FJ

website: www.beryldarbybooks.com

For the 'little girls'
– Lily, Grace, Melissa, and Raiya –
who have given everyone so much pleasure.

Reviews for *Yannis* – the first title in the series

The Daily Mail (National Newspaper)

Yannis makes for a most interesting and enjoyable read.

Evening Argus (Local Newspaper)

Brighton based Beryl Darby is a compulsive writer and *Yannis* is the first of six novels she has written about the same Cretan family. Her saga is built around actual events in the island's history, although the characters are fictitious.

Essentially Worthing (Local Magazine)

A gripping read. You'll get hooked into the atmosphere of this exciting and sometimes harrowing tale, based on actual happenings at the leper colony of Spinalonga near Crete.

C.M.P.C.A (Local Area Magazine)

This is a chilling story, and even more disturbing because it all actually happened. But while everything certainly doesn't end happily ever after, you are not left sad. In fact, after living through the many triumphs and tragedies of these people for 700 odd pages, you are sorry to bid them farewell. Beryl has a comfortable style, an acute ear for dialogue, and total mastery of her subject. *Yannis* works on many levels: it tells a story too long untold, depicts a Greece few of us know at all – with human emotions at their most intense. I promise, once you've been drawn into this close Cretan community you'll be hooked.

Written by D. Shorley FCLIP Sussex University

Uckfield Lending Library (Michael Hollands)

I asked the library to buy *Yannis* and finished it at Easter. I thought it was absolutely wonderful how you got into the minds and situations of the characters and brought it all so vividly to life. There were moments that were really moving.

Ian Rees – Elektros Bookshop, Elounda

A remarkable read, I was unable to put the book down.

Readers' Reviews for Yannis

I started to read *Yannis* at 9.00 p.m. and when I lifted my eyes from it the time was 3.00 a.m.!!

* * *

Thank you so much for such a lovely story. I don't have a lot of time to read, but I couldn't put *Yannis* down.

* * *

Have only this morning closed *Yannis* with regret. There are moments in life when words seem so inadequate to the occasion – and this is another. A massive story – full of the keenest observation of the human condition and the compassion that strings us all together.

* * *

I just had to write to tell you how much I loved your book. It was compulsive reading and beautifully written – I read every single word! I found that whilst I was reading I was also seeing all the characters, places and situations in my mind and I think that is the sign of a great author. You are up there with the best of them and I can't wait to read *Anna* when it is published.

* * *

I just wanted to say how much I enjoyed the novel – if enjoy is the right word to use for such a tragic subject. I didn't realise leprosy was still a problem in this century, particularly the way the lepers were treated so thank you for opening my eyes to this subject. I kept imagining it as a film. It's got all the ingredients. Such a mixture of emotions and human conditions.

* * *

I have just finished reading *Yannis* and really enjoyed it.

* * *

I have read *Yannis* during my holiday and thoroughly enjoyed it. Wonderful! It made me cry.

Readers' Reviews for Anna

I couldn't put *ANNA* down and was trying to finish it with misty eyes when it all comes together at the end – that wonderful mixture of happiness, sadness and completion.
M. Hollands (Uckfield Library)

* * *

I have just finished reading *ANNA* wonderful. The end had me in tears.
S. Beard

* * *

I just had to tell you how much I enjoyed *ANNA*. I just could not put it down.
P. Jones

* * *

The characters are so real that I feel I know them.
D. Mason

* * *

I fell in love with Anna's nephew.
Y. Owens

* * *

I loved *YANNIS*. I thought *ANNA* was even better and I cannot wait to get my hands on *GIOVANNI*.
G.. Newman

* * *

I become so involved in the plot of each book that I await the outcome as anxiously as if the fictitious characters were my own family.
G.. King

* * *

Each time I finish a book by Beryl Darby I am eagerly anticipating the next. Please write many more about this family.
J. Wilson

Readers' Reviews for Giovanni

The plot widens out even more internationally and into the realms of crime. I think it is incredible the way you construct and move the plot forward, handle the dialogue and relationships, the scope and complexities of the places and situations. I put you up there with Maeve Binchy, Jeffrey Archer, and Colleen McCullough.
M. Hollands (Uckfield Library)

* * *

Thank you for giving me so much pleasure with your writing.
R.. Shepherd

* * *

This series of books is the best I have read in thirty years.
C. Taylor

* * *

I absolutely love your books and cannot wait for *JOSEPH*.
S. Wood

* * *

These characters have become a part of our family. We talk about them as if they were real.
G. Hiscox

Readers' Reviews for Joseph

I could not put *JOSEPH* down.
C. Grant

* * *

I cannot tell you how much I enjoyed *JOSEPH*. The characters have become so real to me.
J. Evans

Family Tree

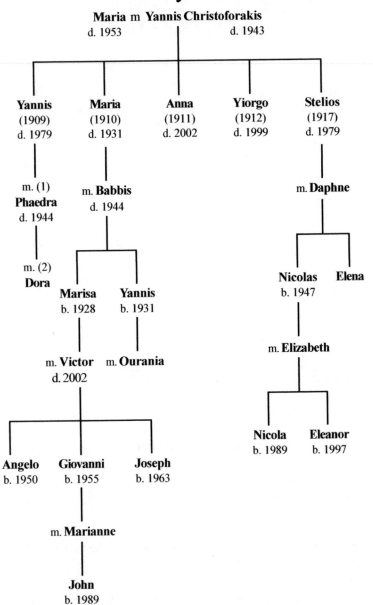

Maria m Yannis Christoforakis
d. 1953   d. 1943

Yannis (1909) d. 1979
Maria (1910) d. 1931
Anna (1911) d. 2002
Yiorgo (1912) d. 1999
Stelios (1917) d. 1979

m. (1) Phaedra d. 1944

m. Babbis d. 1944

m. Daphne

m. (2) Dora

Marisa b. 1928
Yannis b. 1931

Nicolas b. 1947
Elena

m. Victor d. 2002
m. Ourania

m. Elizabeth

Angelo b. 1950
Giovanni b. 1955
Joseph b. 1963

Nicola b. 1989
Eleanor b. 1997

m. Marianne

John b. 1989

Family Tree

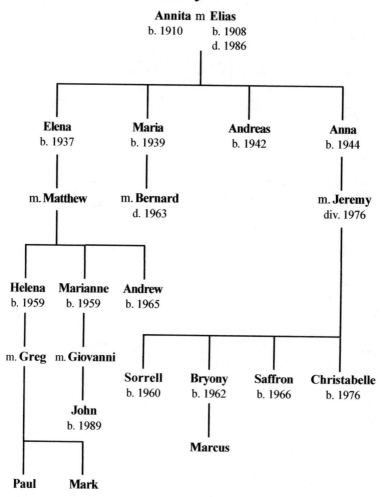

Author's Note

All the characters in this novel are entirely fictitious.
Any resemblance to actual persons, living or dead,
is entirely coincidental.

1976 – 1997

When Jeremy packed his belongings and those of his daughter, Saffron, he had no clear idea of his intentions. He needed to leave and put as much space as possible between himself and his wife. Their relationship had deteriorated over the ten years they had been married and this time he was not prepared to forgive and forget. Anna had gone too far.

On previous occasions when he had accused her of being unfaithful to him she had cried and pleaded for another chance, assuring him it would not happen again, but he was not prepared to pretend to be the father of the child she was carrying. The responsibility he felt for his daughter weighed on him and it was a haggard man who booked them into a motel on the outskirts of the town.

He had explained to Saffron that he could no longer live with her mother for various reasons and in future she would be living solely with him. Saffron had cried, not for her mother, but for her two stepsisters, Bryony in particular. Holding her to him Jeremy assured her that it would not be forever and when she was older she would be able to spend time with them again.

A difficult telephone call to his office had followed and he had agreed to visit the firm to discuss his options. They were more sympathetic than he had dared to hope and offered him a transfer to their London branch. He had accepted gratefully, not sure what the future would hold for him in a strange country, but willing to take the opportunity of building a stable environment where his daughter could grow up. He regretted cutting the ties with Anna's parents, who had always been good to him, but the break from his wife had to be final.

Now he looked around the small flat he had rented and wondered if he should have stayed in America. Everywhere seemed so cramped and dark by comparison and was certainly more expensive. He smiled as Saffron entered the lounge that doubled as his bedroom.

'How's my girl today?'

'I'm okay. Did you sleep all right on that thing?' She pointed to the couch where Jeremy had slept.

'Better than I have for weeks,' he lied. 'Now, plans for today. We need to go round some of the local schools to get you enrolled and see how soon you can start. Once we have done that I think we'll start looking for somewhere better to live. This flat is adequate at the moment, but I don't want you to be embarrassed when you start to bring friends home.'

Saffron shrugged. She knew she would have to go to school, but she did not relish the idea. She was an American and had no idea what would be expected of her. Would the pupils laugh at her accent? Would she be able to make any friends? She thought of her close friend Gina in America and felt tears coming into her eyes.

'I'll go and get dressed.'

Jeremy watched her leave the room and hoped once again that he had done the right thing in uprooting her from all that was familiar in her life.

Jeremy sat at the table in the staff rest room and ate his sandwiches morosely. Financially he could not refuse the offer from his employers. They might even declare him redundant if he did so. If Saffron were older there would be no problem leaving her alone, but she was only twelve. He had felt guilty expecting her to arrive home at least an hour before him each evening, although she had assured him she used the time to complete her homework and an hour alone did not worry her. Now he was being asked to spend two weeks in Ireland to go through the accounts of a firm that seemed to be on the brink of bankruptcy. He could not leave her alone in their flat, but nor did he want to take her with him and leave her in a hotel room all day. There was also her education to consider. She had settled so well at the secondary school, but a two-week absence could be detrimental to any friendships she was making as well as keeping up with the work.

He returned to his desk and frowned at the note he found there. He had sent the file to his secretary the previous day. Why did she need to see him about it? He crumpled the note and threw it into his rubbish bin. He doubted it was important. The ringing of his telephone interrupted his scrutiny of a new file. He answered it automatically.

'Jeremy Bartlett. How can I help you?'

'It's Marjorie, Mr Bartlett. I left a message on your desk asking you to see me about the Coltrane file. Can you spare a few minutes?'

'What's the problem?'

'I really need to see you, Mr Bartlett.'

Jeremy sighed. 'Very well. Come in now.'

Marjorie entered, clutching the file he had returned to her the previous day. She placed it on his desk and opened it at a page she had marked. 'I know I'm not an accountant, but these figures don't make sense, Mr Bartlett.'

Jeremy scowled as he re-calculated the column and checked it against the final balance. Marjorie was right. The figures were incorrect by a considerable amount. He turned to the previous page and looked at the figures he had written there. They were wrong also. He would have to go through the whole file again.

'Leave it with me, Marjorie. I'll go through it again. It was well spotted by you.' He tried to smile at her.

'I was asked to make sure it went into the post tonight.'

15

'I'll give it priority.'

As Marjorie left his office, Jeremy gave a deep sigh. It was already two thirty, to check the whole file would take him at least two hours. The post was always collected ten minutes before Marjorie left at five and there was no way she would be able to have it ready. It was Friday, that would mean it did not go until Monday. Coltrane, one of the firm's largest customers, was depending upon the accounts to present at their shareholders' meeting the following week. He groaned and placed his head in his hands. It was concern over his forthcoming trip to Ireland that was making him lose his concentration.

Marjorie entered without knocking. 'I thought .... What's the matter, Mr Bartlett? Aren't you well?'

Jeremy lifted his head and gave a wan smile. 'I've rather a lot on my mind. I'm never going to have this ready for the post and we promised Coltrane. It's already been delayed by a month due to their accountant taking sick leave.'

'There's a late collection from the main post office. I don't mind staying on a bit and taking it to the post myself.'

'Would you really? It would be one worry off my mind.'

'Just let me know when it's ready.'

Jeremy worked doggedly, checking and re-checking the figures until he was finally happy that they were correct. It was nearly six when he entered the small separate room where Marjorie worked. She looked up at him with a smile.

'I've got a template ready. All I need to do is insert the new figures. If you read them out to me it will be quicker still.'

Jeremy obliged and watched as her fingers sped over the keys. 'You are the most efficient secretary I've ever had. You must claim overtime for this.'

Marjorie shook her head as she stuffed the papers into the envelope. 'You know the firm hates paying overtime, besides, the tax man will only take it away from me.'

'Would you accept a gift from me?'

'Don't be silly. Of course not; just buy me a drink some time.'

'You're on. Let me know when you're free. Now, I must rush. My daughter is on her own until I get home.'

'Is that what's on your mind?'

Jeremy shook his head. 'She's used to being home from school before me. The firm wants to send me to Ireland for a couple of weeks. I can't afford to refuse, but I don't know what to do about her. She's too young to leave alone.'

'Haven't you any relatives who would look after her for a couple of weeks?' Marjorie shrugged herself into her coat and picked up the envelope.

'All her relatives are in America.'

'A neighbour, maybe?'

'I don't know my neighbours. We pass the time of day if we meet, but I don't know any of them well enough to ask them to look after her.'

'A school friend?'

'She has no particular friend. She only started secondary school a short while ago.' Jeremy picked up his jacket and held the door for Marjorie. 'Thanks for the suggestions, anyway.'

Marjorie approached Jeremy hesitantly. 'I don't want you to think that I'm interfering, but I spoke to my mother last night about your daughter. She said she could stay with us for a couple of weeks.'

Jeremy looked at his secretary in disbelief. 'You don't mean it?'

Marjorie nodded. 'If you're both happy with the arrangement, of course. We have a spare room and we're no further from her school than you are. She'd be company for Mum until I get home.'

'She won't have a choice.' Jeremy spoke firmly. 'She's a pretty good kid. She can manage to behave for a fortnight. I'll pay you, of course. She can eat forever; hasn't got to the age of watching her weight yet.'

'I think you ought to bring her over to meet us. Come this

evening and have a meal. That will give us time to get to know her and you can tell us the rules and regulations.'

'There aren't that many; straight home from school, homework done each night before the television goes on, bath and bed by nine thirty at the latest.'

'Sounds easy. What does she like to eat?'

'Just about anything except sprouts.'

'Fine. Shall we say six thirty for seven?'

'We'll be there – and, Marjorie, I can't tell you how grateful I am.'

Saffron looked up from her homework. 'Granny Harris, do you know how to do trigonometry?'

'Trigonometry? What's that?'

'It's something to do with dropping perpendiculars and measuring angles. I don't understand it.'

'Didn't your teacher explain?'

'Yes, but I found it hard to concentrate.' Saffron giggled. 'She kept writing things on the blackboard and when she finished she would stand back and say to us "now watch the board whilst I run through it." Every time she said it we all laughed and she didn't know why.'

Mrs Harris smiled. 'Maybe your dad can help you. We didn't do complicated things like that when I was at school.'

'I really wanted to get this finished before he and Marjorie came home.'

'Haven't you something else you can get on with?'

Saffron shook her head. 'I've done everything else. I did my biology first because I like that best of all. I want to be a doctor.' She closed her exercise books and placed them into her satchel. 'Can we play a game of cards until they come?'

'If you want; you know where they're kept.'

Jeremy opened the car door for Marjorie; then took his seat behind the driving wheel. He gave a deep sigh. 'Could we have a little chat before I take you home?'

'Of course. Is it about Saffron?'

'Partly; it's also about me.'

Marjorie looked at him curiously. 'What's wrong?'

Jeremy took a deep breath. 'Hopefully nothing. I went to the doctor last week. I thought I had a wart under my arm, but the doctor said it was a cyst. He wants me to go in and have it removed and they'll do a biopsy to make sure it's not malignant, besides it itches sometimes and I must look like a monkey scratching away.'

'Oh, Jeremy!' Instinctively Marjorie gripped his hand.

'It's probably nothing. They want me to stay in for a couple of days as I'm having a full anaesthetic and I was wondering if Saffron could stay with you.'

'Of course she can.'

'I don't want her to know. I thought if we said I had to go away for the firm. I don't want to worry her unnecessarily.'

Marjorie nodded. 'That's no problem. Why don't you tell her you'll be away a week? You might feel a bit groggy after the anaesthetic. If you feel fine you can always say you finished more quickly than you thought you would.'

'There's another thing, Marjorie. I know this is asking a lot of you, but I have no one else. Would you be willing to be her legal guardian? If anything did go wrong I'd like to know she was being cared for properly.'

Marjorie frowned. 'Are you telling me the truth, Jeremy? Is it just a cyst they're removing?'

'That's all they've told me, I swear. I've thought about asking you about Saffron before, but this has brought it to a head.'

'What about her mother? Surely she would contest the arrangement?'

Jeremy's lip curled. 'I don't know where her mother is and I doubt if she'd want her anyway. I certainly wouldn't want her returning to America to live with her.'

'If you're quite sure, Jeremy.'

'I am.' Jeremy smiled at her. 'I know you and your mother would be good to her.'

Jeremy sat in the solicitor's office. He felt ignorant and ill at ease, as the man made notes of his request for Marjorie to become Saffron's legal guardian should anything happen to him.

'Is that all, Mr Bartlett? I presume you have made a will?'

'Naturally. I did that as soon as I came to England.'

'And Miss Marjorie Harris is the beneficiary?'

Jeremy frowned. 'No, of course not. My daughter is.'

'Have you really thought this through Mr Bartlett? Should anything happen to you in the immediate future Miss Harris would care for your child.'

Jeremy nodded. 'She's perfectly willing and I know she'd look after her well.'

'I'm sure she would, but have you thought of the cost involved?'

'The cost?'

'You say you have, quite naturally, bequeathed all your assets to your daughter. That would mean that Miss Harris would be responsible for her food and clothing and any other expenses. Is she able to afford to take on such a financial responsibility?'

Jeremy looked bewildered. 'I didn't ask her. I hadn't thought about it. She would get the child benefit, of course.'

Mr Coster sighed. 'Mr Bartlett, may I ask exactly what your assets are?'

'I have my monthly salary; it's paid directly into my bank account. From that I have standing orders set up to cover my rent and utility bills, the outstanding loan on the car, my breakdown cover, life insurance and a sum goes into a trust fund for my daughter. She says she wants to become a doctor. The fund should cover some of the expense of her going to Medical School or University if she changes her mind. Marjorie wouldn't have to worry about that.'

'That doesn't sound as if you have very much left over.'

'I'm never overdrawn,' Jeremy assured him.

'I'm not suggesting that. What I am concerned about is if anything untoward happened to you. An accident, shall we say, on your way home from work next week, what income would Miss Harris have to support your daughter? You say you rent your flat, so you cannot consider that as an asset. You have an outstanding loan on your car so that would fetch very little. I assume your life insurance policy is in favour of your daughter?'

Jeremy nodded.

'I obviously do not wish to meddle in your affairs, Mr Bartlett, but is there any reason why you should not marry this lady? You see, if you did, and then anything happened to you she would be entitled to a widow's pension as well as the child benefit. It could make a tremendous amount of difference to her standard of living, and that of your daughter.'

Jeremy swallowed hard. 'I'd not thought about marrying her – and I'm not sure if she would want to marry me. She's my secretary and we have a good working relationship, we're friends, but nothing more.'

Mr Coster smiled. 'It's entirely up to you, of course. It's just my duty as your solicitor to bring certain things to your attention.'

'Yes, yes, I understand. I'll give it some thought, maybe discuss it with Miss Harris, and see how she feels. I don't know her financial situation. She might have more than enough to bring up Saffron without causing any hardship to either of them.'

'I'll leave it with you, Mr Bartlett. You give it your consideration and get back to me when you're ready.' Mr Coster held out his hand and Jeremy shook it automatically.

Jeremy dialled Marjorie's telephone number slowly. He had spent the last week mulling the problem over in his mind. He was fond of Marjorie as a friend, grateful for her efficiency as his secretary, but did he want to marry her? Even if he did, would she want to

21

marry him? She had never given any indication that she considered him more than a friend. He sighed as the telephone connected and he heard her voice.

'Hello, Marjorie. It's Jeremy. I wondered what you were doing this afternoon.'

Marjorie hesitated. Jeremy never usually telephoned her at the weekends. 'Is everything all right?'

'Yes, fine. I just need to talk to you. Saffron's going ice skating and I thought it could be a good opportunity.'

'Do you want to come over?'

'No, it's a nice day. Why don't we meet at the park gates? We could find a quiet place to sit and chat and go to the tea room afterwards.'

'What time?'

'Whenever it suits you. Saffron won't be home until five.'

Marjorie looked at her watch. 'I'm just about to wash my mother's hair. Give me an hour to get that finished. I can meet you about three.'

'That's fine. I'll see you there.' Jeremy replaced the receiver and took a deep breath. He was not sure how Marjorie would react to his proposal and hoped it would not damage their friendship.

She was already waiting at the park gates when he parked his car in a convenient space. 'That was lucky.' He tried to smile at her, but his face felt frozen. 'It's a beautiful day. I was surprised to find somewhere so easily.'

Marjorie nodded. She could sense there was something on Jeremy's mind and hoped it was not bad news from the doctor about his cyst. 'Where do you want to go?'

'Anywhere we can find a seat to ourselves.'

They walked in silence until Marjorie pointed to a bench beneath a tree. 'Will that do?'

'I guess so. You won't be cold? It's not in the sun.'

'I've got a woolly with me.' Marjorie placed her cardigan on the bench and sat down. 'Tell me what's troubling you, Jeremy.'

'I don't quite know where to start.' He shifted uncomfortably. 'I consider you to be a very good friend, both to Saffron and myself. I don't want what I'm going to say to change that. You can tell me not to be stupid and I won't take offence.'

'I can't tell you anything until you tell me what's on your mind.'

Jeremy took his time lighting a cigarette. 'I saw a solicitor the other day, about you becoming Saffron's legal guardian.'

Marjorie nodded. 'I'm pleased that's all sorted.'

'That's the problem, it isn't really. I told the solicitor what I wanted to do and he asked if you could afford to bring up a child. I don't want to pry into your financial affairs, Marjorie, but had you thought of that? I hadn't.'

Marjorie frowned. 'How do you mean?'

'Well, the way things stand I've got a life insurance policy that Saffron can cash if anything happens to me. I have also set up a trust fund for her, with the idea of her using it to pay for Medical School if she's still set on going when the time comes, but there's nothing else. I haven't any property or more than a few hundred in savings. The solicitor said you would get child benefit for her whilst she's in full time education, but that would only cover her food. There are clothes and things to be considered.'

Marjorie took a cigarette for herself from Jeremy's packet. 'Well, I guess a lot of people manage on a lot less than we would have. I'm working, besides, there's no reason to think that anything is going to happen to you, is there?'

Jeremy shook his head. 'I hope not. It was just that the solicitor said that if I had a car accident then Saffron would become a terrible liability to you. I wouldn't want to put you in a difficult position.'

Marjorie shrugged. 'All the time my mother is alive she has her pension and she gives most of it to me for the running costs of the house and her food. I don't have much in the way of savings. A secretary's job doesn't pay that much, as you know. After Dad died we had to be pretty careful until we had paid off the mortgage, then we needed to have the outside repaired and painted, some work on the roof and other things that we had put off doing.'

'So all you would have to help with Saffron would be the child benefit.'

'I'm sure we'd manage.'

'I wouldn't want to think of you as just managing, which brings me to the other point the solicitor mentioned.' Jeremy ground his cigarette stub out with his heel. 'He said if I married you and anything happened to me you would get a widow's pension.'

Marjorie sat silently, the cigarette burning away in her fingers.

'It was only a suggestion from him. I don't expect you to answer me now. If you said yes, it could be on your terms. It could be in name only if that was what you wanted. Saffron and I could continue to live at the flat and she would come to you after school and stay if I was sent away anywhere just the same as she does now.'

Marjorie sighed deeply. 'I always imagined that if a man proposed to me again it would be in a romantic situation, not a business arrangement sitting on a park bench.'

Jeremy groaned. 'I've made a right mess of this, haven't I? I knew I would.'

Marjorie rose and picked up her cardigan. 'I think we ought to go for that cup of tea, don't you?'

Silently Jeremy followed her, inwardly cursing the solicitor and himself for approaching Marjorie. A few yards from the rotunda that served tea and cakes Marjorie stopped and turned to Jeremy.

'If I said I wanted a proper marriage, living together and – all that, what would you say?'

'I'm very fond of you, Marjorie. I don't think that would be a problem for me.'

Marjorie led the way inside to a table. 'I'll have a cup of tea and a rock cake, please.' Her legs felt wobbly and she wanted to sit down again. Her emotions were in turmoil. She had been engaged when she was twenty-two, but six weeks before the wedding her fiancé had decided he would prefer a single life in Australia. Since then she had avoided friendships that could have led to emotional involvements not wishing to be hurt a second time. As the time passed, she was no longer asked to make up a party for an evening out and her friends married or moved away. Now, twenty years later, she was being offered an opportunity that would probably never come again. Too late for the children she had hoped to have, but not too late for a comforting relationship and a companion in her old age.

Jeremy sat down opposite and stirred his tea. Marjorie lifted her cup and held it out. 'To us,' she said. 'I think both Saffron and my mother would understand a proper marriage rather than a financial arrangement.'

Jeremy looked at his wife of six months sleeping by his side. He did not feel the same impatient passion he had felt for Anna, but he did feel comfortable and satisfied. It was good to have an adult companion once again.

Jeremy smiled to himself. Marjorie thought of ways to please his daughter that would never have occurred to him. She insisted they did things as a family; a picnic in the park, a boat trip up the Thames, a visit to the Tower of London, the museums, or just walking through the fashionable London streets window-shopping. When Saffron reached her fifteenth birthday, Marjorie had said she could have a party. Jeremy remembered the look on Saffron's face as she visualised the girls sitting round a table with ice cream and jelly, playing musical chairs or pass the parcel. Instead, Marjorie had told her she could invite half a dozen girls to go skating and to visit the Wimpy Bar afterwards. Marjorie and Jeremy had escorted them, sitting discreetly at a table a short distance away and producing a small box of chocolates for each girl as a parent came to collect her. To see Saffron hug Marjorie and thank her made Jeremy's heart swell with pride and affection for both of them.

Carefully he slipped out of bed and into the bathroom. He would shower and dress; then bring a cup of tea up for Marjorie to have in bed; a luxury they could only ever enjoy at the weekend. He towelled himself dry and began to apply his deodorant. As he did so, he felt the small lump beneath his arm. He turned and raised his arm to the mirror, then cursed silently. Another cyst. That would mean a two-day stay in hospital again to have it removed and this time he would have to tell Saffron. He frowned. It was strange that he had noticed nothing earlier, but maybe he had just been in a hurry each day.

He returned to the bedroom as Marjorie opened her eyes. 'Stay there,' he smiled. 'It's Sunday. My turn to make the tea.'

Marjorie yawned. 'I do wish we could have two Sundays in a week.'

'Four would be even better. Where shall we go today? Covent Garden or Battersea Fun Fair?'

'Ask Saffron which she would prefer. I really don't mind.'

Jeremy frowned at the doctor. 'I can't possibly go into hospital that quickly. It's only a cyst. My daughter is taking her O levels in a couple of weeks. I don't want her worrying about me whilst she's doing them.'

Doctor Murphy shrugged. 'It's up to you. Personally, I would like to see it removed and biopsied as quickly as possible. Another cyst so soon after the first can sometimes spell trouble.'

'I'm sure waiting another month won't hurt. Saffron's exams are so important to her. She plans to become a doctor.'

'I wish her well. If I can help her in any way do let me know.'

'That's really good of you. I'll tell her. I'll make another appointment on my way out for a month's time and then we can arrange hospitalization.' Jeremy picked up his jacket, feeling a twinge of discomfort in his armpit as he did so. He had probably been stupid to come to the doctor and let him push and prod it around. The cyst had not given him any pain before.

The tears coursed down Marjorie's face as she sat in the specialist's room. 'Are you sure? Quite sure? Could there be a mistake?'

'There's no mistake, Mrs Bartlett. I wish there was. The biopsy revealed a small number of cancerous cells on this occasion. Your husband will have to undergo a course of radiotherapy. There's no reason to think this won't be effective and the end of the matter.'

'Will it cure him?'

'I can't promise that, of course, but it has been caught in the early stages so there is a very good chance that it can be cleared completely.'

'Have you told him?'

'I spoke to him this morning. At first he was adamant that you and his daughter were not to be told. I explained that it was necessary. Unfortunately there are side effects from the treatment and you need to be aware of them and maybe make allowances for irritability or depression on occasions.'

'How long will the treatment last?' Marjorie was trying hard to think clearly.

'I have recommended that it takes place over a period of six months.'

'Will he be well enough to work?'

'Most of the time. There may be an odd day when he feels he cannot make the effort.'

Marjorie took a deep, shuddering breath. 'I'll have to tell Saffron. She's planning to be a doctor so no doubt she knows a good deal more about it than I do.'

The specialist frowned. 'She'll be sensible, I hope. Not try to make any predictions herself on the effects or outcome and tell him anything negative. Every case is different and a positive outlook is very necessary. Radiotherapy can be depressing in itself. You don't want to add to that depression in any way.'

'She is intelligent enough to know that.'

'I'm sure she is, but when the patient is a close member of the family the situation can be more difficult. That is why doctors never treat their own.'

Marjorie scrubbed at her face with a tissue. 'Thank you for telling me. I'll go and wash my face, then call a taxi and take Jeremy home.'

Marjorie's eyes misted over as she gazed with pride as Saffron mounted the platform wearing her cap and gown. How she wished Jeremy could be there to see his daughter. The money Saffron had received from Jeremy's trust fund had not covered the expenses of her years at Medical School, and the life policy had refused their renewal when he declared he had cancer; but Marjorie felt the sacrifices she had made had been worth it. To support Saffron for a further two years whilst she specialized as an Orthopaedic surgeon had meant both of them taking out large loans, but she had no regrets.

After Jeremy had died Marjorie realised just how much she had cared for him. Seven short years of complete happiness. Saffron had been her consolation. Their relationship had become as close as a true mother and daughter. Her hand touched the gold locket that she always wore. 'Thank you, Jeremy,' she whispered to herself.

1998 – 2000

Marjorie looked up in annoyance as the light bulb flickered twice, gave a loud pop, and left her in darkness. She fumbled around in the kitchen drawer for the torch that she kept there, hoping the batteries had not run out since she had last needed to use it. She opened the door to the fuse box and looked to see which switch was down. To her surprise all the switches were in the 'off' position including the main control button. She pushed it back into place and it immediately clicked back to 'off'. Marjorie frowned and tried again with the same result. There must be a fault somewhere that needed the attention of an electrician.

With the light of the torch she ran her finger down the advertisements in the telephone book for electricians, hoping to find one that was close to her address. There was no point in calling one from the other side of London as that would add considerably to the call out fee. She made a note of three numbers in the margin and lifted the telephone, realising as she did so that she would not be able to use it if the power was off. It was connected through the mains.

Finding a sheet of paper she copied the numbers down and placed them in her purse. She would go to her neighbours and ask if she could borrow their telephone. She took her coat from behind the door, checked that she had her keys, and let herself out into the cold, dark evening. She stood outside and looked at the houses of her immediate neighbours. No lights were showing. Maybe it was a general power cut in the whole area, yet the streetlights were on and she could see the traffic lights at the end of the road. Then it dawned on her. It was only five in the afternoon; most of the people who lived along their road would still be at work. There was nothing for it, she would have to wait until Saffron returned from her hospital shift and ask her to use her mobile.

Marjorie scrabbled in the kitchen drawer again until she found the matches and lit two candles that were left over from the previous Christmas. She was no longer dependant upon the torch, but there was not enough light for her to see to read. She was becoming colder by the minute and finally she climbed the stairs slowly and pulled a blanket from her bed, returning cautiously to the lounge. It seemed an eternity before she heard Saffron's key in the door and she immediately called out to her.

'The lights have gone, Saffie. Be careful as you come in.'

Saffron opened the door. 'Have they all gone?'

'Everything. Each time I tried to switch them back on they just blew again.'

'Have you 'phoned for an electrician?'

'I can't. The telephone runs off the mains. It's dead.'

'I'll have to sort you out with a mobile. Suppose I'd been on a late shift? You'd have been sitting here until midnight in the dark.' Saffron threw her coat over a chair and rummaged in her handbag for her telephone.

'I would have gone to the neighbours if that was the case. I went out earlier, then I realised they would probably not be home until about the same time as you. I decided I'd wait. I didn't want to go and knock on a stranger's door.'

'Who do you usually 'phone?'

'I've never needed an electrician before. I found some numbers in the Yellow Pages.' Marjorie handed the sheet of paper to Saffron. 'I doubt if any one is better than the other. I just made a note of the first three that seemed to be local.'

Saffron nodded, squinted at the paper, and began to dial the numbers. She pulled a face. 'That was an answer machine. Their hours are nine 'til five.' She tried again and began to make frantic signals to Marjorie. 'I need a pen. They have an emergency out of hour's number.'

By the time Marjorie had produced a pencil the message had ended and Saffron had to dial again, writing the number alongside the others. She frowned with annoyance as she listened to yet another answer machine asking her to leave her number and assuring her that someone would return her call within the hour. She left her mobile number and said the call was urgent.

'Third time lucky,' she said to Marjorie. 'If I get another machine I reckon we'll look at the directory again and see who else might be available.'

Saffron could hear the telephone ringing in the distance but no one answered and no machine kicked in asking her for a message. She turned off her telephone in disgust. 'So much for people wanting business. Those two can certainly be crossed off the list. I'll get the book and we'll just have to keep trying.'

'Maybe it would be better to leave it until the morning,' suggested Marjorie.

Saffron shook her head. 'We don't want to spend the evening sitting in the dark and it's bad enough getting up early and needing the light on as it is. I don't fancy trying to get washed and dressed by candle light.' She picked up her coat and placed it back on. 'I hadn't realised how cold it was.'

'I can't even make you a cup of tea.'

'That's another problem. Do you want to have a drink of water in the morning rather than your usual coffee? Besides, if the fridge is off all night the milk could have gone sour.' Saffron opened the telephone directory and began to run her finger down the numbers listed, copying those that appeared to be in the locality. She had almost finished when her mobile rang.

'Hello, there. This is Martin. You called me.'

Saffron frowned. 'Martin? I don't think so. You must have a wrong number.'

'You left a message on my answering machine. I'm an electrician.'

'Oh!' Saffron gave a sigh of relief. 'Why didn't you say you were an electrician?'

'Sorry. What's your problem?'

'We don't have any power. No electricity at all.'

'Don't panic. Martin will sort out all your problems in a blink of an eye.'

'I'm not panicking,' snapped Saffron. 'I'd just like to know if you would be willing to come out this evening and fix the problem for us.'

'Of course I will. That's what a man like me is here for. I solve all problems for damsels in distress. Give me your address.'

Saffron rolled her eyes and gave it to him.

'I'll be with you in about, say fifteen minutes. Don't go away.'

'Stupid man!' commented Saffron as she turned off her mobile. She turned to Marjorie. 'He said he'd be here in about fifteen minutes. I hope he knows what he's doing.'

'I'm sure he does. He wouldn't be listed as an electrician otherwise. What shall we do about supper? I had just started preparing a toad in the hole when the electrics failed.'

'We can send out for a takeaway or I can get fish and chips from the corner when he leaves.'

'I hope he won't want cash. I only have a few pounds in my purse. It's pension day tomorrow,' explained Marjorie.

'I'm sure he'll take a cheque. I can guarantee it with my bank card.'

'Maybe we should ask him first?'

'No way! If he refuses a cheque he'll have to come back tomorrow evening for the cash.'

Saffron answered the front door with alacrity as Martin knocked. He greeted her with a broad smile. 'I'm pleased to meet you.

I'm Martin.' He held up a photograph that was around his neck and she gave it a cursory glance. There was no way she could see it clearly in the darkness.

'Please come in. I'll show you where the fuse box is.' She stood aside to allow him access.

Martin followed her into the kitchen and placed a large container of tools on the floor. He removed a high-powered torch and examined the switches whilst Saffron watched him. He pursed his lips and shook his head.

'You've got a bit of a problem here, I think.'

'What do you mean?'

'When were your electrics last checked?'

'I've no idea.'

'That's the problem. All the time the lights work no one thinks about the wiring. It's like everything else. It gets worn out.' He turned the torch round to illuminate Saffron. 'I'll tell you what I'll do. I'll get you some light for tonight, and then I'll come back tomorrow and give it a thorough check. I don't think it will be good news, though.'

'What do you mean?' Saffron lifted her hand to shield her eyes from the beam of the torch.

'I reckon, at first glance, that you'll need a complete re-wire. I could be wrong, but....' He shrugged and shook his head dolefully.

'How much will that be?'

'Difficult to say until I examine the wiring properly. If you want any more sockets it's a good time to have them fitted. It only costs a fraction more.'

Saffron sighed. 'We'll talk about that later. Can you just get us some light for tonight and maybe a bit of heating?'

'You leave it to me. Just one thing, though. If it does trip out again you're not to touch it. I wouldn't want you to get a shock.'

'Is it that dangerous?' Saffron was horrified.

'Just a safety precaution. Electricity is a dangerous thing unless you know what you're doing with it.'

'We won't touch it,' promised Saffron. 'What time will you be back tomorrow?'

'What time would suit you?'

'I'll check with Marjorie. I shall be at work.'

'What kind of work do you do? You're obviously not an electrician.'

'I'm a doctor. If you could start to fix it I'll have a word with Marjorie.' Saffron returned to the lounge and relayed the news to her stepmother.

'I've no idea how much it will be, but it will obviously have to be done. What time would you like him to come back tomorrow?'

Marjorie shrugged. 'Whenever suits him. I shall be pleased if he can get the heating back on. I'm fed up with sitting here wrapped in a blanket like some old lady.'

The centre light came on briefly, only to go off and plunge them back into darkness. Saffron sighed with exasperation. 'I'll tell him.'

Martin greeted her cheerfully. 'I've found the main fault. It's the shower. It's had it. You need a new one. I'm going to isolate it and then everything else should be in working order for twenty four hours.'

'Marjorie said you could come at whatever time it suited you tomorrow.'

As the light came on Saffron saw Martin nod. 'I'll check my diary. See what I've got on tomorrow.'

He replaced his torch into his tool kit and followed Saffron back into the lounge. He pulled his diary from his pocket and studied it carefully. 'I'm on emergency call out until midnight. I don't book jobs for the next morning. It can often be the early hours when I finally get home and I need my beauty sleep. I'm booked for a visit at three. I'm not sure how long that will take. My colleague has just finished a rewire job and I have to check it out for him. I check his work; he checks mine. That way we avoid making any mistakes. He'll issue you with a certificate that

34

will be valid for the next ten years. In the awful event that you had a fire the insurance company wouldn't be able to blame it on faulty wiring. You might even find that it's a requirement on your house insurance policy.' He smiled complacently at Saffron. 'It would probably be best if I said I'd be here between five and five thirty. How would that suit you ladies?'

'Provided the electricity stays on until you get here that's fine by me.'

'Would you like me to bring a new shower with me and fit it?

'Yes,' answered Saffron immediately. 'I can't be without a shower, but we don't need anything fancy.'

Martin grinned. 'I presume you'd like me to give you an estimate for the rest of the work?'

Saffron sighed. 'It will have to be done if it's dangerous.'

Martin snapped his diary shut. 'Believe me, it is. We'll make that a date then. I look forward to seeing you both again tomorrow. Have a good evening.' He picked up his toolbox and Saffron escorted him to the door.

'Thank you for coming out.'

'My pleasure, believe me.'

Martin arrived the following evening just before six. He apologised profusely. 'I'm sorry to be later than I said. I went to check my colleague's work and the woman there wanted to ask about having a new electric fire fitted in her lounge. It's quite amazing the jobs people will come up with just when you think you've finished.'

Marjorie smiled at him. 'Would you like a cup of tea? Saffron should be in shortly and I know she'll want one.'

'That would be great, but I'm happy to wait until she arrives. When I've had a look around we might be able to sit down together and discuss your problems. Are you happy for me to wander over your house and put my little machine on the sockets?'

'You do whatever needs to be done. I'll put the kettle on in about five minutes.'

Martin nodded. 'I'll start upstairs.'

Marjorie listened to him moving from room to room. She hoped he was wrong about the house needing rewiring. She had almost finished paying back the bank loan she had taken out to enable Saffron to finish Medical School and she did not want to take out another one if she could avoid it.

Martin entered the largest of the three bedrooms. On the bedside table was a photograph of a smiling man with his arms around both the women. Martin presumed he was the husband and father. He opened the wardrobe door and closed it again quietly. There appeared to be only female clothing inside. Making a note in his book that there were four sockets, a light over the bed and the main light he left the room and went next door.

The room had been converted into an office with a computer and work desk. On the shelves were medical books and files with an adjustable angle lamp standing at the side. The third room was the same as the first and he assumed it was the younger woman's bedroom. A small television stood on a table in the corner, a novel sat on the bedside table and a bookcase held more books and cassettes. Martin made a note of some of the authors and music titles. Again he made a quick investigation of the wardrobe and was pleased to find only clothing that would belong to a woman.

The bathroom yielded no surprises and there were two sockets on the landing and the central light. Looking up he could see the trap that led to the loft. Whistling cheerfully he made his way back down the stairs just as Saffron opened the front door.

'Perfect timing,' he remarked. 'Your Mum is just about to put the kettle on. Here, let me take that from you.'

He took Saffron's brief case from her hands whilst she removed her coat and followed her into the lounge. 'How was your day?' he asked.

'Pretty routine.' Saffron felt slightly uncomfortable in his presence. He seemed so familiar and at home.

'Mind if I sit down, then when the tea arrives we can have a chat.'

Saffron shrugged. 'You must let me know how much we owe you for the call out last night.'

Martin smiled. 'Let's talk about the job first. Then if you agree we can put everything on one bill.'

'Have you fitted the new shower?'

'I can't do that until I've renewed the cable. It would only blow everything again. I'm afraid you'll have to make do with a bath in the meantime.'

Saffron sighed. 'It's so time consuming, running a bath.'

'Better than the old days, though, when it was a tin bath by the fire once a week.'

'Thankfully I don't remember that.'

'I bet your grandma would.'

'I'm not her grandmother.' Marjorie spoke indignantly from the doorway as she carried in a tray of tea.

Martin sprang to his feet and took it from her. 'I thought you were her sister.' He shook his head. 'I was just saying that her grandmother would remember the old days when you had a bath once a week.'

'Martin says he can't fit the new shower until he has renewed the cable.'

'Oh, well, we'll just have to use the bath for a few days. It will only be a few days, won't it?' Marjorie poured a cup of tea and handed it across to Martin, offering him the sugar.

'I'm sweet enough, thank you.' He sipped appreciatively. 'This is good. I haven't had a cup of tea since mid-day.'

Saffron frowned. 'I hope you've at least had a drink of water. You'll end up dehydrated otherwise.'

'Yes, Doctor.'

'I'm sorry. It was an automatic reaction.'

'I appreciate your concern. I keep a bottle in the van, but it's no substitute for a cuppa. What kind of doctor are you?'

'Orthopaedic surgeon.'

Martin frowned. 'That's to do with bones, isn't it?'

Saffron nodded. 'Do you have an estimate for us?' She really wanted the man to leave so she and Marjorie could have their evening meal.

Martin smiled at her easily. 'Are you sure you want to hear? It's not good news. You need a complete rewire. You have the choice. I can run new cables up the walls and across the ceilings. That's the cheapest option, but they're pretty unsightly and it would be a shame to spoil a nice looking house like this. To do the job properly I need to get into the loft to renew the main lights and have the floorboards up to reach the sockets. With the new shower and the call out fee we're talking in the region of six thousand.'

'Six thousand!' Marjorie gasped.

'Unfortunately electrical work doesn't come cheap. I tell you what I could do for you.' Martin leaned forward and placed his empty cup on the tray. 'If you could put up with me being around in the evenings I could probably knock about a thousand off.'

'What do you mean?'

'When I'm on call I often sit around in the office all evening doing nothing. I could come and work here three evenings a week for a few hours. You'd only be in a bit of a mess a little longer. Have a chat and give me a ring when you've made your decision.'

'How long would it take if you worked in the evenings?'

Martin looked up at the ceiling. 'I'd say about three weeks, maybe four.'

'It would be worth it, Saffron.'

'You'll be the one who's inconvenienced most Marjorie.'

'Saffron? That's a pretty unusual name.'

Saffron ignored him. If the work was going to cost five thousand pounds, her idea of driving lessons and getting a small car would have to be put off for a while longer.

'I think I could manage. It will only be a month at the most. We won't be left without electricity at any time, will we?'

'Only for a few hours on the last day when I make all the connections,' Martin assured her.

'Then let's go for that option, Saffron.'

'Are you sure?'

Marjorie nodded. 'When can you start?'

'Let me just consult my diary.' Martin opened it up and began to flick through the pages, pursing his lips with concentration. 'I'm with Mrs Wilmslow tomorrow, she's a rewire job. I'm on call again on Thursday. I could make a start then and also Friday evening. I might have to go off if someone has an emergency, but they can usually wait for half an hour. I wouldn't abandon you without power. The following week I could do Tuesday, then we'd have to take it from there depending upon the jobs that come in.'

'Will you want any money in advance? What about the new shower?' Saffron did not want to draw any money out of her account until after the end of the month. She was still paying back the rather large loan that she had accumulated whilst she was at Medical School and a generous rent to Marjorie. It left very little for extras and she had been thinking of another loan to enable her to buy a car. Now it looked more likely that she would have a loan to help Marjorie pay the electrician's bill.

'How about five hundred? That would pay for the shower and the new cable I need for it.'

'Five hundred for a shower!' Saffron was horrified.

Martin shook his head at her. 'No, the shower is only a hundred. It's the cable that's so expensive. It's heavy duty. Has to carry a lot of power.'

'What about the other wiring?' Saffron could see the final bill coming to considerably more than five thousand pounds.

'The other cables are not so expensive. They don't have to carry the same load. I shall be able to use the same fuse box, that will save you at least fifty. Most electricians insist that you have a new one, but there's often no need. No point in spending money unnecessarily, I say.'

Saffron nodded miserably. She would have to go to the cash point and draw some money on her way home from work. She would be paying for the privilege of her account being overdrawn again.

Martin left the house feeling very satisfied with life. He had quoted a vastly inflated price for a job that was not necessary and they had accepted it without a qualm. A heavier cable and a new shower was all that was needed to put the electrics back into perfect working order. It could be worth his while to get to know the family considerably better; after all the girl was a surgeon. Surgeons earned good money.

Martin arrived as arranged on Thursday. He placed his ladder beneath the trap to the loft area and asked Marjorie to pass some boards up to him. 'There's no flooring up here,' he explained. 'I shall need to crawl around and I don't want to put my foot through your ceiling.'

'Do you need me to help with anything else?' asked Marjorie.

Martin shook his head. 'No, I shall be fine now. I plan to remove the cable from the shower so I shall have to turn off the electrics for about ten minutes. I'm hoping I shall be able to pull the old cable out through the wall with the new one attached to it. Save a lot of time and mess. When I've done that I can fix up the new shower. Electric off for another few minutes whilst I connect up and the job should be complete. You won't mind if I play some music whilst I work, will you? I find it helps me to concentrate.'

'Go ahead.' Marjorie hoped the music the electrician liked would not be too loud and penetrate the whole house.

Martin removed the skirting board up to the shower exposing a short piece of shower cable. So far so good, it was where he had expected to find it. He removed the shower unit from the wall and joined a new length of cable to the projecting end. Now all he had to do was pull it through the wall cavity. Martin struggled with the cable, cursing under his breath as it refused to move. He guessed the tile cement was holding it firmly in place. Now he would have to remove eight wall tiles and hope they did not crack or break. He went down to the kitchen to find Marjorie. There was just a chance they might have some matching tiles stored somewhere.

Marjorie shook her head. 'Not that I know of. Have you looked up in the loft? That's the only place they would be.'

'There's nothing up there,' Martin assured her. 'Just about the cleanest loft space I've ever been in. I'm rather concerned that if I break a tile I won't be able to match it up.'

Marjorie shrugged. 'We'll just have to take a chance. A few odd tiles are better than no shower.'

Martin returned to the bathroom and placed a chisel behind the first tile. He tapped gently with his hammer, seeing small flakes of tile cement falling onto his dustsheet until the tile cracked in half and fell. He heard the front door open and Saffron call out that she was home. He turned the volume on his cassette player a little higher and began to hum along to the music.

Saffron smiled. That was one of her favourite numbers. It was not often played on the radio. As she hung up her coat, the music changed and she frowned. Had that electrician dared to help himself to her cassettes? She mounted the stairs rapidly and looked in at the bathroom door. Martin greeted her with a broad smile and turned down the volume.

'Did you want to use the bathroom? I can always go downstairs for a few minutes.'

Saffron shook her head. 'I can use the cloakroom. Is that one of my cassettes?'

'Yours? No, of course not. It's mine. These are some of my favourite numbers.'

'Oh!' Saffron relaxed and smiled. 'I'm sorry, I jumped to conclusions. There's no reason why you shouldn't like the same music as I do.'

'Have you got their latest release? I bought it last week.'

Saffron shook her head. 'I haven't had a chance to get into town yet. I plan to get it at the weekend.'

'You can have my copy. I have it with me. I can easily buy another one tomorrow.'

'That's kind of you. Thanks.' Saffron returned to where Marjorie was serving their meal. She felt quite unsettled by Martin and was not at all sure why that should be.

Martin measured the gap left on the wall by the old shower unit. He then checked the measurements on the box of the new one. That was no help; the new shower was slightly larger, but would not cover the line of broken tiles. Not one had come off complete.

He attached the cable to the shower unit and ran a length down the wall where he clipped it loosely into place. Balancing the shower on his knee whilst standing precariously on the steps he coupled up the water inlet pipes and proceeded to fix the brackets to the wall. Finally satisfied that the appliance was safe he tightened all the joints and turned the water back on. He placed a dustsheet underneath and decided he would go down to the kitchen where the women were having their meal and see if a cup of tea was available.

'Have you finished?' asked Sorrell in surprise as he entered.

Martin shook his head. 'I'm just taking five minutes to make sure there aren't any leaks from the pipes. Provided I'm happy I'll run the cable down to the fuse box and reconnect. Would you mind if I put the kettle on? I'm parched.'

'I'll do it.' Marjorie started to rise from her chair.

'You finish your supper. I'm used to looking after myself. Shall I make a pot for all of us?'

Martin busied himself whilst the women finished eating and Saffron cleared the table. He brought over the teapot and sat down at the table with them. 'When we've had a cuppa I'd like you to come up and give me a bit of advice.'

Saffron looked at him warily.

'I'm afraid the tiles broke as I took them off the wall. I want to know if you'll be happy with me patching the area up or if you want to get some new tiles. I don't want to waste my time and your money by doing the job twice.'

'Money!' Saffron remembered. 'I have the five hundred you asked for. Let me give it to you now.' She opened her handbag and took out an envelope. 'I'd like a receipt, please.'

'Naturally.' Martin placed the envelope into his pocket.

'Aren't you going to count it?'

'I trust you. If I didn't I'd have asked for the money up front before I bought the new shower.'

Saffron felt guilty for asking for a receipt. Maybe he would think she did not trust him. 'I'll find a piece of paper.' She rose and went upstairs to the room she used as an office, returning with a blank sheet. 'What shall I put on it?'

'I'll do it.' Martin reached out, took the paper from her hand, and produced a pen from his pocket.

> *£500 cash received from Mrs Bartlett for the*
> *purchase and fitting of a new shower unit,*
> *including original call out fee.*

He signed it Martin Burton and the date before he handed it back to Saffron. 'Satisfied?'

'Thank you.'

Martin finished his tea. 'Well, back to work. If you two ladies would like to come up when you're ready we'll discuss the tiles. Whatever you say I won't be doing that job tonight so there's no rush.'

Martin appeared at the house two evenings each week and worked steadily. Grudgingly Saffron admitted to herself that she missed him when he was not there. He always had an amusing story to tell them and on a number of occasions she had asked him to help her with a small running repair.

'You need a man about the house,' he observed.

Saffron shook her head and smiled. 'I need a handyman on call.'

'Well, you've got my number. You can give me a call anytime. I can turn my hand to most things.'

'Do you mean that?'

'I certainly do. For a lovely young lady like you I'd be willing to do an awful lot.'

Saffron blushed and turned away. Martin caught her arm. 'Don't go. I've wanted to ask you something since I first met you.' He looked at her steadily, a small smile twitching at his lips. 'Would you consider coming out with me? Cinema, concert, dinner – you name it.'

'Maybe.'

Martin grinned at her. 'Let's make that a definite yes and arrange an evening next week.'

Saffron enjoyed her evening. She had met Martin outside the cinema when she had finished work and they had shared a pizza before going in for the film. He had insisted on escorting her home in a taxi.

'I'm not insured to carry passengers in my van. Besides, I wouldn't insult you by expecting you to sit in there amongst all the rubbish and bits of wire,' he explained. 'One day I'll be able to afford a car; then you won't be ashamed to be seen with me.'

'There's nothing wrong with riding in a van,' Saffron assured him. 'Can't you change your insurance policy?'

'For the extra it would cost me it's probably cheaper for me to pay for a taxi.' He grinned at her. 'It won't be every night of the week anyway as I have to work. Still got to get your job finished.'

'How much longer will that be?'

'Shouldn't be more than another three evenings. Why? In a hurry to get rid of me?'

Saffron shook her head. 'No, just working out when I shall need to pay your bill.'

'I'll let you know a couple of days beforehand.' Martin dug in his pocket for the note he had ready for the driver as they drew up outside Saffron's home.

'Would you like to come in for coffee?'

'I'd love to, but I need to get back home. I should manage to get to the tube station before they start the night schedule. I don't want to be stuck there for half an hour on a platform.'

'You shouldn't have come back with me,' Saffron remonstrated.

'I want to see you safely inside before I leave. You read about terrible things happening to women when they were only a few doors from their house.' He leaned over and kissed her cheek. 'Thank you, Saffron. I really enjoyed this evening. I'll see you tomorrow. Off you go now.'

Dutifully Saffron walked up to the front door and unlocked it. Her cheek was tingling from his kiss and she was certain that had he come in for coffee there would have been more passionate kisses between them.

Martin raised his hand and walked back down the road towards the tube station where he had parked his van earlier in the evening. Provided he was careful this could be a very satisfying relationship.

Martin sat at the kitchen table with Marjorie and Saffron. 'You'll be pleased to know that I've finished the wiring. I'll get those new shower tiles in place for you this evening, then I can 'phone Gary and ask him to come in to check my work and sign the certificate.'

'And don't forget your bill,' Saffron reminded him.

'I wish it wasn't necessary,' remarked Martin ruefully. 'I wish I could afford to work for friends for nothing.'

'Business is business,' answered Saffron briskly. 'I don't expect anything for nothing.' She took his hand. 'We're pleased with the work you've done and you made hardly any mess. I'm so pleased you answered our original 'phone call.'

'So am I.' Martin lifted her hand up and kissed it. 'Mustn't linger, much as I'd like to, or that tile cement won't be set by the morning for you to have your shower.' He pushed back his chair, trailed his fingers across Saffron's neck sending shivers down her spine, winked at Marjorie, and returned to the bathroom.

'All set, then, Gary. You go up to the loft as we arranged and check out my work up there. Then you can put your little gadget on the sockets and plugs and sign the certificate.' Martin winked broadly at the man who had accompanied him to the house. 'I'll lift the trap and put the ladder in place. I'm sure there'll be a cup of tea ready for you when you've finished.'

Martin led the way up the stairs. 'Just put it in your tool box when you come down,' he said quietly.

Gary climbed the ladder and Martin waited for him to return. 'That's all fine,' he announced. 'The ladies do appear to have a problem, though.'

'What's that?' Martin frowned.

'Water coming through the roof. Luckily it's well away from any of the wiring, but they ought to get it seen to.'

'Show me. I haven't been up there since I finished the overhead lights.' Martin climbed the ladder and poked his head up through the trap looking where Gary indicated at the small pools of water on the ceiling. Martin shook his head. 'Not good. We'd better break the news to them.'

Saffron frowned. 'What does that mean?'

Martin shrugged. 'Could be a slipped tile, cracked tile or maybe your flashing needs attention. Couldn't say without looking at the roof. Lucky we had that drop of rain the other night or you might not have found out until a ceiling collapsed.'

'Can you go up and have a look?'

Martin shook his head. 'I'm not a roofer and I have no head

for heights. Who's the chap you know, Gary? He might be willing to come out and have a look.'

'I can give him a ring; if that's agreeable to you Mrs Bartlett?'

Marjorie tried to smile. This sounded like yet more money needed. Saffron had finally persuaded her that they should share the cost of the rewire as they both lived there. She wouldn't want to ask her to share the cost of roof repairs as well. 'I suppose we should have it looked at as soon as possible.'

'Only sensible. Won't get better on its own. Catch it whilst it's a small job.' Martin nodded to Gary who dialled a number on his mobile, then looked at his 'phone in consternation.

'I'm not getting a signal in here. I'll have to go outside.'

Saffron and Marjorie sat and waited until Gary returned. 'I've spoken to Sam. He said he could come along tomorrow, about eleven, if that suits you.'

Marjorie nodded. 'I'll make sure I'm in.'

'No need to wait 'specially. He'll only want to put his ladders up outside. If you're not around he can always 'phone you later to tell you what he finds.'

'I'd rather be here.' Marjorie spoke firmly. 'Apart from the leak in the roof are you happy with the job Martin has done? Are you able to issue the certificate?'

'I've never found a problem yet with Martin's work.' Gary opened his toolbox, pushed an empty water bottle to one side, and drew out a pad. He ticked various boxes, inserted Marjorie's name and address, signed it with a flourish, and handed it to her.

Marjorie waited miserably for Saffron to return from the hospital. The news from Sam had been far worse than she had anticipated. He had found a number of cracked tiles and the flashing around the chimneys needed renewing, a down pipe was blocked, the gutters needed to be cleaned out and one of them was cracked. The necessary repairs would be in the region of three and a half thousand pounds and he recommended that it all be completed as soon as possible. One or two heavy downpours during the winter months could see them with a collapsed ceiling and extensive damage inside. If they accepted his estimate he would be able to start the job the following week, weather permitting.

Saffron shrugged when she told her. 'It will have to be. We haven't thought about any outside maintenance since Dad died. Maybe we should get the whole house checked over. If we knew there was going to be a problem we could at least budget for it.'

'Maybe Martin would have a look at things,' suggested Marjorie.

'I'm sure he would. I'll ask him next week.'

Martin sat with Sam and Gary in their local pub. Martin raised his glass to Sam.

'How much do you reckon to make on that one?'

Sam grinned. 'Clean the gutters out and renew the piece that's cracked. I'll stick a tarp over the roof by the chimney and go up and down a few times. They're neither of them likely to come up to check on me. Should make us a thou' each.'

Martin nodded. He knew Sam would pocket more than a thousand for himself; but that was the way they worked. Find a vulnerable household and quote inflated prices for a job that was completely unnecessary. On the rare occasions when they had been challenged by people who had asked another firm for an estimate they had excused themselves by saying they had muddled the address, apologised and sent a new estimate for a more viable amount.

'I'm over at the Spencer's next week. Should be able to con them the same way. Who's for another quick one?' Martin put his hand in his pocket. Life was pretty good at the moment.

Saffron revelled in her relationship with Martin as it developed. He would often send her a text message three or four times during the day to say he was missing her and he became her main topic of conversation with Marjorie. She had always wanted to be married and have a family and it looked as if her wish would be fulfilled with a man that she was head over heels in love with. Although having had a number of boyfriends in the past, she had never felt like this about any one of them.

She forgave him readily when he telephoned to say he would have to break their date as he was late on a job or had been called out for an emergency. He always made up for it by bringing her flowers or chocolates the next time they met. She had been desperately disappointed when he told her he had to go to Manchester for two weeks and would be unable to meet her.

'It's called a refresher course. I have to go up to prove to the electricity board that I know all the latest regulations. Why they have to make it Manchester instead of London I don't know.'

'Won't you be back at the weekend?'

'No, we're expected to stay up there and study.'

'Maybe I could come up?' suggested Saffron.

'That wouldn't be much fun for you. I tell you what, to make up for it, why don't we go away somewhere nice for a weekend? Just the two of us.' He squeezed her arm. 'How about a couple of days down by the sea?'

'What are you suggesting?'

Martin grinned. 'What do you think I'm suggesting? We would probably be able to see the sea from the bedroom window. No need to go out at all if we used room service.'

'What would I tell Marjorie?'

'Tell her the truth. You're just checking me out. Finding out if I come up to your expectations.'

Martin examined his credit cards. He had quite a collection and selected one that was due for renewal within the next six weeks. He rubbed at his signature on the strip until it was virtually erased, then took a piece of glass paper to the numbers. He worked carefully until the first and last two numbers were almost flat. He would try his experiment tomorrow.

Stopping outside the cash point he inserted his card into the machine and punched in his security number. The machine flashed, then denied his request and asked him to try again. He did so and received the same message. Smiling happily he removed the card and replaced it in his wallet. He entered the bank and took his place in the queue.

He handed his card to the cashier. 'I've just tried to withdraw fifty pounds and the machine has refused my card. I know I have plenty of money in the account.'

The cashier ran his card thought her machine and frowned, withdrew it and tried again. She held the card up and examined it carefully.

'I think the problem is the card, sir. You appear to have used it a considerable amount and worn the numbers down. You're due for a new one soon. Do you have any others you can use until the new one arrives?'

'Oh, that's a relief. If it's just a worn card that's no problem.' Martin selected another from his wallet. 'Could you try that one for me, please? I only want fifty pounds, just to get some petrol.'

The different card went through the machine easily and the cashier handed over the money. Martin smiled. That should solve the problem of the hotel bill.

'So where do you fancy for the weekend?' Martin sat with his arm around Saffron's shoulders.

'I really don't mind. Anywhere with you would be enjoyable.'

'I'll make it a surprise then. You be packed and ready on Friday evening and we'll take off. I'll book a dinner at the hotel so don't eat too much during the day. When we've had dinner we can do whatever you fancy.'

'You know what I fancy! I've been fancying you for ages.'

'Not as long as I've wanted you. The first time I set eyes on you I wanted to crush you into my arms.'

Saffron gave a little giggle. 'Is that all?'

Martin shook his head. 'You had to be naked at the time. I can't wait to see you undressed.' He stroked her breasts gently, hearing her quick intake of breath. 'All you've allowed me is a quick fumble in the cinema. I want more than that. Why can't Marjorie be addicted to bingo or something and go out in the evenings?'

'We couldn't, not here. I wouldn't feel right.'

Martin slipped his hand between her legs. 'This feels right, doesn't it?'

'Mmmm.' Saffron closed her eyes and let the delicious feeling wash over her.

'Let's take a chance. I can't wait until the weekend.'

Saffron pushed his hand away. 'Marjorie will be back in any minute. Besides, we want to be able to relax and enjoy ourselves. Have all the time in the world.' She clasped her hands around Martin's neck and pulled his face down to hers, kissing him hard. 'I want you just as much as you want me,' she assured him. 'It will be all the better for waiting.'

Saffron was surprised when Martin drew up in a car to collect her on the Friday evening. 'Borrowed it from a friend 'specially for you. I didn't want to arrive like trippers at the station and have a taxi. Besides, if we find there's nothing to do we can always go for a drive.' He raised his eyebrows speculatively at her.

Saffron placed her hand on his knee and giggled. 'I think we'll find there's plenty to do. I wish you had a car all the time, then maybe you could teach me to drive.'

Martin nodded. That was a good idea. 'Why don't you book some lessons up for yourself? When you've had a few I could probably borrow a mate's car occasionally and take you out in that. We could find somewhere quiet for you to practise your manoeuvres and then somewhere even quieter and we could do a few manoeuvres together.' He grinned. 'How does that sound?'

'A possibility. I'll consider it.'

'After this weekend I guarantee you'll be signing up for those lessons on Monday morning.'

'You have an inflated ego.'

'It's not my ego that's inflated. You wait and see.'

'I wish we'd booked into a local hotel.' Saffron snuggled herself up against him. 'We could be there by now.'

'Next time. I want this weekend to be special.'

Martin looked quite sick. 'Saffron, this is so embarrassing. The hotel can't accept my credit card. They say there's something wrong with it.'

'What do you mean?'

'The machine keeps rejecting it.'

Saffron frowned. 'Have you asked them to phone the twenty four hour number and asked why?'

'It's Sunday.'

'It's also a twenty four hour number so there has to be someone there.'

Martin returned to the reception desk and asked for the number to be dialled. The receptionist handed him the receiver as the call was connected. A look of relief spread over Martin's face. He turned back to Saffron.

'They say the card is worn so it isn't registering properly. They're going to put a new one in the post. For a moment there I thought someone had withdrawn everything from my account.'

Saffron opened her handbag. 'Fine, but that doesn't solve the immediate problem. Here, I'll use my card.' She slipped it into the machine and punched in her numbers, horrified at the amount the weekend in the hotel had cost. She hoped Martin would repay her quickly as the transaction had taken her almost to her credit limit.

'So did you have a good time?' asked Marjorie.

Saffron smiled; a satisfied look on her face. 'Yes, we did, and we were lucky with the weather.'

'You and Martin are a serious item, then?'

'I presume so. We haven't made any long term plans yet.'

'So long as you're happy.' Marjorie liked the young man who had come into their lives so unexpectedly. 'Are you going away next weekend?'

'Martin hasn't mentioned it. I don't think he can take me away again at the moment.' Saffron giggled. 'They refused to take his credit card at the hotel and I had to pay.'

'What!' Marjorie was horrified.

'Oh, it's no problem. Apparently his card is worn and wouldn't register. They said they would put a new one in the post. I don't know what would have happened if I hadn't had mine with me.'

'I'm sure they would have been able to confirm his in some way.'

Saffron shrugged. 'Probably; but we were ready to leave and it seemed easier to use mine than mess around for ages. Martin's going to teach me to drive,' she added.

'I thought he wasn't allowed passengers in his van.'

Saffron shook her head. 'He suggested I signed up for some lessons and when I've had a few he'll borrow a friend's car and take me out.'

'Provided it's all insured and everything,' Marjorie warned.

'Oh, it will be. Martin wouldn't do anything underhand.' Saffron spoke confidently.

2001 – 2003

Ranjit sat across the room from his wife and looked at her with distaste. He had been deceived. When his father had introduced him to her and her sister, she was fourteen years old, not beautiful but reasonably attractive. The arrangement that their father would pay his university tuition fees to enable him to become a surgeon in exchange for marrying his daughter was the deciding factor. He thought he was betrothed to Sanya, slim, with large eyes that were full of fun and with a ready smile.

Upon his return to Hyderabad he sought out Mr Kavira immediately, anxious to fulfil his side of the agreement, only to be told that Sanya was already married. He was to marry Nandita and he was shocked. She was over-weight; any promise of adult beauty had completely disappeared. He should never have agreed to marry her. Somehow he should have found a way to repay the money loaned to him and broken the contract.

His father had been adamant that he could do no such thing. He would never be able to hold his head up again in the community. And what of poor Nandita? She had turned down other offers of marriage on the understanding that she was already betrothed to Ranjit Patel. She would be too old now at twenty-six to be sought after and courted. Ranjit must fulfil his obligations. Finally Ranjit gave in to his father's pressurized persuasion, married Nandita and brought her back to England with him to the house his father-in-law had provided.

The first few months had been tolerable. He had quickly realised that he and Nandita had nothing in common, but he was engrossed in his work and happy to spend his evenings reading. He sent payments to his father-in-law on a regular basis and after a year requested a statement to show the amount that he still owed. He was horrified to find that he was being charged interest and had not even started to repay the initial loan. The knowledge only served to increase his resentment and gave him a determination to work even harder.

Nandita was an embarrassment to him. He did not introduce her to his friends and colleagues and did not talk about her as they did about their partners. She had quickly discovered frozen meals and most evenings he would return home to something unpalatable that had been defrosted and heated through. He had begun to make excuses about consultations after hours and the demands of surgery to arrive home later in the evening having had a lonely meal in the staff cafeteria or a local restaurant. Now he looked over at her, slumped in her chair, eyes glued to the television.

'Have you had a good day?' he asked.

Nandita shrugged, still watching the television. 'Same as usual.'

'Did you go out?'

'Just to the grocer.'

'It was a pleasant day. Why didn't you go for a walk in the park?'

Nandita shrugged again.

'What did you do when you came back?'

'I read.' Nandita pointed to the Bible that was beside her. Having converted to Christianity the only book she ever opened was the Bible. As soon as she finished it, she began to read again from the beginning.

'Why don't you try reading something else?' suggested Ranjit, trying hard to hide his irritation. 'There are plenty of other good books. You could join the library.'

'I like this one.'

Ranjit sighed. The conversation was virtually the same every evening. He really did dislike the woman. Something would have to be done. He could not send her back to Hyderabad; that would be the ultimate disgrace for her and her family, nor could he divorce her and leave her to fend for herself in London. He also knew that if he took either course his father-in-law would demand the outstanding money owed to him immediately and that was impossible. He lit a cigarette, rising from his chair and making his way into the kitchen as he saw the look of disgust on her face.

'That's a disgusting and heathenish habit,' she murmured as always.

Ranjit leant against the doorjamb and looked out into the tiny back garden. He wished he had never wanted to be a surgeon; then he would have stayed in Hyderabad and run the grocery store with his father. He would have married a girl that he wanted to return home to in the evening, eaten well-cooked meals, and been proud to show her off to his peers. The cigarette finished he flicked it onto the garden to join the pile of others that were gradually disintegrating and lit another.

The kitchen floorboards creaked as he walked and he looked around the kitchen. When he first brought Nandita to the house on the outskirts of London he had promised her he would have the kitchen renewed, but when he had discovered how little time she was prepared to spend in there he had discarded the idea. Maybe the ready meals were his fault. If she had a pleasant kitchen she might use it. The first thing would be the repair and renewal of the floorboards. He could at least do that job himself, but he must be careful to protect his hands from damage.

Nandita's eyes were still on the television when he returned. He turned it off and sat down opposite her again.

'I was watching that,' she complained.

'I want to talk to you.'

Nandita looked down at the rug.

'I want to talk to you about the kitchen,' persisted Ranjit. 'I promised you could have a new one and I've never done anything about it. Would you like a new kitchen?'

Nandita shrugged.

'I thought if it was modernised you might enjoy cooking in there.'

'I don't like cooking.'

'I don't like ready made meals.'

Nandita shrugged again. 'I don't mind them.'

Ranjit had a desire to shake her. 'So even if the kitchen was renewed you wouldn't use it?'

'What would I use it for?'

Ranjit reached out and switched the television back on. 'I know you speak English but I sometimes wonder if you comprehend the language.' He rose and made his way back to the kitchen, lighting another cigarette as he went.

Ranjit lay in the double bed, looking at the ceiling and listening to the rhythmic breathing of his wife. He would measure the kitchen and then visit the local store. He would enlist their help in the design and it should be simple for him to remove the old cupboards and replace them. Before starting the work, he would lift the floorboards and see how many of them needed to be renewed. He began to make a mental list of the tools he would need and gradually drifted off to sleep.

The next day he returned home with a variety of tools and various lengths of board. He swallowed the unpalatable meal that Nandita set before him and washed the three-day accumulation of dirty dishes that sat around on the worktop. He would need space if he were to start pulling up floorboards.

He moved the table into the corner and placed the two chairs on top of it. Having drawn on a pair of surgical gloves and covered them with a pair of gardening gloves, he began to lift the floor covering. As he pulled it free it began to crack and then split. In

57

exasperation he tore at it vigorously and tossed the pieces outside into the garden. Now he had exposed the boards he could see where they were sagging and many were riddled with small holes. He placed the chisel into the crack and as he levered it up the edges began to crumble in his hands. As he pulled up the next four he could see they were all in the same condition. Throwing them outside to join the floor covering, he lit a cigarette and considered the problem.

It would make sense to remove the kitchen units and renew the whole floor, but the tools and the boards he had already bought had cost considerably more than he had estimated and when the repairs were complete he would have to buy new floor covering. Despite being a heart surgeon, he was a poor man, thanks to his father-in-law. Their general living expenses and running his car took care of the remainder of his salary each month. His plans for renewing the kitchen were fading rapidly. If Nandita did not care what her kitchen looked like why should he?

He pulled up more boards and was now able to see that there was quite a large cavity between the joists and the earth below. Maybe that was what had caused the little holes in the boards. He would take a piece to the hardware store and ask the man if he knew what it was and if there was a solution.

Nandita entered the kitchen and looked at the gaping hole. 'What are you doing?'

'Trying to repair the floor. I'll ask the man at the shop tomorrow about the holes in the wood and see what he suggests.'

'You can't leave it like that. It's dangerous. I could fall down there and break my neck.'

'I'll move the table over it when I've finished. You won't be able to fall down then.'

'A snake might come up.'

'You don't have snakes in England like we do at home. You'll be quite safe.'

'I don't like it. Why don't you put the boards back now?'

'There's something wrong with them. I shall need to take them all up and buy some more.'

'I don't know why you started something you can't finish.' Nandita sniffed and walked back into the lounge carrying a packet of chocolate biscuits.

Ranjit felt a surge of uncontrollable anger go through his body. Maybe if he left the hole exposed she would fall down it and break her neck. He lit a cigarette and stood at the door trying to calm himself. He saw himself as the grieving widower, accepting the consolation of his colleagues, bravely continuing with his work, putting his patients before his own feelings.

The cigarette burned his fingers and he realised he had been so engrossed in his thoughts that he had not actually put it between his lips. He lit another and turned to study the exposed joists. It was certainly an idea.

'You've got woodworm. Pretty bad, too, by the look of it.'

'What's woodworm?'

'A little fly that burrows its way into wood to lay its eggs. The chances are there's a cupboard in there that's become infested and it's gone into the floorboards. My advice would be to rip the 'ole lot out, joists and all. 'Ave a complete new floor.'

'How much would that cost?'

'I couldn't say. I'm not a builder. It would depend on the size of the room.'

'Is there anything I could do about it myself?'

'Well,' Mr Taylor considered, 'I s'pose you could douse the joists in wood preservative and 'ope that stops the rot, so to speak. You'd still need new floorboards. Anythin' else you 'ave in the room that's made of wood will need to be sprayed with woodworm killer. Even if there are no signs of any 'oles it's a good precaution. You only need one or two of the little blighters an' you'll find that within a year or so the problem is back.'

'And spraying would cure the problem?'

'I can't say for certain. You'd need to check regular like and at the first sign use the spray again, or if it is a cupboard or table chuck it out and get a new one.'

Ranjit nodded. 'I appreciate your help.'

Ranjit examined the cupboard under the sink. He could not see any of the small holes and he doused it liberally with woodworm spray.

'What's that awful smell?' Nandita stood at the doorway, glowering at him.

'I'm making sure there isn't any rot in the cupboards. The man at the hardware shop told me what I needed to do.'

'You're trying to poison me.'

'The smell will soon go away. I've left the back door open. It isn't poisonous anyway, not unless you're a wood worm.'

Nandita slammed the door to the kitchen shut. If the spray were poisonous, he would be very tempted to spray her from head to foot. He turned his attention to the other cupboards, removing the contents and spraying them all in turn. He heard Nandita shut the living room door and mount the stairs to their bedroom. It was past eleven, and he was tired, but also determined to finish spraying everything that evening.

Once in bed he could not sleep. He must now measure the kitchen and see how much more flooring he needed. He would have to buy it on his credit card as his account was already overdrawn at the bank. He sighed and shifted his position as Nandita snored beside him. Irritation towards her rose in him. It was impossible to sleep. He would go back down to the kitchen and have a cigarette. Maybe that would calm him down.

He made his way carefully over the loose boards he had placed on the joists and stood at the open kitchen door. There was at least a foot between the joists and the earth below, which would give enough space for him to climb down and paint the joists with wood preservative. He would do that before he bought the new boards. Provided his caseload was not too heavy over the next few days he could be finished by the weekend. With that comforting thought, he threw his cigarette stub out onto the rubbish and returned to his bed.

Ranjit lowered himself carefully between the joists. It was deeper than he had realised. Assiduously he began to paint the joists, reaching as far as he was able under the units that he had left in situ, screwing his upper body round in the small space to paint the floorboards also. It was exhausting working in the cramped space and the smell was making him feel somewhat lightheaded. Although he had only painted three joists and a couple of floorboards, it would not hurt for him to take a break, besides he needed to think carefully. He stood at the back door and lit a cigarette.

'You'll never get it finished if you stand there smoking.' Nandita had appeared at the kitchen door.

'I'm just having a quick break; then I'll get back to it. You don't realise what it's like trying to work in that small space.'

'I would have thought it big enough for you. You're not exactly a large man.' She slammed the door shut and Ranjit took a deep breath. He must be patient with her, he must not lose his temper.

A further visit to the hardware store saw him purchase three sacks of ready mix cement.

'Are you planning to concrete the floor?' asked Mr Taylor.

Ranjit shook his head. 'I'd need far more than three bags if I was doing that. I can't remove the fitments that are by the walls although I've treated the joists and boards beneath them. I thought it would be sensible to prop them up on timbers and concrete them in at the base.'

Mr Taylor pursed his lips. 'You'd do better to have a proper builder in and have the whole of the floor renewed. You'd be certain then that you'd cured the problem.'

'I can't afford to go to those lengths.'

Ranjit worked hard. He cleared the compacted earth between

two of the joists until he considered the depression deep enough for his purpose. Nandita had commented on the length of time it was taking for him to return the kitchen to rights and asked why he needed to dig such a hole.

'I want to make sure it is completely safe. I plan to lay some concrete down,' Ranjit explained patiently.

'If you're going to dig holes like that under the whole floor it will take you for ever.'

Ranjit shook his head. 'It will not be very much longer now,' he promised.

Ranjit removed all the signs that work had taken place in the kitchen. He cleaned it thoroughly; laid new floor covering and then set about cleaning the rest of the house. Now he must think carefully. In a couple of months he would send a very distressing letter to his father-in-law. He would wait a few months before he placed the house on the market. There was no need to tell his father-in-law about the sale. He would open a second bank account where he would earn interest on the money. He could rent a small flat which would be adequate for his needs. If he found someone he felt was suitable, he might marry again, solely with the object of increasing his finances. He sat in his chair in the lounge and smoked a cigarette in comfort as he made his plans for the future.

Saffron waited for Martin to suggest another weekend away, and also to repay her for the hotel bill she had paid, but he made no mention of either. Twice he had cancelled a date with her, saying he had been called out on an emergency and promised to make up for her disappointment.

'How about a really nice dinner somewhere in a smart restaurant next week? You choose and I'll make the booking.'

Saffron felt mollified but also decided that as he had not repaid her for the hotel he would certainly find he had a large bill for their dinner. She chose an expensive bottle of wine and selected lobster from the menu.

Martin raised his eyebrows. 'I've not had lobster before, but I'll follow your choice. I can't go far wrong.'

'I'm sure you'll like it. Don't have anything too heavy to start with. Pate would probably be best, and something like a fresh fruit salad afterwards.'

Martin nodded. 'If you say so. We'll have to make the most of this evening. I may have to do a bit of overtime.'

Saffron frowned. 'Why?'

'Gary's wife isn't feeling too good. She's expecting. I've offered to do his emergency call out shifts for a couple of months. All you can do for a mate.'

'Maybe we could go away this weekend? If I'm not going to see you for a few weeks I'd at least like a weekend with you.'

'I'll see what I can manage. I'll have to leave my 'phone on and we'll have to be pretty local.'

'That's no problem,' Saffron assured him. 'I wouldn't even mind if we just stayed at your place for a couple of days.'

Martin shook his head. 'That's not possible. I've got a tiny little room with a single bed. The old lady where I live made it quite clear when I took it that visitors were not allowed. The curtains twitch whenever I go in or out. Besides, the walls are like paper. You can hear a pin drop, let alone a condom.'

Saffron blushed. 'You say the most awful things sometimes.'

Martin laughed. 'You're a doctor. You're not supposed to get embarrassed.' He raised his glass. 'How's the driving going?'

Saffron sighed. 'It all seems so easy when I'm out with you. My instructor keeps telling me I'm doing things wrong.'

'Maybe it would be better if you didn't come out with me for a while. You're probably picking up my bad habits. Once you've passed your test you can always have a bit more practice with me before you get your own car. That will give you the confidence to drive on your own.'

'I guess so.'

Martin smiled. 'I love the way you say that. You're so English and then you suddenly sound totally American. Ah, is this the lobster?'

Saffron demonstrated how to remove the lobster from the shell and Martin agreed that it was one of the best meals he had ever had. 'When I'm rich I shall eat lobster at least once a week,' he announced.

'I don't know if I would be able to cook it properly.'

'That's no problem. We can eat out every night.'

'Be careful what you say. I might keep you up to your promise.'

'I think the wine must have gone to my head. Are you ready? Shall I ask for the bill?'

Saffron nodded. 'A quick trip to the cloakroom and I'll be ready.'

Saffron returned and saw Martin looking extremely uncomfortable and worried. The contents of his pockets were strewn about the table and the waiter was standing beside him patiently.

'What's the problem?'

'My wallet. I've lost my wallet. I know I had it earlier because I drew out some money from the cash point and now it's not in my pocket.'

'It's probably out in the car. I'll stay here whilst you go and look.' Saffron sat down. 'Go on. It's sure to be there.'

Martin looked relieved. 'You're probably right. I'll be as quick as I can. Don't go away.'

'I don't think the waiter would let me!' Saffron smiled at the man, hoping to relieve the tension.

Martin returned a few moments later. 'Need the keys,' he explained and picked them up from the table.

Saffron giggled and shook her head. Why didn't men carry handbags? Women did not have things slip out of their pockets at inopportune moments.

Martin was gone for some time before he returned, his face red. 'It's not there, Saffron. I must have dropped it in the street.'

'Oh, no. I doubt if whoever finds it will hand it in. Was there very much in there?'

'A couple of hundred and my credit card.'

'You must put a stop on that immediately.'

'They'll think I'm pretty stupid. I've only just received my new one.'

The waiter cleared his throat, reminding them of his presence and the unpaid bill. Saffron stretched out her hand. 'I'll cover it.' As she handed over her credit card she wished she had been more frugal in her choice that evening.

To Saffron's surprise Martin telephoned her half an hour after he had left her at her door.

'Not too late to 'phone, is it? I just wanted to tell you I had found my wallet. I returned the car to my mate and when I opened the van door there it was on the seat.'

'I'm so relieved for you, but why are you whispering?'

'Don't want to wake Marjorie.'

'You silly man!' Saffron giggled. 'She can't possibly hear you. I'm in bed.'

She heard Martin groan at the other end of the telephone. 'Fancy telling me that when I'm miles away. What are you wearing?'

'Oh, no,' Saffron answered firmly. 'I'm not getting into one of those conversations. You know what you have to do if you want to see what I'm wearing in bed. Goodnight.'

Saffron switched off her mobile 'phone and snuggled down beneath her bedclothes, a happy smile on her face.

'What have you been up to, young man?' Martin looked at the boy with his leg in plaster.

'Slipped off the kerb on the way home from school.'

'Daft thing to do.'

'I didn't do it on purpose.'

Martin ruffled the boy's hair. 'Course you didn't. Does it hurt?'

'Not now. It did until they put me in plaster.'

'How long has it got to stay like that?'

'Six weeks they said. Mum's got the date when I go back to have it off.'

'You'll have to get all your mates to sign it; then you can keep it as a souvenir.'

The boy's face lit up with a grin. 'That's cool. Dominic broke his arm once, but no one in my class has ever broken their leg before.'

Martin and Saffron checked into the elegant hotel. 'Not quite up to the standard we had last time, but the best I could do in this area.'

'It doesn't matter.' Saffron put her arms around him and pulled him close. 'I just like being with you. I'd like to be with you all the time.' She hoped he would take the hint and finally ask her to marry him.

Martin kissed her. 'You'd soon be fed up with me if I was under your feet all the time.' He began to pull down the zip fastener of her dress. 'You'd better help me get my trousers off. There's going to be an explosion any minute.'

Saffron giggled. She knew exactly what he wanted her to do and she would enjoy it as much as he would.

Martin left her packing whilst he went down to reception to check them out and pay the bill. Saffron gave a sigh. The weekend spent together had been idyllic. She knew Martin had put himself out to please her in every way he could as they might not be able to see each other on such a regular basis for a couple of months. She wished Gary's wife was not having a baby, or if she had to have one that she was not ill whilst she was carrying. She felt mean at the thought. The poor woman couldn't help not being well. She and Martin had plenty of time before them. She must not begrudge him doing a favour for his friend.

Martin returned and sat slumped on the side of the bed. 'I'm such a fool, Saffron.'

'What's wrong?'

'My credit card has been refused again. I've forgotten to activate it.'

'Well do so now.'

'I tried. All I got was an answering machine telling me they would be open from six on Monday morning. Have you got yours with you?'

Saffron nodded. She was still waiting to be repaid for the first hotel bill. 'We'll go down together and there won't be a problem.' The problem would arise when her monthly statement came in and she saw how much interest she was being charged for paying back only the minimum amount.

Martin sent her a text regularly, assuring her how much he was missing her and at the end of the week he telephoned to arrange to meet her.

'I'm finishing at four, then I've another evening job. Shall I pick you up from work? I need to talk to you and we could at least go and have a quick drink together.'

'Why don't I meet you somewhere near where you're working? I could have a taxi.'

'No, it's better that I collect you. I don't know anywhere decent in Wandsworth.'

Saffron agreed readily. Secretly she was relieved. To get to Wandsworth would have been at least half an hour in a taxi and she dreaded to think of the fare. She really must ask Martin to pay her back the money for the hotels where they had spent weekends so she could clear her credit card. She did not feel she could ask him to pay for their meal as the expensive food and wine had been her choice.

Martin greeted her rapturously. 'How long is it since I've seen you? Nearly two weeks? It seems more like two months, no two years! Where can we go? I need you desperately.'

Saffron considered. It was risky, but she could lock the door on the inside and the cleaners were not due for another hour. 'Follow me,' she said.

Martin followed her along a maze of corridors until she stopped outside of a small room, opened the door and beckoned him in. She locked the door behind them and virtually fell into his arms. Their mouths locked together as they sank to the floor and removed the minimum amount of clothing.

Martin kissed the tip of her nose. 'That feels better. I haven't been able to sleep thinking about you, wanting you.' He stroked her leg and Saffron shook her head.

'We must go. I took a terrible chance bringing you in here. If we were found I'd probably get the sack.'

'Where are we?'

'One of the doctor's rooms. Come on Martin. Make yourself respectable. We really must go.' Saffron smoothed her hair and unlocked the door. 'Just follow me. Don't speak to anybody. Once we're back in the main area they'll think you're a visitor or patient.'

She led the way back to the main entrance and out to the car park, finally breathing a sigh of relief when they reached the car. What could have made her take such a foolish risk? She must speak to Marjorie and see if she objected to Martin staying over some nights.

Martin placed his arm round her shoulders. 'That was really good. I don't know what I'd do without you.' He squeezed her gently to him. 'Actually there's something I wanted to ask you.'

Saffron held her breath. Was this going to be the moment?

'Would you be able to do me a tremendous favour? I'm waiting on a large payment for my last job. They're dragging their feet and my landlady is after me for two months rent. Would you be able to give me a loan?'

Saffron felt her mouth go dry. 'How much?'

'A thousand would see me through; unless you could manage a bit more. The trouble is, I've got to go away for a couple of weeks, another big job, and they'll send the cheque through to my address. I won't be able to pick it up and bank it.'

'Oh, Martin! Where are you off to this time?'

'I've agreed to do the job in Birmingham that Gary was contracted for.'

'Can't he give you an advance?'

Martin shook his head. 'Gary's over his ears in debt. He's behind with his mortgage and as I'm doing so much of his work at the moment he's not picking up the money.'

Saffron frowned. 'When would you be able to pay me back?'

'As soon as I've finished in Birmingham. That's a promise.'

'How quickly do you need it?'

'Could we go to a cash point now? If I paid my landlady tonight it would keep her happy. I don't want to come back in a couple of weeks and find she's put my meagre possessions out on the street.'

'I guess so,' Saffron sighed.

Lorna straightened up and winced. That was a familiar pain. She picked up the telephone and waited until the spasm passed before dialling the number.

'The baby's on her way. How soon can you get home to look after the children?'

She listened to the answer. 'Try to make it within the next half hour. I don't think this one will hang around.'

Supporting her bulging stomach with her hand she climbed the stairs slowly and picked up the over night case she had ready packed. 'Tommy, come and help Mummy,' she called.

Tommy appeared at the bottom of the stairs. 'What do you want?'

'I'm going to slide this case down the stairs to you and I want you to catch it and put it by the front door for me.'

'Why?'

'Daddy's coming home to look after you and Rosie as I'm going into hospital to collect your new baby sister.'

A broad grin spread across Tommy's face. 'Really? Can we come in with you to collect her?'

'Not today. You'll be able to come in and see her tomorrow.'

'I've got to have my plaster off tomorrow,' Tommy pouted.

'That's no problem.' Lorna took a deep breath as the pain came again. 'Daddy can take you up to have your plaster off and then you can come and see me and baby Emily. I'm going to push the case now, Tommy.'

Saffron returned from her coffee break. She hated Wednesdays. It was her day for working in the fracture clinic. Those patients whose limbs had been released from a plaster cast were X-rayed and then she checked them over and gave any advice that was needed before sending them on their way. She much preferred the days when she was operating or gave consultations to people who had a long-term problem and tried to find a solution to help them.

'I'm ready for my next patient, nurse.' She pulled the top file across her desk and placed it in front of her, a smile on her face to greet the patient.

Her smile froze. Martin entered, a small girl in his arms and a young boy limping by his side. For a moment they looked at each other. Saffron swallowed hard. She must be professional.

'Hello, Tommy, isn't it? Tommy Burton. You've had a broken leg I understand.'

Tommy nodded. 'I fell off the kerb. Dad said it was a stupid thing to do, didn't you, Dad?' He looked at Martin for confirmation and Martin nodded.

'So how does it feel now?' Saffron looked down at the address on the file. It was in one of the best areas near Golders Green. So much for Martin living in a bed-sit and not having any money!

'A bit odd, but it doesn't hurt. I've had the plaster off. I got all my mates to sign it and Dad said I could keep it as a souvenir.

I'm going to show it to Mum in a minute when we go to see our new sister. She's called Emily.'

Saffron examined the X-ray and was satisfied the injury had healed completely. 'That all looks fine to me,' she smiled at him. 'You and your sister go into the side room with the nurse. I just need a quick word with your father.'

Saffron waited until the door had closed behind them. Martin took a step towards her and Saffron backed away. 'Don't touch me. How dare you have an affair with me when you're a married man with children! I don't ever want to see you again.'

'Hey, not so fast, let me explain.'

'There's nothing to explain. I thought you loved me.' Saffron's voice broke.

'I fancied you like crazy. I still do. Remember last time...'

'I don't want to even think about it. You fancied me! That's no excuse for leading me on; taking me away for weekends, letting me think you cared for me. What excuse did you give to your wife? That you were working away that weekend? Where were you when you told me you were in Manchester for two weeks?'

Martin had the grace to bow his head. 'Lorna had booked a holiday in Benidorme. I couldn't let her and the kids down. It doesn't make any difference to us, though. I still fancy you.'

Saffron gave him a scathing look. 'Well I certainly don't fancy you! I just feel sorry for your poor wife. Get out, Martin.'

'Please, Saffron, we can work this out.'

'Get out, Martin,' repeated Saffron and sat back behind her desk. She pulled her next case file towards her. 'I have patients to see.' She raised her voice. 'Nurse, can you bring the children back in, please. I have finished with Mr Burton.' She looked him steadily in the eye as she said the last words.

Without speaking Martin shepherded his children out and Saffron took a deep breath. 'Give me five minutes, nurse. I need to go to the bathroom.'

71

Saffron leant her forehead against the cold glass of the mirror. What a fool she had been to be taken in by the smooth talking, charming young man. She was shaking and she was not sure whether it was from anger or distress. She had loved Martin. She had dreamt that one day they would be married. She had even taken that awful chance of allowing him to make love to her in her own office. Her face became hot again at the thought. She was so ashamed. She heard the outer door to the cloakroom opening and hurriedly turned on a tap and washed her hands. She was a doctor; a professional person. Her personal life must not get in the way of her duty to others.

'Did you have a good day?' asked Marjorie as she entered the lounge.

Saffron threw her bag and coat onto the chair. 'No.'

Marjorie raised her eyebrows. 'What's wrong?'

'Martin.'

'Have you two had a tiff?'

'Not as such. Did you know he was married, Marjorie?'

Marjorie looked both horrified and amazed. 'I had no idea. Oh, Saffie, how awful. How did you find out? Did he tell you?'

'His son had the plaster off his leg today. Martin brought him as his wife is in the maternity wing having just given birth to their third child. Can you believe it! He couldn't even make the excuse that they were separated or just together for the sake of the children. He's – he's scum!'

Marjorie moved and sat on the sofa beside Saffron, placing her arm around her shoulders. 'I don't know what to say. I'm so sorry, Saffie.'

'There's nothing to say. I wish we'd never needed an electrician!'

2004

Saffron gathered the notes she had taken during the lecture. She needed to read the case notes again and check that she had understood everything the heart surgeon had mentioned. If she was convinced he was able to help her patient she must then set up an appointment with him to discuss the implications. Deep in thought, she made her way towards the cafeteria. She had time for a cup of tea before she was due to see her first appointment.

Juggling her handbag, her notes, and the cup, she threaded her way through the other staff towards an empty table. Someone pushed her and the cup flew from her hand. She turned in annoyance to find she was looking at the heart specialist who had so recently been speaking to the gathering of doctors and nurses.

'I do apologise. I moved to avoid someone and just did not see you. Find a seat, there's a spare table over there, and I'll get another cup – tea, wasn't it?'

Saffron looked at the number of people in the queue and sighed. 'I doubt if there will be time. I have an appointment in half an hour.'

'There's plenty of time.' Ranjit Patel raised his hand and attracted the attention of one of the counter staff, made a 'T' with his fingers and indicated two cups. The woman nodded and the surgeon followed Saffron towards the empty table. He slid into the seat opposite and smiled easily at her.

'I'm afraid it is always so crowded after a lecture. They know I will have a dry throat and they usually look out for me to make sure I get served quickly. You obviously know who I am. May I ask who you are?'

Saffron smiled. 'I'm Saffron Bartlett. I'm an orthopaedic surgeon.'

'Well, I'm pleased to meet you, Saffron. If you are in orthopaedics what made you decide to come to a talk about heart surgery?'

'I have a patient who I believe might benefit from your techniques. There's a small boy who needs surgery on his hips. His legs are splayed outwards, he may be able to stand, but walking would be out of the question.'

Ranjit raised his eyebrows. 'I am a heart surgeon,' he reminded her.

'I know. The orthopaedic surgery is fairly straight forward, but the child has a heart condition. I was hoping to make an appointment to discuss the case with you; then I saw you were lecturing and I thought it would be sensible for me to attend. From your talk I could have decided that I would be wasting your time.'

'And will you be?'

Saffron frowned. 'I'm still not sure. I need to read my case notes again.'

Ranjit consulted his watch. 'I am due to operate in an hour. If all goes well I shall be free at five. You could bring your case notes to my office and when I have read them I could give you my opinion.'

Saffron smiled in delight. 'Would you really? I thought I would have to make an appointment, and I'd be lucky if I could see you within a fortnight.'

'I do make exceptions.' Ranjit smiled back at her. He drained his cup and stood up. 'I'll expect you at five. Should I be delayed I'll leave a message for you.'

Saffron rose also. 'Thank you, sir. I really appreciate you making time for me.'

'Please, call me Ranjit. "Sir" is far too formal.' He touched her shoulder. 'Five o'clock in my office.'

Saffron watched as he made his way towards the exit, raising his hand to members of staff as he passed them or exchanging a word. At the door he turned and looked back at her before giving an almost imperceptible nod and disappearing.

She nursed her cup, the tea growing cold. She had expected him to be aloof and informal, but he had appeared so friendly and approachable. All she could do was present the case of the sick child as best she could and hope he would feel the operation was feasible.

Ranjit examined the X-rays and notes Saffron brought to him with care. 'On the evidence it looks as if I could operate successfully on him, but I would need to see him first and make my own examination. I can't promise anything, of course.' He gazed at her intently, his deep brown eyes having a hypnotic quality.

Saffron smiled in delight. 'I'm so relieved. His mother is devastated to think he will never be able to walk or play like other children, but she seems to think his heart condition will get better on its own.'

'Is she simple?' asked Ranjit.

Saffron shook her head. 'I would say she is of average intelligence. The problem is she can see what is wrong with his legs, but she can't see his heart. What she cannot see she cannot comprehend. I'll contact her and set up an appointment with you.' Saffron collected up the papers and slid the X-rays back into the envelope. 'I do appreciate the time you have given me. I mustn't keep you any longer.'

'It was no problem. I have no need to rush home. I often stay on and work late.' Ranjit shook her hand and opened the door of his office. 'Don't hesitate to come to me again if you have a similar problem.'

Ranjit opened his briefcase, took out a small notebook and studied the figures he had entered there. He found the young doctor attractive. He would certainly find out more about her and calculate if she could help his long term plans to come to fruition more quickly. He would be willing to play a part for a couple of years if it were to be to his advantage.

Saffron pulled her coat collar a little higher as she stood at the exposed bus stop and waited for the bus that was invariably late. She wished she had a car, but that was out of the question until she had finished paying back her overdraft and the amount that had accumulated on her credit card. The re-wiring of the house, the roof repairs, and the money that she had given Martin had left her in debt. After they had parted she had insisted she paid to have the bathroom re-tiled, saying she could not face looking at the old tiles that were a slightly different colour.

'Every time I have a shower I'm reminded of Martin,' she had explained to Marjorie.

Now she was struggling to manage on her salary, determined to put aside an amount, however small, each month into her savings account. She had even cancelled her driving lessons. By the time she reckoned she could afford to take some more she would be like a novice.

'Can I give you a lift somewhere?' Ranjit opened the car window to call to her.

Saffron smiled. 'If you could take me into the town I'd be grateful. I have a choice of buses from there.'

'Jump in.' He opened the door and Saffron slid into the shelter and warmth of his car. 'Where do you live?'

'The other side of the town. If you could drop me near the bus terminal that would be wonderful.'

'Nonsense, I'll take you home. I also live on the other side of the town so it must be on my way. Just give me directions as we get nearer.'

He drew away carefully from the bus stop. 'What are your plans for this evening?'

'Oh, nothing much. I expect Marjorie and I will watch some television when we've eaten.'

'Who's Marjorie? Your flat mate?'

'No, my stepmother. We live together.'

Ranjit raised his eyebrows. 'How does that work out?'

'Very well. We're good friends.'

'What about your father?'

'My father died some years ago. What about you?' Saffron was not really interested, but she felt she should show some curiosity.

'I haven't decided yet. I will probably read.'

'Work or pleasure?'

'Pleasure. I no longer take work home with me.'

'I shall be pleased when I can say that. I still have so much to learn it seems.'

'But you can spend time watching television?'

Saffron felt herself blush. 'I owe it to Marjorie to spend some time with her. She's lonely without Dad and she has been so supportive of me. I usually catch up on my reading when I go to bed.'

'You should be going out with your friends, not staying home.'

'I do go out occasionally, to the cinema or the theatre, but you can't do that every night of the week.' Saffron spoke defensively. 'Turn left here; it's quicker than going down to the bus station if you're taking me right home.'

Ranjit swung the wheel of the car. 'I said I would take you home. When do you get your car back?'

'I haven't got a car. I haven't taken my driving test yet.'

'You have no car at all? I thought it must be in the garage when I saw you waiting at the bus stop. You mean you make the journey by bus each day?'

'Left again at the junction. Sometimes I walk to the terminus or home from there when the weather is good.'

'And when the weather is bad you get soaked to the skin or frozen. I will be your chauffer until you have a driving licence and buy a car.'

'You can't do that! I mean, it's very kind of you to offer, but I may not be ready to go until after you, then you'd be hanging around waiting for me. Turn right at the end of the road and I'm just a couple of houses along.'

Ranjit shrugged. 'I can always occupy my time if I have to wait. What time shall I collect you in the morning? Between eight and eight fifteen?' He drew to a halt outside Saffron's house.

'I'm really embarrassed. I would have lied about having a car if I'd thought you were going to offer to take me backwards and forwards.'

'Why should you be embarrassed? I live a short distance further on than you and we work at the same place. It makes sense to have two people in the car rather than one.'

'It's terribly kind of you.'

'Not at all, as I say, it's just a short detour for me. I'll see you tomorrow. Enjoy your evening watching television.' The hypnotic brown eyes held Saffron's gaze, sending a frisson of excitement tingling down her spine.

'Thank you,' she replied stiffly as she opened the door.

'Don't forget, eight to eight fifteen. I'll be here.'

'I'll be ready. Thank you, Ranjit.'

Ranjit watched as Saffron walked to the door of the house. He wondered if her stepmother owned the property or if it was rented . No doubt her father had left her well provided for when he died. She could be very suitable. He lit a cigarette and drove slowly away. He had much to think about.

'Are you frozen?' asked Marjorie as Saffron walked through the door.

'No, I had a lift. I talked to a surgeon about one of my caseload and he offered me a lift home when he saw me at the bus stop.

He lives quite close and he's offered to take me in each morning and bring me home.'

'That's very kind of him. I'll have to start getting the supper ready a bit earlier in future. Do you want a cup of tea whilst you wait?'

Saffron nodded. 'I'll put something comfortable on; then I'd love one.'

The transport arrangement between Ranjit and Saffron worked well, but was not unnoticed by the other staff.

'What's between you and Mr Patel?' asked Lisa.

'He gives me a lift to work, that's all.'

'Does he bring you in every day?' asked Lisa.

Saffron nodded. 'It's made so much difference. I was often soaked when I got home, or when I arrived here for that matter.'

'I thought he was married. Doesn't his wife mind?'

'His wife?' Sorrell felt cold inside. Ranjit Patel had never made any overtures to her, but there was no way she would risk her name being linked with a married man again after the deception she had experienced with Martin.

'Yes. Most women would object to their husband running their life around the working hours of a colleague.'

Saffron frowned. 'He's never mentioned her.'

'Maybe you should ask him. It's not natural for a man not to mention his wife, even if it's to complain about her.' Lisa smiled smugly. 'He's probably not mentioned her because he has designs on you.'

Saffron flushed. 'He's always behaved like a perfect gentleman. I wouldn't go in his car with him otherwise. You said you'd heard a rumour and you know you shouldn't believe half of what you hear.'

Lisa shrugged and turned away. She had hoped for a bit of gossip to relay to her friends.

The conversation niggled at the back of Saffron's mind for the rest of the day. Ranjit rarely spoke about himself, however hard she had tried to draw him out. She realised most of their conversation consisted of him asking her questions which she always answered easily. When she settled herself into the seat beside Ranjit, she decided to broach the subject. She took a deep breath.

'Ranjit, how does your wife feel about you giving me a lift all the time? It must upset her arrangements on occasions.'

Ranjit appeared to be concentrating on the traffic around them and at first Saffron thought he was not going to answer her question. Finally, he gave a hard smile. 'My wife is dead.'

'Oh!' Saffron felt humiliated and embarrassed. If that interfering Lisa had not mentioned a wife she would never have brought the subject up. 'I'm so sorry.'

'It was quite a while ago now.'

Saffron bit her lip. She could not say that she was sorry again!

Ranjit banged his hand on the steering wheel. 'Hospital gossip! Is that why you asked about Nandita? Has someone accused you of going out with a married man?'

Saffron shook her head. 'It wasn't like that. Lisa just asked if your wife minded you giving me a lift every day and I thought I ought to ask.'

'Well now you know the answer.' Ranjit compressed his lips together and continued to drive in silence until he drew up outside her house. 'Do you want a lift tomorrow – or is your reputation too precious to be seen with me?'

Saffron felt her eyes filling with tears. 'I'm sorry if I offended you by asking about your wife. I didn't mean to open old wounds.'

'Do you want a lift?' he asked again.

'Yes, please.' She released her seat belt and opened the car door. 'Goodnight, Ranjit.'

He did not answer and Saffron hurried up the path and let herself in. 'I'll just get changed,' she called to Marjorie and escaped to the privacy of her bedroom. Why should she have been hurt when he accused her of caring about her reputation?

She wished she had never broached the subject. She had obviously offended him. Maybe she should have refused to meet him the following day as usual, but that could have offended him further, suggesting that she did not trust him. She shook her head. She would definitely not mention his wife again.

Ranjit collected her as usual from the bus stop in the morning and they drove to the hospital in silence. Saffron determined that she would tell him that evening that she would no longer accept a lift from him. She felt the atmosphere between them was hostile, and that she was guilty of instigating the situation.

She tried to concentrate on case notes, but found her mind was continually straying to Ranjit. She had never thought that much about the man behind the doctor. Now she assumed he must be very unhappy and hiding it behind a mask of efficiency and courtesy whilst he was working. She was plagued by feelings of guilt mixed with pity. He seemed such a very nice man that it was not fair for life to have treated him so cruelly. She must not assume that every man was as unscrupulous as Martin.

Ranjit opened the car door for her and she slid inside. She felt tongue-tied. How could she tell him she would no longer accept the lifts he offered without offending him further? To her surprise he did not take the usual route to her house, but swung in towards the town and drew into a parking space.

'I need to talk to you, and I thought it would be friendlier if we talked over a cup of tea.'

Saffron did not answer, but followed him to the teashop where he held the door open for her. The woman behind the counter frowned. It was only half an hour before she was due to close. Pasting a smile on her face, she approached and asked what they would like, being relieved when they just asked for a pot of tea.

'Pastries?' she asked and Ranjit shook his head.

As the waitress left Ranjit leaned forward. 'I'm sorry, Saffron. I was rather rude last night.' He had thought long and hard during

81

the evening how to present his position to Saffron. It was an ideal time to elicit her sympathy and move their relationship forward.

'I should not have asked you. It was my fault.'

'Not at all. I would just like to explain to you.' He waited whilst the woman brought two cups of tea to their table and laid the bill down at the same time. Once she had returned behind the counter he continued.

'I had an arranged marriage. I met Nandita only once before we were married. Her father paid all my tuition fees to enable me to become a surgeon. In return, my family arranged for me to marry her. I had to fulfil my side of the bargain. Unfortunately, we were not happy together and she did not like living in England. Nandita returned to Hyderabad to visit her family and there was a cholera outbreak whilst she was there. She did not return to England.' Ranjit sipped at his tea.

'Oh, Ranjit; I am sorry. Sorry that you should have had an unhappy marriage and sorry that she died whilst she was visiting her family.'

'I don't talk about it. If people ask where my wife is, I say she is in India. It is my private life and people do not have to know about that. I never saw the need to tell people at the hospital. It made no difference to any of them. They did not know her.'

Saffron frowned. 'I appreciate you telling me. I can also see that you felt there was no need to tell anyone at the hospital, but maybe they should know. Suppose you met someone else and wanted to get married? Unfounded rumours could cause a problem.'

'There would be no problem because the person I wished to marry would know my situation. They would not listen to idle gossip.' Ranjit's eyes seemed to be giving her a message.

Saffron felt herself flush and bent her head to her cup, hoping Ranjit would not notice. She would put Lisa well and truly in her place when she saw her the next morning.

'Now, are we friends again?'

'Of course.' Saffron smiled.

'That is good, because I have two tickets for a concert tomorrow night and I would like to ask you to come with me.'

Saffron's blush deepened. There was no way she could refuse and she was not sure that she wanted to. 'What kind of concert?' she heard herself asking.

'Don't worry, it is not Indian music. I know that can be somewhat hard on the Western ear. It is the London Philharmonic. It should be very enjoyable.'

Saffron accepted the occasional invitations that Ranjit extended to her and she found she enjoyed being with him. They visited the cinema or theatre together and attended an occasional concert; afterwards they would stroll through the streets or along the Embankment. Ranjit did not attempt to hold her hand or place his arm around her and Saffron felt at ease in his company.

When Saffron realised Ranjit had not visited the tourist attractions in London she suggested various ones that she thought would interest him. He appeared happy to fall in with her plans and together they toured the London museums, churches, parks, Buckingham Palace and the Tower of London.

She persuaded him that a trip on the London Eye on a clear day was an experience he should not miss and after the visit he was forced to agree with her.

Marjorie was relieved that Saffron appeared to be having a social life again after becoming a near recluse when she had discovered Martin was married. One evening Ranjit announced he had booked a table at a restaurant and asked that Marjorie joined them.

'Why do you want Marjorie to come?' asked Saffron curiously. Ranjit had never suggested including her before wherever they had gone.

'I feel that we should meet each other. Do you object? Is there a problem?'

'No, none at all. I'm sure she'll be delighted.'

'That is settled then.'

Marjorie was surprised by the invitation. 'What should I wear? How formal is it?'

'I'll ask Ranjit. I'm sure whatever you wear will be suitable.'

Ranjit told Saffron the name of the restaurant and she was impressed. It was not evening dress, but certainly smart clothes were required. Marjorie searched through her wardrobe. She had one long skirt that she had not worn for a considerable time and she hoped it would still fit her. If she bought a new blouse and visited the hairdresser earlier in the day, she should be presentable.

'You look gorgeous,' Saffron assured her. 'You know, Ranjit thought at first that you were my flat mate. It's a good job I disillusioned him. He'd fall for you looking like that. Mind you, when you see his wonderful eyes you'll probably fall for him.'

'Mmm.' Marjorie hoped she would find the man as attractive as Saffron said. According to Saffron, Ranjit was delightful and she would be bound to like him. Had her stepdaughter romantic feelings for the Indian doctor? After her affair with Martin she had avoided dating for a long time and Marjorie hoped she would not be hurt again. Was there more to this dinner invitation than Saffron realised?

To her relief Marjorie found that her skirt and blouse were eminently suitable and after a glass of wine she relaxed. Ranjit was a charming host and spoke of his childhood in India, bringing the country alive for both of them.

'Have you no desire to return?' asked Marjorie.

Ranjit shook his head. 'I know it is a wonderful country. I love India and at heart I will always be Indian.' He spread his hands. 'I would not fit in now. I have spent too long in the west. The disorganisation and inconveniences that I took no notice of when I lived there would now become an annoyance to me.'

'What about your family? Wouldn't you like to see them again?'

Ranjit shrugged. 'My mother died when I was a small child, and my father a few years ago.' He began to weave a fictitious account of his early life, knowing Saffron would believe him and had no way of proving he was lying. 'I have many cousins, of course, but many have moved away from the country to the towns. Some of them would not remember me after all this time. No,' Ranjit shook his head. 'I have no plans to return to India to live.'

'I'd like to go to America to see if I could find my family! I guess it would be pretty hopeless. I expect they've moved on, even getting married and changing their names would make them difficult to trace.' Saffron sighed.

'Talking of getting married brings me to the reason I asked you both out to dinner.' Ranjit turned to Marjorie. 'May I have permission to court your stepdaughter?'

'My permission?' Marjorie was astonished.

Ranjit nodded. 'I have known Saffron for some months now. I find her delightful and would like our relationship to develop. I am sure she would make me very happy if she eventually agreed to marry me.'

Saffron blushed to the roots of her hair and Marjorie looked bemused.

'Why ask me? Surely it is Saffron you should be asking.'

'It is a courtesy to ask you first. I am an Indian. My background and upbringing has been very different from Saffron's. I would not want to take our relationship any further and then find that you disapprove and cause trouble between you.'

Marjorie shrugged. 'I think Saffron must be left to make up her own mind. All I would want is for her to be happy.'

'Thank you.' Ranjit smiled and turned to Saffron. 'How do you feel? Are you happy to get to know me better?'

Saffron twisted her fingers together. 'I'm happy to do that.

See how things turn out. I'm not prepared to make any commitment at this stage.'

'I would not expect it. After a few months we could both end up realising that it would be a mistake to go any further.' Ranjit took Saffron's hand in his. 'I very much hope we will not find it is a mistake.'

Saffron looked at the plain gold ring on her finger. They had been married a month. When Saffron had declared her intention of continuing to work using the name Bartlett, not Patel, it had caused an acrimonious exchange of words between them. Ranjit had regarded her coldly and accused her of being ashamed of him and his name. Despite all her protestations, he had only spoken to her with an icy politeness for the next two days.

She wondered if she had made a wise decision. She did not feel the uncontrollable passion for him that she had for Martin. He was so different from Martin, so sensible and reliable. He had never suggested they had a weekend away or done more than kiss her lips. She had told him about the affair, thankful that the full extent of her foolishness had never come to light.

'In my culture,' he had explained, 'you wait until you are married to experience the pleasure your wife can give you. I would not dream of cheating on my wife. Even when I was unhappily married I did not look at another woman and lust after her. It is a shame now that I have sold my house. We could have moved in there. My flat is far too small for two people to share.'

Saffron considered her words carefully. 'I wouldn't want to live in the house you shared with Nandita. I would feel she was looking over my shoulder. I don't think I would be comfortable. Maybe we could look for a larger flat or take out a mortgage on a small house?'

Ranjit shook his head. 'I think a mortgage is out of the question. When I sold the house I had to repay my father-in-law. That was only fair. He had bought the house as a wedding gift for Nandita.

I am still repaying him for my tuition fees. I did not know that he would charge an extortionate amount of interest on the money whilst it was outstanding. Why do you think I rent a small flat? I am a poor man, Saffron; despite the fact that people think a surgeon should be rich.'

'I don't mind you being poor, Ranjit.'

Ranjit sighed. 'I should not have asked you to marry me. I should have waited until I could provide for you properly. If I could only clear this debt that is hanging over me.'

Saffron was tempted to offer to help. She bit back the urge. She could not afford to let Ranjit take advantage of her financially. She had only just cleared the overdraft and credit card debts that she had accrued during her affair with Martin.

'I'm sure we'll find something. In the meantime we shall just have to be patient and wait.'

Saffron had confided their problems to Marjorie and was surprised by her tentative suggestion that they should move in with her.

'The house will be yours eventually. I have no one else to leave it to. If it doesn't work out living together then would be the time to think about buying another property. Hopefully you would have a bit of capital behind you then.'

To Saffron's surprise, Ranjit had accepted the idea enthusiastically. 'It would solve our problems. I would still have to repay my outstanding debt in India. It would give us the opportunity to start saving.'

Now she looked around the room she shared with her husband. Marjorie had insisted she gave up her bedroom to the couple and moved into the one Saffron had previously occupied. Saffron had bought a new carpet and new bedroom furniture for them and Ranjit had insisted they had wardrobes built into the alcoves of the chimneybreast before the room was repainted.

'That will save money,' he announced. 'We will not have to buy a wardrobe.'

When Saffron looked at the bill from the carpenter she thought new wardrobes could have been cheaper, and suggested to Ranjit that they did the painting themselves.

'I am a surgeon,' he explained patiently. 'I have to look after my hands. I cannot use them for manual labour.'

'Did you not do any decorating in the house where you lived with Nandita?'

Ranjit shrugged. 'I did very little. Nandita did not like any disruption. After she died I saw no point in bothering. It was just somewhere to sleep until I sold it.'

Saffron hugged him. 'You've had such an unhappy life, Ranjit. I want you to be happy all the time now.'

Ranjit hugged her back. 'If you are happy then I shall be happy too.'

Marjorie was not entirely sure about her feelings for the man Saffron had married. He was always charmingly polite to her and he and Saffron appeared to be happy together but they never seemed to have any money. Saffron paid more housekeeping to her to cover the extra expenses, but when she had mentioned that the house needed to be repainted and asked if they would be able to help with the cost Ranjit had refused.

'Of course we would like to be able to help, but we have no money. I have had to buy the new car. The old one needed so much work on it that it was only suitable for scrap. I'm so sorry, Marjorie.'

She felt slightly annoyed. Despite both of them having excellent jobs he gave the impression that they were struggling financially, yet only a couple of weeks ago Ranjit had bought a new suit, saying he had to keep up appearances at the hospital. She knew he had thirty shirts, all crisp and white, hanging in his wardrobe and at least twelve pairs of shoes. She doubted if Jeremy had ever possessed that many in his lifetime.

When Marjorie questioned the excessive number of shirts he possessed Saffron had smiled complacently at her.

'Ranjit always changes his shirt mid-day. You can't always rely on the laundry to have them back on time and you know how fussy he is. Being such an important surgeon he needs to look clean and smart all the time.'

What Marjorie did not know was that each month Saffron paid any debts Ranjit had accumulated on his credit cards and also paid the monthly instalments on the new car, often having to dip into her savings account. He had explained to her that he needed to send a large sum to India each month as there was still a considerable amount outstanding to Nandita's father. He showed Saffron his earlier bank statements and the amount that he transferred each month to a separate account, which left him with very little to live on.

Ranjit had discouraged Saffron from continuing with her driving lessons. 'There is no need for you to learn to drive. Once you had a licence, you would want a car of your own. We could not afford a second car; besides, it would be stupid for us to drive separate cars to work each day.'

Saffron had not argued. Ranjit was right. They did not need a second car. She pushed her hair back from her eyes. It needed cutting, but Ranjit had told her he would prefer her to keep it long. It was annoying her and she scraped it back into a rubber band.

Ranjit looked at her coldly. 'Take down your hair. It looks a mess like that.'

'It's getting in my eyes. I really should have it cut, Ranjit. My parting is showing. I'll have to make an appointment to have it bleached. Maybe they could re-shape it for me, without cutting the length,' she added.

By way of an answer, Ranjit inserted his finger beneath the band and pulled vigorously, making Saffron cry out in pain. 'I have told you how you are to wear your hair. It should look natural. It should not be bleached.'

With tears in her eyes, Saffron brushed her hair back from her face. He ran his hand across her shoulders. 'I am sorry if I hurt you. I just found it so offensive pulled back into a rubber band.'

Saffron was finding to her cost that if she disagreed with her husband he had an unpredictable temper for which he always immediately apologised for after the incident. She tried to smile.

'No doubt in a month or so it will have grown long enough not to worry me. I would like it to look nice when I meet up with my old friends next week.'

Ranjit frowned. 'I am not sure I agree with this meeting.'

Saffron looked at him in surprise. 'You didn't say anything when Katy 'phoned.'

'I have thought about it since. You have not seen these so-called friends for some years. Why should you bother to see them now?'

'We've all been working in different parts of the country. It's just lucky that four of us will be in London at the same time. It means we can catch up with each other's news.'

Ranjit shook his head. 'I do not want you to go.'

Saffron looked at him in surprise. 'Why not? I'm only meeting three girl friends I was at Medical School with.'

'And what time will this meeting end? How do you propose to get home?'

'I don't know what time we shall break up. We're meeting at seven, so it will probably be about eleven. I'll call a taxi and I can 'phone you when I'm leaving.'

Ranjit shook his head. 'If you insist on going then I shall come to collect you.'

'There's really no need.'

'I shall be there for you at eleven. I will expect you to be ready.'

Saffron pursed her lips. She would have to compromise.

July 2005

John arrived at Diagoras airport in the company of Lester. He had an hour before his flight to Crete, whereas Lester had five hours before he would be called for his flight to Heathrow, but once there he had an immediate connection for a direct flight to New Orleans.

'What are you going to do with yourself?' asked John.

'I'm going to type up a full report and e-mail it to Rory. What about you?'

'The first thing is to get rid of this disgusting stubble. That will probably take me the best part of an hour.'

Lester shook John's hand. 'Thanks for your help. I'll be in touch.'

John looked at his clean chin in the mirror. That felt better and he resembled his old self. He still did not know what his mother's reaction would be to his shaved head, but his hair would grow back and the henna tattoos on his arms were already fading. He bought a local newspaper to pass the time on the flight and tucked it under his arm until he had boarded.

Pleased to have a row of seats to himself he sat back and began to look through the pages. The Greek football team was doing well and he read the report avidly before moving on to other news.

A small paragraph caught his eye.

MURDER SUSPECT DIES IN ACCIDENT

Mr Joseph Konstandides was found dead at the bottom of the hill known as The Street of the Knights in Rhodes Old Town. Mr Konstandides had been confined to a wheelchair for some years due to an earlier accident when he fell over the perimeter wall of the castle into the moat. It was thought that he had tried to negotiate the steep hill and lost control of his wheelchair.

Since his death it has become known that his real name was Joseph Pirenzi and he had been involved in a shooting incident at an Athens hotel some sixteen years previously. The owner of the night club and his manager had both been shot and injured. The hotel receptionist was killed. Mr Pirenzi stood trial for the murder, but was acquitted due to lack of evidence against him.

John sucked in his breath. Pirenzi was his surname. He knew his father had a brother called Joseph about whom he would never talk. Could the man in the wheelchair have been his uncle? John shuddered. He had felt guilty that he had been unable to stop Christabelle pushing the crippled man down the hill, but this made the whole situation very much worse. Had his mother's cousin killed his father's brother. He closed his eyes and sat back in his seat. He would have to think about this.

Once able to switch on his mobile 'phone John called his father and asked if he would be able to collect him from Heraklion Airport, warning him that he had shaved his head. He had decided that he would say he was unable to tell them anything about the events in Rhodes due to legal restrictions. They would be curious, but they would accept that, at least as a temporary stall.

Giovanni hugged his son to him. 'Your mother is relieved to know you're home.' Giovanni did not mention his own relief at having him safely back. 'We're longing to hear all about your trip.'

John nodded. 'I'm pretty tired, actually. I seem to have spent the last week walking around on cobbled streets. How's Nick? Has she heard how Eleanor is getting on?'

'She spoke to her mother earlier today. I gather the news is good.'

John looked at the familiar surroundings as they drove towards his home. Finally he decided he must ask his father about the newspaper report.

'Dad, could we stop somewhere for a quick drink? I want to ask you something.'

Giovanni frowned. 'Won't it wait? We're nearly home.'

John shook his head. 'I'd like to do it now, whilst we're alone.'

Giovanni shot his son a wary glance. What had he been up to in Rhodes with Lester? Had he been duped into believing he was a private investigator? Had Marianne been correct in thinking the man was a paedophile? He drew into a parking space in Malia and looked along the road. There were a number of tavernas catering for the tourists, but none of them appeared particularly busy at this time of the afternoon.

They sat outside and having ordered John pulled the newspaper out of his rucksack and opened it to the page where the report of Joseph Pirenzi's death was featured. He pushed it across to his father.

'Was he a relative, Dad? Was he your brother?' asked John.

Giovanni shrugged. 'It's a very long story. Let's just say he was no good.'

John frowned. 'That was Uncle Yannis's hotel. Did Uncle Yannis sell it because of the murder?'

'It was a long time ago. Best forgotten now.'

'I'd like to know more about him,' persisted John.

Giovanni shook his head. 'Believe me when I say he was not a relative to be proud of. I don't ever want to hear you mention his name again.' Giovanni tore the item out of the paper and crumpled it in his hand. 'There's no need for your mother to know about this and under no circumstances do you tell your grandmother. It would only upset both of them.'

John watched as his father walked back to where he had parked his car. That decided him. He could certainly not tell his family what had taken place in Rhodes. He swallowed the remainder of his drink and followed his father.

Giovanni drove in silence. He felt guilty for not having tried to contact Joseph and inform him of their father's death. Would he have cared anyway? There had never been any love lost between them. He wondered vaguely what had become of Sorrell; no doubt she was continuing to dupe people into providing her with a living.

'So what did you do whilst you were in Rhodes?' asked Nicola. 'I'm longing to hear all about it.'

John shook his head. 'I can't tell you any details. Lester said I must keep it to myself. Something to do with discussing a case before it has been brought to trial. Most of the time we just wandered around the Old Town and I filmed whatever he said.'

Nicola looked at him in surprise. 'Is that all? It sounds pretty boring.'

'It was. I'd have liked to wander around on my own and see the Old Town properly. Most of the time we were in the tourist shopping area or down at the harbour. We did manage a visit to the Grand Master's Palace, but that was about all. I wanted to walk around the walls and the moat but I didn't have the opportunity.'

'Did you take any photographs of your own?'

John shook his head. 'No, I couldn't. You know how long it can take me to set up a specimen. Besides, the wild life over there is the same as here. I tried to persuade Lester to take me back to the States with him. I'm sure I would have found different species to photograph over there. Do you think I could come over and stay with you next year, Nick? I really do want to go to America.' John was desperate to turn the conversation away from his visit to Rhodes.

'I don't see why you shouldn't. After all, I've stayed here all summer.'

'How is Eleanor? Dad said you spoke to your Mum earlier.'

Nicola spoke enthusiastically. 'She's doing really well apparently. Mum said if she continues to recover at this rate she'll be able to return to school in the fall.'

'That's really good news. You'll stay here until you have to go back to High School, won't you?'

'If your Mum can put up with me that long.'

Marianne smiled. 'You're no trouble, Nicola. You've been a tremendous help to me this season.'

'How about a swim?' suggested John. 'I haven't had one for a week.'

Nicola looked at Marianne. 'Do you need me any more this afternoon?'

Marianne shook her head. 'No, you two go off and enjoy yourselves.' Marianne watched them as they disappeared to their bedrooms to change. She was so relieved her son was safely home, despite the shaven head and the horrible tattoos that he was sporting on his arms.

John and Nicola lay side by side on the beach. John stretched out his arm and placed it around her shoulders.

'I've really missed you, Nick. Did you miss me?'

'Mmm. It wasn't much fun lying down here on my own.'

John held her a little more tightly. 'I mean I *really* missed you. I realised we're wasting our holiday together.'

Nicola turned her face towards him. 'What do you mean?'

'We're not children any more.' John could feel himself blushing. 'I went to a chemist whilst I was on Rhodes.'

'A chemist?'

'Yes, you know, for some protection. I've been thinking about getting some for a while now, but I knew if I bought them locally someone would tell Mum or Dad. Will you, Nick?'

'Will I what?' Nicola looked at John mischievously.

John blush deepened. 'You know. Let me,' he bent closer and whispered in her ear.

'That's a horrid word to use, John!' Nicola pulled herself away from him. 'I'm going for another swim. You've made me all hot and sticky with your arm round me.'

John watched her walk the few steps into the water and strike out strongly. He had really made a mess of that!

Nicola returned ten minutes later and dropped down beside him. 'Where would we go?' she asked.

John swallowed hard. Maybe he hadn't made such a mess of his proposal to her. 'I thought I'd come along to your room tonight.'

'What! In your parent's house? Suppose they found out?'

John shrugged. 'They'll have to realise that we're adults at some time. Dad was no angel, that I do know. I was over a year old when they were married. He'd understand, besides your room is at the end and there's the spare room that used to be Uncle Yiorgo's next to you. No one will hear us. Leave your patio window open and I'll creep along when everyone has gone to bed.'

Nicola considered the idea. During the day they were often in and out of each other's rooms and no one thought anything of it.

'Don't be too late or I'll be asleep,' she warned him.

Alecos grinned maliciously at Sorrell. 'I've come for the rent.'

'The rent?'

'Joseph may have let you live here rent free, but I can't afford to. I have a business to run.'

'I haven't any rent. I've not been working this week. I'll try to make it up next week.' Sorrell had been surprised how affected she had been by Joseph's death. She still felt numb.

Alecos shook his head. 'I need it now. Lakkis is due to be released from prison in two weeks time and I need the accounts up to date.'

Sorrell paled at the mention of the man's name. 'Are you sure?'

'Quite sure. Now, the rent.'

'I haven't got it, Alecos, honestly.'

'You had money yesterday when you came to *The Grapevine* and bought some stuff.'

'That was all I had and I needed a shot.'

'So where are you going to get the next one if you haven't got enough money to pay the rent or for your next shot?'

Sorrell shook her head miserably. 'I don't know.'

'You must have something.' Alecos's eyes swivelled around the small dwelling.

'If I managed to find something to sell would you give me a fair price?'

'That would depend what it was,' sneered Alecos. 'I'd want enough to cover the rent and a commission for buying whatever it was.'

'I'll see what I can do. I'll come down to *The Grapevine* this evening if I can find anything worth your while.'

Alecos placed a hand on her shoulder. 'I don't suggest you try to run out on me.' His grip strengthened. 'I'd only have to put the word out and you'd be found. Lakkis might even reward me for my efforts.'

Sorrell's face whitened even more and she began to tremble. 'I won't run out on you. I just need a bit of time. I'll be there this evening.'

Alecos released her and nodded grimly. 'With the money or something I would be willing to take in exchange.'

'Yes, Alecos. I promise.'

Sorrell removed one of the uncut diamonds from the screw of paper. She replaced the others into the heel of her shoes and rewrapped them carefully before returning them to their box. She hoped Alecos would give her enough money for her to be able to take a ferry to Athens. Once in the city she was sure she would find somewhere she could sell the other stones.

She looked around the mean house she had shared for so long with Joseph. She felt a tinge of apprehension. She had always known that she could rely upon Joseph to fund her habit and find her customers to bring in the rent money. Now she was on her own. Shrugging the feeling aside she took a case from under her bed. Once it had held her glamorous and expensive wardrobe. Now she had very little to put in it. She pushed it back to gather more dust. It would be more practical to take the bag she used for the laundry and would not attract the attention of anyone who happened to see her.

On her way to *The Grapevine* she would find out the time of the first ferry to Piraeus the following morning.

'Come on, Bartlett, stir yourself. The doctor's here to see you.'

Christabelle looked at the woman venomously. That was no way to address her; she was called Miss Christabelle. 'I haven't finished doing my hair.'

'Finished or not, you're to come now. You don't keep the doctor waiting.'

'I have no need to see a doctor. I am not ill.'

'He's a head doctor, a psychiatrist, and you have to see him. Come on, move.'

Sulkily Christabelle rose to her feet. For two days she had been confined to the small room, allowed out to shower and exercise, always accompanied by a warden. She had protested against her treatment to no avail, being told that the alternative to being held in the hospital wing was to be in jail sharing a cell with common criminals. Christabelle had shuddered. At least she had the room to herself.

She smoothed her skirt over her hips. She was grateful that she had her own clothes and had not been forced to wear hideous orange overalls. Another warden waited outside her room and she walked between them along the corridor until they halted before a locked door. Taking a large bunch of keys from her belt the warden unlocked the door and pushed Christabelle unceremoniously through before locking it behind them.

'Wait there.'

Christabelle looked around. She had not been to this part of the building before. There were a number of small rooms leading off a central area, they all had a long glass panel in the door, and she could see most of them were occupied with a warden standing outside.

One of the wardens accompanying her knocked on a door, opened it, and held a brief conversation with the occupant. The warden opened the door wider. 'In there,' she directed Christabelle. The door closed behind her and the warden took up her position outside.

Not knowing what was expected of her Christabelle stood just inside the doorway. The man looked up from his notes and smiled at her.

'Please take a seat, Miss Bartlett.'

'I'm known as Miss Christabelle,' she corrected him.

The doctor made no comment. 'I have to advise you that the interviews that are held between us will be recorded. Do you have any objection?'

'And if I do object?'

'I would not be able to proceed any further. You don't have to talk to me, of course, but if you refuse I will have to report your un-co-operation. That would mean you would be removed from this wing and sent back to the prison area.' Doctor Ferguson switched on the tape recorder. 'Please repeat after me – I give permission for my interviews with Doctor Ferguson to be recorded.'

Christabelle considered. She could always terminate the interviews, but it could be to her advantage to comply with the Doctor's request. No doubt she would be able to charm him and he would realise that she was totally innocent of the accusations that had been levelled at her. There was no way she wanted to be sent to a prison cell.

Doctor Ferguson sat with his head in his hands after Christabelle had left. She was quite unbelievable. She appeared to have no concern for anyone but herself and no conception of the enormity of her actions. He sighed. He would have to speak to the Prosecutor General and ask him to appoint lawyers and attorneys to present her defence on medical grounds. There was no way he could recommend she should stand trial for her crimes.

Once she had a lawyer assigned to her, he would have to see her one final time and explain the position to her. He hoped Janet Green might be available and willing to take on the case. He had worked with her before, and found her sympathetic and understanding of his work. If Janet was willing to enter a plea of insanity due to Narcissistic Personality Disorder it was likely that Christabelle would be detained under the Mental Health Act rather than sitting in a prison cell with the death penalty hanging over her.

For a week, Christabelle fretted, continually asking the wardens when she would be released and was relieved when she was told Doctor Ferguson wanted to see her again. She was surprised when she entered his room to find an elderly grey haired woman sitting there. Doctor Ferguson introduced them and explained that Janet would be representing Christabelle in a legal capacity.

'What do you mean? Representing me legally? I am planning to sue the police department for wrongful arrest. I will choose my own lawyer, not one who is already biased by being in your employ.' Christabelle's eyes flashed dangerously.

Doctor Ferguson sat back. 'Let me explain the position to you. You are going to be charged with the first degree murder of your mother and possibly Mr Brajowski.' Doctor Ferguson held up his hand as Christabelle was about to interrupt him. 'If the jury should acquit you, which I think most unlikely, you will then have to face the charges to be brought against you in Italy for causing the death of Mr Verri.'

Christabelle paled. 'You can't do this to me. I'm Christabelle. No one will believe you. They have no proof.'

Doctor Ferguson continued as if she had not spoken. 'Again should you be acquitted, you will be sent to Greece to stand trial for the deliberate murder of Mr Pirenzi. There is irrefutable proof that you caused his death.'

'Was that the man in the wheelchair? He was a pimp. He hit me. He's better off out of the way. Everyone must realise that.'

'As I see it, you have only one option. Mrs Green will put forward a plea of insanity on your behalf.'

'Insanity? How dare you! I'm not insane. I'll sue you for defamation of character. These are trumped up charges. You tricked me into talking to you. You said if I told you about various events you would arrange for my release.'

Doctor Ferguson shook his head slowly. 'I said no such thing, Miss Bartlett. I said I would help you to solve your problems. I have diagnosed your problem as suffering from Narcissistic Personality Disorder. That is a form of insanity and you will need some years of psychotherapy. I can only recommend that you accept Mrs Green as your lawyer and allow her to put forward the plea. Provided it is accepted you will be detained under the mental health act. It will enable you to avoid a prison sentence or worse.'

Christabelle ignored the doctor's words. 'I need to contact my agents. Once they know I am back in New Orleans they will have contracts waiting for me to sign. I cannot hang around here any longer.' She leaned towards him. 'I have money, plenty of money. How much do you want to drop these ridiculous charges and allow me to leave?'

'I am sorry. There is no way I can recommend your release at present.' Doctor Ferguson spoke firmly.

Christabelle glared at him. 'You will regret that decision. I don't take kindly to people who try to stand in my way. Once the newspapers hear about my wrongful arrest I will make sure you are ruined. You will never be able to call yourself a doctor again. I will tell them you tricked me into making false statements. They will believe me. I am a household name, I am Miss Christabelle.'

Doctor Ferguson looked at Janet Green in despair as Christabelle left the room. He shrugged. 'I fear she has a hopeless condition. She appears to think that being a famous model makes her above the law. I'm still not sure that she even understands the seriousness of the crimes she has committed. You should have no problem convincing the prosecutor that she needs medical treatment.' He rubbed a hand over his forehead.

Janet Green nodded her agreement. 'I do think she will need continual monitoring and further assessment. I get the impression that she is putting on an act to avoid standing trial. I think she understands exactly what she has done and knows she would be given the death penalty.'

'You could be right, Janet. I must admit I find her a most disconcerting young woman. So beautiful, yet so obviously evil.'

Janet eyed the doctor keenly. 'Can I give you a bit of advice? Don't ever be alone with her.'

Doctor Ferguson nodded. 'I'll take that advice on board. Now I suppose I'll have to compose a statement for the press. They've been clamouring for days for a news release.'

August 2005

Bryony looked across the small garden towards the sea. 'I absolutely love this house, Marcus. Could we go into town at the weekend and buy the furniture we want for the roof patio?'

Marcus smiled at her indulgently. 'If you want to.'

'It will be the final touch.'

'I certainly hope so. We've spent far more than we originally intended.'

'Oh, but it's worth it. I know we have loans to repay and we can't afford to go over to Crete again for a while, but I don't mind. This house is worth everything.'

'This house is everything! All our money is tied up in this property forever more.'

Bryony hugged her husband. 'That doesn't matter. What else would we do with it? We can live here forever and grow old. I shall never want to leave. When we've had the patio furniture delivered I'll invite grandmother over again. It's a shame she can't get up to the patio, but she'll be able to see it from the garden and I can take her a photograph of the view from up here.'

'I'm surprised she doesn't manage to climb up here. She never ceases to amaze me. She is quite incredible for her age.'

'Greek peasant genes. Her generation had to be extremely tough to survive. I hope I've inherited them.'

'You probably have. You never even seem to have a cold.'

'I do get colds, I just don't complain about them like you men.'

Bryony smiled up at him. 'Let's have a look at the catalogue and decide what we want up here. Do you think there will be enough space for four chairs?'

'That depends upon the size of the table you want and how many pots you decide to put everywhere.'

Bryony shrugged. 'I can always move some pots downstairs if they begin to make it look cramped.'

'I can, you mean,' muttered Marcus under his breath, as he followed his wife back down to their lounge.

Bryony looked at the patio furniture that Marcus had carried up the stairs for her. It was a good choice. The oval table and the backs of the chairs were inset with coloured tiles making a flower design. She had chosen matching cushions and in a moment of extravagance insisted on a lamp with a glass shade made in the same mosaic of colours. Now she moved from one side of the patio to the other, admiring the overall effect.

'What do you think, Marcus?'

Marcus nodded. 'I like it. There's only one problem. We need another lamp. That one looks rather isolated and stupid standing on its own, besides, it would only throw light on that side of the table. Anyone sitting the other side would be in darkness.'

Bryony looked at her husband in delight. 'I hoped you would say that. Do you think if we telephoned them now they would be able to deliver it tomorrow?'

Marcus smiled at her enthusiasm. He looked at his watch. 'It's not that late. They might even be able to deliver it tonight.'

'If they do we'll eat supper out here.'

'We can still eat out here, even with one light,' Marcus chided her gently.

Bryony shook her head. 'I want it to be perfect. I feel like hanging a notice outside saying *'OUR HOUSE IS FINISHED'*. I promise I won't ask for anything more, Marcus.'

Bryony stood back and surveyed the table. The second light had been delivered and she had spent more than half an hour running up and down the stairs from the kitchen to the patio with cutlery and dishes. She would have to organise herself better so she would not have to make so many trips in future. She felt quite exhausted.

'Supper's ready, Marcus,' she called and stood and waited to hear his heavy tread on the stairs. He did not appear as she had expected and she called again a little louder. 'Marcus. Did you hear me? Supper's ready.'

She heard his voice but could not make out his answer. If she could not hear him clearly, he could probably not hear her. With a sigh she made another trip down the stairs to the lounge. Marcus was sitting hunched forward on the sofa listening intently to the news on the television. He held up his hand as she entered and she waited patiently. Finally he switched it off and turned to her, a worried frown on his face.

'What's wrong?'

'Apparently Christabelle has been arrested.'

'Arrested? Christabelle? Whatever for? Tax evasion?'

'No,' Marcus shook his head sadly. 'It's rather more serious than that. Come and sit down.'

'But, Marcus, supper is ready.'

'I think you ought to hear this first.' He patted the seat beside him on the sofa.

'According to the news she has been arrested for murder.'

'What!' Bryony's face paled. 'I don't believe you.'

Marcus continued as if she had not spoken. He took both his wife's hands in his own. 'There's no easy way to say this, Bry. She killed your mother.'

Bryony looked at him wide-eyed. 'Killed mother? She can't have done. There's a man in custody for her murder.'

Marcus shook his head. 'She's admitted that she did it, and to some other murders as well.'

SAFFRON

Bryony shook her head. 'It's not true. Why would she want to kill people?'

'She's sick, very sick. She's being detained in a mental hospital. The news reader said she had Narcissistic something or other.'

Tears began to course their way down Bryony's cheeks. 'Poor Christabelle. She can't have *meant* to kill anyone. Maybe she had blackouts. Maybe she's one of these people with a dual personality.'

Marcus looked at his wife sadly. 'You always think the best of people, Bryony.' Marcus took his wife in to his arms to try to comfort her. The supper sat upstairs on the patio untouched.

Marianne added the figures up a second time. They were making a profit again over the summer months, not as much as she would have liked, but that was due to employing more women to clean the bungalows. She would sit down with her husband and uncle and see what plans they had for the following year.

She stretched her hand out and turned on the television for the news. It was already half way through and she only caught the last few words of the newsreader.

'...*according to the psychiatrist Miss Christabelle is unfit to stand trial.*

The Governor of New England ...'

Marianne changed channels in annoyance. What had Christabelle been charged with that she would need to stand trial and subsequently been declared mentally unfit? It was probably to do with her tax whilst she had worked overseas. She listened carefully to the Greek news channel and there was no mention of her cousin. She would have to listen to the International News in an hour's time.

The telephone rang and Marianne picked it up, expecting to have a booking enquiry and prepared to tell the caller they were full until the last week of the season.

'Bryony! How lovely. How are you?'

'Have you heard the news, Marianne? It's so awful.'

'What is? What's happened? Are you all safe?'

'It's Christabelle. I wanted to 'phone you earlier, but Marcus made me wait until I had calmed down. They say she's confessed, but they can't charge her because she has some mental condition.' Bryony's words came tumbling out.

'Now hold on, Bryony. I don't know what you're talking about. I heard the tail end of some news saying she couldn't stand trial. It's for tax evasion I presume.'

'Oh, no, it's far worse than that! It's murder! She murdered her mother, my mother...' Bryony broke into a torrent of sobbing, her words unintelligible.

'Bryony, is Marcus there? If he is let me speak to him. Bryony, put Marcus on the phone.'

'I'm here Marianne.' Marcus sounded weary. 'Bryony's in a terrible state, of course. I don't know how to comfort her. I heard the news first and then I had to break it to Bryony. I hoped it wasn't true, but it appears she has confessed.'

Marianne sat down hard in the chair and took a deep breath. 'Tell me from the beginning, Marcus.'

'I'm not sure when she returned to New Orleans, but apparently the police were waiting for her. She was asked about the death of an Italian photographer. They have matched his blood to some that was found on a pair of jeans that belonged to her. That could have been co-incidence, of course, but then they said they had evidence that she had killed someone whilst she was on Rhodes. They have a film to prove it.'

'What! I don't believe it!' Marianne gripped the arms of the chair and her head swam. It could not be true. John had gone to Rhodes with the private detective from America to take a cine film for him. Surely he was not involved in this!

'I didn't believe it at first either,' continued Marcus. 'I thought there had to be a mistake. According to the news reports she has been seen by a psychiatrist and has confessed to any number of murders, including her mother.'

'What will happen to her?' Marianne was taking deep breaths trying to regain her composure.

'I've no idea. I've only ever heard about murders and not taken much notice. I've never known anyone who was involved in any way. Bryony is absolutely distraught, of course. I've asked the doctor to prescribe a sedative for her and a neighbour is collecting it at this moment. I'll have to answer the door when they arrive.'

'Of course. Is there anything we can do?'

'I don't think anyone can do anything. I just hope Christabelle doesn't mention Bryony. We don't want reporters on the doorstep.'

Marianne gasped. 'Are they likely to start hounding you?'

'You know what reporters can be like once they sense a story.'

'If that happens you know you're welcome over here any time.'

'Thank you, Marianne. I have to go. I'll call you again when we have any further news.'

'Give Bryony my love and tell her I'm terribly sorry.' Marianne replaced the receiver and sat with her head in her hands. She needed to speak to her son, but she wanted his father present when she did so. Had Giovanni and John known who Lester was investigating and why? They both of them had some very serious explaining to do.

She waited impatiently for Giovanni to return from the taverna, unable to sit still, her thoughts in turmoil. Finally she picked up the telephone and called him.

'I need to speak to you, urgently. Can you close up and come back here now?'

'What's wrong? Has something happened to John?'

'Not yet.' Marianne spoke through gritted teeth. 'I need you here.' She replaced the receiver and when the telephone rang she did not answer it, guessing it would be Giovanni asking for an explanation from her.

John looked at his mother's face in consternation. This was obviously serious. He could never remember seeing his mother looking so angry before.

'Sit down, both of you. Nicola, maybe you could go and start making some lunch?'

Nicola nodded. What had happened? Silently she slipped into the kitchen and closed the door. She felt slightly sick. Had Marianne discovered that John was spending most of each night in her bed? Was she going to be sent back home to the States in disgrace? She realised her hands were shaking as she pulled the lettuce apart and began to wash it.

Marianne looked first at her husband and then at her son. 'Have either of you heard the news?'

Both men shook their heads.

'I haven't heard it fully either, but I have had a telephone call from Bryony. Have you any idea what it may have been about? I think you might know, John.'

John hung his head. 'I'm sorry, Mum.'

'You're sorry! Sorry for what? Sorry for not telling us the truth when you returned from Rhodes? Sorry for putting your life in danger? And you, Giovanni, did you know who John was supposed to be filming?' Marianne's voice rose hysterically.

Giovanni shook his head. 'Lester never gave me a name. Just said it was someone they suspected of committing crimes and an innocent man was taking the blame.'

'You didn't think to ask him?'

'I felt it was confidential. He was a private detective. I had the assurance of the Inspector in Italy that he was bone fide.'

'I knew who it was, Mum.' John spoke quietly. 'I knew if I told you, you wouldn't let me go.'

Giovanni looked at John in surprise. 'Who was it?'

'Christabelle.'

'Christabelle!'

'Please, let me explain. Maybe I should have told you when I came back, but I didn't know what would happen then.' John looked pleadingly at his parents. 'When Christabelle came here she deliberately damaged the brake cable on my bike. I had filmed her doing it so I knew it was no accident. Lester came here trying to track her down and I took a sneaky look at his notebook. I tackled him about the information he had and told him about the film and the brake cable. When he asked me to go over to Rhodes as his photographer it was an opportunity too good to pass up. I just looked on it as a bit of fun, an adventure. She had tried to hurt me and probably Nicola as well. It seemed like a way to get my own back. I didn't realise how serious it was then.

'We followed Christabelle around whilst she went shopping and it was all pretty boring. She then met up with someone at a taverna and arranged to meet her again down at the harbour. She kept on meeting this woman and once she went back to her house. There was obviously something going on between them.

'I don't know why Christabelle took a man in a wheelchair from the taverna where he was drinking. Maybe this was what she had been meeting the woman about. She took the man back into the Old Town. When she got to the top of a steep hill she hit him and gave the wheelchair a push. He went speeding down, eventually crashing onto the cobbles.'

'Why didn't you stop her?'

'It all happened so fast. I was filming her pushing him along the road one minute and the next I was filming her giving him an almighty push and then running away.'

'Where was Lester whilst this was happening?'

'Right behind me. I suggested we went down to help the man, but he said not to interfere. There was already someone on their way up the road who had found him and would get help.' John shrugged. 'Maybe this woman and Christabelle arranged it between them. Anyway Lester took my film and went back to the States and I came back home. I showed Dad a small piece in the newspaper that reported the death of Joseph Pirenzi and asked him if he was his brother.' John turned accusing eyes on his father. 'You refused to talk about him. You said I was never to mention his name again. How could I tell you about the film? How do you think I felt?' For the first time John's voice faltered. 'Mum's cousin had killed my uncle and I had filmed the murder.'

Marianne put her hands up to her mouth. She was still horrified that John had been in such a dangerous situation – Christabelle could have turned on him – but she also had a desire to laugh. It was poetic justice. After all, Joseph had shot her husband and his cousin before killing the hotel clerk and never been brought to justice for the crime. She was filled with an overwhelming sense of relief that Joseph could never be a threat to anyone ever again. But Christabelle – a murderess – it was unbelievable.

Giovanni ran his hand across his head. 'I'm sorry, John. It was wrong of me. You had a right to know about him.'

John shrugged. 'It wouldn't have changed anything. When I received the letter and cheque from Lester he also sent me a cutting from their local newspaper. Apparently Christabelle has some sort of mental problem and she will be in an institution for the rest of her life. I thought that would be he end of the matter. I didn't think she would make international news. That's why I didn't tell you.'

Giovanni took Marianne's hand. It was cold and she was trembling. 'You go and help Nicola. I think it's time John and I had a talk. He has a right to know about Joseph.'

Marianne went out onto the patio. John looked after her. He hated to see his mother so upset. He looked away and then back again. Who did she suddenly remind him of? It was the tilt of her head that seemed familiar.

His attention was drawn back to his father who had poured each of them a glass of wine. Suddenly he looked his age and he touched his shirt beneath which John knew he had a large, ugly scar.

'I am truly sorry, Dad.'

Giovanni waved away the apology. 'I should probably have told you about your uncle before. I was more concerned for your grandmother and I thought you could be too young to keep the information to yourself.' Giovanni sighed. 'The problem with Joseph goes back a long way. Your mother was visiting Crete with her friend. She had a telephone call to say her father was seriously ill and she rushed back to the States. I had been planning to ask her to marry me, but,' Giovanni spread his hands 'she wrote me a brief note to thank me for my help. I thought she didn't care about me the way I cared about her. I had no idea about you.'

John flushed and looked uncomfortable.

'I continued working for Uncle Yannis and at my night club where Nicola's father was the manager. I happened to be there on the night of the robbery. I saw who shot us and killed the night clerk.'

John's eyes widened. 'You mean you knew who it was and never said?'

'How could I? He was my brother. Think of your grandparents. They would not have forgiven him, nor would they have forgiven me for causing him to be in prison for the rest of his life, possibly with a death penalty hanging over him. Nicolas and I survived. There was nothing to be gained by identifying the man responsible. I decided to cut him out of my life forever. I would not become bitter thinking about him and wishing for revenge.

'I succeeded, until your mother and I went over to Rhodes for a holiday. We inadvertently wandered into the red light area and there he was. I swallowed my hatred, my pride, call it what you will, and spoke to him. He had not changed, despite being a cripple in a wheelchair.' Giovanni shook his head sadly at the memory. 'When I spoke to Lester I made it quite clear that you were not to go into that area. I didn't expect you to recognise him and he doesn't – didn't – know about you. There were other reasons.'

'I didn't know what area I was going into,' John interrupted. 'I was just following her. I doubt if she knew where she was.'

'Who was the woman Christabelle met up with?'

'I've no idea.'

Giovanni smiled grimly. 'I imagine it was her half sister.' He held up his hand as John was about to interrupt him again. 'Before I met your mother, her cousin, Sorrell joined forces with Joseph and they had worked out a scheme to rob the hotels. They were very successful, but Uncle Yannis's was not touched. A very beautiful young woman came to stay, and, I admit, I fell for her. I tried to persuade her to stay in Crete. She tricked me and managed to be alone in the office for long enough to remove the contents of the safe, and, I found out later, copies of the keys. I felt rather foolish and thought that was the end of the matter, until the shooting. She was there with Joseph. He tried to blame the shooting on her. Had it not been for your mother coming over here to help Elizabeth, she would probably have been convicted for the murder of the night receptionist. Once Uncle Yannis knew she was a relative he managed to get her sentence commuted to deportation. I don't know when Sorrell returned to Greece or how she found Joseph again, but when we went to Rhodes they were together and she was working in the red light area.'

John looked out to where his mother was still standing on the patio. Now he knew who it was she reminded him of; the woman he had seen Christabelle meeting in Rhodes. He swallowed hard. For years he had wanted to know why his father would never speak about his younger brother, and why his uncle had sold the profitable hotels he had owned.

'Thank you for telling me, Dad. Maybe, at another time, we could talk about it a bit more? I'd like to get a few more details from you so I fully understand.' John looked at his father. 'Not that I think knowing about it would have made any difference to the outcome. I was convinced Christabelle was mad by the way she behaved on the beach.' John pushed back his chair. 'Now I think I ought to go and talk to Mum for a bit.'

Giovanni nodded and watched as his son went out onto the patio and placed his arms around his mother.

Nicola found she could hardly eat any lunch. When she had laid the table she had raised her eyebrows at John and he shook his head at her. What did that mean? She longed for the meal to be over and to be able to have a few minutes alone with him to find out what had made his mother so furious with him.

She cleared the table and was relieved when John entered the kitchen carrying the last of the plates.

'What was the problem? Does your mum know about us?' she whispered.

John shook his head. 'I'll tell you later. Nothing for you to worry over.' He raised his voice. 'Do you need either of us this afternoon? I'd quite like to go into the nature trail and take some photos. I can check for any damage whilst we're there.'

Giovanni looked at his wife and she shook her head. 'If you're going up there would you do the late opening of the taverna and shop for me, please? There's little point in me going up if you two are already there.'

'No problem. You get the keys, Nick, and we'll be off. See you all later.'

John parked the scooter outside the taverna and Nicola checked her pocket to ensure the keys were safe. 'Please, John, tell me what the problem was. I was convinced your mum had found out about us and I was going to be sent back to the States.'

John squeezed her hand. 'That was the last thing on Mum's mind. It was about my time in Rhodes. I was going to talk to them about what happened over there; then I spoke to Dad because I'd read a bit in the newspaper. He told me about his brother and said I was never to talk about him again. I didn't feel I could tell them after that, and I didn't think they'd find out anyway.'

Nicola frowned at him. 'John, I haven't the faintest idea what you're on about. You're talking in riddles.'

'Has your dad never told you about being shot?'

'No. When was he shot?'

John looked at her in surprise. 'Do you really not know? He's got a pretty big scar.'

'That's from an operation.'

'Yes, an operation to take out a bullet and repair the damage it had done. Come on, we'll find a secluded spot and then I'll tell you what my Dad told me. Then I'll tell you what happened whilst I was on Rhodes.'

Ranjit read the letter in delight. An invitation to go to Paris to speak at the Cardiac Conference that was to be held there in September. Of course he would attend. He would also make quite sure that Saffron accompanied him. He did not like the idea of leaving her alone in London for a week. She would no doubt plan to meet up with some of her old friends and he was not sure he approved of the few he had met. When he had collected her from her evening out with them she had not been ready when he arrived, despite him telling her he would be there at eleven. They had all kissed and hugged each other and promised to meet up again as soon as possible. He was sure some of them had drunk rather too much and he certainly did not want Saffron to be influenced by them.

He spoke to her after their evening meal and Saffron frowned. 'I can't just cancel my appointments and go off for a week. My patients are relying on me.'

'Your patients will still be there when you return. If you were sick they would have to wait until you returned to work. I have already informed your department that you will not be available the second week in September and they will reschedule all your appointments or pass them to a colleague if necessary.'

Saffron's face flamed. 'How dare you do that Ranjit without speaking to me first?'

Ranjit raised his eyebrows. 'There was no need for me to speak to you. You do as I say.'

Saffron stood up and looked down at her husband. 'You seem to forget that I have not been brought up in your culture. I am an independent woman. I am a doctor and as such I have a sense of responsibility. I don't just cancel my appointments to go away for a week at such short notice.'

Ranjit shrugged and ignored her objections. 'I have made the arrangements now. There is time to have your passport changed into your married name and I have collected the appropriate papers from the post office. There is nothing more to be said.'

'Why should I change my passport? There are another three years before I need to renew it.'

'We cannot go to Paris as a married couple if your passport is in your maiden name. People would think we were there for an illicit weekend. You can fill in the application form this evening.'

'I am not a child to be ordered around.' Saffron stamped her foot in anger. 'I absolutely refuse to change the name on my passport until it is time for it to be renewed.'

'You may not be a child, but you behave in a very immature fashion on occasions.' He looked pointedly down at the foot she had stamped at him. 'You will complete the forms this evening and I will take them to the post office tomorrow to ensure you receive your new passport in time for the trip to Paris.'

'Marjorie, do you think I would be terribly disloyal to Dad if I tried to contact my relatives in America?'

'Do you think that's a good idea after all this time?'

'I'd like to be in touch with my sisters again.'

'Did your father give you any reason for not contacting them?'

'He always discouraged me; he said I might be disappointed with the reply. I think he thought they might not want to know me.'

Marjorie shrugged. 'He could have been right. After all, it's years since you saw them last.' Marjorie thought it more likely that Jeremy was worried about his ex-wife knowing where he was living.

'It's not as though I would be asking them for anything. I'm a doctor and I'm married. I'd just like to know about them. It seems wrong, somehow, not to know about your family. Look at Ranjit, he has no contact with his family any more.'

Marjorie frowned. 'Is it his idea to contact them?'

'I haven't mentioned it to him. I'll ask him and see what he says.'

Marjorie raised her eyebrows, but said nothing. She did not think it had anything to do with Ranjit.'

'Don't be silly. I'm sure they could have traced you if they wanted to. You don't need them. You have me now. I'm your family.' Ranjit spoke firmly, as if to a child.

Saffron shook her head. 'No, Ranjit, you're my husband. I spent the first ten years of my life with these people. I loved my grandparents and sisters.'

Ranjit shrugged. 'You are very foolish and sentimental. Suppose one of them did write back to you? What then? They are too far away to visit.'

'At the moment, but maybe one day we could go to America.'

Ranjit shook his head. 'It would be out of the question. If we had enough money to travel anywhere we would have to go to India to introduce you to my family.'

'I thought you didn't want to go back to India and had no contact with your family.'

'To live, definitely not. One day, when the time is right, we will go on a holiday and I will take you to meet them. Just because

117

we do not keep in constant contact does not mean we would not be welcome.'

'But if I had contacted my American family we could go to New Orleans and I could take you to meet them.'

Ranjit compressed his lips. 'I have said no. That is the end of the matter.'

Saffron shook her head. 'I'll think about it.'

Ranjit placed his hands on her shoulders, his fingers digging into her collarbone painfully. 'I have said you are not to write. I forbid you to write.' There had been no sign of this rebellious streak in Saffron before he had married her.

Saffron tried to wriggle away from him. 'You forbid me? You cannot forbid me. I'm not a child.'

'You are my wife and you do as I say. Let's hear no more of this silliness.' He released her. 'You can tell Marjorie we are ready for our meal now.'

Saffron looked at him in surprise. 'I'll *ask* Marjorie if it is ready. She's not a servant to be ordered around.'

Ranjit shrugged. 'You have a lot to learn, my dear.' He pulled out a chair and sat in his usual place at the dining table. 'I am ready.'

Saffron went through to the kitchen. 'Can I help you dish up, Marjorie?'

'Not for another five minutes at least. These potatoes are like rocks still.'

'I'll tell Ranjit.' Saffron returned to the dining room. 'Supper is not ready yet. The potatoes are not cooked.'

Ranjit frowned. 'Then she should have started cooking earlier. Such incompetence!'

'She's not incompetent. Sometimes potatoes do take longer than you expect.'

'I call it incompetence. Maybe she would benefit from some lessons.'

'That's insulting. Marjorie is a superb cook.'

'In your opinion.' Ranjit picked up the evening paper and opened it on the table over his plate.

Saffron looked at his action with distaste. 'Don't put the newspaper on your plate. The print might come off.'

Ranjit looked at her coldly. 'I am the head of the house. I shall do as I please. You can bring me a clean plate.'

Completely nonplussed Saffron returned to the kitchen where she took a deep steadying breath. Ranjit had never spoken to her like this before.

'What's wrong?' Marjorie looked at her keenly.

'Oh, Ranjit decided to go macho-man on me again. He forbade me to try to contact my relatives in America.'

'So?'

'So I have every intention of writing them a letter.'

Marjorie smiled to herself. At last Saffron seemed to be standing up for herself against her domineering husband. It was not before time.

Saffron began to compose a letter to her relatives in her head. She remembered the name of her grandparents, but not the address. She knew her grandfather had worked in the research department of the large local hospital and was sure they would have a record of his last known address. She could send the letter there and ask them to forward it. If it was returned to her, she would just have to accept that they could not be traced.

'One plain, one purl, one plain, one purl, one plain....'

'Stop that!'

'One purl, one plain....'

'Stop it, I said.'

'Stop what?'

'That silly one plain, one purl.'

'I have to count or I'll forget where I am.'

'Don't be stupid. It's only a piece of knitting.'

'It's going to be a coat for my baby.'

'What baby?'

A secretive smile came over the woman's face. 'I'm having a baby.' She laid her hand on her stomach. 'Do you want to feel her kicking?'

Christabelle rose in disgust. 'No I do not. You stupid old woman.' She walked over to the far side of the communal lounge where the warden sat. 'When do I get out of here? She's driving me crazy. Talking about a baby at her age!'

'If it keeps her happy. There's no harm in her.'

'It doesn't keep me happy. She should be locked in her room.'

'Why don't you sit a bit further away and put the television on? You wouldn't hear her then.'

Christabelle flounced across the room, switched on the television and turned it up as loudly as she dared.

Nancy finished her row of knitting and placed it in her lap. 'Could you turn that down a bit, please. I find it difficult to concentrate with it as loud as that.'

By way of an answer, Christabelle turned the volume even louder. Nancy rose placed her knitting on her chair and approached Christabelle.

'I asked if you could turn it down, not up.' She stretched out her hand for the control knob, but Christabelle slapped it away.

Nancy looked at her with a puzzled frown and stretched her hand out again. Christabelle pushed her roughly away and went over to Nancy's chair. She snatched the knitting up and pulled the stitches off the needles.

For a moment Nancy stood and looked at Christabelle, then she rushed across to her. 'You did that deliberately. You've spoilt my baby's coat.' She grabbed a handful of Christabelle's hair and began to tug at it viciously.

The warden pressed the alarm bell in the wall as Christabelle screamed. 'Get her off me!'

Christabelle twisted and turned trying to loosen the firm grip on her hair. She punched Nancy hard in the chest and as she gasped in surprise, Christabelle thrust the knitting needles into her stomach with all the force she could muster.

Nancy released Christabelle's hair and clutched her stomach. 'My baby! You've killed my baby!' She sank down in a chair doubled over and sobbing.

'Good thing too. Now you won't need to do that ridiculous knitting all the time.'

Two wardens entered the room and took hold of Christabelle's arms. 'I think you ought to return to your room. Give both of you time to calm down.'

Christabelle tried to shake them off. 'Did you see? She attacked me. She's pulled my hair out.'

'We weren't in here at the time, but no doubt Doctor Ferguson will speak to you about the incident tomorrow. Let's get you up to your room and find you a nice cup of tea.'

'Stop talking to me as if I was five years old. I do not want to go to my room. I do not want a cup of tea. I don't even like tea.' Christabelle tried to pull free of the restraining hands.

'Whenever there's an incident the people involved have to go to their rooms. Betty will talk to Nancy and we'll ask Doctor Ferguson to speak to you. No one is blaming either of you. Tempers do flare every so often.'

'I do not want to go to my room.'

'We have to insist.' The warden tightened her grip on Christabelle's arm. 'We don't like having to use force, so please don't make us.'

Christabelle's eyes glittered dangerously. 'You'll regret this,' she muttered. 'I should be treated with respect. I am Miss Christabelle.'

Marcus drew up outside his house, relieved to see that his wife's car was already there. The news he had broken about Christabelle had hit her hard. At first she had refused to believe it, then she had wanted to visit her, to see if she could help in any way. Finally, she had promised Marcus she would not go without speaking to him first. This was one promise Bryony had made that he did not feel he could depend upon her keeping. Marcus had spoken to her firmly.

'There's nothing you can do at this stage. The police say they have evidence against her and the psychiatrists say she has a mental condition. Let them fight it out between them. If the case goes to trial and you want to go to support her, I'll not stop you. I'll even come with you. If she's committed to a mental hospital we can visit her there. I don't think we should do anything at the moment.'

'But Marcus, she's all alone in the world.'

'That's her choice. She didn't want to get to know the family, she hardly wanted to know us if you think about it. Whenever you suggested a meeting she decided she had something urgent she had to do.'

'She was busy with her modelling.' Bryony tried to excuse her half sister.

'I'm sure she was, but I'm also sure she used it as an excuse whenever it pleased her. In retrospect I'm glad she did. We might have upset her and goodness knows what she would have tried to do to either or both of us.'

'Maybe I could write to her?'

'What would you say?'

Bryony bit at her lip. 'I don't know,' she confessed.

'Believe me, it's better to leave things as they are at present.'

'You really think so?'

'I do. If she should write to you, there's no reason why you shouldn't write back to her. Let her make the first move.' Marcus squeezed his wife's shoulders. 'I know you feel she's family and you want to do the right thing, but give it time. How about if we had supper on the patio tonight?' he suggested, wanting to distract

Bryony from her present train of thought. 'We've not been up there since we heard the news.'

Annita looked at the letter from the hospital curiously. Why would they be writing to her? With arthritic fingers, she opened it carefully and was surprised to find another thick envelope inside with an English stamp. If it was meant for her why was it sent to the hospital? There was a request that the letter should be returned to an address in London if it was not delivered.

Annita turned it over in her hands. There was a time when she and Elias received correspondence from all over the world, but since his death she received only an occasional Christmas card from anywhere other than Crete. She slit the envelope with a paper opener – she did not want to spoil the stamp, Paul would want it to add to his collection. She turned to the last page and caught her breath. The signature was *'Saffron'*.

Why would she be writing to her after all the years of silence? Annita sniffed. She was probably hoping she had died and left her something in her will. Well, she would be sadly disappointed on both counts there! She turned back to the first page and began to read.

Dear Grandfather and Grandmother
I hope after all these years you are both in good health
and have not completely forgotten me. I have never
forgotten you, but I could not remember your address so I
had to send this letter care of the hospital and ask them to
forward it to you. This is a very difficult letter for me to
write and I hope you will understand when you read it.

Anna sniffed again. She was after money.

When my father, Jeremy Bartlett, left my mother, Anna, he
took me to England. He never told me the reason for the

breakdown of their marriage, but obviously he felt that there could be no reconciliation. Dad worked for his same firm of accountants in the English office. We rented a small flat on the outskirts of London and I attended the local school. Not long after I started secondary school Dad was sent away to Ireland to work for a couple of weeks and he arranged for me to stay with his secretary and her mother.

I got to know them both well as I used to go to their house every day after school and do my homework until Dad came home from work. He didn't like me being in the flat alone, particularly if he had to work late, as sometimes happened.

I was not unduly surprised when Dad and Marjorie were married and we moved in to her house. Marjorie, his ex-secretary, is a lovely person and I have come to love her dearly. Shortly after they were married Dad went into hospital to have a lump removed from under his arm. A year later he found he had another lump and this time the diagnosis was cancer. I won't go into the details, but as you can imagine, it was not an easy time for any of us. After bouts of treatment he would appear to be well, but sooner or later another lump would appear.

At quite an early age I had decided that I wanted to become a doctor. I gained a place at Medical School, but sadly Dad died a year before I graduated. I am now an orthopaedic surgeon, working in the local hospital. I love my work.

Whilst Dad was alive I suggested on many occasions that I wrote to you. I would so much like to see my sisters again. Are they married? Do they have children? How is my mother? What about my aunts and uncle? Are my cousins married with families of their own? Dad did not forbid me to write, but he asked me not to do so. When I discussed this later with Marjorie she thought he may

*have discouraged me to avoid me being disappointed if I
received no reply.*

*I do hope someone will reply to me. I am married now to
a heart surgeon. He is Indian and we are living with
Marjorie at the moment. It works out well and I would not
have wanted to leave Marjorie alone as she has been so
good to me. I do not know what would have happened to
me after Dad died if she had not been there to look after
me.*

*If this letter reaches my grandparents or someone else
in the family PLEASE write back to me.*

*Although I think of myself as English after all these
years I guess I am still an American Greek at heart and
family is important to me.*

Sincerely
Saffron

Annita read the letter through a second time. She had not
mentioned money or an impending visit. All she asked for was
information. Surely there could be no harm in asking Bryony to
write back and give the girl news about her family? She would
ask her the next time she visited *Green Vistas* and see what she
suggested. Annita tucked the letter safely inside her address book.

Christabelle marched imperiously over to the warden who sat at
the chair at the side of the room, watching every move the inmates
made.

'Who's in charge here?' she demanded.

'I am.'

Christabelle regarded her scornfully. 'I mean properly in
charge. Who do I need to speak to. I have a number of complaints
that I need to make.'

The woman raised her eyebrows. 'Really? Then I suggest I
make you an appointment with Doctor Ferguson.'

'I would like one immediately.'

'When I am relieved from this duty I will have a look at his appointment book and let you know tomorrow when he can fit you in.'

'Fit me in? I'm Christabelle. He should be only too eager to talk to me.'

The woman shrugged. 'I'll see what I can do.'

Christabelle glared at her mutinously, then walked back to where she had been sitting and continued to leaf through a magazine. It was ridiculous. How much longer were they going to keep her hanging around in this place? They even locked her in her room at night. It was disgraceful.

Three days later Dr Ferguson welcomed her with a smile. 'What can I do for you? I was told you had a complaint.'

'I have a number of complaints.'

'Then please sit down and we'll see if we can solve them.'

Christabelle glared at him. 'Why is she here?'

'Miss Green is an associate of mine. You were introduced to her the last time we met.'

Christabelle gave her a venomous look. 'I was told you were in charge.'

'That is so, but I often find that a second opinion is helpful. Now, please, tell me what you wish to complain about, Miss Bartlett.'

'I am Miss Christabelle. I have told you before how to address me.'

'Of course. I do apologise.'

Christabelle continued as if he had not spoken. 'Why am I locked in my room at night? I demand that in future the door is left unlocked.'

Dr Ferguson shook his head. 'Everyone is locked in at night. It is for their own safety. Some people do not sleep well and they might wander into another room and disturb the occupant. You would not want to wake up and find an intruder standing by your bed.'

Christabelle regarded him scornfully. 'Then in future I will have the key on my side. I will then be in control. I can lock the door when I go to bed.'

'I'm afraid I cannot allow that.'

'Why ever not? I have no problem sleeping.'

'The doors are constructed in such a way that there is no key hole on your side.'

'Then in my case I demand that you make that facility available immediately.'

'Miss – er – Christabelle, do you understand why you are here?'

'Oh,' Christabelle tossed her head. 'There are some ridiculous charges against me. No doubt made by someone who is jealous of my fame and popularity. There's no reason why I should be here. I really do need to leave and return to my modelling?'

Doctor Ferguson placed his hands together. 'Miss Christabelle, you are here because you have committed some very serious crimes. If I allowed you to have a key to your room I would not feel convinced that you would not commit another crime if you felt so inclined. There has already been one violent incident involving you.'

Christabelle curled her lip scornfully. 'That stupid woman with her knitting. She was the one who attacked me. I was only defending myself.'

'Quite so, but we have to take the facts into account.'

'It's not good enough! It's like being in a prison.'

'Miss Christabelle, this is a prison.'

Christabelle's eyes opened wide. 'I was told it was a hospital.'

Doctor Ferguson nodded. 'Yes, a prison hospital.'

'I refuse to stay here any longer.'

Doctor Ferguson shrugged. 'As you wish. I can arrange your transfer to the penitentiary centre if that is what you want. I do not think you will find the conditions there as pleasant as they are here. You would be confined to your cell for most of the day, not allowed to share a communal sitting room and mix freely with the other inmates. It is unlikely you would be able to receive the counselling you need in there, but the choice is yours.'

Christabelle took a deep breath. 'It isn't right that I should be treated like this. Anyone would think I was a common criminal. I'm Miss Christabelle. When are you going to understand that?'

'I do understand, Miss Christabelle. Now, would you like me to arrange for a transfer or would you prefer to stay here?'

'Heard the news, Marcus?'

Marcus looked up from the insurance policy he was examining. 'What news?' He hoped his colleagues were not going to want to discuss Christabelle with him.

'They say we're in for a big blow.'

'What's news about that? We've had big blows before.'

'Yeah, but this one is forecast to be the mother of all blows. If it keeps to its present course they say New Orleans is due for a direct hit.'

'We'll survive. We have before.'

'That was when you lived inland. You live down by the coast now. You'll take the full brunt of it. I'm going to get some timber after work tonight before they sell out. You ought to do the same.'

Marcus frowned. 'I suppose it would be practical. When do they forecast it will hit?'

'Middle of next week. Where've you been these last few days? The forecast has been mentioning it on every bulletin, telling people to be prepared.'

'I've had one or two other things on my mind.'

'Have you heard about that model that's accused of being a serial murderess? Or have you managed to miss that as well?'

Marcus smiled thinly. 'I did hear something about it. Now, I really must get this finished or I shall be working too late to go and get any timber.'

'Have you got an electric drill and masonry screws? You'll need them to fix it firmly.'

'I'll buy some.' Marcus bent his head back to the papers. They had suffered from hurricanes before and he wondered if Frank was exaggerating. Maybe he would have a look at the weather forecast before he went to the expense of buying timber and covering the windows.

'Supper's ready, Marcus.'

Marcus did not reply. He was listening intently to the weather forecast as the man explained how the hurricane was building in strength and appeared to be readying itself to make a direct hit on New Orleans.

'Marcus.' Bryony stood in the doorway and he held up his hand. 'Just a minute.'

'What is it?' asked Bryony. 'More about Christabelle?'

'Let me listen.'

Bryony perched on the arm of a chair. Marcus was not usually so abrupt with her. Finally he turned off the television and smiled reassuringly at her.

'Frank was telling me about a hurricane that is supposed to be heading our way. I wanted to find out if he was right, and unfortunately it seems that he is. We're in for a direct hit.'

'Oh, Marcus.' Bryony's face paled. 'What are we going to do?'

'I'll get the windows boarded up tomorrow and you'd better get some supplies in. It will probably be no worse than any of the others we've had.'

'I suppose we'll have to bring the patio furniture inside. I wouldn't want that to get damaged as we've only just bought it.'

'We'll do that after supper.'

Marcus surveyed his handiwork. The windows and the back door were boarded up and as an extra precaution he had covered those on the upper floor as well. If the hurricane missed them he was going to be annoyed that he had spent so much money. The builders' merchants had raised their prices due to demand and he knew he had paid twice as much as the usual going rate. Bryony had also complained about the amount her shopping had cost. Tinned goods and bottled water were in short supply as everyone purchased as much as they could carry or afford.

Bryony and Marcus sat together in the dark room listening to the latest weather forecast.

'They can't mean it!' Bryony turned to her husband in amazement. 'They want us to leave the area?'

Marcus held up his hand. 'Let me listen.' He frowned in concentration as the areas considered prone to flooding damage were coloured in on the map of Louisiana. Finally he switched off the television. 'We're leaving,' he announced.

Bryony's face paled. 'Where will we go?'

'We'll drive to Dallas. That should be far enough.'

'That's six hundred miles away! Surely we don't need to go that far?'

'You saw the same as I did, Bryony. The government are advising a mass evacuation. They're predicting that our area is going to have severe flooding. That will mean no electricity for days. No sewerage system. We could run out of food or water, or both. I'd rather drive an extra hundred miles and be safe.'

'But we don't know anyone there.'

'We'll stay in a hotel for a couple of days.'

'What about Grandma?'

Marcus frowned. 'What do you mean?'

'She's in the same area. *Green Vistas* will have the same problems as we would have. Can we take her with us?'

Marcus hesitated. Bryony's grandmother was ninety-five. Would she be able to stand a long car journey?

'Telephone Helena or Aunt Elena. They may have made arrangements for her.'

Bryony gave her husband a dubious glance and lifted the receiver.

Bryony drew up in front of the care home where her grandmother lived. There was a flurry of activity, ambulances drawn up outside and orderlies loading a van with bedding. She found a parking space where she hoped her car would not be in the way and went inside. In the reception area a harassed woman glanced up at her and then stretched out her hand to answer the telephone that began to ring. Bryony listened to the one sided conversation impatiently. As soon as the call finished she placed her hand on the telephone to prevent another incoming call.

The receptionist frowned. 'Please, take your hand off the telephone. What do you want?'

'My grandmother lives here. Please tell me where you're taking your patients.'

'They'll be accommodated in various hospitals round and about.'

'Where is my grandmother going? She's Mrs Annita Kzantari.'

'I don't have individual lists.'

'Who can I talk to?' Bryony looked round wildly. 'I have to know what's happening to her.'

The receptionist shrugged. 'If your telephone number is in her records we'll contact you when she is settled in somewhere. Now please take your hand off my telephone. I have calls to make.'

Bryony stood uncertainly in the foyer. She heard the woman begging a hospital to take some patients, saw her strike through a name on a pad, and dial another number. After listening to three calls she surmised that the woman was getting the same answer whichever hospital she contacted. They had no space. They were already full. Bryony's mouth set in a grim line as she made her way down the corridor to where her grandmother's room was situated.

Annita looked up with a pleased smile when she saw she had a visitor. 'This is an unexpected pleasure.'

Bryony bent and kissed her. 'Have you heard the news, Grandmother? There's a big storm on the way.'

Annita nodded. 'So they said on the news yesterday. They're advising people to leave the area. I can't think why. We've had hurricanes before.'

'This is going to be a particularly bad one. The care home is trying to make arrangements to move all of you to local hospitals, but everywhere appears to be full. I want you to come with me. Marcus and I are planning to drive to Dallas.'

Annita raised her eyebrows. 'That's rather a drastic move. What will you do when you get there?'

'We'll book into a hotel for a few days. Please, Grandma, come with us.'

Annita shook her head. 'I'll be safe enough wherever they send me. You and Marcus look after yourselves. What about Helena and Greg? What are they doing?'

'I think they may have already left. All I can get is their answer phone.'

The door opened and a nurse entered. She smiled when she saw Bryony. 'Nice of you to visit your grandmother before we move her. I've come to get you packed up, Mrs Kzantari.'

'Where is she going?'

'Just a few miles up the road.'

'That's not far enough. The forecast is terrible. They say there could be flooding at least ten miles inland. If the levies give way it could be even worse.'

'It's the best we can do. The hospitals are squeezing extra people in wherever they can.'

'Please, Grandma,' begged Bryony. 'Come with us to Dallas.'

'Now that's a good idea.' The nurse bent over Annita. 'Why don't you do as she says? You'll be safe enough there.'

'I'll think about it.'

'There's no time to think about it. Marcus wants us to leave this morning. We're not going to be the only people wanting to get out of the area. The roads are going to be clogged with traffic very soon.'

'You should go, Mrs Kzantari. You'd be one less person for us to worry over.'

Annita hesitated. 'Do you really think I am in danger if I stay here?'

Bryony nodded. 'You know how level headed Marcus is. He wouldn't suggest this unless he was seriously worried. Where's your passport?'

'In my drawer by the bed I think. I'm not sure if it's still valid.'

Bryony pulled open the drawer and gave a sigh of relief. Not only was the passport there it was also still valid for a further year. 'What does she need with her as regards medicine?' asked Bryony of the nurse.

'I'll check and bring you a supply. There's a suitcase here you can use.'

Bryony nodded and laid it on the bed. She began to open drawers and remove underclothes and nightwear, checking there was enough for a week before placing it in the suitcase. She added a pair of slippers, two skirts, a jumper and a blouse before selecting basic toiletries from the bathroom. As an afterthought she added a toilet roll and a towel. 'Is there anything else you need?'

'Elias's photograph and my spare pair of spectacles.' The initial resistance seemed to have left Annita.

Bryony added them to the suitcase, placed a coat over the back of the wheelchair and covered her grandmother's legs with a blanket.

'I don't need that. It's not cold,' remonstrated Annita.

'It could turn cold later,' said Bryony as she handed her grandmother her purse. 'All we need now is your medication.'

Bryony waited impatiently until the nurse reappeared and handed Bryony a small box. 'There's a week's supply in there and you shouldn't have any trouble getting any more if you need them.' She beckoned Bryony to one side. 'I'm glad you're taking her,' she whispered. 'There will be nowhere safe down here.'

Doctor Ferguson looked at the patients whom he had requested to be assembled together in the dining room.

He cleared his throat. 'Ladies, you have no doubt heard on the news that we are in the path of a severe hurricane. This area is forecast to receive a direct hit. I want to reassure all of you that this building is one of the strongest and safest in the area, but as a precaution we are going to board up the windows. This will mean that you have no natural light. Should the electricity fail the emergency generator will automatically start up. In the unlikely event of a complete power failure we will issue everyone with a torch and spare batteries that they can use. The kitchen is well stocked with food that can be eaten cold and we have containers filled with water. We may have to suffer a little hardship for a few days, but nothing more. I will ask you to stay in your rooms whilst the hurricane passes overhead. This is for your own safety. Thank you for your time.'

The doctor looked at the assortment of women before him. He had made some very difficult decisions. He could not lock them in their rooms, much as he would have liked to. If they needed to be rescued during the hurricane they all had to be able to reach the ground floor. The best he could do was to lock all the doors on the ground floor except the emergency exit and hope they would not start arguments between themselves. Only Hazel and Marcella had volunteered to stay on duty with him. He felt he had insufficient staff at the mental hospital during normal times, and he knew the next few days were certainly not going to be classed as normal.

Christabelle prowled around her room. She hated not being able to see out and know what was going on. She could hear the wind

134

howling and the rain lashing against the building. The electricity had gone off some hours ago and she was dependent upon the light of her torch. Already she had inserted the spare batteries she had been given. How long would they last? The beam seemed to have dimmed considerably and she dreaded being in total darkness.

There was a crash, it sounded like breaking glass, but she was certain it was not her window that had smashed. More noises followed, creaking, bangs, crashes, the sound of metal, and all the time the wind shrieked. She shuddered. She should not be here. She should have been allowed to leave and go somewhere safe. It was all very well for the doctor to say the building was one of the safest in the area, but he would say that. It was only to lull them all into a false sense of security.

Her torch flickered and she shook it; the batteries must be nearly dead. She could be in total darkness for hours. She switched off the torch and took some deep breaths whilst she waited for her eyes to become adjusted to the darkness. Finally she was able to make out the shape of her bed and dressing table. Someone began to scream and she guessed it was another resident whose torch had failed and was frightened of being in total darkness. Her screams were added to by another and Christabelle covered her ears.

A resounding crash shook her room and decided Christabelle. She was not going to stay there any longer. She did not doubt that she would be able to find someone outside who would be willing to help her to safety. She fumbled with her wardrobe door and pulled on a waterproof jacket and a pair of fashionable, high-heeled boots, tucking her trouser legs into them. They would not offer very much protection, but a little more than shoes. She took her purse in one hand and the torch in the other. She would use the torch to break the lock on her door. She tried the handle and to her surprise the door opened easily. Cautiously she pulled it wider until she was able to see into the dark corridor. She looked both ways and she realised why the door had not been locked as usual. Sitting near the top of the stairs was a warden.

Walking quietly on tiptoe to avoid her heels tapping on the floor, she felt her way along the wall until she reached where the woman was sitting. She raised her arm and brought the torch down heavily on the woman's head. With no more than a grunt, the warden toppled over. Christabelle hit her again. She did not want the woman to blow her whistle and alarm the wardens or Doctor Ferguson. Swiftly she moved to the top of the stairs and began to descend them carefully, counting each one as she went.

She shuddered as another crash rent the air. The building must be falling around them. She must get out. She pulled at the door leading to the garden and it did not yield. Panic began to overtake her. They had been locked in and left to die there. She took a deep steadying breath. She knew there were other doors. She just had to find one that she could open.

Moving methodically around the walls she registered the position of the windows by their boards. Her eyes could pick out shapes, but she was unable to see clearly. She passed through an unlocked door into a corridor and felt her way along it, opening doors and entering rooms, trying to gauge where she was. The noise of falling items and the roaring of the wind assaulted her ears continually. She reached the end of the corridor and felt the texture beneath her hands change from cement to metal. Where was she? For a moment she was disorientated, then she realised. She had reached the emergency exit. She switched on her torch, hoping it would work one more time. The beam flickered twice before the batteries finally gave out and she dropped it to the ground.

Feverishly she moved her hands over the metal door. What kind of fastening mechanism did it have? Did she have to lift a bar or just push it? By chance she found the bar moved upwards and she pushed with all her might, although it only moved a few inches. She leant against the door and felt it give slightly. Taking a deep breath she stepped back and launched her shoulder at it. It gave way easily and she almost catapulted out through the doorway. Christabelle steadied herself and stood there trying to get her bearings. The wind was beating against her and she was already soaked by the rain. Her hair was whipped into her face and she took her hand from the door to brush the strands out of her eyes.

Something landed a few feet away from her and she shrunk back into the doorway. As she did so a huge gust of wind caught the open door and slammed it back into her, breaking her breast bone and snapping a number of ribs. It happened so fast she had no time to move out of the way. Her purse dropped from her numb hands to be swirled away by the wind as she struggled to free herself. She tried to cry out for help, but only a faint sound came from her lips as the wind pushed the door harder against her bruised and broken body. Her legs crumpled beneath her and she felt the door hit her for the last time before the surge of water submerged her.

September 2005

Marianne lifted the receiver. 'Reservations. Can I help you?'

'Marianne, it's Helena. Have you seen the news?'

'Of course I have. I've tried and tried to 'phone you. Are you all safe?'

'Oh, yes. Greg insisted that we left as soon as he saw were in for a direct hit. We're staying with some of Paul's friends. We're planning to return next week and see what the damage is.'

'How's Mother?'

'Mother's with Andrew and Sarah. She was already visiting them, so she stayed on.'

'And Grandma?'

'Grandma?'

'Yes. Is she safe?'

'I expect so.'

'What do you mean? You expect so? Haven't you found out?'

There was a sulky silence. 'I expect the care home moved everyone in time.'

'Haven't you tried to phone and find out?'

'I've been busy trying to get organised here. You don't know what it's like. We've only got a small room and Mark is sleeping on the floor in with us. There's no space, no privacy, it's a nightmare.'

'Have you telephoned Bryony or uncle Andreas?'

'No. Why should I? They haven't called me.'

Marianne sighed in exasperation. 'One of them might have some news of Grandma. Please, Helena, telephone them and then call me back. I'm so relieved to hear that you are all safe, but I'd like to know about Grandma.'

'I'm not sure if I have their telephone numbers with me.'

'Then use the directory services. They'll be able to help you.'

The telephone line went dead and Marianne looked at it furiously. Had her sister put the receiver down on her or was there a fault on the line? She slammed her fist down on the desk. 'My sister is quite unbelievable!'

'What's she done?' Giovanni smiled easily at his wife.

'She finally called to tell me they were all safe. She and Greg left Louisiana a week ago. She could have called me earlier. No wonder I couldn't get through to her. When I asked about Grandma she didn't know where she was.'

Giovanni frowned. 'She was probably moved out and no one knows which hospital she's been sent to.'

'Giovanni, she's ninety-five. She needs to be looked after, not dumped into a hospital somewhere. I've asked Helena to call Uncle Andreas and Bryony to see if they have any news of her. Goodness knows when she'll bother to do that!'

'So why don't you call them?'

'I tried their number when I couldn't get through to Helena. The lines were dead. I tried Uncle Andreas's mobile number and left a message on his voice mail. He hasn't answered me.'

Giovanni hugged Marianne to him. 'So what makes you think Helena will have any success? Think logically. We've seen the pictures on the news. It stands to reason that all the telephone wires are down. There's probably a problem trying to communicate by mobile, everyone will be using one. Voice mail could be so clogged up that the message doesn't get through. Have you called Elizabeth?'

Marianne shrugged herself away from him. 'Not since she telephoned to say they were all safe with Bob in Atlanta. My friend calls within twenty four hours and it takes my sister two days!'

'Why don't you call her? You ought to ask her if Eleanor is recovering after her relapse and she should be able to tell you the latest situation over there. You could ask her to try to telephone Bryony and Uncle Andreas.'

Marianne passed a trembling hand over her forehead. 'I'll try her. She might be able to help.'

Elizabeth was sympathetic but totally unable to help. 'I'm sure the lines are down. Most everywhere seems to be under water since the levies gave way. People are being rescued from the roof of their house; there are rumours that there's no fresh water or food to be had and bodies are floating around. I've tried calling a number of friends but the lines are dead.'

'What about mobile numbers?'

'They were fine for a while, but once the electricity went no one would be able to recharge their 'phone.'

Marianne gave a little choking sob. 'I guess my grandmother must be dead. She's ninety-five and could never survive without help.'

'You mustn't think that, Marianne. Someone will have helped the elderly. I'm sure they've all been moved away to safety.' Elizabeth did not add that the roads from New Orleans and the surrounding area had been so clogged up with people trying to escape at the last minute that traffic had been at a standstill. 'The whole area is closed off; no one is allowed back in to see the state of their property so we're staying with Bob for at least another week. As soon as Eleanor has picked up a bit we'll return. I'll see what I can find out. Are you able to put up with Nicola for a bit longer?'

'Of course. She's no problem. She can stay with us as long as you want.'

'Thank you, Marianne. There's really no point in her coming

back over to the States until we know what the situation is. Give her our love. If you have any news you know where to find me.'

'Thank you, Elizabeth. Let me know when you're leaving Atlanta.'

Marianne replaced the receiver and sat with her head in her hands. She had been prepared for years for the news that her grandmother had died in her sleep, but she did not want to think of her drowning in floodwater or dying of starvation and neglect.

Marcus switched on the television and watched the latest reports coming in from New Orleans. The devastation was beyond belief. The cameras on a helicopter panned across the shoreline and focused in on the breached levies. They cut across and showed houses submerged, people waving from the roof tops waiting to be rescued, others wading chest deep through the dirty waters that swirled along the thoroughfares.

Where the water was not so deep, people were looting from the damaged shops, others crowded together on a patch of dry land begging for water and food. Mothers cradled their babies in their arms, a look of both horror and desperation on their faces. Men sat with their heads in their hands, they were helpless against the destruction nature had thrown at them.

Marcus looked at his wife. She was drained of emotion, exhausted by their long, slow journey out of New Orleans and attending to her grandmother. The first time she had seen the newsreel of their hometown she had sobbed in Marcus's arms, now she sat and looked at the pictures with a closed, blank look on her face. The disaster had become unreal to her. Her grandmother looked no better.

Marcus held her hand tightly.

'What are we going to do, Marcus?' asked Bryony fearfully.

'There's nothing we can do. We're safe and well. We just have to sit it out until the government say we can return.'

'I don't think there's going to be very much to return to.'

'Don't be pessimistic. We won't know how bad it is for a few days yet.'

'But suppose we go back and find *Green Vistas* has gone? What would we do? What would happen to my grandmother? What about our house?'

'I'm not taking either of you back until I know it's safe. As soon as they give the all clear I'll drive back down and assess the situation. Once everything has calmed down we'll find out about compensation for any damage and I'm sure that within a few months everything will be back to normal.' Marcus spoke with more optimism than he felt.

Bryony picked up the hotel telephone. It had been out of order for three days due to the high winds Dallas had suffered. She was relieved to finally hear a dialling tone. 'I must try to call Marianne and tell her where we are.'

Marianne lifted the receiver. 'Hello?'

'Marianne? It's Bryony here. I'm sorry I haven't called before. The telephone lines have been down and we haven't been able to recharge our mobiles. I just wanted to let you know that we're safe and Grandma is with us.'

'Oh, Bryony!' Tears of relief began to roll down Marianne's cheeks. 'Where are you?'

'In Dallas. Marcus wanted us to get as far away as possible.'

Marianne gulped and wiped her face with the back of her hand. 'How is Grandma?'

'She's fine. She offered to share the driving with Marcus,' Bryony gave a little giggle. 'Then she slept through most of the journey and said how much she'd enjoyed it.'

Marianne gave a shaky smile. 'I'm so grateful to you. Are you staying with friends in Dallas?'

'No, a hotel. As soon as the government says we can return Marcus has said he will drive back and see what the damage is to our house and *Green Vistas*.'

'Give me your number. I'll call you back.'

'There's no need. I just wanted you to know about Grandma. I'll call you again in a few days when Marcus has been home and we know what the situation is.'

'Thank you, Bryony, and thank Marcus also. You don't know how relieved I am. Give Grandma my love.' With shaking hands Marianne replaced the receiver and went to search out Giovanni and tell him the news.

It was a further three days before Bryony telephoned Marianne. 'We're still in Dallas,' she announced miserably. 'Marcus drove back down and he wasn't allowed through. The National Guard have roadblocks in place. They say the situation is 'volatile' whatever that means, and no one is allowed back to check on their property at present. At least we are staying in a hotel. Marcus said he saw people living in their cars at the side of the road.'

Marianne had followed the news on the Greek television and she was not surprised at Bryony's news. For some days people were stranded and thousands had been forced to wait without shelter, food or water before rescuers had been able to reach them and move them to safety. The death toll was rising and she dreaded to think of the conditions that would confront the inhabitants when they were finally allowed to return to their homes.

'That must be costing you a fortune!'

Bryony hedged around the remark. 'Necessity. We'll probably be able to claim it back from the insurance company.'

'Give me your number. I need to speak to Uncle Yannis and Giovanni urgently. I'll call you back later.'

'There's no need.' Bryony felt unreasonably annoyed that Marianne was not prepared to talk to her for longer.

'Please, Bryony. This is important. Just tell me your telephone number.'

Bryony read the number from the dial and Marianne repeated

it back to her. 'I'll call you back, hopefully within the hour,' she promised.

Marianne unclipped her mobile phone from the back of her shorts and dialled Giovanni's number. 'Where are you?' she asked as soon as he answered.

Giovanni frowned. 'In Aghios Nikolaos; at the wholesalers. I told you where I was going. What's the problem?'

'I have something important to talk to you about. I don't want to do it over the phone. I need to talk to Uncle Yannis as well. Can you meet me back at the house as soon as possible?'

'Tell me, Marianne, what has happened?'

'Nothing. It's to do with Bryony and Marcus.'

'Your Grandmother?'

'No, they're all safe and well. Please, Giovanni, meet me at the house as soon as you can.' Marianne finished the call. Maybe her idea was crazy; after all, her grandmother was ninety-five.

'Marianne, that's impossible.'

'No it isn't. Let me speak to Marcus.'

Shaking her head Bryony handed the telephone to her husband.

'Hello, Marcus?' Marianne suddenly felt nervous. Would he think she was interfering? 'I've just asked Bryony to come to Crete. No, please listen to me. You are staying in a hotel and don't know when you'll be able to return home or what you'll find when you get there. We've seen the news over here and it's going to take a considerable time for life to get back to normal in Louisiana. There will be many more elderly people needing care home places. Grandmother can't be shunted around from place to place at her age. I've spoken to Giovanni's aunt and uncle. They want to offer her a home here, with them. You know we looked after Aunt Anna and Uncle Yiorgo for years and we have plenty of space available. She obviously can't make the journey alone so we would like you and Bryony to come out with her. You could stay for a couple of weeks or more, think of it as an impromptu holiday, and see her settled in. At least when you return home you won't have to worry about Grandma.'

There was silence on the other end of the telephone.

'Are you there, Marcus?'

'Yes, I'm sorry. You have just taken me by surprise. I don't know what to say.'

'Please, Marcus. Put the cost of the flights against staying in a hotel for an indefinite amount of time and you'll hardly be out of pocket.'

Marcus ran a hand over his forehead. 'I don't know. I'll have to talk to Bryony.'

'Have you got access to the internet?' asked Marianne.

'The hotel has facilities.'

'Then have a look at the news they are showing and then look up flights. You might be able to get one direct to Athens and change there, or go via England. Phone me back as soon as you've decided what route you'll take and when you should arrive. We'll be at the airport to meet you.'

Marcus looked at his wife with a bewildered expression. 'I'll have to talk to Bryony. Grandma might not want to leave America.'

'Don't ask her. Just do it. Tell her she's coming for a visit. Please, Marcus.' Marianne felt on the verge of tears. Suddenly she was desperate to see her grandmother again.

Marianne waited anxiously at Heraklion airport. She had been relieved when Marcus and Bryony had finally capitulated and agreed to bring her grandmother to Crete. She dreaded the telephone bill they would receive that month after the number of calls she had made to America and then to an old University friend in England, arranging for them to be met and looked after for twenty four hours until they could catch their connecting flight from Heathrow.

Visitors to the island made their way down the steps from the aeroplane and onto the waiting buses to transport them to the terminal. There was no sign of her relatives disembarking and she felt panic surging through her. Had they changed their minds at the last minute and decided to return to America after all?

Two burly airport workers climbed the steps and held a brief conversation with the steward at the door before disappearing inside, returning moments later, one on each side of a wheelchair containing an old lady who they carried carefully down to the runway. A man and woman followed them and they stood in an uncertain group. An empty bus drew up and the men placed Annita in her wheelchair on board and indicated that Bryony and Marcus should join her.

A delighted smile on her face Marianne raced down the stairs from the cafeteria that overlooked the runway and took her place amongst the throng of people waiting at arrivals. To her surprise it was only a matter of minutes before she saw her grandmother being pushed through by the same attendants with Bryony by her side. She waved wildly and began to push her way forwards.

Marianne enfolded her in her arms. 'Where's Marcus?' she asked.

'Waiting for the luggage. He shouldn't be too long. We haven't got much.'

Marianne turned her attention to her grandmother. 'It's wonderful to see you, grandma.' She spoke loudly and clearly.

Annita looked at her granddaughter critically. 'I may not be able to walk very far, but there's nothing wrong with my hearing.'

Marianne blushed. 'I'm sorry. I always had to raise my voice when I spoke to Aunt Anna or Uncle Yiorgo. I tend to assume that everyone over the age of seventy is deaf.'

'Well I'm not. Can we move to one side? There are so many people around that I'm getting a crick in my neck looking up at you.' Annita began to push at the wheels on her chair.

'How did Grandma cope with the journey?' asked Marianne quietly.

'She was fine. She said she enjoyed the flight.' Bryony gave a little giggle. 'She kept telling the steward that when she first came to America she had to travel by ship to New York and then take a train to Louisiana. I think she had told him her life story by the time the plane landed in Athens. He insisted she had a motorised buggy instead of using a wheelchair and he cleared us through the checkout in a matter of minutes. We didn't have to queue at all.'

'Do either of you need the rest room?' asked Marianne. 'It will take us at least an hour to get home.'

Bryony nodded. 'I think it would be a good idea. We could go now whilst we're waiting for Marcus. If you see him looking very lost with two cases and a holdall please rescue him.'

Marcus did indeed look lost. Nowhere could he see his wife or her grandmother. He placed his burdens at his feet. Hopefully Marianne had met them and between them they were getting Annita settled into whatever transport there was to take them to Aghios Nikolaos and they would return for him.

'Hello, Marcus?'

'Marianne.' He enfolded her in his arms. 'It's good to see you.'

'Bryony and Grandma are in the rest room. I'll stand with your luggage if you want to go over.' Marianne pointed to the door.

Bryony leaned back and closed her eyes. She had not appreciated how much stress she had suffered in the past weeks and now she felt exhausted. She was still not convinced that bringing their grandmother to Crete had been a good idea and had not dared to tell her that they planned to leave her there when they returned to America.

Marianne slowed as she pulled her mobile phone from the pocket of her shorts and dialled a number before tucking it into the crook of her neck. 'Five more minutes,' she said and listened to a reply. 'Unbelievable!' was her answer.

Bryony opened her eyes and caught her breath. As they rounded a corner and drove down a hill the view across the sea was just as she remembered, the small island of Spinalonga shimmering like a mirage in the distance.

'There's Giovanni. Oh, good, John and Nicola are here to meet you as well. Now we can get you all settled in and relax.'

Annita looked around the spacious room in surprise and delight. Large windows opened onto the patio outside that ran the whole width of the house and gave a view over the sea. There was a settee and easy chair, as well as a small table and two upright chairs. A television stood on a swivel base that turned it towards the bed or settee. Through an archway was her own bathroom, a handrail beside the toilet and a bath with an electric hoist to enable her to get in and out easily. There was also a shower with a seat fixed into the wall and again a handrail.

'This is better than the room I had at the care home,' she told Marianne. 'It was only half this size.'

Marianne smiled with pleasure. 'This was Uncle Yiorgo's room. Marcus decorated Aunt Anna's when they stayed here before and we gave that to Giovanni's mother. The windows and doors open electronically.' She indicated the push button in the wall. 'There's a bell pull over your bed that you can use in the night if you want anything or during the day as well. It connects through to all the rooms in the house. We turn the bedroom ones off during the day and take it in turns to have one on over night. That way there is always someone who can come to you.'

'You seem to have thought of everything.'

'That was Uncle Yannis. He knew Aunt Anna and Uncle Yiorgo would have to live with them eventually and he wanted to make life for everyone as easy as possible. Is there anything you want now? If not, I'll take you out on the patio and see if Bryony and Marcus are ready for coffee. I'm planning an early meal this evening as I'm sure you're all exhausted.'

Annita smiled at her granddaughter appreciatively. 'You're a good girl, Marianne. You and Bryony are certainly the best of the bunch.'

Marianne patted the old lady's wrinkled hand. 'I've wanted you to come and visit us for years. Tomorrow we'll take you along to Plaka. You'll not believe the difference we've made along there.'

'Your mother's told me about the bungalows and the taverna, but I'll be pleased to see for myself.'

Marianne wheeled her grandmother out onto the patio where Giovanni was sitting with a glass of wine. He rose to meet her; his hands outstretched, and planted a kiss on each cheek. 'I was so busy getting everything out of the car and showing Marcus and Bryony their room that I didn't have time to greet you properly. How was your journey? Did you find it very tiring?'

'I was pleasantly surprised. It took us less time to fly to Athens than to drive to Dallas. We weren't stuck in traffic jams of course.'

'I should hope not, not in the air anyway. Now,' Giovanni winked at her, 'I know Marianne is making coffee, but would you like to join me with a glass of wine?'

'I'd love to.' Annita lowered her voice. 'Bryony and Marcus are teetotal. That's their choice and nothing to do with me, but I don't feel that I can drink a glass of wine on my own in front of them. It seems rude, somehow.'

Giovanni poured a generous glass and held his own up in salutation. 'Welcome home,' he said and Annita felt a lump come into her throat.

Annita held the photograph of her dead husband in her hand. 'Well, Elias, who would have thought I would come back over here at my age. I wish you could be with me. Marianne and Giovanni are a lovely couple. They seem so happy together, and their John is a nice boy. So is the girl, Nicola, who is staying with them.' She replaced the photo on her bedside table. 'I'll talk to you again tomorrow.' she promised, shaking her head sadly. 'I'm not as young as I was and I am feeling rather tired.'

Marianne parked her car and joined Bryony and Marcus on the

patio. She waved gaily at them. 'Sorry about running out on you, but I had to go up and open the taverna. I'm pleased to see you raided the kitchen.' She helped herself to one of the rolls that were one the table. 'How did you sleep?'

'Fantastically well,' admitted Bryony. 'I'm not sure whether it was the time difference or just the travelling but I was unconscious the moment my head touched the pillow.'

Marcus smiled. 'I haven't slept so well in weeks.'

'Grandma seems to have slept well also. She didn't call during the night and I crept in before I left and she was still asleep. I switched the call button over to Aunt Ourania whilst I was gone.'

'You seem terribly well organised already,' remarked Marcus.

'We've just gone back to the system we used with Aunt Anna and Uncle Yiorgo. Giovanni and I will go off to work first thing. Aunt Ourania can help grandma shower and dress as necessary. I shall be back by the time Uncle Yannis takes Aunt Ourania into Aghios Nikolaos to open up the shop. Giovanni's mother is here during the morning. She has taken on the task of packing the herbs and olives. We usually do a bit of housework together and prepare some lunch. John and Nicola are also around so you two can relax and enjoy yourselves. Grandma can choose if she wants to have her evening meal with us, or she can eat it in her room if she prefers. After Uncle Yannis and Aunt Ourania have left we could drive along to Plaka and I'll show Grandma our bungalows and taverna. She might like to go up to the cemetery.'

A bell sounded in the house and Marianne rose to her feet. 'That's Grandma. I'll go and see what she wants.'

Ourania had already reached Annita's room by the time Marianne arrived. 'I wasn't sure if you were back.'

'Thanks, Aunt Ourania. You carry on. I'll see to Grandma. Bryony and Marcus are on the patio. You and Uncle Yannis go and join them. Remember Marcus doesn't speak Greek.'

Ourania shook her head in despair as Marianne smiled and entered her grandmother's room.

Annita was dressed and sitting in her chair. 'I wasn't sure if anyone was up yet. I thought I ought to find out before I started making myself at home.'

'All I ask is that you stay in your room overnight. There aren't alarm pulls anywhere except in your room so we wouldn't know if you needed help. Also, you could inadvertently set the intruder alarms off and then we'd have the police out. During the day you can do exactly as you please. You're not confined to your room. Are you ready for some breakfast? Marcus and Bryony have had theirs, and Uncle Yannis and Aunt Ourania should be with them. Shall I push you or do you want to wheel yourself? You can walk with your sticks if you prefer.'

'I think I'll use my chair until I know how far we're going. You'd better push me. I don't want to scrape the walls.'

'It wouldn't be the first time. We just paint the marks over. We'll go straight out onto the patio.'

Annita took a deep breath of the sea air. 'Nowhere else in the world smells like Crete. The moment we landed I could smell the mixture of sunshine and herbs.'

Annita walked into the old farmhouse with the aid of her sticks and looked around. She remembered when her aunt and uncle had their bed in the corner and the children slept upstairs in the loft area. The room had been crowded with tables and chairs, dominated by a large cupboard where Maria had kept her table wear, bedding, and winter or summer clothes according to the season. She had used one drawer to store her completed embroidery and no one was allowed near it for fear of damage or soiling. Even when she had visited Plaka with Elias, after Yannis had died, it had still looked exactly the same, only the large bed had been removed.

Now all was gone. Patio windows had been installed and led out to a paved area with tables and chairs. A large kitchen ran the entire length of a wall with a counter for serving food before it. The opposite wall was shelved and held an array of everyday commodities for the visitors to purchase. The door that had led to the upper level was marked '*PRIVATE*' and Annita was immediately curious.

'What's behind there?' she asked.

'A small toilet for the staff to use and a stock room. Upstairs we had a shower installed and a room where we could keep some clean clothes and change.'

'Whatever for?'

'You'd be amazed at how sticky and dirty you feel when you've finished the cleaning, not to mention the odd drain that needs to be unblocked. It was fine when I used to go home afterwards and Giovanni came out to run the shop and taverna, but if I had to do both I didn't feel I should be wearing the same clothes to prepare food as I had worn whilst I was cleaning showers and toilets. Some of our staff from Aghios Nikolaos stay on to help in the shop at busy times and they appreciate being able to have a proper wash and change their clothes.'

Annita nodded. 'That photograph? Where did that come from?' She pointed to the large framed photograph adorning the far wall.

Marianne flushed. 'I believe that was Anna. She was the girl that old Uncle Yannis and his wife adopted. She died during the war. It must have been her ghost appearing to me when I took the photo.' Marianne felt the usual lump coming into her throat as she talked about the young girl who had died from blood poisoning.

Annita crossed herself. 'I read about her in Yannis's book.' She wheeled herself closer to the photograph and looked at it for some minutes. 'She was supposed to be the school teacher's daughter, wasn't she?'

Marianne nodded. Annita rose from her chair and scrutinized it more closely. 'Hmm,' she said finally and sat back down.

'Would you like to go over to Spinalonga?' she asked, once again in control of her emotions and wishing to divert her grandmother's attention away from the photograph. 'It looks very different now from the way it used to. There has been so much restoration, and there is an education centre in some of the old buildings. The main road looks like any other village now, but you can still wander around some of the areas that haven't been touched and get a feel for the place. It's definitely worth a visit.'

Annita shook her head. 'I have no wish to visit. I'm pleased it has been restored and is being put to good use. When Elias and I visited Plaka years ago he went over and I refused to go with him. I know how difficult life was for my cousin, Yannis, when he lived there. I don't need to see for myself. I still have the letters he sent to me when he asked our help to present the new treatment for leprosy to the government and force them to give it to the islanders. He described the conditions and his life over there very vividly, far more so than in his book.'

'Where are those letters, Grandma?'

'Safe enough in the strong box at the bank. Can we go up to the cemetery? I ought to pay my respects to my relatives whilst I'm here. If I'm not polite to them they might insist that I join them!'

'Grandma!' Marianne and Bryony spoke in horrified unison.

Annita retired to her room, finally admitting to being tired, and saying she would rest until Yannis and Ourania arrived and it was time for their meal. She was determined to return to the Greek way of life, resting in the afternoon and eating late.

'Well, Elias, you would never believe the change they have brought to the area. That awful old farmhouse has gone and everywhere looks so attractive. Just thinking about all the hard work they have put in makes me feel tired. I'm going to have a little rest now, then I shall be able to join everyone for supper.' She sighed deeply. 'I just wish you could be here with us.'

Bryony sat with Marianne on the patio as the sun went down. Marcus had accompanied Giovanni to his office to look at the news from Louisiana on the internet.

Marianne stretched her arms above her head. 'Grandma is amazing. I was expecting another Aunt Anna. For the last few years of her life she seemed to be in a dream world. I know Uncle Yannis found it very hard to accept, she'd brought him up and he thought of her as his mother, but she seemed happy enough.' Marianne shrugged. 'Maybe it was because she'd had to work physically hard all her life.'

'Maybe.' Bryony seemed ill at ease as Marianne made conversation.

'What's wrong, Bryony? Are you worried about the situation at home?'

Bryony shrugged. 'Of course I am, but there's nothing I can do about that. Well, it's Grandma, really. She thinks she is just over here for a couple of weeks for a holiday with us. I haven't mentioned that she won't be returning to America.'

Marianne frowned. 'Go on.'

'She's seen the news, but I don't think she comprehends just how serious the hurricane was. She knows there were floods and loss of life, but she also talks about going back to the care home. She only brought a picture of Grandpa and her spare glasses with her and she keeps mentioning little keepsakes and souvenirs that she will be pleased to see again.'

Marianne nodded. 'I'll do my best, but we can't make her stay if she is really unhappy. I thought it would be my mother and Uncle Andreas that she would miss.'

Bryony shook her head. 'From what I've gathered your mother is very involved with your sister and her boys. She also plays golf, belongs to the bridge club, and arranges coffee mornings and outings for them. It's obviously very good for her, but it doesn't leave her much spare time to visit Grandma.'

'Don't make excuses for her,' smiled Marianne. 'She is always welcome to visit. She might find it easier to come over once or twice a year than feeling committed to regular visits at home. What about Uncle Andreas?'

'He lives in New York. He telephones her every week. He managed to visit a couple of times last year. He is very busy now he's so successful, and he's also looking after Laurie. You know he has Alzheimer's Disease?'

'How sad. I didn't know. Poor Uncle Andreas. Has he no one to help him?'

'He arranges care for Laurie when he has to go away. I saw him briefly the last time he came down and he said Laurie is always worse when he returns. It takes him out of his usual routine. I also feel guilty. You have such a busy life it doesn't seem fair to add caring for Grandma to your jobs.'

'You don't have to worry about us looking after Grandma. You've seen the system we have. I'm busiest when we have new arrivals. The shop has to be open for most of the day. It's amazing how many people forget their toothbrush. John's very good during the holidays now he's older. He runs the shop and waters all the pot plants, as well as running odd errands. Nicola has also been a great help this year.'

'I've hardly seen him, he's such a nice boy; a credit to you both. You never thought about having more children?' asked Bryony.

Marianne shook her head. 'We couldn't possibly have afforded another child whilst we were trying to get this project off the ground. By the time this was up and running successfully we were too busy for me to be able to cope with another child. Now I would hate to have a baby around again to care for.'

'I wish I could have had children.' Bryony sighed. 'It was not to be. The fault appeared to be with Marcus, but don't tell him I told you. He's a bit sensitive about it.'

'I won't mention it. It's none of my business. Is that all that's worrying you?'

Bryony frowned. 'If we went into Aghios Nikolaos would we be able to go to a drug store? Grandma will need some more medication within the week.'

'Of course. There is one in Elounda, but if they haven't got the medicine in stock they have to send to Aghios Nikolaos so if it's urgent you might as well make the journey yourself.'

'She has five days supply left.'

'We'll need to take it in with us. The pharmacist will be able to look it up and then give her the Greek equivalent.'

'Would there be anywhere I could buy a bathing costume? I know it's getting towards the end of the season and I do feel rather guilty about spending the money, but I'd like to take advantage of the weather whilst we're here. Grandma could do with a few more clothes also. I only packed the minimum when we left for Dallas.'

Marianne's heart sank. She hated shopping for clothes. 'I've got an idea. Make a list of what you want. We can go to the chemist first, then I'll take you to Aunt Ourania's shop. She loves going shopping and would have a far better idea than me which shops would stock suitable clothes for Grandma.'

'Do you think Grandma will want to come with us?'

'I hope not,' frowned Marianne. 'It would be a bit difficult getting her wheelchair around. I'll suggest that she stays here and John spends the morning with her. Nicola can go up to the shop. I know he wants to talk to her. He wants to know what America was like when she went there in the nineteen thirties. I can take her in another day if she wants to go. I'm sure she'd like to see Aunt Ourania's shop, but most of Aghios Nikolaos has changed since she lived there as a girl.'

John sat outside with his great grandmother. 'I really am interested,' he insisted. 'I know you went to Athens as a nurse and worked for a microbiologist who you married and that's how you ended up in America. I want to know what life in America was like then. How did you manage without air travel? It must have taken ages to get anywhere.'

'It was such an adventure. We had only just married and were off to a new life in a new country. We had to go by ship, of course. Elias had never been on a boat before and he was sea sick. I wasn't, of course. I'd been out on my father's fishing boat since I was a child. The last time I went out with him was to go to Spinalonga to speak to Yannis.' Annita's eyes took on a far away look as she reminisced about her early life with Elias, and John listened entranced.

Marianne drew up outside the house and was amused to see John was taking photographs of Annita. She waved to them as she removed the packages from the car and took them into the kitchen, returning with a glass of fruit juice and an apple.

'Has John been looking after you properly, Grandma?'

Annita smiled. 'He's drained me dry of memories.'

'You mustn't let him tire you out.'

John looked at his mother, his eyes glowing. 'Grandma's better than a history book. You've no idea how much I've learned about the family. Far more than you've ever told me,' he added accusingly. 'Did you know that her father had a fish shop when he went to America?'

Marianne looked surprised. 'Did he? I don't remember him and I suppose it never occurred to me to ask if he did any work over there.'

'And her mother looked after Grandma's children whilst they were small so she could go back to work.'

'That I did know.'

'Let me have a photograph of you both together; then I ought to go up to the taverna and relieve Nicola – unless you need to go off and do anything else.'

Marianne complied and John took a further half a dozen photographs of his mother and Annita before finally declaring himself satisfied and packing his camera away.

'Will you talk to me again, Grandma? We've only got as far as the war,' explained John to Marianne. 'There are years to go yet.'

'I hope he wasn't a nuisance,' apologised Marianne. 'He is genuinely interested.'

'Not at all. I wish I had my photographs with me so he could look at them. I'll make sure Bryony sends copies of them over when we go back.'

'I'm sure John would love to see them. He says he wants to be a photographer and you'll never see him without his camera. He spends a good deal of his pocket money on film and does his own developing. He's just bought an underwater camera.'

Annita nodded. Maybe she could give the boy some money that he could put towards his photographic expenses as a present. It would be a way of thanking his parents for their hospitality. She had probably been foolish to give Helena so much and then setting the same amount aside for her other children. She would have to speak to Bryony and Marcus at an appropriate moment. She still owed them for her hotel bills and the flight to Crete.

London: September 2005

'Close your eyes. Don't open them until I say.' David put his arms round his wife and thrust a piece of paper into her hands. 'You can open now. What do you think of that?'

Carol looked at the cheque she held for fifteen thousand pounds. 'Where did you get this? Is it real?'

'Last week's lottery. I couldn't believe it myself when I checked the numbers. What shall we spend it on?'

Carol shook her head in disbelief. 'I don't know. We need to think carefully. We don't want to waste it. Maybe we could pay off some of the mortgage?'

'That's a bit uninteresting. We'll have nothing to show for it.'

'Lower mortgage repayments.'

David sniffed. 'What about a holiday?'

'And when we come back we'll have nothing to show for that apart from a sun tan and some photos.'

'You come up with some ideas, then. I'm going down to the bank to open up a deposit account. Until we make up our minds we can at least earn some interest on it.'

Carol spent the rest of the day thinking about the money they had won on the lottery. There was so much that needed to be done in the house. They had known that when they had purchased the property, deciding they were young enough to complete a certain amount themselves and only employ a professional for the essential services. This could change everything.

She purchased a bottle of wine, spending more than usual, and a joint of beef. She would cook David his favourite meal and then they could talk through her ideas.

She raised her glass. 'To the house, and my clever husband who chose the winning numbers.'

David grinned at her. 'Have you had any thoughts how to spend it?'

'I've thought of nothing else all day. I think we ought to get some estimates for the essentials. We know the roof is sound and we have the certificate for the electrics. We ought to have the double glazed windows we've talked about put in as a priority. That should still leave a sizable sum.'

David nodded. 'And then?'

'Then we tackle the central heating. Maybe we could even have the kitchen and bathroom renewed. After that it would just be the decorating and we said we could do that ourselves.'

'Better start to look in the Yellow Pages. I'll ask around at work and see if any of the chaps can recommend a plumber.'

'I could ask the neighbours. Shall we tell our parents?'

'No, let's leave it as a surprise. When it's done we can ask them down for a weekend. We can tell them we've managed to do a few improvements and we'd like them to tell us what they think.'

Carol laughed delightedly. 'I can't wait to get started.'

Mr Goodman sat in the lounge with Carol and David. He spread a sheaf of papers out before him.

'I'll leave this lot with you to have a look at. You don't have to accept my estimate, but I'd like to give you a bit of advice. If you're going to have central heating put in, now is the time to update your bathroom and kitchen. The floorboards will need to come up to do the plumbing runs to the radiators so the other plumbing runs could be done at the same time. If you decide where you want your appliances the pipes can always be capped off until a later date.'

'That makes sense,' David agreed. 'Give us a couple of days to compare estimates and we'll let you know our decision. If we agreed your price when would you be able to start?'

Mr Goodman looked in his diary. 'At the moment I could start in a couple of weeks. I'd appreciate a call even if you turn me down. Helps me to plan ahead.'

David held out his hand. 'Thanks for your time and your advice. I'll phone you as soon as possible.'

'Well, what do you think?' David placed three sheets of paper covered with his small, neat handwriting in front of Carol. 'Mr Goodman's estimate falls between the other two, but he was the only one who suggested the other plumbing work should be done at the same time.'

'Has he allowed for the extra in his estimate?'

David nodded. 'It's not an exact figure and he's made it clear that it's for the plumbing run only, not fixing appliances, old or new.'

Carol frowned. 'I just don't know. Mrs Whitworth said he had worked for her. She was pleased with the job, had no reason to call him back. He started and finished when he said he would and didn't leave a load of mess behind.'

'So what do you want to do? Toss a coin?'

'No, let's go with Mr Goodman.'

'Assuming he doesn't suddenly start coming up with extras we can't afford it makes sense to have the bathroom and kitchen sorted out at the same time. Only one lot of disruption. Why don't we call him back and ask him to quote for the rest of the work? That would also give us an idea how much we could afford for new fixtures and fittings. We don't want to do either on the cheap and regret it afterwards. Again, we don't want to spend an extortionate amount on something that will be out of fashion by next year and look hideous and unnecessary.'

'Is my taste that bad?'

David smiled. 'I have complete faith in your taste, but you know what some of these sales people are like. I don't want to come home and find they've talked you into a Jacuzzi when all we want is a conventional bath.'

'I promise. No Jacuzzi. I think a shower would be more practical anyway. Maybe we could ask Mr Goodman to give us separate quotes for fitting the bathroom and kitchen. It might be a good idea to discuss the layout with him. I know what I'd like but he might say it isn't practical.'

'I'll 'phone him tomorrow. You could always pick up a few brochures on your way home tomorrow night. We can have a look through them and get some firm ideas before he comes.'

Mr Goodman stood with a notebook in his hand. 'Be guided by me for the size of the radiators you need. You don't want anything too big for these rooms, but you need to have sufficient heat. The pipe runs are no problem, they can go behind the skirting boards. Have you decided what you want in the bathroom?'

Carol nodded. 'We're going to do away with the bath altogether. If we have a double shower it will give us enough space to have a small chest of drawers in here where we can keep the spare towels and a small chair. We want a white toilet and basin, but they can be in the same place as they are now. I really would like a heated towel rail so we shouldn't need a separate radiator.'

Mr Goodman looked around approvingly. 'Sensible decision. I can do all the fitting for you, but you'll need a separate contractor for the tiles. I know a man who's good and reliable. He's worked with me before.'

'How much will the tiling cost?'

'I can't say. Charlie charges by the metre and it depends upon the size of the tiles and how much cutting is needed. You decide what you want and I'll ask him to come over and give you a quote.'

David was calculating mentally. If they had the bathroom completely refurbished would they be able to afford to have the kitchen done at the same time? Fifteen thousand pounds had seemed like a fortune when they had first received the cheque, but having replaced the windows and installing central heating was taking a sizeable amount.

Mr Goodman led the way back down stairs. 'Small radiator in the hall; saves you having a cold spot and the heat rushing out of the rooms. I suggest you have one large radiator in each of your living rooms; again, the pipe runs can go behind the skirting boards. Now, let's have a proper look at the kitchen.'

Carol looked at David for reassurance. 'We obviously need to have some heating in here and I thought we could have the boiler in that corner. What I'd really like is to have all the old units ripped out and new ones put in. There's hardly any worktop available. I'd also like an eating bench under the window.'

Mr Goodman pursed his lips. 'The boiler in that corner is no problem. If you want an eating bench under the window it will mean moving your sink and the washing machine. I'll need to have a quick look at your main drains to see if it's feasible.'

'It might mean more work but we really want the bench. We can always delay the tiling in the kitchen for a few months if necessary, provided the basics are done.'

'Do you have any plans of the house?'

David shook his head. 'I suppose we could get some.'

'I'll have a quick look this evening and pop down to the Council tomorrow and ask them to dig them out. I don't want to start something that could lead to a problem later for you. You're obviously prepared to spend a good bit of money in one go, but I presume there is a limit?'

'There certainly is,' David assured him.

Mr Goodman arrived and sat in the lounge with Carol and David. He was not sure how they were going to take his news about the drains. He spread a photocopied plan out on the coffee table before them.

'I've had a good look at this and your kitchen. If you're determined to have the sink and washing machine moved I will have to do a plumbing run diagonally under the kitchen floor. That's no problem to me as a plumber. The thing is, we don't know what is under there. Sometimes there's a good depth between the floor joists and the ground, other times we need to drill through the joists as they are sitting too low to pass a pipe under.'

David frowned. 'Will that cost a lot more if you have to drill through?'

'A couple of hundred. It's more the disruption. I'll need the floorboards up, of course. The snag is, until I've had a look underneath I don't know the state of the joists. The worst scenario is that some or all could be rotten. That would mean I was unable to drill through safely. They would need to be replaced, but if that was the case we could leave enough space underneath to run the pipes. If the joists did need to be replaced you're looking at a good bit more than two hundred.'

'And you're not going to know this until you've lifted the boards?'

'That's right. It would be no good me lifting an odd one and looking. The joist there could look fine and a couple of feet further along be quite rotten.'

Carol bit her lip. 'It won't affect the installation of the central heating in the rest of the house?'

'Not a bit,' confirmed Mr Goodman. 'If there's any problem where the boiler will be situated that's just a small area that could be rectified, even a bit of concrete to give it a firm foundation. The choice is yours. If you want to leave the kitchen as it is I don't need the floorboards up. I've jumped up and down out there a couple of times and the floor seems pretty firm in the centre. If you start to take out the units that are in position it might be a different story at the sides. Joists often begin to rot where they are inset in the wall. Provided it hasn't spread too far they can be strengthened.'

David scribbled some figures on a piece of paper. If they allowed a thousand pounds for possible floor repairs they would have to delay the re-tiling of the kitchen. They had considered that possibility earlier and now it seemed a sensible option. Carol's heart was set on having an eating bench under the window and getting rid of the table and two chairs.

'Well, I think we should go ahead. There's no point in doing half the job. We'd be in the same position regarding the joists in the future. If we decided in a year's time to have the eating bench fitted we'd need to have all the floor ripped so the plumbing work could be done. I think it's better that it's done now.'

Mr Goodman nodded. 'You'd not be very happy if you'd had your new units fitted and then had to have them taken out. Let's hope the joists are just the way I would like them, sound and with a cavity underneath.'

Mr Goodman started the work on the agreed date and each evening when Carol and David returned from work they would inspect his progress. The skirting boards had been removed where necessary and gleaming new pipes were in situ, a radiator had been placed in each room and bracketed to the wall. Carol was less happy when she found a note stuck on the bathroom door saying the new shower was out of commission for twenty-four hours.

'I'd planned to wash my hair this evening,' she grumbled.

'You can wash your hair in the sink,' David tried to console her; he too, was disconcerted by the fact that he would be unable to bathe as usual in the morning. 'I'll phone Mr Goodman and ask what the problem is.'

'There's no problem,' Mr Goodman assured him. 'I didn't want to start connecting up to the water supply just in case I found a leak somewhere. It can take a bit of time to trace and I wouldn't want to leave you without water over night. You can use the toilet, but I've capped the other supply pipes off. I'll connect up and test first thing tomorrow. If I do find any problem I shall have all day to put it right.'

'What about the kitchen?'

'You've water there. I've installed a separate stopcock for the bathroom. There'll be another for the kitchen. That way if you have any work done in the future you will still have a water supply.'

David relayed the message to Carol. 'I'm glad we decided on Mr Goodman. He seems to think of every eventuality.'

Mr Goodman was enjoying his work in Carol and David Wright's house. It was far more satisfying installing a new system rather than doing running repairs. They were a co-operative couple and obviously trusted his judgement and expertise as a plumber. He had asked them to clear the kitchen for him ready to start work on moving the sink and washing machine pipes and they had done it over the weekend. He would make himself a cup of tea whilst he waited for Brett to arrive. Between them, they would remove the old units and Brett would cart them away, leaving him with an empty kitchen. If all went well he could even have the new plumbing runs installed that day. By the end of the week the new boiler would be in and connected up.

He was surprised by the sound of the doorbell. Brett would have come to the back door that stood open. He frowned. Should he answer it? It could be a delivery. His cup in his hand he walked along the hall and opened the front door.

'Can I help you?'

For a moment the man on the doorstep looked puzzled, then smiled. 'Mr Patel? Is he in, please?'

Mr Goodman shook his head. 'I don't know a Mr Patel. I'm only working here. If you come back this evening and see Mr or Mrs Wright they may know him.'

'No, this is his house. This is where Mr Patel lives.'

'I think you must have the wrong address. Come back this evening.' Mr Goodman pushed the door closed and returned to the kitchen. He began to unscrew the doors from the cupboards. It would all save time when Brett arrived.

David looked around the bare kitchen critically. It had taken Mr Goodman longer than he had anticipated to remove the units and then he had been called away to attend to a burst pipe. The sink and washing machine were capped off with notices attached saying 'Do Not Use' and the new boiler stood in the corner. Chunks of plaster had come away from the walls and David groaned. The walls would have to be repaired before the new units could be fixed in place. He could see they had been over ambitious. They would have to take out a loan to complete the refurbishment. He had secretly hoped there would be enough money left from the lottery win to redecorate the whole house, but common sense told him that would have to wait a while.

The front door bell rang and he wondered if Carol had forgotten her key, although it was unlike her. It would probably be Mr Goodman coming to tell him about the walls. He opened the door to a stranger.

'Can I help you?'

'I am looking for Mr Patel. He lives here.'

David shook his head. 'I'm sorry. Mr Patel moved away when we bought the house.'

'No, that cannot be. I still write to him at this address. This is his house; where he lives.'

'As I said, he's moved. He sold the house to us a few months ago.'

'So what happens to the letters I send to him?'

David shrugged. 'I send them on to the hospital where he works. I presume they pass them on to him.'

'You do not have his new address?'

'I'm sorry, no. Maybe the hospital could help you.'

'I see.' The man hesitated. 'You can give me the address of this hospital?'

'Of course. Step inside a moment and I'll write it down for you. Excuse the mess. We're having a new kitchen fitted.'

The man approached the reception desk tentatively. 'Could I see Mr Patel, please?'

'When is your appointment?' The receptionist did not raise her eyes.

'I don't have an appointment. Mr Patel is my brother-in-law.'

The woman looked up and removed her glasses. 'Mr Patel is away at present. He is in Paris for a conference.'

'When will he be back?'

'I'm not sure. I expect his secretary would know.'

'Please, ask her for me.'

The receptionist lifted the phone and dialled an extension. 'Can you tell me when Mr Patel will be back from Paris?' She frowned at the answer. 'I thought the conference finished on the Thursday.' She listened to the person on the other end of the line, finally saying 'I see,' and replacing the receiver.

She turned back to the waiting man. 'Mr Patel is at the conference until Thursday evening. He will not be back in the hospital until Monday. He and his wife are spending a few days in Paris together.'

Tariq Kavira looked at her in surprise. 'His wife? His wife is dead. She was hit by a bus.'

The receptionist shook her head. 'No, she died when she returned to India to visit her family. If you are her brother you must know that.'

'Nandita never returned to India. He wrote and told us she had been involved in an accident.'

With a sigh the woman turned to her colleague. 'I am right, aren't I? Mr Patel's first wife died when she was in India.'

'So I heard. What's the problem?'

'This gentleman insists she was killed in a road accident in England.'

'Are we talking about the same Mr Patel? Maybe the one you need works at another hospital.'

Tariq shook his head. 'I went to his address and the man there told me that he had moved. They have forwarded any mail that comes for him to this hospital.'

'I don't think we can help you. As I said, our Mr Patel is in Paris at the moment.'

Tariq shook his head. 'I don't understand. Why didn't he tell us he had remarried and changed his address?'

'I have no idea.'

'Do you have his current address?'

The receptionist pursed her lips. 'I'm not able to divulge confidential information. If you wish to leave a letter for him I will ensure he receives it as soon as he returns.'

Tariq Kavira purchased a notepad and envelopes as he returned to the small bed and breakfast room he had rented. He felt totally confused. His brother-in-law had never written and told him he had sold the house or remarried, the hospital had a doctor of that name working there, but it seemed unlikely that he was the man he was looking for, so where was his sister's husband?

He wrote a brief note, saying he was looking for his dead sister's husband and asking the surgeon, Mr Patel, at the hospital to speak to him. He would call at the hospital again on Monday and wait until it was convenient for the surgeon to have a quick word with him.

Tariq walked through the busy streets to the hospital and left his letter at the reception desk where he had been assured it would be given to Mr Patel immediately upon his return. He walked back, looking in the shops, aghast at the prices he saw displayed. He had found out how expensive London was. To rent the mean room had cost him six weeks of his Indian wages and for the price he had paid for the stationery, he could have eaten a dozen meals in his own country. He now began to realise why Ranjit claimed he could only pay back so little of the debt outstanding to his father each month. How could people afford to live here?

Mr Goodman lifted the first three floorboards and peered into the cavity. His luck was in. There was a space beneath the joists that would easily accommodate the pipe runs. He measured the amount of piping needed from the boiler to the ground and made a note on a scrap of paper. He would check it later when he had the main pipe in position.

He pulled up three more floorboards and examined them. They appeared to have been treated for woodworm at some time in the past, but seemed to be sound enough now. He prised the nails from another three and then looked in consternation at what confronted him. Just where he wanted to run his main pipe was a large slab of concrete. It oozed beneath the joists filling the cavity below them and between two of them it reached up almost to the floorboards.

Mr Goodman scratched his head. Why should anyone put concrete under a section of the floor? If the joists were unsafe and not renewed, the concrete would be needed under the whole floor area, not just in the middle. He could make bends in the pipe from the boiler, but certainly not in the waste pipes from the washing machine and sink; that would be asking for a blockage. He gave a deep sigh and pulled out his chisel and a hammer. He would try to chip a channel out. It would be time consuming, but certainly the most practical solution.

An hour later, hot and perspiring, he stood back and gazed morosely at the concrete. He had hardly made any impression on it. It would need to be drilled or smashed into small pieces and removed. He took his mobile 'phone from his overall pocket and dialled the number of an equipment rental shop and arranged to drive over and collect the small pneumatic drill that they had assured him would be ideal for the job. Half a day virtually wasted! By the time he had finished sorting out the concrete the remainder of the day would be gone and nothing to show for his labour.

Mr Goodman read the instructions carefully, although the man who had handed the drill over to him had already told him how to use it. He had purchased goggles and accepted a hard hat.

'It's a wise precaution, sir,' smiled the assistant. 'Quite large chippings can fly up into the air; can cause quite a bit of damage if they land on your head.'

He donned his protective clothing, plugged the drill into the electric supply and took a firm stance beside the concrete, the drill bit in position. He pressed the 'on' switch and almost fell backwards as the power surged through, switching it off again rapidly. He would take up his position again and be ready this time.

The whine of the drill made his ears ring as it began to eat away at the concrete, sparks flying up at the point of contact. Mr Goodman switched off and knelt down on the floor, pulling up the pieces that he had broken free of the main bulk. He placed them in a sack and started again. At this rate it was going to take him more than the remainder of the afternoon to clear the obstruction. It was definitely time for a cup of tea.

He walked outside and leaned against the doorpost. Once he had cleared the concrete it should be a straightforward job to run the pipes and connect up to the boiler and the waste. Provided he did not have to spend any time attending to leaks he should be able to have the floorboards back down by the following afternoon and that would be the end of the job. He drained his mug and walked back inside.

He nibbled away at the concrete, then stopped and began to pull out the pieces again and place them in the sack. To his surprise, someone had put some plastic sheeting beneath the joists. They must have had a problem with damp and thought that would prevent it. He pulled at it, a small piece mixed with material coming away

171

in his hand. It was firmly embedded. He took up the drill again and the familiar whine began to fill his ears. Suddenly the drill went straight through and he almost lost his balance on the joists. This was good news. If it was a hollow piece of cement he might not have to take very much more out.

He knelt down and began to pull out a few more pieces. There was more material adhering to it and a rather strange smell reached his nostrils. He put his hand down into the cavity again and touched something that was neither plastic nor material. Had someone buried an animal down there? The thought made him recoil in disgust. Cursing again, he rose and rummaged in his toolbox until he found his torch and directed the beam into the hole to see what he had touched.

This time he did lose his footing on the joists and slipped astride them, barking his shins and twisting his ankle. He tried to take a deep breath. He felt ill. He could not stay in the kitchen any longer. He scrambled back up onto the joists, relieved to find that he had not hurt himself seriously, and shone the torch into the hole once more. He then made a dash for the back door.

David went to draw in his car off the pathway and was surprised to see a length of police tape saying 'DO NOT CROSS' and a police officer standing outside his front door. Further up the road two police cars were parked and a van that he did not recognise. Carol! What had happened to Carol? It must be serious for police to be there waiting for him. He abandoned the car on the pavement and jumped out.

'You can't leave that car there,' the police officer called.

'Where's my wife? Where's Carol? What's happened to her?'

The police officer moved forward. 'Is this your house, sir?'

'Yes, where's my wife? Is she all right?'

The police officer ignored his question. 'If you'd just wait there a moment, sir. I'll let Superintendent Rawlings know you're here. He'll come and have a word with you.'

'What's happened?' shouted David. 'Tell me what's happened.'

The Superintendent emerged and the police officer spoke quietly to him. Alan Rawlings looked at David, taking in his distraught manner.

'If I could just have a quick word, sir.'

'Where's my wife? What's happened to my wife?'

'Why should you think anything untoward has happened to your wife?'

'Where is she? Why are you here if nothing's happened to her? Why won't someone answer me?' David tried to push his way past and enter the house.

'Not so fast, sir. No one is allowed in there at the moment. Where do you believe your wife to be?'

David looked at him, dazed. 'Inside. Where else?'

'When did you last see your wife?'

'This morning; when I left for work.' David bunched his fists. 'If you don't tell me what's happened... My God, has Mr Goodman touched her? I'll kill him if he has.'

'There's no need for violence, sir. Where does your wife work?'

'She's a librarian. City Library. Tell me what's happened!'

The Superintendent ignored him. 'What time does she usually arrive home?'

'That depends; some evenings the library stays open later.' David ran a hand through his hair and looked around wildly. 'What's going on?'

'And you say she went in to work this morning?'

'Yes, yes, of course she did.'

'What time would that have been?'

'Probably about half an hour after I left.'

'Can anyone vouch for that?'

'The neighbours may have seen her leave. Her colleagues will have been with her all day. Please tell me,' David spoke miserably, his first anger having left him. 'What's happened to her?'

For the first time the Superintendent gave a thin smile. 'Mr Goodman made rather a nasty discovery when he took up the floorboards in your kitchen. Assuming that you are telling me the truth when you say your wife has been at work all day I don't think you need to have any concerns about her well being.'

David relaxed visibly. 'She's all right? She's not hurt – or anything?' He took his mobile 'phone from his jacket pocket. 'Can I 'phone her? I just want to make sure.'

The Superintendent nodded. 'Go ahead.'

David dialled Carol's number and was relieved when she answered the call.

'What's wrong, David? You sound awful. Aren't you well? You haven't had an accident, have you?'

'No, no, I'm fine, Carol. Listen, I've just got home and there are police everywhere. They won't let me into the house.'

'What's happened? Mr Goodman hasn't had an accident, has he?'

'I don't know. You speak to the Superintendent. He won't tell me anything.'

David held out his 'phone, but the man shook his head. 'I suggest you ask your wife to return home now. Then we can all go down to the station together.'

David swallowed. 'Carol, he won't speak to you. He says you are to return home now and then we both have to go to the police station. I don't know what it's all about.' He held the 'phone away from his ear. 'Are we being arrested?'

The Superintendent Rawlings shook his head. 'We would just like you to answer some questions for us, help us with our enquiries.'

David relayed the message to his wife, closed his 'phone, and looked again at the Superintendent. He felt much calmer now he had actually spoken to Carol.

'Can you tell me what has happened? Why can't I go into my own house?'

'Everything will be explained when we get to the station, sir.

Now, if you will excuse me, I am probably needed back inside. Officer, let me know when the gentleman's wife arrives.' He turned his back on David, went inside the front door and closed it firmly behind him.

David sensed the neighbours were watching from behind their curtains and he felt most uncomfortable. They probably thought they had some criminals living amongst them instead of a librarian and a printer. He pulled his cigarettes from his pocket. He was trying hard to give up the habit, but he felt in need of one after the nasty shock he had been given.

Carol and David were taken to separate interview rooms when they arrived at the police station.

'Why can't my wife be with me?' asked David of Superintendent Rawlings.

'We wish to speak to you alone in the first instance. It's just procedure, sir. Nothing to be alarmed about. This is Detective Inspector Baker.' He waved his hand towards the other officer who had accompanied them into the room.

'I wish to make a complaint. I have been refused entry to my own house and no one has told me what the problem is. It took some time before I was even reassured that my wife was safe. We were told we both had to come down to the station and now you say you wish to speak only to me!'

'As I said, in the first instance, sir. We will then speak to your wife and probably both of you together. You have no objection to us recording the interview?'

David shook his head.

'Very well. First, I will read you your rights. I will then ask you some questions and if you decide you want to have your solicitor present you can request that at any time.'

David looked totally bemused. The police officer switched on the tape recorder, stated the date and time, his own name and confirmed that he was interviewing David Wright.

'Mr Wright, I should first like to ask you the date when you purchased your house.'

'February of this year.'

'And from whom did you make the purchase?'

'Wilson and Smith, the estate agents.'

'Do you know the name of the vendor?'

'I understood it was a Mr Patel.'

'Did you ever meet this man?'

'No.'

'Did you meet his wife?'

'No.'

'Did you have a survey carried out before you completed the purchase?'

'Of course.'

'And what were the results of the survey? Were any problems highlighted?'

David frowned. 'No. There was no sign of subsidence. There were signs of damp round a couple of the windows. The roof was declared sound and they said there were no signs of dry rot in any of the timbers. It needed modernising and decorating, but we were prepared for that.'

'When did you decide to start the renovations?' asked Detective Inspector Baker.

'We thought we'd have to do things over a number of years, but we had a win on the lottery. We discussed it and decided we could afford to replace all the windows and have central heating put in. We had some estimates and decided it would be practical to have the bathroom and kitchen refurbished at the same time provided we could afford it.'

'What made you choose Mr Goodman?'

'A neighbour recommended him. He's all right isn't he? I mean, he hasn't had an accident or anything?'

Superintendent Rawlings shook his head. 'It was Mr Goodman who called us. Why was he taking up the floor of your kitchen?'

London: September 2005

'My wife wanted an eating bar beneath the window. That meant the washing machine and sink had to be moved and Mr Goodman said he would have to alter the plumbing runs.'

'Had you attempted to do any of this work yourself, Mr Wright?'

David managed a weak smile. 'I'm a printer. I can wield a paintbrush but nothing more. Please can you tell me what the problem is? Is the house in danger of collapsing?'

'Unfortunately there was a large slab of concrete beneath the floor. Whilst Mr Goodman was attempting to remove it he discovered a body.' Detective Inspector Baker sat back and watched David's reaction to the news.

David's jaw gaped, he could feel sweat breaking out on his forehead and his hands were clammy. 'A body?' he whispered. 'You mean – a dead body – buried there?'

Tony Baker leaned forward. 'Are you able to throw any light on this discovery? Did you know about the concrete beneath the floor?'

David shook his head.

'Please answer 'yes' or 'no', Mr Wright.'

'No, no, I had no idea. Where did the body come from?'

'We were hoping you might be able to tell us.'

'Me?' David drew a deep breath. 'Is that why I was being asked about my wife? You thought I had – had – murdered her and put her under the floor? I wouldn't touch a hair on her head. I love my wife.'

'Quite so, Mr Wright, but we have to investigate every possibility in a case like this. Unfortunately the owner of the property is always the first person who falls under suspicion.'

'But I had nothing to do with it! I'd be pretty stupid anyway to ask a plumber to have the floor up if I'd hidden a body underneath.'

'You'd be surprised at the stupid things some people do. We will close the interview now and in a short while you will be able to be reunited with your wife. I'll arrange to have a cup of tea brought in to both of you.'

'Can I have a cigarette?'

Superintendent Rawlings nodded and pushed a polystyrene lid towards him. 'You can use that as an ash tray.'

Detective Inspector Baker lit up a cigarette and leaned back against the wall, inhaling deeply. 'I'm certain neither of them know anything about it. For a minute I thought he was going to pass out when I told him. According to the first observations by forensics the body has been there a considerable amount of time. Let them have half an hour together. Then you can break the news to them that they can't go back to their house until our investigations have been completed. We'll need to have a team out there to take all the floors up. There could be a few more bodies lying around.'

David and Carol sat on the side of the bed in the hotel room where the police had taken them. They had been allowed home accompanied by a police officer. Under their supervision they had been told to pack a case each and told to take enough clothes with them for a week. David held Carol's hand tightly.

'I was so frightened when they wouldn't tell me what was happening. I thought it was you, something awful must have happened to you.'

Carol squeezed his hand back. 'You shouldn't have worried. You knew it was my late night.'

'When I saw the police I had no idea what night it was! I wish I had told them you were working late in the first place. I told them you were in the house!'

'I feel sorry for Mr Goodman. It must have been horrible for him. Fancy,' Carol shuddered involuntarily, 'you're just doing your job and you come across a body.'

David frowned. 'We ought to visit him. He might refuse to come back and finish.'

'Are we allowed to?'

'They didn't say we couldn't. They asked us not to talk about it to anyone, particularly the press, but they didn't say we couldn't speak to Mr Goodman. All we want to know from him is if he's willing to come back and work for us.'

'Suppose he refuses?'

'Then we find someone else and he doesn't get the money we owe him so far.' David spoke more confidently than he felt. 'We say he walked off the job.'

Carol sniffed. 'He'll say he was traumatised and probably ask us for compensation. I'm not sure I want to go back there to live anyway.'

'Maybe we should consult a lawyer?'

'It's too late for that tonight, besides we ought to see what he has to say first. We don't want to pay a lawyer for nothing.'

'Shall I 'phone him?'

Carol nodded. 'It is only nine, I doubt if he's in bed yet.'

The police visited Wilson and Smith requesting information about Mr Patel, the previous owner of David and Carol's house. Mr Lambert shook his head.

'I can't tell you anything very much about the man. He said he was selling up and returning to India. All the paperwork was in order and the contracts exchanged. Our bill was settled without a problem and that was the end of the matter as far as we were concerned.'

'Did he leave any forwarding address with you?'

'There was no need. All the service bills were paid up to date as he had moved out a couple of months earlier. He said he didn't like the idea of strangers wandering around amongst his personal possessions and he could not be there when we made appointments for a viewing.'

'So where did he stay when he had moved out?'

'He said he was renting a flat temporarily.'

'Do you have that address?'

Mr Lambert looked through the file. 'I can give you that, but he's not likely to be there now. From the way he spoke he was planning to leave the country as soon as the formalities were completed.'

'We'll have to check it out anyway, just for the record. If there is anything you do recall about him that you think might help us just give me a call on that number. There will be someone there to take a message and I'll get back to you personally.'

Mr Lambert nodded. 'You can't tell me what this is all about, I suppose?'

Detective Inspector Baker shook his head. 'Not at this stage, sir. Thank you for your time.'

Paris: September 2005

Saffron found that she was looking forward to spending a week in Paris, despite still resenting the way Ranjit had arranged for her to accompany him. She had been to France on a number of occasions whilst she was at Medical School and enjoyed being in the country, sampling the different foods, and hearing the language around her. She planned to visit the Eiffel Tower, Galleries Lafayette, the Pompidou Centre and as many museums and art galleries as she could manage whilst they were there.

'I don't know when you will have the time for all that,' Ranjit commented. 'You will be at the conference with me during the day.'

Saffron shook her head. This time she was determined to stand up to her husband. 'I am not spending all my time sitting listening to eminent doctors talking about things I know absolutely nothing about. I understand how interesting it will be for you and that it is an honour for you to be asked to speak, but I would be bored to tears.'

'You have to be there with me,' Ranjit insisted.

'I certainly do not. I will come to the opening reception, I will attend when you give your talk and for the closing ceremony. The rest of the time I plan to see as much of Paris as I can.'

'That's impossible. You do not know the city.'

'I've visited before and never had a problem finding my way around. There are plenty of signs in English and I speak enough French to ask for directions; besides, I could always take a taxi.'

Ranjit shook his head. 'I cannot allow that.' His penetrating eyes bored into her. Daring her to contradict him.

'You cannot allow it! I am not a prisoner, Ranjit. I can do as I please. If you have any thoughts of forcing me to attend the conference every day you can forget them now. Either I spend the week as I please or I don't come at all. It was your idea that I should go with you, not mine.'

Saffron walked out of the room shaking with anger. There were times when she really disliked her husband, and although only married a few months, she was beginning to feel she had made a big mistake. He no longer seemed to be the charming, caring man she had thought him to be.

Saffron accompanied her husband to the opening of the conference. She chatted genially to those who were introduced to her, accepting modestly the accolades regarding her husband. Yes, he was a marvellous surgeon; yes, they were very lucky to have him at the hospital; yes, he had pioneered innovative surgery; yes, he was a charming man. The same things were said repeatedly to her.

By the end of three hours Saffron's jaw felt stiff from smiling, her feet ached, having been forced to stand for most of the time and she longed to go back to the hotel and have a luxurious bath and sink into bed. She had only consumed one glass of wine all evening, but her head throbbed. She shouldered her way through to Ranjit's side.

'Could we go soon, please? My head is fit to burst.'

Ranjit frowned. 'Have you had too much to drink?'

'I'm still on my first glass of wine. It's just so stuffy in here and my feet ache.'

'I still have various people to meet. It would look most discourteous if I left before speaking with them.'

'I'll ask them to call a taxi for me and see you back at the hotel.'

'You will not! You will stay until I say it is time to leave.'

Saffron shook her head. 'I can't. I feel ill. You wouldn't want me to embarrass you by being sick all over the floor.'

Ranjit looked at her furiously. 'Call a taxi. I'll speak to you later.'

Saffron slipped away to the reception desk and took a deep breath. It was cooler out there. No doubt Ranjit would stay until the early hours of the morning, enjoying the adulation of his peers. She would just have to face his wrath the next day.

Ranjit shook Saffron's shoulder roughly and woke her up. 'What was that behaviour all about?'

Saffron blinked at him bemused. 'What do you mean?'

'You had no right to leave the reception so early. You had been invited as my wife and you had a duty to stay and support me.'

Saffron pulled herself up into a sitting position. 'Ranjit, I was feeling ill. I honestly thought that if I stayed very much longer I would be sick. It was hot and airless in there. The flowers were beautiful, but they had an overpowering scent that made my head ache. Besides, none of those people wanted to meet me. They only wanted to speak to you.'

Ranjit's lips compressed into a thin line. He gripped her arm firmly. 'Tomorrow you will come and stay all day, regardless of how you are feeling.'

Saffron tried to pull her arm away and she shook her head. 'I am not coming again until you are speaking. That was our arrangement.'

'You did not keep to the arrangement. You left early.'

'I could have claimed to feel ill and not attended at all. I am visiting the Louvre tomorrow and maybe some of the shops. You should be finished at four and I shall be back here waiting for you then. We can spend the evening together.'

'You should be with me during the day. It is not often we are able to spend so much time in each other's company. You should appreciate it.'

'We won't be spending quality time together. You will be listening to the speeches and having discussions with the other surgeons. We have the evenings when we can spend time together and also the weekend when the conference has finished. I'd like you to visit Versailles with me and we must take a trip to the top of the Eiffel Tower together. I've been up once before and the view is spectacular.'

'If you want us behave as tourists at the weekend there is no reason why you cannot come to the conference each day.' His fingers dug harder into the muscle at the top of her arm.

'You're hurting me, Ranjit. I shall have bruises on my arm. I have very little knowledge of cardiac surgery and will be quite happy to amuse myself by visiting the museums and art galleries. Either I do as I please whilst you're at the conference or I shall return to England tomorrow.'

'Don't be foolish and do not threaten me with ultimatums. You could not get a flight at such short notice.'

'I can always take a train and catch a ferry. Let me go. I'm tired and I want to go back to sleep.'

Ranjit's dark eyes narrowed. He had not expected Saffron to have such determination and oppose him. Whilst he had courted her she had seemed so pliable and amenable to his will. He was not prepared to tolerate such rebellion. He released her arm. Maybe the marriage had been a mistake. He must consult his little private book. It was possible he could bring his plans for the future forward. This time it would have to appear to be a tragic accident, preferably in full view of witnesses.

Saffron enjoyed her time in the Louvre. She wandered leisurely from one gallery to another, pleased to be alone and able to stay as long as she wanted studying the works of art. Finally looking at her watch she was surprised to see it was nearly two and if she wanted to have something to eat she really should leave. She would have to postpone her visit to the Paris shops until the following day.

Ranjit did not ask if she had enjoyed her day, although she made a point of asking about the conference.

He shrugged. 'You have made it quite clear that you are not interested, so why do you bother to ask me?'

'I thought you would like to tell me about the discussions that took place today. You can explain procedures in words that I can understand.'

'Really?' He raised his eyebrows. 'Do you wish to go for a walk before we have dinner?'

Saffron sighed; obviously her husband was not going to be placated. 'That would be very nice. It's a beautiful evening. We could go down to the banks of the Seine. Another place we should go at the weekend is Montmartre so you can see the artists at work.'

'I am not interested in art.'

'This is different. The artists sit around and offer to draw your portrait. They are very talented. Who knows, you could find they have become a famous artist and you have a masterpiece.' Saffron realised Ranjit was not going to respond. 'We could also visit Notre Dame.'

'Why should I wish to visit a church? I am not a Christian, you know that.'

'You don't have to believe in the religion to admire the architecture. We visited St Paul's Cathedral together.'

'At your insistence.' Ranjit hung up his suit carefully. 'Are you ready?'

Saffron felt her desire for the walk waning. She just hoped that when the conference had finished Ranjit would be more enthusiastic about their sight seeing at the weekend.

Saffron visited Notre Dame alone and wandered disconsolately around the Montmartre district. It could have been so much more enjoyable if Ranjit had wanted to share the experience with her. He had said no more about her attending the conference each day and did not ask her opinion of the speech he gave, despite the fact that she had sat in his full view in the front row and applauded at length when he finished.

He at least seemed enthusiastic about visiting the Eiffel Tower and had spent a good deal of time looking at the brochure that described the various levels and gave the height from the ground and the surrounding area that they should be able to see on a clear day.

As a surprise for her husband Saffron had booked dinner at the Eiffel Tower followed by a cruise up the River Seine by night on their last evening and hoped that Ranjit would accept it as an unspoken peace offering. Now she wandered through the Pompidou Centre looking for a gift to take back for Marjorie, maybe she would buy Ranjit a new tie if she saw something she thought he would like.

She walked from floor to floor, admiring the expensive items on offer. Finally she reached the glassware department and wished she could afford to buy something spectacular for Marjorie to add to her collection. She had always given her a piece for Christmas and her birthday and Marjorie displayed each item in a cabinet Jeremy had bought her specifically for the purpose.

Everything that attracted her was highly priced. She would use her credit card. That way she would not have to let Ranjit know the cost of the gift. She sighed and made further excuses for him. His parsimony was due to the enormous debt that he was repaying to his father-in-law. She selected a small vase, delicately engraved with entwined flowers and leaves and waited whilst her purchase was wrapped and the transaction completed.

She looked at her watch and bit her lip anxiously. She was going to be late returning to the hotel and Ranjit would be waiting impatiently for her. She hurried out and looked for a taxi to flag down, relieved that she was able to get one almost immediately.

Having given the driver the address she needed he pulled out into the traffic and began to crawl along in the unending stream.

Traffic lights were against them and the journey took far longer than she had anticipated. She rushed into the hotel and took the lift to their floor, her heart sinking as she saw Ranjit standing in the doorway waiting for her.

'I'm so sorry. I was longer than I expected being served and the traffic was heavy.'

Ranjit scowled. 'You are supposed to be here waiting for me. Where have you been?'

'The Pompidou Centre. I wanted to buy a present for Marjorie.'

'Why does Marjorie need a present?'

'It's just something that is nice to do for someone when you have been away. It shows you care for them.'

Ranjit shrugged. 'An unnecessary waste of money.'

'I'm not asking you to pay for it,' snapped Saffron. 'It's a present from me to her.'

Ranjit regarded her coldly. 'I suggest you get yourself washed and changed. We are meeting colleagues for a meal tonight. I would like my wife to be a credit to me.'

Saffron swallowed her indignation. 'Of course. What would you like me to wear?'

'The same dress as you wore for the opening ceremony would be suitable. I trust you will not feel unwell halfway through the evening.'

Saffron did not reply. She placed the vase she had purchased safely inside her case. 'I'll go and shower,' she said meekly.

'How shall we do it?' asked Saffron eagerly. 'Shall we go up one level at a time until we reach the top, or go to the top and come down one level at a time?'

'To the top first. The view should be best from there.'

Saffron approached the ticket kiosk and asked in her faltering French for two tickets for the lift to go to the top. The attendant smiled. It was a good job she was used to these foreigners whose accent was so bad it made them almost unintelligible.

To Ranjit's surprise the lift was nearly full. He had not expected to find so many people were interested in paying to see a view. They stepped out onto the viewing platform and Ranjit sucked in his breath angrily. There were people everywhere and a high wire fence that ran the whole way around for safety. The idea he had at the back of his mind for a fatal accident to take place was impractical. He pretended enthusiasm as Saffron pointed out the landmarks to him, but had no desire to linger, claiming to be chilled by the wind.

'I did say you might need a jacket,' Saffron chided him.

'I don't want to spend all day carrying a jacket with me just so that I am warm for a few minutes. Once we are back down at ground level I certainly won't need one.'

'Promise me you'll bring one with you when we go out this evening,' urged Saffron.

Ranjit shrugged. 'It is hardly any cooler in the evening than during the day.'

'Just to please me. Believe me when I say you may need it this time.'

Ranjit raise his eyebrows. 'We are not planning to come up here again at night are we?'

Saffron blushed. 'I wanted it to be a surprise. I've booked dinner up here and a river cruise afterwards. That's why I want you to bring a jacket. I'm sure it will be warm enough in the restaurant, but it might be rather cool on the river.'

'That was rather extravagant of you, my dear.'

'I wanted to do it, to say thank you for bringing me with you and letting me have such an enjoyable week.' Saffron spoke sincerely, all her previous animosity towards her husband forgotten.

London: September 2005

Ranjit parked his car in the space that was reserved for him at the hospital. 'I will see you this evening. Try not to be late.'

'I'll do my best.' Saffron leant over and gave him a peck on the cheek. 'I'll tell everyone how well you spoke at the conference and how we enjoyed out last few days.'

'If you wish.'

'Don't be grumpy, just because you've had to return to work,' Saffron chided him.

'I am not grumpy. That is such a silly word anyway. I am just rather tired. The conference was exhausting. I needed to rest, but you insisted on running half way round Paris pointing out monuments and the like. We had to go to the Bastille. I was expecting a large prison and what do I see? An obelisk in the middle of the square. The Bastille has long gone.' Ranjit got out of the car and slammed the door behind him.

He waited until Saffron had climbed out also, and then locked the doors.

'Try not to be late,' he instructed her again and strode off to the entrance of his department.

Saffron bit her lip. She had thought Ranjit would be interested in seeing Paris and the outings she had planned so carefully for the weekend. She had obviously misjudged things badly. She gave a slight shrug. At least Marjorie had been delighted with her glass vase and wanted to hear where she had visited.

'Mr Patel, I have a message for you.'

Ranjit turned and gave a patient smile to his receptionist. 'I am sure I have a considerable number of messages waiting.'

'This one is a little different. A man came here looking for you last week. He thought you were his relative and asked me to give you this as soon as you returned from Paris.'

Ranjit frowned. Who had come looking for him?

'Thank you, Jane.' He pushed the envelope into his pocket. He would open it in the privacy of his office.

'Did you enjoy Paris? Were you able to go out and see everything after the conference?'

Ranjit smiled at her again. What was this fixation with having to go sight seeing? 'It is a very beautiful city.'

'Did your wife enjoy herself?'

'Very much.' Ranjit opened the door to his office. 'I shall be ready for my first appointment in fifteen minutes.' He closed the door firmly behind him. That should now be an end to talk about Paris and sight seeing.

He pulled the letter out of his pocket and slit the envelope. A single sheet of paper was inside.

FOR THE ATTENTION OF MR RANJIT PATEL
My name is Tariq Kavira, the brother of Nandita who married Ranjit Patel.

I have come to England from India in the hope of visiting my sister's grave and taking a photograph of it back to my father.

I have visited the address where I have sent correspondence in the past only to be told that Mr Patel has moved away and any letters that come for him are sent on to this hospital.

I visited the hospital and they said that Mr Ranjit Patel was in Paris and would return on Monday. I understand that you are probably not my brother-in-law and it is just a coincidence of name. I will visit the hospital and wait until you have a moment to speak to me before I move on to search elsewhere for him.

If you can help me with any information I would be very grateful.

Sincerely

Tariq Kavira

Ranjit read the letter through a second time. There was no way he could meet the man. Tariq would immediately know who he was and he could not possibly show him a grave where his sister was buried. He pressed the bell for his secretary.

'I believe there could be an Indian gentleman waiting outside. He is hoping to see me on a personal matter. I am far too busy to see him today. Please be kind enough to give the receptionist a message to pass on from me.'

'Yes, sir.' She stood waiting.

'I wish you to write it down. I do not want any mistakes.'

Mandy fumbled for her pad and pen whilst Ranjit glared at her.

'Mr Patel regrets that he is unable to help you. He knows no one of the names you mention. Unfortunately he is quite unable to meet with you as his appointment diary is full. I suggest you try elsewhere for your relative.'

Please give that to Jane and ask her to pass it on to this man if he should be waiting or when he calls again.'

'Yes, sir.'

'I will see my appointments until eleven then I should like you available for an hour to take my notes.'

Mandy left the room. She did not enjoy being secretary to Mr Patel. The other two doctors who shared her time were far less formal and if she was five or ten minutes late arriving for her duties they accepted that she had been held up and did not ask her to account for every minute of her day.

Ranjit opened his office door quietly and walked along the corridor. He stood half hidden by the wall and looked at the people waiting for their appointments. They looked bored or apprehensive, but none of them looked like the man who was seeking him. He looked towards the reception desk and stiffened. There was Tariq Kavira. There was no mistaking him, despite having put on a considerable amount of weight. He watched as Tariq read the note he had dictated to Mandy only a short while earlier. The man appeared to be pleading with the receptionist who shook her head vehemently. Finally, his shoulders slumped, Tariq turned away, and Ranjit retreated to his room. This was going to alter all his plans.

Ranjit picked up the telephone to the receptionist. 'I'm sorry, Jane. I'm afraid I will have to go home. I'm not feeling at all well. I must have picked up something whilst I was in Paris.'

'Do you want me to cancel all your appointments for today?'

'Yes, Jane. I can hardly see patients if I am not here,' Ranjit snapped back at her. He placed his head in his hands. It was true that he did not feel well. The sight of Tariq Kavira in the hospital had given him a severe fright. He must clear his head and think carefully.

Tariq pocketed the note and left the hospital with a feeling of hopelessness. London was a large, sprawling city. Where did he start to look now? He consulted his map. There were hospitals everywhere, probably private clinics as well and his brother-in-law could easily be working in one of those. He walked slowly along the road, taking in the array of small shops as he went. Many of them seemed to be staffed by Indians or Pakistanis. It was possible that one of them would be able to help him. He entered a newsagent and waited his turn to be served.

'I've really come in to ask for some advice,' he apologised.

'Do you need directions?'

'Well, not really. I'm looking for someone.'

The assistant looked back at him suspiciously. 'Well unless it's me you want there's no one else in here.'

Tariq shook his head. 'I'm looking for my brother-in-law. He's a surgeon...'

'Try the hospital, then.'

'I've been there and they say he doesn't work there, although I'm sure he used to.'

'People move around a good bit over here.'

'I've been to the house address I have for him and they said he had moved. Where can I look now?'

The man shrugged. 'How should I know? They say the Salvation Army are good at finding people. You could try them.'

'Where are they?'

'No idea. Now, is there anything I can serve you with? If not, I have work to do.'

'I'll have a newspaper.' Tariq picked up the one nearest to him and paid for it, once again horrified by the price. 'Who could I ask about the Salvation Army?'

'Try the police. They're supposed to know these things.'

Tariq nodded. 'I'll do that.'

Dispirited he wandered on up the road to where there was a small patch of greenery with two seats. He sat down and looked at the paper. Having bought it, he might as well read it, although the events it related would probably mean nothing to him. He skimmed through the headlines and one or two smaller items then folded it and placed it on his knees. He should have saved his money.

A woman, a loaded plastic bag in each hand, sat down heavily on the seat beside him. She placed her bags on the ground beside her and flexed her fingers. Tariq was not sure how he should react. If he spoke to her would she think he was going to rob her? If he ignored her, would she think him rude?

'Gonna be annuver 'ot one,' she observed and Tariq nodded.
''Spose you're used to it, bein' from over there.'

Tariq nodded again.

'Don't spik English?'

'Yes, yes, I do.'

'Cat got your tongue?'

'Pardon?'

'Fergit it. Bad bis'ness 'bout that body, in'it?'

'Body?'

'Yer – the one farnd in the 'ouse. Under the floorboards, they say. It's in the paper.'

She lifted the newspaper from Tariq's knees and opened it towards the centre, pointing at a small paragraph and the photograph with a dirty fingernail.

Dutifully Tariq took the newspaper from her and read the information.

> Police were called to a house where a workman had discovered a body beneath the floorboards. The owners have lived there for only six months having purchased the house from an Indian. As yet the police do not know the identity of the victim or how long it has been incarcerated. The previous owner of the house has been asked to come forward to help the police with their enquiries.

Tariq read the article a second time. He squinted at the photograph that had been taken from a distance. There had been a workman at his brother-in-law's house when he had visited a few days ago. He continued to sit and look at the paragraph.

'Comes to summin' when yer not safe in yer own 'ome.'

Tariq stood up. He debated the wisdom of asking the way to the nearest police station and decided against it. 'Thank you for showing me.'

He would pay another visit to the house before he went to the police. He could be mistaken. Many of the houses in the residential districts looked identical.

Tariq waited at the bus stop. He hoped he had remembered correctly the number of the bus he had caught before and would recognise the bus stop where he should get off. He did not want to ask for directions. He was Indian, and to most Westerners, all Indians looked the same.

He walked slowly down the road towards the house he was seeking. There was no mistake. Police tape was stretched across the frontage of the property and down one side. A small group of people stood outside, but there was no sign of any activity. Before he reached it, he crossed the road. He did not want anyone to recognise him as having been a visitor to the house twice in quick succession the previous week.

Tariq walked on, crossed the intersection, and continued until he found himself back on the main road. He had to go to the police. It would be quite awful if the body that had been found were that of his brother-in-law. He must find out, besides, the newsagent had said the police would know where he could find the Salvation Army. There might be no need for him to contact them if the situation was as he feared.

The sign outside a shop declared that it was a post office. Tariq hesitated. He would go in there and ask directions to the nearest police station, he would say wished to report that his dog had run off whilst he was exercising her. They would hardly be likely to remember him amongst all the other customers they would have during a day. He shook himself. What did it matter is they did recall him? He had done nothing wrong; he merely wanted directions.

Tariq stood in the queue and waited patiently whilst the people in front of him drew their pensions and purchased their stamps. His turn finally came and he cleared his throat nervously.

'Could you direct me to the nearest police station, please?'

The man scratched his nose. 'It's quite a distance from here.'

Tariq nodded and waited.

'You'd have to catch the forty seven bus up to the High Street. The station isn't there, mind, it's tucked back a few streets. You'd need to ask for directions again. What's the problem?'

'I've lost my dog.'

'Hope you find it.' The counter clerk was not interested in anything as mundane as a lost dog; after all a body had been discovered only a few streets away.

Ranjit checked the contents of his desk ensuring that he left nothing of a personal nature behind. He walked out to his car and drove slowly out of the hospital grounds in the direction of north London and the bank where he held his 'private' account. He was told the manager was not available to him as he had not made an appointment, but if he cared to wait a short while an adviser would be able to help him.

Curbing his impatience Ranjit took a seat and concentrated on his next movements.

His money safely transferred to a bank in Venezuela and with an assurance that it would be there within the next three days he left with a satisfied smile on his face.

He used his credit card in the cash point of a different bank to withdraw as much as he was permitted in a single transaction from the current account he had with Sorrell; and walked around the corner to a travel agent.

'I would like to make a booking for a flight to Venezuela.'

The assistant smiled at him. Venezuela. She would earn good commission for selling that. 'When would you like to travel, sir?'

'As soon as possible.'

Her fingers flicked over the keys of her computer. 'I don't think you'd be able to make today's flight unless you have your luggage with you. It leaves Heathrow in just under three hours.

There's a two hour check in, of course, and the drive from here would take at least three quarters of an hour.'

'So when is the next one?' Ranjit knew it would take him far longer than three quarters of an hour to finalise his arrangements.

'The next one is Wednesday, sir. It leaves at three thirty in the afternoon. You would need to be there by one thirty at the latest. When do you propose to return?'

'I have no idea. I shall have to take a one way ticket, first class, of course, as my expenses will be refunded.'

'You realise that you are only allowed to stay for thirty days without a visa, sir?'

'That should be long enough for me to complete my business.' Ranjit smiled at her.

'We have to advise people,' she smiled back at him. 'You can extend your stay if necessary. Do you wish me to book you into a hotel?'

Ranjit shook his head. 'That will be taken care of by my colleagues.'

'How would you like to pay, sir?'

'Cash. Is there any other way?'

'Some people prefer to use their credit card. Of course, they then have to face a large bill when they return home.'

Ranjit counted out the notes he had so recently withdrawn. 'I believe you will find that is correct.'

'You will be able to collect your ticket when you check in, sir. It will be waiting for you.' She handed Ranjit a slip of paper. 'You will need to give them proof of your identity and purchase. I will give you our business card also. Should you experience any problem at all just ask them to call us.'

The assistant placed the ticket purchase slip, a business card and a map into a folder before handing it to Ranjit. 'Have a very enjoyable trip, sir.'

'Thank you.' Ranjit placed the folder carefully into his briefcase.

He drove to the bank, where he and Saffron had a joint account. Once there he withdrew all the money from their current account, leaving a small balance. To his annoyance the earlier withdrawal from the cash point had already been deducted from the account.

'I am returning to India,' he explained. 'My family need me there and I do not know when I will be able to return.'

'We could transfer the money to our branch in Hyderabad,' offered the cashier. 'It would be safer than carrying so much cash around with you.'

Ranjit shook his head. 'I will need this for my travelling expenses. I am sure it will be quite simple for me to open a new account if I need to. Thank you for your offer.'

Feeling pleased that he had accomplished a number of transactions in such a short space of time Ranjit returned to where he had left his car.

He had ignored the regulations regarding parking there. Taped to his windscreen was a summons. He looked at it and threw it into the gutter. It was no concern of his. By the time the fixed penalty arrived at his address he would be long gone. All he needed to do was pack his belongings.

He drove back to the house where he lived with Saffron and her stepmother and let himself in quietly. He could hear the radio playing in the kitchen and pushed open the door.

'Hello, Marjorie.'

Marjorie looked up from her ironing; her hand flew to her heart. 'You gave me a fright. I wasn't expecting you. What's wrong?'

Ranjit gave a weak smile. 'Nothing really. I'm just feeling ill. I think I must have picked up something whilst I was in Paris. I just wanted to tell you I was home and I shall go and lay down upstairs for a while. Have my shirts been returned from the laundry?'

'They came this morning. I've left the box on your bed. Would you like a cup of tea or anything?'

'No thank you, Marjorie. I think I would be better just drinking water at the moment.'

'Does Saffron know you're not well?'

'I haven't told her. She's busy. She doesn't need to be worrying about me.'

'Maybe I should 'phone her to see if she's all right.'

'I'm sure she is or she would have called me. Don't bother her. I'm sure I shall feel well enough to collect her at the end of the day.'

'If you're sure,' Marjorie answered dubiously.

Ranjit nodded and closed the door. Once in the privacy of the room he shared with Saffron, he took both the suitcases down from the top shelf of the cupboard. Placing his clothes on the bed, he began to pack carefully. Shoes at the bottom, with his socks neatly rolled up inside, followed by his underwear, pyjamas, dressing gown and mackintosh. In the second suitcase he placed his carefully folded suits and the freshly laundered shirts. He placed his razor and washing kit, box of cuff links, private bank statements, the certificates qualifying him as a surgeon, and letters recommending him for the position of a cardiac specialist into his briefcase. He should have no problem finding a suitable position in Venezuela. If he encountered any problem, he could always move on to another South American country.

He checked the time by his watch. It was nearly four. He would have to leave by four thirty if Marjorie thought he was collecting Saffron from the hospital. He waited ten minutes, then returned to the ground floor. Marjorie had completed the ironing and was sitting in front of the television with a cup of tea.

'Marjorie, I hate to bother you, but could you do me a great favour?'

'What's that, Ranjit? Changed your mind about the cup of tea?'

Ranjit shook his head. 'I really need a prescription from the chemist. I'm not going to have time to collect that before I meet Saffron. They'll be closed by the time we get back. Would you be a dear and go and collect it for me?'

'Have I time to finish my tea first?'

'Of course.' Ranjit forced himself to smile. He really wanted her out of the way now.

He returned upstairs and did a mental check. He had his ticket arranged; his passport was in his briefcase along with his money. The paper from the bank confirming the transfer of his account was there also. He checked the drawers and wardrobe to ensure that he had left nothing behind that he wanted, then hovered by the window waiting to see Marjorie leave the house.

It seemed an age before he heard the front door close and he shrank back from the window until he calculated she would be a short distance down the road. He watched as she stopped to speak to a neighbour, waving her hand back towards the house. No doubt she was telling the woman that he was there. As soon as she continued on her way Ranjit moved swiftly.

He carried his cases down the stairs and stood them in the hall whilst he opened the boot of the car. He placed them inside and then put the briefcase on the passenger seat beside him. He would not want to lose his suitcases, but the contents of his briefcase were vital to him and he wanted to be quite sure that it was safe.

Once in the car Ranjit drove to Heathrow airport. He parked legally, displaying his ticket prominently and returned to the terminal where he studied the advertisements for hotel accommodation. Finally selecting one that he decided was reasonably priced and within a short distance of Heathrow Air Terminal, he returned to his car and drove the few miles.

Having completed the formalities for checking in he deposited his cases in his room and smiled. Everything was going to plan. Taking his briefcase, he returned to his car and began the drive to Gatwick airport. He parked his car in the long stay car park and returned by bus to the terminal along with the other travellers, made his way down to the railway line and waited for the train to Victoria. He caught a tube train to Green Park and changed on to the Piccadilly line where he stood and waited in the taxi queue to return him to his hotel. The drain by his foot made an ideal place to dispose of his old mobile 'phone as he bent, ostensibly to tie his shoelace.

Tariq entered the police station hesitantly. Was he being foolish? Would they just send him away?

He approached the desk and waited until the police officer looked up from the paperwork he was completing.

'How can I help you, sir?'

Tariq lowered his voice. 'It's about the body that has been found. I'd like to speak to someone.'

The officer frowned. 'Are you Mr Patel?'

Tariq shook his head. 'No, he's my brother-in-law, well, at least I think that's him. I've been trying to find him. I went to the house and the owner said they didn't know him. I went to...'

The officer held up his hand. 'Just a moment, sir. I think it might be better if you spoke to my colleague, maybe go somewhere a little more private.'

The officer spoke into his telephone, continually glancing towards Tariq. Tariq shifted uncomfortably. He was sure the officer was giving a description of him to someone and he felt like a criminal. Finally the officer replaced the receiver.

'If you would care to take a seat, sir. Someone will be with you shortly.'

Tariq sat on the hard bench, his hands clasped between his knees and his head bent. Would they understand that all he wanted was help to find his brother-in-law?

'Mr Kavira?'

Tariq stood up, hoping the Detective would not realise how nervous he was.

'I'm Detective Inspector Baker.' He held out his hand and Tariq touched it briefly. 'I understand you wish to speak to someone as you may have some information to help us with our enquiries. Please follow me.'

Tariq followed the officer into a small side room.

'Please sit down. Would you like tea or coffee?'

Tariq shook his head. His eyes strayed to the door. He had not seen the officer turn a key, but it could have an automatic lock.

'Now, sir, how can I help? Maybe you could give me your name and address to start with.'

Tariq moistened his lips. 'My name is Tariq Kavira. I have come from India to look for my brother-in-law.'

'And his name is?'

'Ranjit Patel.'

'How do you think we will be able to help you?' Tony Baker, through long experience, showed no reaction to the name.

'Ranjit married my sister. She died in London after an accident with a bus. My father is ill. He is probably dying. He knows he will never see Nandita again, but I wanted to take him a photograph of her grave. I also wanted Ranjit to send him more of the money he owes him. The debt should have been repaid long ago, but he continually makes excuses.'

The Detective nodded. 'And where have you looked for your brother-in-law?'

'I went to the address I had for him. There was only a workman there. I returned in the evening and spoke to the man who lives there. He bought the house from Ranjit some months ago. Ranjit did not tell us he had sold the house. It was my father's house. He had bought it for them when they married.'

Detective Inspector Baker frowned. This was beginning to sound more like a debt collection search and would have no bearing on their current investigation. 'So why have you come to the police?'

'I went to the hospital where he works and they told me he was in Paris. They said he would return today. They did not think the man was my brother-in-law, but I left a message with them. I asked Mr Patel to contact me when he returned. I said I would wait all day until he was free. The receptionist gave me a note from the doctor. It said I had the wrong Mr Patel and he was too busy to meet with me.' Tariq looked up at the Detective for the first time. 'Then I saw the newspaper. It said a workman had found a body hidden beneath the floor of a house. The photograph looked like the house I had visited.'

Tony Baker raised his eyebrows. 'Houses in London can look very much the same.'

'I know.' Tariq nodded. 'I caught a bus and went back to the address. There is police tape around it. It is the same house. I need to know what has happened to my brother-in-law. Has he been murdered?'

The Detective glanced more keenly at the man before him. Maybe he did have some useful information. 'At this stage of our enquiries I am not in a position to release the identity of the body, sir. Can you give me the address of Mr Patel's house and also the hospital where you believed him to be working?'

Tariq opened his wallet and pulled out a letter that his father had received three years earlier breaking the news of Nandita's death. At the top was the address of the house and Ranjit had also written to say Nandita had initially been taken to the hospital where he worked. He assured them that he and his colleagues had done their best to save her life.

Detective Inspector Baker copied both addresses onto a pad of paper. 'This is the hospital where you made your enquiries?'

Tariq nodded. 'Ranjit is a heart surgeon. There is a Mr Patel who works in the cardiac department, but in his message to me, he said he knew no one of Nandita's name and did not know me. I have it here.'

Tariq passed the short note across the table.

'It is possible that your relative has moved to another hospital to work. Doctors often move around quite frequently.'

Tariq shook his head. 'The man I spoke to at his house said he forwarded any letters on to him at that hospital. If he no longer works there surely they would return them?'

'They would not know they were intended for a different Mr Patel. It would be up to the doctor to point out the error. He probably just disregarded them and threw them away.'

'So what are you going to do to help me find my brother-in-law?'

Tony Baker placed his elbows on the table. 'First I am going to ask you to make a statement. I would like you to write down all the information you have given to me. I can ask an officer to be with you if you wish or you can sit here alone if you feel more comfortable. Whilst you do that, I will make a few telephone enquiries. Hopefully by the time you have finished writing and I have made the telephone calls we will have found your brother-in-law.'

Tariq looked at the Detective and shook his head. 'I think my brother-in-law has been murdered.'

'Why would you think that, sir?'

'It's obvious. These people who live in his house – they murdered him.'

'I think it most unlikely, sir. We have contacted the estate agent who dealt with the sale.'

Tariq shook his head in disbelief.

'There's just one more thing, Mr Kavira. Would you have a photograph of your sister?'

'Why should you want a photo of Nandita? I know she has died.'

'It could help us in our enquiries for your brother-in-law.' Tony smiled at him. 'A photograph can help jog people's memories.'

Tariq opened his wallet and took out a passport size photograph of his sister. 'I will want it back.'

'You can have it back in just a few minutes. I will take a copy.'

Tony looked at the small photograph. There was nothing attractive about the woman. Her eyes were small, her nose too large for her face and her crooked teeth were noticeable in her smile, but it was the kind of face people were likely to remember.

Detective Inspector Baker returned to the office where his colleagues were working and began to give orders.

'Simon, Elaine and Mark, you three get on to all the hospitals in the London area and find out if they have a Doctor or Mr Ranjit Patel working for them. Try every department. He could be a porter or even a cleaner and just told his family he was a doctor. Get their current address and the length of time they've lived there. Show them a copy of the woman's photograph when you interview them and ask if they recognise her. Get back to me immediately if you have anything positive. Mick, you get out to the house and see if anything else has been unearthed over there. I'm going to get on to forensics to see if they have any more information for me.'

Saffron locked her office and made her way out of the hospital. She stood in the car park and looked around. Where was Ranjit's car? Maybe he had been called to another hospital for an emergency and the receptionist had forgotten to give her his message.

She returned to the reception area where Angela was closing her computer for the day.

'Have you had a message from my husband?' she asked.

Angela shook her head. 'I've not taken one today, Saffie. What's the problem?'

'His car isn't there.'

'Maybe Mandy or Jane has forgotten to send one through. Do you want me to try the department?'

'Yes, please.' Saffron waited impatiently whilst Angela dialled the internal number. There was no answer.

'They were pretty prompt today,' observed Angela. 'Reception isn't answering. They must have left for the day.'

Saffron shrugged. 'I'll wait around for a while, then call him on his mobile. He may have left a message on that for me.'

'Is it all right if I leave?' Angela looked pointedly at the clock.

'Yes, of course.'

'You don't want me to give you a lift anywhere?'

Saffron smiled. 'No, thanks for the offer. Ranjit will no doubt be here soon.' She returned to her office and unlocked the door. So much for Ranjit telling her not to be late! To pass the time she began to study her case files for the following day. They all appeared to be very routine appointments. She looked at the clock. It was only five fifteen. She would go back to the reception area and have another look at the car park to see if Ranjit had arrived.

Saffron waited until five thirty and there was still no sign of her husband. Finally she dialled his mobile number. The 'phone was switched off. She frowned with annoyance. He must be in the operating theatre. She would just have to sit and wait until he returned.

By six, Saffron was feeling annoyed. Why hadn't he sent her a message? If he had told her he would be so late she would have caught the bus home as she had on a few previous occasions. With a sigh she placed her cardigan around her bare shoulders and began to walk across to the operating block of the hospital. She made her way through the corridors leading to the three theatres. Two were in darkness and she peered through the door of the third. She raised her hand across the glass pane until she finally caught the attention of a nurse.

The nurse opened the door a crack. 'What's the problem?'

'Is Ranjit Patel operating?' asked Saffron.

The nurse shook her head. 'He's not in here.' She closed the door, stripped off her gloves and took a fresh pair from the box.

Saffron turned away. If Ranjit were not waiting for her when she returned to the car park she would telephone Marjorie and see if he had contacted her.

Marjorie turned the oven down as low as possible. The lasagne she had cooked would be hopelessly crisp if Saffron and Ranjit did not return home soon. It was not like them to be so late without letting her know. She hoped Ranjit had not had an accident, maybe he should not have been driving if he was feeling unwell. The prescription he had asked her to collect stood unopened in a white chemist's bag on the table.

She debated whether she should open it and decided that it was none of her business. Despite having asked her to collect it, he might not wish her to know what medication he was taking. Maybe, unknown to her, he was diabetic, and it contained his insulin. In that case, he might well have needed to inject himself before he left the house and she should alert Saffron. As her fingers touched the paper bag the telephone began to ring.

'Saffie. Where are you? I was beginning to get quite worried about you. Has Ranjit had to stay late at the hospital?'

Marjorie listened, a frown creasing her forehead. 'What do you mean; you don't know where he is? He left here to collect you. Didn't you know? He came home from the hospital saying he was unwell. Have you tried to 'phone him?'

Marjorie listened again. 'I expect he forgot to charge his 'phone if you say it's dead. Take a taxi, Saffie. Don't hang around waiting for buses. If he hasn't returned or called you when you get home we'll try 'phoning him from here. I'll see you in about half an hour.'

Marjorie turned the oven off. The lasagne would just have to be reheated through, despite Ranjit's aversion to microwave meals. An awful thought crossed her mind and she rose from her chair. Had Ranjit been taken really ill whilst she was collecting his prescription? She had not thought to check upstairs. Then she remembered his car was not parked in the driveway as it had been when she had left, so he must have driven to collect Saffron. Her curiosity overcame her and she opened the bag from the chemist and looked at the contents in surprise. Milk of Magnesia for indigestion. It was hardly an urgent prescription. It could be bought quite freely over the counter from any chemist. Indigestion could be a sign of heart trouble. Ranjit would know that. Had he suffered a heart attack on his way to collect his wife?

Marjorie sat in an agony of apprehension until Saffron arrived home.

'Where can he be? It is so unlike him not to tell me if he's delayed. I checked in the theatre and he wasn't there and you tell me he came home ill anyway. Why didn't he 'phone and tell me or get his secretary to do so?'

'Saffie, has Ranjit ever told you if he has a heart condition?'

Saffron raised her eyebrows. 'A heart condition! He's never mentioned it. He always insists he has nothing wrong with him.' She frowned. 'That's another thing that's strange. He's never missed a day's work through illness before and he was fine when he left me this morning.'

'He told me he was going to collect you and asked if I would collect an urgent prescription for him. By the time I returned he had gone. The prescription was for Milk of Magnesia – indigestion.'

Saffron's frowned deepened. 'What would he want that for? I've never known him suffer from indigestion. Is that why you were asking about his heart?'

Marjorie nodded. 'I know people often complain of indigestion, but it can also be a warning sign of an impending heart attack.'

'But he would know all the symptoms. He wouldn't be so foolish as to ignore them. He would know that Milk of Magnesia was only a palliative for ordinary indigestion, not heart pains.' Saffron paled. 'Marjorie, you don't think he's had a heart attack whilst he was driving, do you? I'm phoning the police.'

'I think you should wait a little longer. Ranjit won't thank you if he arrives home and finds the house full of police officers. Have something to eat first. Give him another half an hour. I'm sure there's a logical explanation.'

Saffron shook her head. 'I have to 'phone them now. At least to tell them what I think may have happened and ask them to let me know if anyone is admitted to a hospital in the area. I can give them the number of the car and a description of Ranjit which could help them to identify an accident victim.'

Marjorie sighed. She could see that the lasagne was going to be completely ruined. 'I'll put the kettle on. We can at least have a cup of tea.'

'Yes, madam, I have taken down all the details you have given me. I will pass them on to our traffic division and should there be any accident with an unidentified driver reported that matches the description of your husband we will be in touch with you immediately. I'm sure you have nothing to worry about. He will no doubt turn up shortly.'

The police officer replaced the receiver. Why was that name ringing a bell in his mind? He continued to fill in the form recording the conversation with Saffron, and had almost completed it when he remembered. Elaine had complained that she had been telephoning the hospitals all afternoon asking if they had an employee of that name. He ought to pass the information on to Detective Inspector Baker.

He copied the information from the form onto a new blank sheet, marked it 'COPY – for DI BAKER', and took it through to the office. Simon and Elaine were still there collating their findings from the hospitals.

Elaine looked up and grimaced. 'I think Patel must be the most common name in England after Smith. Do you want to guess how many Patels I found working at three hospitals? Thirty-seven! Simon found another twenty two and Mark fourteen.'

'Is Tony Baker around?'

Elaine shook her head. 'He's gone to a meeting with the house crew. He said he should be back about seven thirty unless they had found any more bodies.'

'Make sure he sees this, will you?'

'What is it?'

'A missing Patel.'

'Get out,' said Elaine as she bent her head back down to her lists.

Half an hour later Elaine stretched her arms above her head. 'I've finished. How about you?'

'I've got a couple that I want to check out further. They've both moved house recently. They were able to tell me when the data was amended but not the previous address. I'll have to go along tomorrow when they're working and ask the men in question. Do you have queries?'

Elaine shook her head. 'Not unless Tony wants me to interview any of them. They're all manual workers, varying age groups and a good many seem to be related, or at least living at the same address. Most of them have lived at the same address and worked there for years. What's this message Brian brought in?'

Elaine walked over to Tony Baker's desk and picked it up, her forehead creasing into a frown as she read the report. 'Simon, come and have a look at this. Tell me what you think.'

Simon took the report from her hand and scanned it. 'I think we ought to 'phone Tony and let him know.'

'Not much point.' Elaine looked at her watch. 'He should be back any minute. I'll hang around until he comes, then I'm off.' She helped herself to a coffee from the machine and grimaced as she took a mouthful.

Tony Baker appeared through the door. 'Still here, Elaine? I thought your shift finished at six thirty.'

'Just wanted to make sure my report was ready for you when you came back. I can't see anyone matching the Patel we appear to be looking for.'

'What about you, Simon?'

'A couple of possibilities. Moved house within the last year. I'll check them out fully tomorrow.'

'Might as well call it a day, then. You'll be pleased to know that no more bodies have shown up so far. They've had the dogs in and they haven't got excited anywhere. They'll lift a few floorboards upstairs, just in case, then tackle the garden. Forensics has confirmed that it's definitely a woman, appears to be of Indian sub-continent origin or thereabouts. Too soon to be definite on that. They've based their assumption on the remainder of her clothes.'

'There's a message on your desk. Brian brought it in a while ago.'

Tony picked up the report and scanned it quickly. 'Hang on, you two. You might be needed.'

Elaine sighed. 'I knew I shouldn't have waited for you to come back.'

Tony ignored her remark. 'Have you read this?'

'I looked at it quickly. When we saw the name Simon was going to 'phone you, but we realised you were due back.'

'I think we'll go and pay this lady a visit. It could be a wild goose chase, but according to this report, her husband is a Patel who works at the hospital. The one where the brother-in-law went searching. Apparently she works there and she and her husband travel in and out together. He didn't meet her as planned and she's worried he's had an accident.'

'What time was he supposed to meet her?'

'Near enough two hours ago.'

'And she's panicking? If my wife called up each time I was two hours late getting home she'd be on the 'phone most days.'

'According to the report,' Tony tapped at the sheet of paper, 'the mother-in-law was at home in the afternoon when he returned unexpectedly saying he was ill. He later said he was going off to collect his wife and never showed up. It's probably just a coincidence that it happens to be the name Patel, but you never know.'

'Are you going to 'phone her first? He could have turned up by now.'

Tony shook his head. 'I don't think so. If hubby has returned I'd quite like a few words with him anyway. It will take a Patel off the list.'

Saffron answered the door and her face paled as she saw the three police officers standing there.

'What's happened to Ranjit?'

Tony Baker flashed his identity card. 'May we come in, madam? We'd like to have a word with Mrs Patel.'

Saffron opened the door wider. 'That's me. Has my husband had an accident?'

'We've not had any reports matching the description you gave. We'd just like to ask you a few more questions and make sure we have the details correct.'

Saffron ushered them into the sitting room. 'What more can I tell you? I'm sorry, please sit down. This is my stepmother, Mrs Bartlett.'

The officers acknowledged Marjorie with a nod and spread themselves around the room. Marjorie leaned over and squeezed Saffron's hand. 'I'll go and make a fresh pot of tea. Would you all like a cup?'

Detective Inspector Baker nodded. 'That would be very welcome. When we've spoken to Mrs Patel maybe we could have a few words with you also.'

Elaine followed Marjorie into the kitchen. 'I'm sorry; we're probably intruding on your supper time.'

Marjorie smiled ruefully. 'I had made a lasagne, but it will be horribly overcooked by now. Saffie says she isn't hungry and I don't feel I can sit and eat on my own at the moment.'

'Are you worried that something has happened to Mr Patel?'

'Yes, I am. He is a stickler for punctuality. They usually arrive home about five thirty and he likes to have supper on the table at six. One of them has always 'phoned if they were going to be delayed.'

'What do you think may have happened?'

'I can only assume he has had an accident. He came home this afternoon saying he didn't feel well. He should have telephoned Saffie and told her to have a taxi home. I just hope it isn't serious.'

'Has he come home early before because he wasn't well?'

'Never.' Marjorie shook her head. 'Would you like some biscuits or a piece of cake?'

'I would,' Elaine smiled. 'I don't remember lunch. Shall I carry the tray through for you?'

Tony Baker sat forward on the settee. 'Mrs Patel, I need to check out a few facts with you. Is that all right?'

Saffron nodded.

'You told us you are married to Mr Ranjit Patel.'

Saffron nodded again. 'Yes.'

'How long have you been married?'

'A few months.'

'And is it a happy marriage?'

Saffron looked at the detective in surprise. 'Yes.'

'Now, I understand that Mr Patel was in Paris last week for a conference. Is that correct?'

'We were there together. Ranjit was speaking at the conference and he wanted me to go with him. We decided to have a few days sight seeing before we returned to work today.'

'So when did you actually return home?'

'Yesterday evening.'

'And your husband showed no signs of being unwell then?'

Saffron shook her head. 'None at all. He seemed quite well this morning when we went in to work.'

213

'I understand you also work at the hospital, Mrs Patel. Are you in the same department as your husband?'

'I'm in orthopaedics.'

'And you and Mr Patel met at the hospital?'

'Yes, Ranjit is their chief heart surgeon. He has pioneered a number of new techniques.'

Detective Inspector Baker frowned. 'So as a heart surgeon he would know all the symptoms of an impending heart attack. Would he be foolish enough to ignore them?'

'I'm sure he wouldn't.'

'Yet when you asked if there had been an accident you implied that he may have had a heart attack. Why was that?'

'He asked Marjorie, Mrs Bartlett, to go to the chemist for a prescription. It was for an indigestion mixture.' Saffron managed a shaky laugh. 'I think we probably both jumped to conclusions.'

'Easily done.' Tony Baker smiled at her. 'If it puts your mind at rest we have had no reports of anyone being involved in an accident who matches your husband's description or the vehicle registration number.' He replaced his empty teacup on the tray. 'Whilst we're here, Mrs Patel, could I ask you one or two other things about your husband?'

'Yes.'

'Do you know Mr Patel's relatives?'

'No, they're all in India. They seem to have very little contact but he has said that one day we will go out to meet them.'

'So do you know the name Tariq Kavira?'

'I've never heard of him.'

'What about Nandita Kavira?'

Saffron frowned. 'Nandita was the name of Mr Patel's first wife. I don't know if her surname was Kavira. She returned to India and died over there.'

'So Mr Patel was a widower when you married him?'

'Yes.'

'How long had he been widowed?'

'I'm not sure. He didn't like to talk about it. It had been an arranged marriage and they were not happy together.'

'Do you happen to know the address where Mr Patel and his first wife lived?'

'No.' Saffron shook her head. 'I've never had any reason to ask.'

'Where was he living when you married?'

'He was living in a flat.'

'Are you able to give us the address of this flat?'

'Yes. Why are you asking all these questions about Ranjit? Where he used to live and his first wife have nothing to do with him not coming home this evening.'

'We are investigating a Mr Patel. As I am sure you are aware the name 'Patel' is very common amongst the Indian population. As we were coming out to see you, we decided we would ask you a few questions. We will be able to tick another Patel off our list.' Tony smiled at her. 'If you could just give us the address of the flat where Mr Patel used to live, then we will leave you in peace.'

Saffron gave them the name of the road and wrinkled her brow. 'I think it was number seventeen. I never went there.'

'Why was that?'

'Mr Patel is very, well, honourable, I suppose you would call it. He would not have wanted our names linked by gossip.'

'I understand, Mrs Patel.' Tony Baker rose. 'Thank you for your time. I'm sure your husband will be returning very soon and have a good reason for his absence. I'll leave you my card and if you have any further cause for concern please call me.'

Saffron closed the door behind the police officers and sank back down on the settee. 'I really do not know why they bothered to come. I had told them all about the car and that Ranjit had not felt well over the 'phone.'

Marjorie patted her hand. 'It was probably a good excuse to get out of the office for an hour. Besides they were able to ask after this other Mr Patel and that will save them a job tomorrow.'

Saffron sighed. 'There's no point in us sitting here looking at each other. I'm going to have a quick shower, then we ought to eat that lasagne before it's totally ruined.'

'Back to the station, please, Simon. Do you want us to drop you off home on the way, Elaine?'

'Are you trying to get rid of me?'

Tony Baker grinned at her. 'I suggest you take me up on my offer and get your beauty sleep. I think there could be quite a bit of work to be done tomorrow.'

Once back in his office Detective Inspector Baker pulled out the statement by Tariq Kavira. He tapped the paper with his finger. 'There's not much to link the two together, but his sister's name was Nandita and the brother-in-law is supposed to be the heart surgeon at the hospital. It's the best we have at the moment. The address the woman gave us for the flat lived in by Mr Patel matches the one the estate agent produced. Simon, get on the 'phone to the letting agents for those flats. They're a fairly big firm so they should have a man on twenty-four hour call. He might know something.'

Simon frowned. 'In Mr Kavira's statement he says his sister died in a traffic accident in London, but in your report Mrs Patel says her husband's first wife died in India. She can't have done both.'

Tony Baker shrugged. 'First thing tomorrow you can get on to the registry office and see if they can trace a death certificate for a Nandita Patel.'

Simon held up his hand as his telephone call was answered and he began to make notes. Finally he walked over to Tony's desk. 'I've spoken to the handyman who's on twenty four seven for the agents. He's worked for them for the last six years and has no recollection of an Indian living in those flats. That's not to say he didn't live there, but he was never called out to do a repair job.'

216

'Get back to the agents tomorrow. See if they can be specific about dates.'

'What next?'

'Now we put out a general call to all traffic units to be on the lookout for Mr Patel's car. Once they've located it we'll put it under surveillance and when he returns he'll find he has a few questions to answer.'

'Do you want me to do that?'

Tony nodded gloomily. 'We'll probably find he's spent the evening with a woman and forgot to tell his wife he would be working late.'

'Do you really think that's the case?'

'No, I'm beginning to feel there is far more to this than an errant husband. Place that call, then get off home or we'll have your wife asking us to look for you.' Tony picked up his jacket, checked his pockets, and made for the door just as his telephone started to ring. He looked over at Simon, who was busy relaying details to traffic control. He would have to answer it himself.

'Mrs Patel. You're telephoning to say your husband has returned safely?' Tony listened with growing disbelief. 'Say that again. All his clothes have been taken?'

Saffron tried hard to control herself. 'I went up to have a shower. There was something missing. I couldn't think what it was at first, then I realised. Ranjit's toiletries and shaving kit were missing. I went into the bedroom thinking he must have put them in there. There was no sign of them. I don't know why, but I opened the wardrobe and it was empty. His suits are gone, his shirts are missing, his underclothes and all his shoes. What's happened to him?'

'Now, Mrs Patel, I'm sure nothing has happened to him. I'll be back round to you. Give me about half an hour. I'm sure there's a very simple explanation.' As Tony listened, he indicated to Simon that he should get his jacket.

'What's happened?'

'Mr Patel appears to have taken his entire wardrobe with him. Hardly the action of a man who was supposed to be feeling ill.'

'He might have some sort of mental disorder.'

Tony gave Simon a scathing look. 'Upgrade that alert to traffic control. Give it priority. We're going to pay Mrs Patel another visit.'

Tony and Simon sat on the settee with Saffron opposite them. 'Thank you for calling me, Mrs Patel. I'm sorry to have to disturb your evening once again, but I think we ought to have a few more details about your husband. I shall have to ask you some rather personal questions. Would you like me to 'phone for a female colleague to be present? The officer who was with us earlier is off duty now.'

Saffron tried to smile. 'There's no need. Marjorie is here with me. Ask me whatever you want. I'll do my best to answer you.'

Tony nodded. 'I'd like to go back to when you first began to work at the hospital. Was Mr Patel already working there?'

'I believe so; in fact I'm sure he was.'

'Have you any idea how long he had worked there?'

Saffron shook her head. 'Not really. I think it was about five years, maybe more.'

'Had he worked at any other hospital before?'

'He never mentioned working anywhere else.'

Tony nodded. 'We can obviously check that out with the hospital tomorrow. Would you care to tell us how you came into contact with him, a contact that obviously led to marriage?'

Saffron blushed. 'I went to a lecture he gave and consulted him about a case I was dealing with. He gave me a lift home and that became a regular arrangement. Occasionally we would spend an evening at a concert or the theatre. Eventually we became engaged and married a short while afterwards.'

'Most newly weds like to have a home of their own, yet you continued to live here with Mrs Bartlett, and your husband moved in. Why was that?'

'Economy, really. Ranjit said the flat he was renting was too small to accommodate the two of us comfortably. He had sold the house where he lived with his first wife and repaid his father-in-law. Consequently we couldn't afford to put down a deposit on a place of our own and it seemed foolish to pay rent to a stranger when we could live here.'

Tony nodded. 'Very practical. The house where Mr Patel lived previously; you say he had repaid his father-in-law so I assume that gentleman owned the property?'

Saffron shook her head. 'I'm not really sure. I believe it was in Ranjit's name, but his father-in-law had lent him the money. He had to repay that along with his tuition fees.'

'I'm sorry; I'm a bit confused here. Can you explain?'

Saffron twisted her wedding ring nervously. 'Ranjit wanted to be a surgeon. He agreed to marry Nandita when he had qualified. Her father loaned him the necessary money to travel to London and study on the understanding that it would be repaid at a future date.'

'And Mr Patel was quite happy about marrying the young lady?'

'I suppose so, at the time.'

Tony raised his eyebrows. 'Can you explain that statement?'

'Ranjit did not see Nandita for a number of years. They did not really know each other. Apparently Nandita did not like England. Presumably that led to friction between them. Ranjit said it was not a happy marriage and Nandita returned to India. Unfortunately there was a cholera outbreak and she subsequently died.'

'And your marriage, Mrs Patel, I have to ask you again; is that a happy marriage?'

'I told you all of this earlier.'

'I have to check. When people have had time to think about the previous answers they have given they sometimes realise they were not always strictly accurate or truthful. Sometimes the marriage is unhappy and the partner decides to leave without advising the other party. For varying reasons the partner left behind does not always want to admit there had been problems.'

Saffron shook her head. 'We had occasional disagreements, but never anything serious enough for either of us to consider ending the marriage. Certainly not on my part, anyway' she added, a cold feeling in the pit of her stomach. Maybe Ranjit had been unhappy with her and decided to leave.

'So you would have no reason to suspect that your husband was interested in anyone else? To put it bluntly, having an affair?'

Saffron shook her head vehemently, despite a sudden feeling of uncertainty. That could explain Ranjit's change of attitude towards her. 'I'm sure he isn't.'

'Yet he appears to have disappeared and taken all his possessions with him. Can you think of any reason why he should do that?'

'No.' Saffron's eyes filled with tears.

Tony rose and patted her shoulder. 'If I could just have a quick look at your room. It's possible he has left a note and you've not discovered it yet.'

'Of course.' Saffron rose also.

'You stay here. I'm sure Mrs Bartlett could show us.'

Looking surprised, Marjorie led Tony up the stairs and into the large bedroom Saffron and Ranjit had shared.

Tony smiled easily at her. 'I just wanted to ask whether you had any theories about the disappearance of Mr Patel.'

Marjorie shook her head. 'I've no idea why he should leave.'

'In your opinion they are happily married?'

Marjorie pursed her lips. 'Ranjit was somewhat overbearing, almost dictatorial at times. Saffron found that a little difficult to accept.'

'And that led to arguments between them?'

'Never in front of me.'

'Why do you think Mr Patel asked you to collect a prescription for him?'

Marjorie frowned. 'I've been wondering about that. I can only think he wanted me out of the house so I wouldn't see him removing his suitcases.'

'I think the same thing, Mrs Bartlett.'

Tony's eyes swept around the room. It was impeccably tidy; any note left would have been immediately visible. He pulled open the wardrobe and the drawers of the dressing table and chest. A woman's clothing took up approximately half of the space; the remainder was bare.

'Thank you, Mrs Bartlett. There's obviously nothing up here to help us. If we return downstairs I'll have a final word with Mrs Patel.'

Saffron looked up at him as he entered the lounge.

'I could see nothing up there that would further our enquiries.' Tony looked steadily at Saffron. 'Mrs Patel I am not able to help you any more at present. Mr Patel is not a child and has no known medical condition. He has to be missing considerably longer before we could add him to our missing persons list and send out an alert. I think you have to accept that Mr Patel has left for reasons known only to him. Hopefully he will contact you to set your mind at rest about his safety. If he does so, please let us know.'

'So why did you ask me all those questions if you can't do anything?'

'As I told you earlier we are pursuing a line of enquiry relating to another matter that involves a man with the name Patel. They were just routine questions, a follow up by way of eliminating a name from our list.'

Saffron frowned. She did not believe the Inspector's glib excuse.

'What now?' asked Simon.

'Back to the station and we put out a red alert for him. All ports and airports. I think we may have struck gold here.'

'Are you going to tell her we've instigated a full scale search?'

Tony shook his head. 'Not at this stage. There's just a chance he'll contact her and we don't want her to give him the tip-off. I could also be wrong, of course.'

Ranjit woke early. He lay in his bed and thought of ways to spend the day that yawned ahead of him. He needed to be amongst a crowd so he would blend in and be inconspicuous. The tube was the obvious choice, but he did not want to spend all day travelling around. He would visit the British Museum, there would be plenty of people there of all nationalities. No one would notice him. When he became too bored, he could walk down to the West End and look at the shops, and then go to a cinema during the evening. His decisions made, he took a leisurely shower and dressed as casually as his wardrobe allowed.

Saffron dozed fitfully during the night. Despite Ranjit having removed all his possessions she could not conceive that he had left her without a word of explanation. The awful thought struck her – maybe Nandita was still alive in India and he had decided to return to her. She would have committed bigamy. Would she be sent to prison?

She rose earlier than usual and showered, surprised when she went down to the kitchen to find Marjorie already there.

'I couldn't sleep,' Marjorie explained. 'Are you able to eat some breakfast?' She took in Saffron's appearance and was sure her stepdaughter had suffered with even less sleep than she had managed.

Saffron shook her head. 'How early can I 'phone the police, do you think?'

Marjorie looked at the clock. 'Not yet. I'm sure the officer we spoke to yesterday won't be in yet. You'll only get the night duty officer and he probably won't be able to help you.'

Saffron heaved a sigh and leant her chin on her hands.

'Have a piece of toast at least, Saffie. You need to eat something.'

'I can get something from the canteen if I feel like it later.'

'You're going in to work?' Marjorie looked at her in surprise.

'I have to. I was away last week and I'm behind with my appointments. Besides, it will stop me thinking about Ranjit and wondering what's happened to him.'

'Take a taxi. It's raining and you don't want to get soaked.'

Saffron nodded. 'I've enough cash on me. I'll go to the cash point later and draw some more. I owe you the housekeeping for this month so I can get that at the same time.'

'There's no rush for that.' Marjorie placed a slice of toast on a plate and pushed it across the table to Saffron.

'If you insist on going in to work then I insist you have something to eat first.' She stood with her arms folded, daring Saffron to refuse.

Detective Inspector Tony Baker looked at the notes he had made. Tariq Kavira had said Patel owed money to his father, and his wife had confirmed that medical tuition fees and the purchase of a house had been a loan from his father-in-law. When Elaine came on duty he would ask her to track down the bank account where the hospital paid the surgeon's salary each month. If Ranjit Patel were transferring money to India there would be a record of that, however irregular the payments.

He would also like to see a copy of the death certificate for Nandita Patel. If she had indeed died in London there would certainly be a record; but why did the current Mrs Patel think her predecessor had died in India?

If forensics could come up with a date for the approximate length of time the body had been beneath the floorboards it would help. If it had been hidden over five years ago they were probably chasing the wrong man. Tony shook his head as if to dispel the thought. There could be no other reason why the surgeon had disappeared. The visit to the hospital by Tariq Kavira had frightened him and he had probably gone into hiding until he knew the man would have returned to India. That could account for him having taken his clothes.

'Morning, Tony. Been here all night?' Elaine hung her bag over her chair.

'Feels like it,' grumbled Tony. 'I want you to get on to payroll at the hospital. Find out which bank they pay Ranjit Patel's salary into each month. If they won't give details over the 'phone get over there. When you've got that we'll see what we can glean from the bank. I'm interested in payments going off to India. How regularly do they go and what is the amount. I want the name of the payee and his account details as well. Whilst you're on the 'phone to the hospital check that Mr Patel hasn't turned up for work this morning.' He fired his instructions to her.

Simon hurried over to Tony's desk. 'We've got the car.'

Tony looked up with interest. 'Where is it?'

'Long term car park at Gatwick.'

'Check with them immediately. See if he flew out within the last twenty-four hours. If he has, find out his destination and contact the police there.'

Elaine looked up in surprise. 'You really think he's left the country?'

'It's beginning to look that way. I think our Mr Ranjit Patel has a guilty conscience. I wish forensics would get a move on. We need the approximate age of the woman and the length of time she's been underneath that floor. Any luck with the bank details, Elaine?'

'They're getting back to me. Said they had to get clearance to give me any information.'

''Phone them again. Tell them it's urgent. If they stall you again get over there and lean on them. Obstruction of a police enquiry should do for a start.'

Elaine nodded, hoping she would not have to make the drive across London.

'Colin, have you got the dates from the letting agency yet?'

'They also said they'd get back to me.'

'Same instructions to you as I've just given to Elaine. I'll try forensics and then the team at the house.' Tony looked over at Simon where he was waiting to be connected to airport security. 'When you've done that get on to the registry office. Get them to check for a death certificate in the name of Nandita Patel or Nandita Kavira going back for ten years.'

'Ten years?' Simon raised his eyebrows.

'We don't know how long ago she died. We don't want to do a second search because we missed it first time round by a few months.'

Simon nodded and turned away as he was finally connected to departures. Tony could hear him explaining patiently that he was interested in departures from Gatwick to anywhere in the world during the previous twenty-four hours. Finally he slammed the 'phone down.

'They'll get back to us. The chap I spoke to said it would take at least a couple of hours to check departure lists. I'll see if the registry office is open for business yet.'

Having taken a taxi Saffron was more than half an hour early for her first appointment and decided it would be practical to go to the cash point situated in the main entrance to the hospital before she went to her office. She inserted her card and pressed in the numbers. She frowned in annoyance as the machine told her it was unable to comply with her request and her card was ejected. She could not have been concentrating and had obviously pressed a wrong number. She inserted it again and very deliberately keyed in the numbers. Her card was delivered back to her again with the same message. She held it in her hand tentatively. If her request was refused a third time the machine might swallow her card. There must be a fault or maybe the machine was waiting for a top up of cash. She would try again during her lunch break.

Tony helped himself to coffee from the vending machine and looked at the members of his team, Colin and Elaine were busy writing notes, and Simon was on the telephone, tapping his pen impatiently as he waited.

'Colin?' he asked.

'The letting agents say he was there for eight months. Paid his rent in cash, six months in advance and a two-month deposit. He never complained or asked for any work to be done. He only visited their office once. That was when he signed the contract and paid the rent. He gave them written notice of his departure date and the last two months of his occupancy was covered by the refundable deposit. They could only confirm that he was an Indian gentleman. References had been taken up by them at the hospital where he claimed to work as a surgeon and they had come back confirming his status. They checked with his bank and his account was conducted in a regular manner, no cheques ever returned for lack of funds, no request for an overdraft.'

Tony raised his eyebrows. 'Any details yet, Elaine?'

Elaine held up her hand and finished writing. 'I've got them here.'

'You and Colin get a warrant signed and make your way over there. I want photocopies of all accounts in his name going back as far as possible. They'll probably tell you they're not available before a certain date, but they'll have them archived somewhere. Bring back whatever is available and tell them you'll collect the others tomorrow.'

Simon pushed back his chair and lifted his jacket from the peg. 'I'm off to the registrars. They won't give any information over the 'phone. I've got to go down and fill out an official form before they'll start a search. I tried telling them it was obstruction, but they're adamant.'

Tony nodded. 'Right. Get off all of you. Report back to me as soon as you have anything tangible. If I'm not in the office use my mobile number.'

'What about the airport? They're supposed to be 'phoning back.'

'I'll speak to Noah. He can take down details and call me if I'm out. I want to have a word with the immediate neighbours. I'll show them the photo I have of the previous Mrs Patel. Surely one of them must have known her to speak to. I'd like to know if she told them she was returning to India. I also want another word with Mr Goodman. He may have seen her when he was working at the neighbour's house.'

Saffron returned to the cash point in the early afternoon and tried to use her card again to draw some money. She was met with the same refusal as before. She leant her head against the machine, the cold metal soothing to her throbbing head.

'Anything wrong, Miss Bartlett?' A nurse waiting to use the machine looked at her curiously.

'It keeps throwing my card back at me. All I want is some cash.'

'Have you tried asking for a balance? Maybe a debit has gone out that you've forgotten about and the balance is too low to give you the amount you're asking for.'

Saffron frowned. It was possible. She tried to remember if she had used her debit card when she had paid for the trip down the Seine and the meal at the Eiffel Tower. 'Go ahead of me,' she said. 'You could be right. I'll ask for a balance in a minute.'

Saffron stood back and waited until the nurse had collected her money. She inserted her card again and keyed in the numbers, this time asking for a balance on her account. She gasped in horror and disbelief. A balance of one pound thirty six pence showed on the screen. She was sure she had not used her debit card in France so there should be at least a thousand pounds available to her. She tried again and the same amount showed again. She asked for a mini statement to be printed and the machine flashed up a message to say it was not programmed to comply with her request. Biting her lips in frustration and annoyance Saffron returned to her office. She would have to take the bus into town at the end of the day and visit the bank for an explanation.

Simon returned from the registry office empty handed. He had sat and waited whilst they searched for a death certificate for Nandita Patel or Nandita Kavira. Finally, the woman had returned.

'I have five Nandita Patels registered, but two of them are children and the other is a lady who was in her eighties. I can let you have the certificates for the other two, but you'll have to fill in another form and pay the fee. I can give you a receipt so you can claim it back on your expenses. I have nothing in the name of Nandita Kavira.'

Grudgingly Simon did as she requested and then studied the two forms she handed over to him. One had committed suicide less than six months earlier and the other was single and in her mid fifties when she died. The suicide had been registered by her husband, Madanial Patel and the woman in her fifties by her mother.

He shook his head. 'I'm sure neither of those are the one we're looking for. I'd be grateful if you'd keep them to one side in case my boss thinks otherwise and sends me back for them, though.'

'I can keep them for a week. After that they will have to be shredded. You'd be amazed at the number of people who ask for certificates and never come back to collect them. We'd be up to our ears in paper if we didn't dispose of them.'

'If we decide we need them I shall probably be back before the day is out. Thanks for your help.'

Elaine telephoned the station only to be told that Tony had left the office to collect the report from the forensics department.

'I'll call him there. I've got his mobile number.' She waited for it him to answer. 'Tony, we've got a problem with the bank. No, listen,' she said as he was about to interrupt. 'We've got photocopies of his bank statement for the last five years up until he married again. It then became a joint account and we're not allowed access unless we have a warrant for the joint bank account or Mrs Patel's permission.'

Tony frowned. 'Anything stand out on those you have?'

'All seems to be conducted in a regular manner. Direct debits for utilities, cash drawn at regular intervals, credit card payments; the usual. There's only one anomaly. A large sum transferred each month to another bank account.'

'Get the bank to give you details of the receiving bank. Colin can get over there with the warrant and you go and visit Mrs Patel. Insist she gives you permission to access the account. It would be quicker to take her down to the bank with you. If she presents a problem bring her in.' Tony closed his mobile 'phone. 'I'm sorry about that. Please continue Dr Moore.'

Dr Moore shrugged. 'I really cannot tell you very much. Obviously female, aged between twenty-five and thirty-five. By her appearance and the clothing that was retrieved we are assuming she was of Indian origin, but we cannot take that as a fact. Many Westerners wear ethnic clothes simply because they like them. The skin looks a bit dark for a European, and the hair appears to be black. I'll send samples off to the lab: They should be able to narrow down her ethnic origins and hopefully ascertain her cause of death. The bones appear undamaged, including the skull, so that seems to rule out physical violence. No disease is apparent in any of her organs.'

Dr Moore peeled off his surgical gloves and rubbed his nose with his thumb. 'Of course, she could be an illegal immigrant. Bit of a problem there if you're not supposed to be in the country and your partner dies suddenly from natural causes. It could be the husband panicked and decided it would be easier and safer for him to place her under the floor.'

'She was married then?'

Dr Moore shrugged. 'A gold ring was on her finger. It could be a wedding ring.'

'Any idea how long she had been under the floor?'

'Difficult to say. The fact that she was wrapped in polythene and covered in concrete has kept out the damp and any insect activity. I would guess a couple of years. I can't be any more specific until the lab: gets back to me.'

Tony nodded. 'We're not talking an old body then? She hasn't been under there since the house was built?'

Dr Moore shook his head. 'Maximum length of time would be five years. When were those houses built; shortly after the war; she certainly doesn't date from then.'

Tony closed his notebook. 'Thanks. You'll fax through the report as soon as it's ready, I take it.'

'Of course. Should be with you this afternoon.'

Tony returned to his car and read the notes he had taken. He was certain when the laboratory results were returned the body would be that of an Indian woman, and he was equally sure she would eventually be named as Nandita Patel. He started the engine; now for the neighbours.

The Detective knocked on the door of the house next to the Wright's, the couple who lived there were only too willing to discuss the grisly find with him. They confirmed the photograph Tony showed them was that of their previous neighbour. He sat in their lounge, sipping a cup of tea and learning very little. The man left at near enough the same time in the morning, they used to hear him slam his car door and drive away. If they met outside they would nod and pass the time of day, but they had never held a conversation with him. They had seen his wife leave the house at various times during the day, but she was never out for long. She may have used the general store at the end of the road for her groceries.

Tony made a note to visit the small parade of shops. 'Did you ever speak to Mrs Patel?' he asked.

The couple exchanged looks. 'I don't think she spoke English,' said the man. 'If you spoke to her she would just bob her head and smile. What about you, Mary? Did she ever speak to you?'

Mary shook her head. 'I'm sure she did speak English. Sometimes you could hear the television and it was an English programme.'

'Maybe she was trying to learn the language.'

'More likely to have been him watching a programme. He spoke English.'

'He was out during the day, couldn't have been him,' Mary's husband countered.

'Sometimes it was in the evening,' she insisted.

Tony cleared his throat. 'I understand that Mrs Patel returned to India at some time. Do you happen to know when that was?'

Mary shook her head. 'A couple of years ago maybe. I didn't see her for a week or so and when Ron saw the husband going in he asked him if she was ill. He said she had returned to India to visit her family. We never saw her again. Hardly ever saw him for that matter. Didn't even know he was moving until a removal van appeared. The young couple who have moved in seem friendly enough. Poor things. Fancy finding something like that under your floor. Bad enough if it had been a dead cat, but...' She gave a mock shudder. 'I don't think I'd want to live there.'

'Quite.' Tony smiled at them. 'Well, thank you for your time and the tea.'

'You're welcome. Sorry we couldn't be more help.'

Tony handed Ron his card. 'If you do happen to think of anything you can always give me a ring on that number. If I'm not around someone will be there to take a message.'

Ron nodded and passed the card to Mary who promptly stuck in into the rim of the mirror over the fireplace to join the collection already there.

Tony knocked on the door the other side of the Wright's house and waited, finally accepting there was no one in. He made a note to request an officer to return at a different time of day and walked to the end of the road. A small parade of shops consisting of a grocer and general store, greengrocer, baker, hairdresser, hardware store and a funeral parlour had been purpose built back from the line of houses. Parking spaces were marked out on the road, all but one empty. Tony debated whether to return and bring his car to the parade, but decided it was safe enough. This was not the kind of area where vehicles were vandalised as a matter of routine.

Tony produced the photograph, but the greengrocer insisted he had no recollection of an Indian woman and the bakery was equally unproductive. The bakery had changed hands eighteen months ago and since then most of the staff had moved elsewhere.

At the grocers and general store he had more success. They recognised Nandita Patel and remembered her as the Indian woman who had come in most days and purchased a couple of items.

'Haven't seen her for a long while now. I presume they moved away. Don't know where. We called her Mrs Frozen,' the grocer smiled. 'Never bought anything fresh, always frozen ready meals. Of course, she may have gone into town to one of the specialist grocers and bought ingredients for making curry. Couldn't say about that.'

'Did she speak English?'

The grocer nodded. 'I think so. We never held a conversation. If I made a remark about the weather she seemed to understand, but only ever answered yes or no. Kept herself very much to herself. I never do remember seeing him, although, come to think of it, I wouldn't know he was Mr Frozen, would I? If they weren't together I wouldn't make the connection.'

'You don't remember an Indian gentleman coming in, possibly buying a newspaper here or cigarettes?'

The grocer scratched his head. 'Well, now you mention it, that could have been him, I suppose. Used to drive up in the morning, early; I'd only just be open, and buy cigarettes. He always sat outside in his car and smoked one. I called him Mr Early Fag. He's not been around for a good while now either.'

'Do you have names for all your customers? Tony asked curiously.

'Most of them have a nickname. I don't take cheques or run a book so I don't know their proper names.'

Tony nodded and thanked him. He looked at the other three shops. It was doubtful she would have patronised any of them, but he ought to check them out. If he had sent a junior officer he would expect them to question every shopkeeper and not use his own judgement regarding the relevance.

As he had expected, the funeral parlour and hairdresser had no knowledge of either of the Patels. There was just the hardware store left and it was unlikely Mrs Patel had ever patronised him. He pushed open the door and held it open to allow a customer to exit.

'Thanks, mate. I'll be back in a mo' for the rest.'

Tony watched as he opened the boot of the car and carefully laid a sack of cement inside, followed by a carrier bag. He returned to the shop, collected some lengths of timber and a pot of paint. Once again Tony held the door open for him.

'Cheers.'

'You sell a wide variety of goods,' observed Tony.

'Need to. Everyone wants somethin' diff'rent. What can I get for yer?'

'I'd like to ask you a few questions.' Tony flashed his badge at the man.

'What about? I'm an 'onest trader. Pay my taxes and fill in V.A.T. forms. I've got an accountant. 'E'll vouch for me.' He glared at Tony belligerently.

Tony shook his head. 'I'm not investigating you. I'd just like to ask a few questions about a man who may have been a customer.'

'I wouldn't know if 'e'd bought tools for a break in.'

233

'Of course not. The customer I'm interested in is a foreign gentleman, lived in this area until a short while ago.'

'Illegal immigrant?'

'Not that I know of. I'm just interested to know if he did any repairs in his house.'

'Most people round 'ere do their own work if they can.'

'This man may have asked your advice. Building was not his trade.'

'They generally ask me. They know I can tell 'em the right thing for the job.'

'Could you think back, probably a few years. A gentleman may have asked how to treat a floor that had woodworm.'

Mr Taylor shook his head. 'Can't say I do. No, wait a mo'.' He wrinkled his brow as he concentrated. 'Somethin's comin' back to me.'

'You remember the man?'

'Indian or Pakistani chap came in with a bit of wood riddled with woodworm and wanted to know what it was. I told 'im. Best to chuck the lot out. Once you've got it, it's a devil to get rid of. 'E said 'e couldn't afford no fancy job and could 'e do it 'imself. I sold 'im the woodworm killer an' a paintbrush an' told 'im what to do. 'E came back later for some cement an' a roll of polythene.'

'Polythene? What would he need that for?'

'No idea. Not up ter me ter ask. 'E also bought some new boards an a bit of new floor cov'ring. Never saw 'im again after that.'

'Your advice must have been very effective then.' Tony smiled. 'Would you know him again if you saw him?'

Mr Taylor frowned. 'I might. They all look the same to me.'

Tony took the photograph of Nandita Patel from a folder. 'Would you have seen this lady around at all?'

The shopkeeper scrutinized the photograph, finally shaking his head. 'Can't say I've ever seen 'er.'

'You've been very helpful,' Tony handed him his card and returned the photograph to the folder. 'I may send an officer along to have another word with you at a later date. You may have remembered something else about the man that could be useful.'

'Is it about the body under the floor?' Suddenly Mr Taylor was interested.

'I can't divulge anything at this stage, sir. We're only making some routine enquiries in the area. Thanks for your help.'

Tony sat in his car and wrote his notes up to date. He had little to show for his questioning, but the man Mr Taylor remembered purchasing materials could certainly be the Mr Patel they were anxious to find and question. He telephoned his office, asking for a progress report.

Simon informed him that he had drawn a blank at the registry office.

'The woman said that registration was necessary in the area where the person died. Where they lived was irrelevant. We only have Mr Kavira's word for it that his sister died in England. Perhaps she did die in India.'

'If she did he must know that. Why come over here and say he wants a photograph of her grave?'

'Could be an excuse to try to find his brother-in-law and recoup the money he says is owed to his father,' suggested Simon.

Tony shook his head. 'I might agree with you if the body had not turned up at his house. No, I think Mr Patel did away with his wife and disposed of her. He took fright when Kavira turned up looking for him and decided to make himself scarce. He may not know we've found the body.'

'Nothing from airport security yet?'

'I'll try 'phoning them again. Give them a reminder that the information is needed urgently.'

'You do that. Has forensics faxed through their report?'

Simon turned and checked the machine sitting silently in the corner. 'Nothing yet.'

Tony sighed. 'I'm on my way back.'

Elaine showed her badge to the receptionist in orthopaedics. 'I would like to see Mrs Patel, please.'

Angela frowned. 'Doctor Bartlett is very busy with appointments at the moment.'

'I'm sure she is, but this is rather important. It should only take a couple of minutes.'

'Very well. I'll slip you in before her next patient. Take a seat whilst you're waiting.'

Elaine waited, knowing the moment the doctor saw her she would be expecting news of her husband. The hopeful look on Saffron's face as she looked up confirmed this and Elaine shook her head.

'I'm sorry, Mrs Patel. I haven't come with any news, I'm afraid. I've come to ask for your help.'

'If I can.'

'As part of our ongoing enquiry it is routine to look at bank accounts. Just a formality to check there are no irregularities, you understand. I have been down to the bank and I am not allowed access without your permission to the joint account you have with your husband. I could get a warrant, of course, but that seems rather excessive. I'd like you to come down to the bank with me.'

'Now?' Saffron looked at her in surprise. 'I can't come now. I have a queue of patients.'

'When would you be able to come?'

'When I finish seeing my appointments at four.'

Elaine shook her head. 'We do need access as soon as possible. I can drive you down, you can give your permission, and then I will drive you back again.'

Saffron frowned. 'How long will it take?'

'No more than a few minutes. It is just a formality.'

'I did want to go to the bank myself.' Saffron hesitated. 'I suppose I could take a break. Angela would have to apologise to my patients and tell them I was running late. Oh, very well. I have two more appointments that I have to see first. I can't keep them waiting any longer.'

Elaine nodded. She was frustrated that she would have to waste the time hanging around in the waiting room, but she had no remit to put pressure on the doctor unless she had met with an outright refusal. 'I'll no doubt be able to get a cup of coffee whilst I wait.'

'There's a vending machine just outside the waiting room.' She opened the door. 'A quick word with you, Angela, then I shall be ready for my next patient.'

Tony was just drawing into his parking space at the police station when his mobile 'phone rang.

'I'm just parking. What is it?'

'Gatwick says they can find no record of him leaving the country through their airport. That's assuming he doesn't possess a second passport in another name. So the car abandoned at Gatwick could be a red herring.'

'It could be.' Tony banged his fist on the steering wheel. 'Get on to Heathrow, Stansted, and Luton. It would be feasible to leave your car at Gatwick and take a train or bus to one of the other airports. He could have caught a flight from one of those to the continent. Get them to check their flight schedules for yesterday. Tell them it's urgent. In the meantime put out an alert – all airports and ports – detain anyone travelling by the name of Ranjit Patel to anywhere in the world. He could have travelled to another airport further up the country. He's had plenty of time.'

'Will do.'

Elaine sat with Saffron in a small, screened area at the bank. There was a minimum of privacy and Elaine wished she had insisted they had had been taken to one of the private rooms to conduct their business there. The young man, wearing a badge that gave his name as Geoff and his title as Customer Adviser, flicked his fingers over the keys of his computer. He swivelled the screen round so that both Elaine and Saffron could see the details.

Saffron caught her breath. 'There must be a mistake. There should be at least a thousand pounds on the account.'

Geoff shook his head and turned the screen back to face him. 'Most of the balance was withdrawn yesterday.' He turned the screen back to them and pointed with his biro. 'There was a cash point withdrawal, then the remainder of the balance was withdrawn inside the branch.'

'Not by me,' stated Saffron.

'I can only assume your husband made the withdrawal and omitted to tell you.'

Elaine made a swift note on her pad of the account number and scanned the page. A large amount had been transferred to another account earlier in the month. 'Would it be possible to have a print out of this, please?'

Geoff looked at Saffron. 'I need your permission for that, Mrs Patel.'

Saffron nodded miserably. 'I'll have to take some money from my savings account, I suppose.'

'Unless you wished to make an overdraft arrangement,' suggested Geoff.

'Could I have a private word with Mrs Patel?' asked Elaine and Geoff nodded.

'Would either of you like a coffee or tea? I'm just going to get one for myself.'

Both women shook their heads and Elaine bent towards Saffron as Geoff left the booth.

'May I suggest that you have your hospital salary paid into another account, one that is only accessible by you.'

Saffron sighed. 'I suppose that would make sense. I just don't understand what is going on. Why should Ranjit draw out all our money and go away without telling me?'

'At this stage I can't answer that question.'

'Meaning you can't or you won't?' asked Saffron sharply.

Elaine smiled sympathetically at her. 'Meaning I don't know the answer. If I did I would tell you.'

Geoff returned, hesitating at the entrance. Saffron gave him a strained smile, her face felt stiff.

'I would like to make arrangements to have my hospital salary paid into my savings account in future, please'

'That's no problem. All you need to do is give your payroll department the new account number.'

Saffron shook her head. 'It isn't quite that simple. This month's pay will already be in transit. Can I give you a letter or something to request that as soon as it reaches this account it is transferred over to my savings account?'

'You can certainly do that.'

'Then I would appreciate a sheet of paper so I can do it now. Can you dictate what I need to say? I don't want there to be any misunderstanding.'

Geoff dictated a few lines and Saffron wrote them and signed her name. 'I'll inform payroll of the new arrangements so there should be no problem next month. Now I suppose I'd better draw out some money and get back to work.'

Tony studied the report sent through to him by forensics. The autopsy carried out on the body showed the woman to have had healthy organs and no immediate cause of death was obvious. Samples had been taken and had been sent off to the toxicology department for further examination. It told him nothing new and he threw it to one side. 'Anything to report?'

Colin handed him a sheet of paper. 'I went over to the bank where Patel had been transferring money each month. The

239

account was in his name, a small transfer to a bank in India each month, no withdrawals. He closed the account yesterday. Transferred the whole balance to a bank in Venezuela.'

'Get back on to the airports. Ask them to have a look at their advance bookings for flights to South America. Reiterate the importance of holding anyone by the name of Patel. What's keeping Elaine?'

Elaine returned to the office and greeted Tony with a satisfied smile. 'I think that clinches it. Our Mr Patel has done a runner. He drew out all the money from their joint account yesterday.'

'We've already drawn that conclusion,' replied Tony drily. 'Colin found he'd closed the other bank account in his name yesterday as well. The problem is, where has he run to?'

Saffron returned home feeling sick. Somehow, she had managed to deal with the remainder of her patients, apologising for keeping them waiting. Marjorie looked at her wan face and knew she had not received any news of her husband during the day.

'Why has he drawn out all the money, Marjorie? Do you think he's going back to India and didn't like to tell me?'

'That sounds most likely.' Marjorie did not believe her answer for one moment. 'He may have had news that he was wanted urgently over there.'

'I just don't know what to do.'

'There's nothing you can do. The police are obviously taking him seriously now as a missing person.'

Saffron frowned. 'There seems to be more to it than that. I'm sure there's something they're not telling me.'

Ranjit took the underground to the British Museum and spent most of the day wandering around the exhibits. He was not truly interested, but he knew he would be unremarkable in the throng of foreigners who patronised the museum each day. He bought a newspaper and sat outside a cafe in the sunshine for a late lunch. He would find out if there were any films on at the local cinemas that interested him. That would fill the remainder of the afternoon for him and by the time he had partaken of an Indian meal in the evening it would be time to return to his lodging for a good nights' sleep. He would then make his way to Heathrow airport ready for his flight. He leaned back in the chair and inhaled his cigarette. No doubt Saffron would be wondering where he was, but he doubted the police would start looking for a missing adult for at least a week.

Simon watched anxiously as the fax came through and pulled it away from the machine the moment it had finished. Heathrow had a list of thirteen Patels who had travelled to various parts of the world the previous day. He was able to eliminate seven on a time basis. They had left before Ranjit Patel had closed his bank account. Two more were doubtful, as he would hardly have had enough time to travel from the bank and check in. Three others were unlikely as they were family groups, but there was a single man travelling to Switzerland.

Excitedly he hurried over to Tony. 'This could be him.'

'Switzerland, departing four fifteen. He could have just made that one.'

'Find out if the ticket was purchased in advance or if he took a stand-by. Get as much information as you can regarding his age and the amount of luggage he had with him. We know he must have left the family home with two suitcases at least.'

Simon returned to his desk, hoping he would be the officer to have tracked him down.

'Stansted seems a possibility,' called Elaine. 'Two single travellers, one to Paris and the other to Dusseldorf.'

Tony nodded glumly. They might be able to find out where he had landed, but once abroad their chances of finding him were slim. He could have moved on to anywhere.

'We'll give it to the newspapers tonight. We might get a response from the public.'

Colin snorted and tried to turn it into a cough. That would mean people claiming they had seen the man throughout London and probably all over Europe.

Saffron looked at the newspaper whilst she drank her coffee. It was more for something to do rather than out of interest. She turned the page, looking for the crossword to distract her thoughts. The name seemed to jump off the page at her.

> Mr Ranjit Patel, the eminent heart surgeon, is being sought by the police.
> He disappeared from his home two days ago without leaving news of his intention to his wife. Mr Patel is asked to contact the police as a matter of urgency to help eliminate him from their enquiries into the identity of the body that was found buried beneath the floor of a London house last week.
> The police are asking anyone who may have any information to contact them on the telephone number below.

Saffron read the few lines a second time. There were probably many men named Ranjit Patel who lived in England, but how many of them would be heart surgeons? She took out her mobile 'phone and dialled the number.

'Could I speak to Detective Inspector Baker, please?'

'Who's calling?'

'It's about Mr Ranjit Patel.'

'Could I have your name, please, madam.'

Saffron sighed. She had hoped to be put straight through to the officer without having to give any details. 'I am Mrs Patel. I reported my husband missing to Detective Inspector Baker.'

'One moment, please.'

'Mrs Patel? It's Elaine Saunders here. I went to the bank with you yesterday. Detective Inspector Baker is with someone at present. Am I able to help you?'

'I've just seen the newspaper.' Saffron's voice faltered. 'Is it my husband you want to speak to about a body that has been found?'

'We would like to eliminate him from our enquiries. Had we been able to speak to him at the hospital or your home I'm sure we would have completed our business with him by now. He hasn't contacted you, I suppose?'

'I've not heard from him.'

'You would telephone us, wouldn't you, Mrs Patel?'

'Of course,' Saffron spoke indignantly.

'I have to ask. Many people would be so relieved to have their husband back safe and well that they would forget to notify us that he had turned up.' Elaine shook her head at Simon who had been listening to her side of the conversation. 'We will contact you if we hear anything, I promise.'

'What was that about?'

'Mrs Patel, wanting to make sure it was her husband we wanted to question about the body.'

'He hasn't contacted her, then?'

Elaine looked at her colleague scornfully. 'Would you, if you'd done away with your first wife, withdrawn all the money from your bank account and done a disappearing act?'

Simon shrugged. 'Some women feel it is their duty to defend their husbands whatever they may have done. She could even be in on it with him and planning to join him wherever at a later date.'

'Got him!' Colin gave a thumbs up sign to Tony who hurried to his side. 'I've just been speaking to Heathrow. They have a Ranjit Patel booked on a three thirty flight this afternoon to Venezuela.'

'Are they sure it's him?'

243

Colin shrugged. 'Well, they can't be certain. A flight was booked on Monday through one of their inner city tour operators.'

'Anything back from the continent about the other Patels?'

'The Swiss one has checked out as legitimate. He's in his seventies.'

'Simon, you're with me. Elaine, find out the name of the tour operator and get all the details you can. 'Phone me as soon as you have them. Colin, get back to Heathrow and make sure they detain him. Any excuse will do.' Tony picked up his jacket. They were going to have to drive fast to get to Heathrow before the flight took off.

Ranjit stood in the smoking area at Heathrow. He was nervous now the final moment to leave had arrived. It would be a long flight, a long time without a cigarette. He drew on it greedily, anxious to have as much nicotine in his body as possible.

'Mr Patel, Mr Ranjit Patel, travelling to Venezuela. Please come to the departure desk immediately.'

Ranjit frowned. Why were they paging him? Having collected his ticket he had checked in, his passport in order, his luggage weighed, and the excess duly paid for. There was probably another Patel catching the flight. He ignored the message as it was broadcast a second time across the airport.

Tony switched on the warning blue light and the siren to clear their passage as they sped up the motorway.

'I bet everyone thinks you're off on a holiday and late for the flight,' grinned Simon.

'I wish! I also wish we hadn't given that press release. If he's seen it he could easily have changed his plans. He could lay low anywhere in England for a few weeks. By the time he emerged we would probably have other enquiries going on and could miss him as he sneaked out of the country.'

'Don't be such a pessimist,' Simon chided him. 'If you really want to look on the black side you could consider that he's not our man anyway. Just an innocent Patel travelling to Venezuela.'

Tony's mobile 'phone rang and he answered it with alacrity. 'Elaine? What have you got?'

'Flight booked on Monday. Would have preferred to travel that afternoon, but unable to make the deadline for check in. Paid cash. The tour operator is only a few doors away from the cash machine where he made the withdrawal from the joint account and one block away from the bank where he held his own account. Assuming it is him the time scale fits together nicely. Ties in with the time he returned to his home according to the woman there.'

'Well done, Elaine. I shall probably need you tomorrow to go with me to break the news to the wife.'

'If it is him,' Simon reminded him and Tony looked at him sourly.

Ranjit heard the call for passengers to go to the departure lounge. He stubbed out his cigarette and lifted his briefcase, joining the swelling group of travellers going towards the same exit. He stood in line, waiting for his boarding card to be handed to him. To his surprise, he was asked to step to one side.

He frowned in annoyance. 'I hope this will not take long. It is imperative that I catch this flight.'

'I'm sure you won't be delayed more than a few moments, sir.'

Ranjit tapped his foot impatiently as he watched the other passengers filing through. Maybe he should have reported to the desk when he had heard his name called. He felt decidedly conspicuous standing there, conscious of the glances of the other travellers as he stood waiting. Finally the last one had been dealt with and the door closed and locked. He glanced around nervously. He did not like this.

'Mr Ranjit Patel?'

Ranjit swung round and was confronted by Detective Inspector Baker holding out his warrant card.

'What do you want?'

'You are Mr Ranjit Patel?'

'Yes.'

'Mr Ranjit Patel, the heart surgeon?'

'Yes, yes. Hurry up. I need to catch my flight.'

'I'm sorry, sir. I have to ask you to accompany us to answer a few questions.'

Ranjit looked at his watch. 'I cannot do that. I am already late boarding the 'plane.'

'I'm afraid I have to insist, sir. I would ask that you are co-operative and come quietly. Should you refuse I would have to arrest you for obstruction to the course of justice.'

Ranjit paled. How had they found him so quickly? 'If my wife has complained that I have drawn money from our joint account it is for my visit to Venezuela. I have been requested to attend at a very complicated operation at short notice.'

Tony raised his eyebrows. 'Really, sir. Well, if you would just like to come into a side room with us I am sure you can show us the paperwork you have from your intended destination. We will then contact the hospital involved and once we have checked that out satisfactorily you will be able to board your flight.'

'It will be too late by then. There is only another twenty minutes before it takes off.'

'All the more reason to come along with us immediately, sir.' Tony took a firm grip on Ranjit's elbow. 'This way, sir.'

'Mrs Patel, Mrs Patel, just a moment, Mrs Patel.'

Saffron stopped in horror at the entrance to the hospital. A camera flashed and she was too late to shield her face.

'What do you want?'

'Just a few words. What can you tell us about your husband? Do you know where he is?'

Saffron turned on her heel and walked back inside. She was shaking. How had the reporter tracked her down? She still worked under the name of Bartlett.

'Angela, has anyone been asking for me?'

Angela shook her head. 'Not that I know of. Are you expecting someone?'

'There's a reporter outside. How would he know that I'm Ranjit's wife? Did he come in and ask you?'

'More or less any member of staff could have told him. He hasn't been in here.'

The reporter walked through the door. 'If I could just have a few words, Mrs Patel. Just to put the record straight.'

Saffron looked in horror at Angela. 'What can I do?'

'Just say 'no comment'.' Angela lifted her telephone. 'Security. We have an intruder in orthopaedics. Could you come and remove him please. Would you like me to call the police as back up?' She waited for a moment. 'Fine. Quick as you can.'

The reporter looked at the receptionist nonplussed. 'There's no need to call security. I'm not doing anything wrong.'

'You are harassing one of our doctors. That's an offence.'

'I only want to ask her a couple of questions.'

'You are on hospital premises. I suggest you leave now before the security guards arrive.'

The reporter looked towards the door. 'I'll wait for you outside,' he muttered and pushed his way out of the door. Angela promptly locked it behind him.

Saffron sat down in a chair. 'Thank you, Angela. I didn't know we had security guards on the premises.'

'We haven't, but that reporter obviously didn't know either. It just seemed like a good way to get rid of him. You sit there for a minute or two. Would you like a cup of tea?'

Saffron shook her head. 'I just want to go home. Can you see if he's waiting outside for me?'

Angela lifted the blind and peered out. 'He's standing by his car.'

'I'll have to order a taxi. I can't stand and wait for the bus with him pestering me with questions all the time. What would people think?'

'Ask the driver to come to the back entrance. I'll keep lifting the blind and he'll probably think you're watching him and waiting for him to leave.'

'I don't want him following me and finding out where I live.' Saffron bit her lip.

Angela looked at the distressed woman before her. 'I don't know what the problem is, but I do know you haven't been yourself these last few days. Do you want to talk about it? You can tell me to mind my own business, I won't be offended.'

'I don't know what's happening and the police won't seem to tell me. Ranjit has gone missing. He's taken all his clothes and the money from our joint account and disappeared. I don't know why. We hadn't had a row or anything. All the police have told me is that they want to question people named Patel, then I saw the bit in the paper today. They want to question him about a body that was found. I'm sure it's nothing to do with him, but why has he gone away?' Saffron looked up at her secretary, her eyes full of tears.

Angela pulled out her cigarettes. 'I know we're not supposed to smoke in here, but what the hell? Do you want one?'

Saffron shook her head. 'I don't, thanks.'

Angela sat down beside her. 'I know you haven't been married that long, but do you think there's another woman involved?'

'I suppose there could be. They always say the wife is the last person to know.'

'That's the answer. He couldn't face telling you so he has just gone away. The fact that the police want to question men named Patel is just coincidence. That reporter is just jumping to conclusions to try to get a story.'

'Do you really think so?' Saffron looked at her hopefully.

'Sure to be the answer. By tomorrow he'll be chasing some other poor woman with the same name. Don't you worry. I'll order a taxi in my name to meet you at the back entrance. If I see him leave I'll 'phone you on your mobile.'

'He might be waiting for me when I come in tomorrow.'

'If he is then I'll certainly telephone the police. That will be harassment. You go on home. You could even find that Ranjit is there waiting for you and begging to be forgiven.'

Saffron managed a watery smile. 'You could be right. Thanks, Angela.'

Marjorie sat beside Saffron and held her hand, hoping she could sense the comfort and support she was offering her. Tony and Elaine sat opposite, having refused Marjorie's offer of refreshment.

'Mrs Patel, I'm pleased to say we have located your husband. The bad news is that he is in custody. He is helping us with our enquiries regarding a body that was found beneath the floor of the house he owned previously.' Detective Inspector Baker watched Saffron's reaction to the news carefully.

'There must be a mistake, officer.'

Tony shook his head. 'We know we have the right Mr Patel that we want to question. More than that I cannot say at present. I realise this has probably come as rather a shock to you, but I do need to ask you some questions also.'

'Are you arresting me?'

'The choice is yours. You can make a statement now. Elaine can record it, or you can come to the station with us and make it there.'

'I'd rather do it here.'

Elaine set up the cassette recorder, stating the date and time, those present and quoting Saffron her legal rights before Tony continued. He went through the formalities of asking Saffron her name and address before confirming with her that she was giving her statement voluntarily and she was not under duress.

'Mrs Saffron Patel is being questioned by Detective Inspector Tony Baker regarding her husband Mr Ranjit Patel.' Tony looked at Saffron as she waited for him to continue. 'The previous week, whilst completing some renovations for a customer, a workman discovered a body hidden beneath the floor of a room that had been used as a kitchen. He naturally reported the find to the police immediately. Upon investigation, we found the house had been purchased, quite legally, through an estate agent, from a Mr Ranjit Patel. We obviously wanted to speak to the gentleman and see if he had any knowledge of the body. It was whilst we were trying to find the correct Mr Patel that Mrs Saffron Patel reported that her husband had left the marital home taking his personal possessions with him.

'Mr Patel's car was traced to the long-term car park at Gatwick airport, but after examining their records we knew he had not left the country from there unless he possessed a second passport in a different name. We put out an alert to all airports and ports requesting that Mr Ranjit Patel should be detained in this country until we were satisfied that he had nothing to add to our enquiries.' Tony looked directly at Saffron. 'Did you ever go to the house previously owned by Mr Patel?'

Saffron shook her head. 'I don't even know the address. I never went there or to the flat where my husband lived before we married.'

'But you did know he had been married previously?'

'Oh, yes. I told you before. It was an arranged marriage and she was not happy in England. She returned to India and died over there.'

'Mr Kavira, the lady's brother, believes her to have died in a traffic accident in London.'

Saffron shook her head. 'He must have it wrong. Ranjit told me she died during a cholera outbreak.' Saffron's hand flew to her mouth. 'You don't mean... you're not implying that Ranjit...'

'At this time we are only making enquiries, Mrs Patel. We do not make accusations without proof. Did you know Mr Patel was planning a trip to Venezuela?'

Saffron looked at him in surprise. 'No. He hadn't mentioned it to me.'

'Had he done so would you have agreed that he could withdraw all the money from your current account?'

'I would have resisted. We owed some of the money to Marjorie to cover living here.'

Tony leaned forward. 'We insisted on examining Mr Patel's papers. There was no written request amongst them to go to Venezuela, no hospital address where he was to report. He had a large sum of money on him and had already transferred an even larger sum to a bank out there. That is hardly the behaviour of a man who is planning to fly out, operate, and return to England.'

'What money did he transfer? Where did he get it from?' Saffron was genuinely puzzled.

'Your husband had an account in his sole name. Each month he had transferred a substantial sum from your joint account to that one.'

Saffron shook her head. 'That can't be right. That transfer was to his father-in-law in India. He explained to me. He had to repay the money that had been loaned to him for his stay in England and his tuition fees. His father-in-law had also bought the house he had shared with his first wife. When he sold the house the money had to be repaid.'

'Unfortunately it seems that your husband was rather unwilling to repay his debts in full. He sent only a small amount to India each month. I'm sorry, Mrs Patel, but it begins to look as if your husband was not strictly honest with you.'

Saffron swallowed. 'What's going to happen to him now?'

'Mr Patel still has some questions to answer. We are waiting for a toxicology report and that could take some days or even weeks. In the meantime we shall be keeping Mr Patel in custody and we will be questioning him further.'

'But you don't know that he has done anything,' Saffron remonstrated.

Tony looked at her sadly. 'If he is innocent then he has nothing to worry about except explaining his behaviour to you.'

'You think... oh, I don't know what you think! Can you turn that machine off now, please?'

Tony nodded to Elaine. 'Your statement will be typed up. If there is anything that you disagree about in the wording when we ask you to sign it, you have a right to listen to the tape again and if necessary any corrections will be made.'

Saffron nodded miserably. 'Can I see my husband?'

'No doubt arrangements can be made for you to visit in a few days time.'

'What about going to work? I can go to the hospital, can't I?'

'Certainly you can. I do have to ask you to be available for further questioning if we feel it is necessary.'

Marjorie placed her arms around Saffron who was sitting motionless, a blank look on her face. 'I'm sure everything will turn out to be a case of mistaken identity and Ranjit will have a reasonable explanation.'

'Are you? Why did he pack his clothes and go away? He deliberately sent you out on a fool's errand so you couldn't question him. Why did he have a separate savings account? He told me the transfer was to his father-in-law each month. Why was he going off to Venezuela?' Saffron spoke bitterly. 'I don't understand and I wish I'd never married him.'

October 2005

Marcus sat with Giovanni at the computer. He looked at the devastation that was being shown of New Orleans and the surrounding area. 'What does the news say?' he asked.

Giovanni shrugged. 'They're just describing what is being shown in the pictures. The waters are receding and they're beginning a big clear up. The electricity supply is back on in some areas. People have been told to boil their water until further notice. Do you know any of the areas?'

Marcus nodded grimly. 'I think that's the area where we live – or lived.'

'You know you're welcome to stay with us for as long as you want.' Giovanni repeated the invitation as he and his wife had done many times over the past few days. 'Elizabeth has asked that Nicola stay a bit longer.'

Marcus sighed. 'Thank you, but we have to go back. We can't tell from this what has happened to our house. We ought to return quickly. Once everywhere is accessible no doubt there will be looters taking whatever they can.'

Giovanni nodded understandingly. 'You boarded up, so hopefully they will leave you untouched and go for easier pickings.'

'Who knows? I wish I could leave Bryony with you and go back alone. I know how distressed she is going to be if the house is badly damaged.'

'She can stay until you send for her. You know that.'

Marcus shook his head. 'She'd not be willing to do that. Provided you can look after her grandmother she will come back with me. Can we have a look at flight availability?'

Bryony held her grandmother's hand. 'We're going back to New Orleans, Grandma. We have to find out what has happened over there.'

Annita's face fell. 'I'm not sure I could undertake that long journey again so soon. Do we have to go?'

Bryony shook her head. 'You don't have to come with us. Marianne is more than happy to have you stay here. Marcus and I have to go back now. We need to get back to work. We're obviously going to be very busy with insurance claims. We also have to go to *Green Vistas* and see if they suffered any damage. We must make sure your possessions are safe.'

'What about my monthly rent to them? Will I have to pay that whilst I'm over here? I still have to reimburse you and Marcus for my flight and hotel accommodation and I'll have to pay Marianne for looking after me here.' Annita frowned. 'I hope my bank account will stand it.'

'Of course it will. You have the money from the sale of the house.'

'Not all of it. I gave some to Elena. She mentioned that Helena and Greg were hard pressed due to the boys going on to University and I thought I should help out. Better to have it now when they need it than have to wait until I'm gone. Having given some to Elena I thought I ought to do the same for Andreas. He was very grateful as the nursing fees for Laurie are horrendous. I also put some into a trust fund for Maria. I can't touch that.'

Bryony looked at her grandmother in consternation. Just how much money had she given away? Had she also opened a trust fund for her mother?

'Why don't you write a letter to your bank asking them to send your statements to you here? You'd know exactly what your position was then.'

Annita smiled. 'I'll write a letter and give you authority to administer my account whilst I'm in Crete. They can give the bank statements to you. They could take forever to arrive here. You can telephone me and let me know my balance.'

'If that's what you want.'

Annita nodded. 'I do. I trust you, Bryony.'

Detective Inspector Baker and Elaine arrived at the hospital and asked to see Mrs Patel.

'Miss *Bartlett*,' Angela emphasised the name, 'has a patient with her. As soon as she is free I will let her know you are here.'

'How long has the doctor been using her maiden name professionally?' asked Elaine.

'She has always worked under that name. Most doctors when they marry continue to work under the name their patients know them by. It saves confusion.'

'Very sensible,' Elaine agreed. 'We'll just hang around, then until she's free.'

Saffron sighed when she saw the police waiting for her. 'Not more questions.'

'Could we go into your office, please? I would prefer to speak to you in private.'

Saffron nodded and held the door open, closing it firmly behind her. She had kept the news that her husband was in custody to herself, telling colleagues he was away on business, but she had an idea they did not believe her.

'Please sit down, Mrs Patel.'

Saffron frowned. This was her office. She did not have to be asked to sit. She remained standing by the side of her desk.

'Will this take very long? I do have more patients waiting.'

'Mrs Patel, I regret that we have come to inform you that we will be holding your husband in custody for the foreseeable future.

We are proposing to charge him with the unlawful disposal of human remains.'

Saffron's face whitened, the room began to spin before her, there was a buzzing in her ears, and everything was going dark. Elaine stepped forward and held her whilst Tony pulled the chair away from her desk and she sank into it gratefully, letting her head fall forward until her head cleared.

'I am sorry, Mrs Patel.' Tony's voice seemed to come from a long way away.

Saffron forced herself to look up at him. 'What do you mean – the unlawful disposal of human remains?'

'The body found beneath the house is that of an Indian woman in her early thirties.'

'That doesn't mean that Ranjit had anything to do with it.' Saffron tried to defend her husband.

'Mr Patel is not able to offer us any satisfactory answers at present. In view of the fact that he was planning to leave the country when he was apprehended, we have no option but to hold him in custody. We are awaiting the toxicologist's report. If that shows death was due to natural causes, then the charge against your husband will be unlawful disposal.'

'And if it shows unnatural causes?' Saffron's voice was almost a whisper.

'We won't jump to any conclusions yet.' Elaine frowned at Tony and shook her head. This was not the time to mention their suspicions. 'I do have to warn you that the press will probably try to contact you. If they do, I suggest you put the telephone down on them or say no comment.'

Bryony and Marcus had flown to Dallas airport and collected their car from the parking lot.

'One good thing,' Marcus tried to be flippant, 'the drive back should be considerably quicker than when we came up.'

Bryony looked at her husband and shrugged. She felt wrapped in a blanket of misery and despair. Everything they had left on the ground floor was going to be ruined. No doubt the insurance company, despite both of them being employees, would be slow to reimburse them and in the meantime they would have to manage as best they could. She wished they had never moved to the house, but stayed in their third floor apartment.

She looked out of the car windows as they drove along. Even this far from New Orleans there were signs that the hurricane had damaged the area. Road and shop signs sat at precarious angles, branches and small trees were piled up on waste ground ready for disposal, shutters hung crookedly on their hinges, and many roofs had a tarpaulin covering them.

As they neared the outskirts of New Orleans, the damage became even more evident. Once busy streets were now vacant lots with piles of rubble where there had once been homes and thriving businesses. Despondent and despairing people were climbing over the remains, pulling timber and bricks aside in the hopes of reclaiming something from their past lives, however trivial.

Marcus took the road leading to the coast and the area where their house was situated. He drew to a halt. He could go no further. A barrier ahead of him told him the road was closed. The message was unnecessary. There was no road. As far as they could see in either direction everywhere was derelict and barren. The buildings gone. Stagnant pools of water were interspersed with low walls – all that was left of the once desirable residential area.

'Marcus, what are we going to do?' Bryony looked at her husband for guidance.

Marcus took a deep breath. 'We'll leave the car here and walk down to our road.'

'What for? We can see there's nothing there!'

'We need to see if we can salvage anything.' Marcus opened the door of the car. He, too, thought the journey was useless, but he had to see with his own eyes that there was nothing remaining of their house.

Bryony scrambled out and joined him, the crust that had formed on the mud giving way and she sank up to her ankles. 'This is horrible.'

Marcus squeezed her hand. 'I'll go first and you walk in my footsteps.'

Making slow progress, they finally reached firmer ground and gradually covered the distance to where their house had stood. Marcus looked at it incredulously. Three walls had disappeared completely into a mass of rubble and broken furniture. The cooker and refrigerator lay on their side amidst broken china and dented saucepans. There was no sign of the washing machine. Flung to one side was Bryony's car, lying on its roof, the buckled wheels in the air. The remaining wall stood at a height of approximately three feet, and wedged against it was one of the patio chairs, distorted and with a leg missing. Beneath it sat three pieces of coloured glass from the lamps they had purchased. Bryony stepped forwards and picked them up carefully, slipping them into her pocket.

Marcus covered his face with his hands and for the first time in her life Bryony could see he was crying. The tears coursing down his cheeks in a silent river.

'Oh, Marcus.' Bryony put her arms around him and tried to draw him close to her. 'Please don't.' Her words were lost as she began to sob with him.

'Marcus, what are we going to do?' Bryony looked at her husband for guidance. 'We can't afford to stay living in a hotel until the insurance money comes through.'

'We can manage for a few weeks,' Marcus assured her. 'We'll drive back into town and see what we can arrange for the next few days, then go to the office and see about getting back to work. We'll probably both be on overtime, so we don't need anywhere luxurious.'

The drive from Gulfport to the centre of New Orleans was depressing. Everywhere there were signs of the destructive force of the hurricane, bewildered people were picking their way through the remains of their homes, or standing in long queues outside the few shops that had re-opened for business. They tramped from one hotel to another asking for a room to rent, only to be turned away. The hotels were full or so badly damaged that they were unable to accommodate guests.

Finally Marcus took the road leading out of town. 'We'll try the motels along the highway.'

'Suppose we can't find anywhere?'

'We're sure to find somewhere eventually.' Marcus spoke more positively than he felt. 'We can always sleep in the car tonight and look again tomorrow.'

'What do we do now?' asked Bryony as she brushed at her skirt, feeling dirty and unkempt, having spent the night huddled under a blanket on the back seat of the car. She had not showered or washed her hair since the morning they had left Crete and that seemed much longer than three days ago.

'What we should have done earlier, contact our company.'

Marcus tried to telephone the insurance company he and Bryony worked for on his mobile. Yet again the line was dead.

'The lines must still be down in that area. We'll drive in anyway. I just wanted to let them know we were coming.'

'I hope they'll understand why we have been away for so long.'

Marcus shrugged. 'We'll explain about taking your grandmother to Crete. They may insist that we take the days from our vacation allowance.'

As they drove back to the city, they were struck anew by the devastation that was around them. So many properties showed signs of irreparable damage, rubbish was strewn around, swarms of flies rose in a cloud as they drove past, only to settle back down on whatever dead carcass they were devouring and people still looked dazed and confused as they tried to continue with their lives.

Marcus found a parking space a short distance from the insurance company and he and Bryony walked around the block. There seemed to be far less damage to the buildings here and the municipal workers were clearing rubbish, power lines were being repaired and many of the shops were open as normal.

They halted outside their offices, surprised to find the door and windows still boarded up. Marcus frowned. 'They must have suffered a good deal of interior damage not be open.'

'Maybe they're operating from a different building,' suggested Bryony. 'Why don't we ask at the shop over there? They might know.'

They crossed the road and entered the drug store, and were greeted with a cheery smile from the owner. 'What can I get you?'

'One espresso and one latte, please.' Marcus sat on the high stool and looked around. The interior was no different from the last time he had visited. 'The insurance company across the road, did it suffer from a lot of damage?'

Their coffees were placed before them and the owner shook his head. 'Not that I know of. We were pretty lucky just here.'

'Why is it boarded up?' asked Bryony.

'Gone bust.'

'What!'

'That's what I've heard. No end of people wanting to put in a claim for damages have been in here asking. They did put a notice up, but someone tore it down.'

'But we work there,' exclaimed Bryony.

The owner looked at her sadly. 'I guess you did. Where've you been that you didn't know about it?'

'We had to take an elderly relative to safety. We've only just returned. Have you any idea where they can be contacted?'

'They certainly didn't leave a forwarding address with me. Maybe one of your work colleagues would know.' He walked to the other end of the counter to serve a customer who was signalling to him for attention.

Marcus took a mouthful of his coffee. He felt sick. They had no home and now it appeared they neither of them had a job. Added to that if the insurance company was bankrupt they would not receive any compensation for their property that had been completely destroyed. Each year he and Bryony had taken their bonus money in shares, calculating that when they retired they would be able to cash them in for a lump sum. Now they were worthless. They had nothing more than a car and a few clothes to their name.

'I'll try 'phoning Harry,' he managed to say.

Marcus drove away from Harry's house in a stunned silence. His colleague had invited them in and led the way upstairs.

'Ground floor's ruined,' he explained ruefully. 'We've moved upstairs until we can afford to do the repairs. How was your house affected?'

'It's gone,' Marcus replied simply. 'Just a heap of rubble where it once stood.'

'Where are you living?'

'We're hoping to find a room in a hotel. I thought we would be able to stay there for a few weeks. I was expecting us to be working all hours. Then when the insurance money came through I thought we'd find a decent apartment to rent. We wouldn't be able to afford to buy another house for a while.'

Harry pursed his lips. 'Now could be a good time to buy. A number of people are planning to move out of the area. They'd be pleased to make a quick sale.'

Marcus shook his head. 'It wouldn't matter how cheap the house was, without the insurance money on the old one we couldn't afford it. Now it appears there's no insurance and no job.'

'Yeah, bad business that. A lot of people were relying on putting in a claim. You're not the only ones who've lost everything. I couldn't believe it when I turned up to work and found the place abandoned. They'd tacked a notice to the door saying due to unforeseen events they were bankrupt. Not even an apology or a telephone number where anyone could contact them.'

'So what are you going to do?'

'Well,' Harry scratched his head. 'The wife and I have talked it over. She's a teacher, so she has work. I'm going to apply to some of the other companies but I've no great hopes. I'm only a couple of years off retirement. In the meantime I'll take anything that comes my way. Delivering, labouring, sweeping the streets even. What about you?'

'I don't know. I haven't had time to think about it yet. Like you, I suppose I'll take anything I'm offered.' Marcus shot a glance at Bryony who was sitting miserably by his side.

'Where are we going to live?' she asked finally.

'Maybe you could rent a trailer,' suggested Harry.

'If we could find one that wasn't damaged beyond repair.'

'I might be able to help you there. The wife's cousin has a trailer park. I can give you the address and you could ask him if he has anything.'

Marcus sighed deeply. 'We'd be grateful, Harry.'

'Oh, Marcus, who would have thought we'd have been brought as low as this.'

'Cheer up, Bry.' Marcus squeezed her shoulders. 'It could be worse, and it won't last for ever.'

Two hours later and more than thirty miles from the city they drew up in what resembled a ploughed field. Standing desolately were a collection of trailers, some had obviously been thrown over and righted again by the mud that caked their sides, others had their windows and doors boarded up, but they appeared to be deserted.

'You stay here. I'll see if there's anyone around.' Marcus climbed stiffly out of the car. He walked over to the nearest trailer and hammered on the door. Receiving no answer he moved on to the next and it was not until he reached the fifth one that a door opened to him.

'What do you want? Are you the social or insurance?'

'I'm actually looking for a trailer to rent.'

The woman pursed her lips. 'I can't help you there. You'll have to speak to the site manager.'

'We were told he would be here.'

'Might be somewhere around. He was here earlier.'

'Where's his office? I could try there.'

'Used to be over there.' She indicated a pile of timber that had once been a small building.

'We'll hang around for a while. Hopefully he'll come back soon.'

'Where've you come from?'

'Gulfport. We were hard hit down there.'

'Everywhere was.' She closed the door in his face and he trudged miserably back to the car.

'Not exactly welcoming,' he tried to smile at Bryony. 'I'll wander around a bit more and see if I can track down this site manager. You stay in the car and keep the doors locked. If anyone comes around put your hand on the horn.'

Bryony looked around in despair. Marcus had finally found the site owner and persuaded him to let them occupy a trailer.

'They're all in a bad state. Take your pick. It will be up to you to make it habitable. I'll try to get the windows re-glazed by the end of the week, but I don't know when the water or electricity will be back on again.'

Marcus pointed to a trailer that still stood upright. 'We'll take that one. What about leaving our belongings here? Will they be safe?'

'Should be secure enough after tomorrow. I'm repairing the perimeter fence at the moment. I'll give you a key to the padlock when I've finished.'

Marcus walked back to the car where Bryony sat waiting for him. 'Well, we've got a trailer. I've no idea what state it's in, but it's better than nothing. He reckons our belongings will be safe enough after tomorrow. Let's have a look and see what we've let ourselves in for.'

Marcus forced the door open and it now hung on one hinge. Inside was dark where the windows were boarded up and they both stood still, waiting for their eyes to become accustomed after the bright sunlight.

Bryony wrinkled her nose. 'It smells horribly damp.'

'Leave the door open; that will let the air in and begin to dry everything out. I'll unblock the windows first, then we can see what we need to do. You go back out and stand well clear. I don't want to hit you with splinters and there might still be some glass in the frames.'

With the help of a tyre wrench Marcus removed the wood from the trailer's windows. The full extent of the damage to the inside was visible now. Mud covered the walls and floor, mixed with grass and weeds; two of the windows were badly cracked; the other three were broken, jagged glass littering the floor and shards still in situ in the frame. Carefully he collected the pieces together and laid them in a heap on one of the boards from the window. He then set about breaking out the remaining pieces that were in the frames.

'Come and help, Bryony.'

'What do you want me to do?'

'Help me to haul the mattresses outside and put them in the sun. They should be dry by tomorrow, until then we'll sleep in the car.'

Bryony nodded miserably, took the end of the mattress, and backed out carefully. She had taken a quick look at the interior and shuddered. She did not relish the thought of sleeping in the car again, but it would be impossible to stay in the trailer as it was. Everywhere needed to be cleaned and there was nothing in the empty trailer, not even a cloth.

Marcus took a mouthful of their precious water. 'Come and sit beside me, Bryony. We must make a list of the things we need. Then you'll have to drive into town and get it.'

'Why don't we go together?'

'I don't want to leave the trailer. We could come back and find squatters or the mattresses stolen. I'll have a word with that woman again. She may be able to lend me a broom and I can at least start sweeping the place out whilst you're gone.'

Desolately Bryony sat beside her husband and wrote down all the items he thought she should purchase.

'A broom or a brush, cleaning cloths and detergents, more water if you can get it, a screwdriver, a pair of hinges, plates and cups, knives, forks and spoons, a kettle and saucepan. Try to get a camping stove. At least then we would be able to have a hot drink and some hot water. Bring back some coffee and tea and any food that we can eat cold. We can make do for a few days. If there's a gas station open top the car up. Whilst you're gone I'll see what other repairs I can tackle. Add a hammer, nails and screws to the list. Buy anything you think might be useful.'

'Surely everyone else will be doing the same?'

Marcus shook his head. 'People whose property has only been slightly damaged will have those necessities to hand. Take some water with you and be careful. Don't accept offers of help from strangers.' He frowned. 'Maybe I should go instead of you.'

Bryony shook her head. 'I can't do anything useful here.' Her cheeks began to redden. 'Marcus, is it awful of me to suggest it? Maybe you could break into the other trailers and see if there is anything useful left inside.'

'That's not awful, that's practical. The previous occupants couldn't have taken everything with them. If I find anything we can always offer to pay for it later and when you return with some tools I can always board them up again.'

Bryony stood up and brushed the dust from her jeans. 'I'll be as quick as I can.'

Marcus knocked on the door of the trailer occupied by the woman. She opened it with a frown on her face. 'What do you want now?'

'We've spoken to the site manager and we're going to stay here for a while. My wife's gone into town to buy some necessities. Would you be able to lend me a broom or a brush until she comes back?'

'I suppose so.' The woman spoke grudgingly. 'I'll want them back, mind.'

'I promise. Just as soon as my wife returns. I'm Marcus, by the way. My wife is called Bryony.' Marcus extended a grubby hand.

'I'm Jenni-Lyn.' She did not offer to shake Marcus's hand, held out a broom and closed the door as soon as he had taken it.

Marcus dragged the broom across the ceiling of the trailer, seeming to make little impact except to leave streaks of damp mud. He did the same down the walls, finally sweeping the accumulation of debris from the floor out of the door.

Finally satisfied that he had done as much as he was able he took up the tyre wrench and walked over to the trailer nearest to them that was lying on its side. Although confident there was no one inside, he knocked on the base of the broken door before inserting the wrench. He waited for his eyes to become accustomed to the dark interior.

A jumble of items had been thrown to one side as the trailer had toppled over and he would have to climb inside to examine them. Using all his strength he hauled himself into the doorway and slithered the few feet across what should have been a wall rather than a floor. Moving to one side to allow as much light as possible to penetrate he began to rummage around with his hands.

The bedding lay in a wet and tangled heap, but he pulled at it and threw each piece as it came away towards the doorway. The ruined sheets would do as cleaning cloths or to place over the open windows of their trailer. He wished he'd asked Bryony to add a pair of scissors to the list. Having salvaged as much as he considered practical, Marcus opened the cupboard doors in the kitchen area. To his delight, he found some cutlery and a tin opener, another thing he should have remembered to ask Bryony to buy. All the crockery was smashed and unusable and any food that had been stored in jars was in a similar state. Finally satisfied there was nothing else of any use he threw the items down to the ground, climbed out, and pushed the door back in place.

Bryony waved gaily to Marcus as she drew up. 'The gas station was open so I've put in as much as he allowed. I managed to get most of the things you put on the list. I couldn't get a camping stove anywhere, and I had to go to four different shops to get the water. They were only allowing two bottles per person. I've bought some pizza. Most of the restaurants and drug stores seem to be open and I've found a job. I start tonight.'

Marcus frowned. 'What kind of job?'

'Washing up. The restaurant had a notice up asking for kitchen staff so I went in and asked if I could apply.'

'Washing up!'

'I know it's not much, but it will bring a bit of cash in. We can't live on our savings for ever.'

'Would they have anything for me?' asked Marcus.

'I could ask them this evening. Better still, you come in with me and you can ask.'

Marcus shook his head. 'I don't want to leave the trailer unattended until that perimeter fence is secure. I might be able to go in tomorrow with you.'

'I really want to go to the bank and *Green Vistas* for Grandma tomorrow. I need to let *Green Vistas* know she won't be returning and also collect her belongings – if there are any left.'

'Suppose she decides she wants to return?'

Bryony shrugged. 'We'll think about that if it happens. Did you find anything useful whilst I was away?'

Marcus showed her the pile of ragged bedding lying on the ground. 'I thought we might find a few decent bits to cover the window openings and the rest could be used for cleaning cloths.'

Bryony pulled a face. 'I suppose we ought to start. I'll leave two bottles of water in the car. They'll be safe there and then we won't use it all by mistake. I thought to buy a bucket and a scrubbing brush,' she announced triumphantly.

'I'll do the ceiling and the walls where the beds are. You start on the kitchen area.'

Bryony returned from the restaurant where she had spent the evening washing dishes and cups feeling exhausted. She was not used to standing for hours at a time. Marcus was waiting anxiously for her when she arrived and she chided him gently.

'You shouldn't have stayed up for me. You must be tired after the work you have done in the trailer. Why didn't you go to bed?'

Marcus smiled at her in amusement. 'You forget, you had my bed with you. The mattresses are not dry enough yet to sleep on. We'll have another night in the car.'

'I remembered to ask the restaurant owner if he had a job for you, but he said no. He suggested you tried one of the building firms. He said they need labourers to clear the streets of rubble.'

Marcus nodded. He did not relish the job, but if Bryony could spend hours each evening washing up he could certainly work as a manual labourer for a few weeks.

Marcus left Bryony at *Green Vistas* and continued driving into the town to see if he would be able to find some work with one of the building firms. Bryony looked at the elegant building in trepidation. The once well-tended garden was now a sea of mud and tangled vegetation, a dirty watermark running along the wall. Everywhere looked deserted and she rang the bell and pushed at the door with a heavy heart.

To her surprise the door opened and she walked into the bare hall. She could hear the sound of a radio playing in the distance and she walked down the hallway.

'Hello. Anyone around?' She called again more loudly. 'Hello. Hello.'

A man poked his head around the doorway.

Bryony smiled at him. 'Hello there. Is there anyone around I can speak to? My grandmother lived here.'

'They're probably upstairs. That's where they've moved everyone for the time being.'

'Thanks.' Bryony walked up the stairs slowly. If everyone had been moved to the upper floor the chances were that all her grandmother's possessions were lost. She reached the landing and listened for any sound of activity. She could hear voices somewhere.

'Hello,' she called out. 'Can I speak to someone?'

A harassed looking woman with a clipboard stepped out of the room. 'We're not able to take any more patients,' she said immediately.

Bryony smiled. 'I'm not here to ask that. My grandmother lived here. Before the hurricane struck my husband and I took her away to Dallas. She isn't going to return so I need to cancel her room and collect any of her belongings that you have around.'

A look of relief came over the woman's face. 'We moved what we could to the top floor. I'll ask someone to go with you to have a look.'

Bryony stood and waited until a young girl appeared. She smiled shyly at Bryony. 'Follow me, please.'

Bryony waited whilst she unlocked a door and led the way up to the top floor rooms. 'We did the best we could. We had to look after the patients first, you understand.'

'Of course.'

'What is it exactly that you're looking for?'

Bryony frowned. 'I'm not really sure. Ornaments and personal bits and pieces. I'm not worried about her clothes.'

'Do you have a list of the belongings she brought in with her?'

'No, I shall just recognise things I hope.'

The girl looked at her suspiciously. 'You won't be allowed to take anything off the premises unless you can prove it belongs to her.'

'How will I do that?'

The girl shrugged. 'I don't know. That's just what I've been told to tell people.'

'Could I just have a look?' begged Bryony. 'I wouldn't try to claim anything that didn't belong to her.'

The girl unlocked another door. The room was stacked with boxes and heaps of clothes and bedding. 'We're trying to get it sorted out,' she explained. 'Once the patients were safe we just moved whatever we could up here.'

Bryony disregarded the clothes and bedding. 'Have you any idea what is in the boxes?'

The girl shook her head. 'Just whatever we could pack up.'

Bryony sighed. It could take her all day to examine the contents. 'May I open them up and have a look?'

'What was your grandmother's name?'

'Annita Kzantari, she was in room three.'

The girl lifted two boxes aside and pointed to a third. 'You could try that one. We tried to keep the boxes marked with the room number and stacked in order.'

Bryony smiled gratefully at her and pulled at the tape that sealed the box. She parted the flaps and let out a sigh of satisfaction. 'I'm sure these are her belongings. May I take out the photo album? There should be a sticker in the back giving the name of a shop in Crete. That will tell me for sure.'

'What's the name?' The girl pulled out the album.

'*Ourania's.* The address is Aghios Nikolaos in Crete.'

Bryony watched as the girl opened the album at the back. There was the small sticker placed there by Ourania years ago when Marianne had purchased the album as a gift.

'That's it.' Bryony pointed to it excitedly.

'We'll take the box down and I'll speak to the manager. She'll have to give permission for you to take anything away with you.'

'Of course. I need to see her anyway. My grandmother is planning to stay with her relatives, so she won't be returning.'

It took Bryony almost an hour to convince the manager that all the items in the box did belong to her grandmother and that no further fees for her care would be forthcoming. She showed the letter signed by her grandmother giving her authority to administer her account and assured the manager that she was visiting the bank later that day to put the instruction into force.

The manager was less than gracious. 'The fees are due until the end of next month. We insist on a month's notice.'

Bryony shook her head. 'These are rather unusual circumstances. My grandmother has not received any care from you for almost three weeks now, so she doesn't owe you for that. I know it was not your fault that there was a hurricane, but had she stayed here and died you would not have received any money over this time for her care. In fact, had she died I would have sued you for negligence for not moving her to safety earlier.' Bryony glared at the manager.

'I stand by my request for a months' notice.' The manager glared back.

Bryony picked up the box containing her grandmother's possessions. 'Then you can sue me,' she announced, and walked out of the door.

Half an hour later Marcus found Bryony standing by the road. 'What are you doing out here?'

'That woman tried to say that Grandma had to give a months' notice and that she owed for three weeks care. The three weeks where we looked after her and took her to Crete! The nerve! I told her I had no intention of paying and she would have to sue me.'

Marcus raised his eyebrows. 'That was a bit strong, wasn't it?'

'Probably, but I thought she was being totally unreasonable. If she had asked for one week I would have paid, but she wanted seven weeks in all. Can you put this box in the trunk? At least they had the sense to pack up peoples' belongings and store them on the top floor. Anyway, how did you get on?'

'I start work tomorrow. From what I can gather it's only shovelling rubble, but it's quite decent pay. It will do until I can find something better.'

'Marcus, I had an idea whilst I was waiting for you. You may think it's silly, but what about Christabelle's house? Could we stay there, do you think? If it's standing there empty maybe she would rent it to us?'

'Would you want to live there?'

'Marcus, at the moment I would be glad to live anywhere. At least let's drive down there and have a look. We owe it to her to at least let her know what kind of a state it's in.'

'I don't actually think we owe her anything,' observed Marcus. He held up his hand as he could see Bryony was about to protest. 'All right. We'll drive down there. If it's habitable we'll move in and ask her if we can rent it.'

The drive was depressing. There did not seem to be a property that was intact. Some had walls missing, windows had been blown out, and many had gaping holes in the roof. Rubbish and rubble was strewn around everywhere, often almost blocking the road.

They turned the corner and Bryony drew in her breath. Christabelle's house was standing. Marcus drew up outside and they both climbed out of the car. As they walked up the short path they could see the front door was lying in the hallway and they had to step over it to enter. All the windows were broken; mud and grass on the sodden carpets and staining the walls. The kitchen was ankle deep in broken glass from the cupboards and there was no sign of her cooker, freezer or fridge units.

Bryony turned to her husband, puzzled. 'Where has her equipment gone?'

Marcus's mouth set in a grim line. 'I think looters have been at work.'

They walked from room to room. Each one was devoid of furnishings. Cautiously they mounted the stairs and halted at the top. Mounds of plaster, bricks, and roof tiles blocked their way.

'Stay there,' Marcus ordered and edged his way forwards gingerly. He peered quickly into each room. All that remained was the soaking carpet, littered with debris and gradually drying as the sun shone through the broken roof. He shook his head. The house was totally uninhabitable.

Carefully he walked back to where Bryony stood waiting for him. 'The roof has gone,' he said bleakly. 'There's no way anyone could live here with the state it's in.'

Bryony bit at her lip. 'We ought to let Christabelle know.'

Marcus shrugged. 'I doubt there's anything she can do – as she's in hospital,' he added.

'There must be something. Even if she can't claim from an insurance company she must have plenty of money in the bank and could get it repaired.'

'What for? From what we've heard she won't be coming back here to live.'

'Please, Marcus. It's not that far to the hospital where she is. We ought to drive up there and at least let her know what's happened. You were quite prepared to visit her to ask if we could rent it,' added Bryony.

Marcus sighed. He thought the journey a waste of time.

The gates leading to the pleasant three-storey building were standing open. Two men were attempting to remove tree branches and other rubbish that had accumulated in the grounds and load it into an open truck. Running around the building was the now familiar dirty watermark, showing how high the floodwater had reached. Two windows on the ground floor were boarded up, but the rest of the building looked intact.

They entered the hall, where a wooden floor had been scrubbed clean. There was no one around.

'They may have moved everyone away from here. There's no sign of life.'

Bryony pushed at a door, which did not yield, then tried another which opened easily. She walked through, Marcus in her wake. Opening another door, they found themselves in the kitchens where four women were busy preparing a meal. They looked up in surprise.

'Can I help you?' A woman wiped her hands on a cloth and walked towards them.

'We really wanted to speak to someone who runs the hospital. I believe there is a resident here who is a relative and we have some news for them.'

'You'll need the manager.'

Marcus nodded. 'Where will we find her?'

'Him.' The woman corrected Marcus.

'If you return to the main entrance I'll see what I can do to contact him. He's very busy at the moment.'

'I'm sure he is. We only need a few minutes of his time.'

Marcus and Bryony waited impatiently in the main hall by the reception desk. Marcus looked at his watch. 'I'll give this manager ten more minutes; then we go,' he said finally.

Bryony nodded. She was doubtful that the woman had made any attempt to contact the manager for them. 'Shall I go back to the kitchen and speak to that woman again?'

Marcus shook his head. 'I doubt it would do any good. As I said, ten more minutes.' He stood looking at his watch, checking the minutes as they ticked away. 'That's it,' he said finally.

'No, wait.' Bryony held up her hand. Someone could be heard unlocking the door.

The middle-aged man eyed them up and down and frowned. He really was too busy to deal with visitors.

'I understand you needed to speak to someone. I'm Doctor Ferguson. How can I help?' He did not offer to shake their hands.

'It's about Christabelle Bartlett.'

Doctor Ferguson held up his hand. 'You have to realise that we were very short staffed that night. The hospital cannot take responsibility for the accident. There will be an enquiry, of course. At present I am not able to discuss it.'

'What accident?' asked Bryony. 'Is she hurt?'

Doctor Ferguson frowned. 'I thought that was why you were here.'

'Is she hurt?' asked Bryony again.

The doctor shook his head. 'It was during the hurricane. For some reason she tried to leave the premises where she was safe.'

'What happened to her?'

'We're not entirely sure.' He was not prepared to describe the mangled wreck that was Christabelle's body. 'I regret she did not survive.'

Marcus felt Bryony slump beside him and he steadied her with his arm. He moistened his lips. 'We actually came to tell her that her house was badly damaged and also appears to have been looted. That is rather irrelevant under the circumstances.'

'Her house?'

'She had a small house. I assume it belonged to her mother and she inherited it after her death.'

Doctor Ferguson raised his eyebrows. 'Really? Maybe you could give me the address. It will have to be added to a list of her assets.'

Marcus shrugged. 'I can, but it has been looted and the roof has totally gone.'

'There is still the plot of land that could be valuable real estate and no doubt the property was insured.'

'I have no idea. What happens with regard to her estate?' Marcus frowned. Had she left all she possessed to Bryony? He felt guilty as he asked. 'Had she made a will?'

'Not that I am aware of. Everything will be frozen, of course, for the time being.'

'What do you mean? Frozen?'

'Whenever anyone dies their estate is usually frozen until such time as a will naming beneficiaries comes to light.'

'But I'm her nearest relative,' protested Bryony.

Doctor Ferguson pursed his lips. 'Do you have any proof of that? Miss Bartlett never mentioned any living relatives.'

Bryony shook her head. 'I have my birth certificate. We shared the same mother so her name would be on Christabelle's birth certificate. Would that be proof enough?'

The doctor shook his head. 'Miss Bartlett appears to have had her purse with her and it has disappeared. We have obviously collected together the personal belongings in her room and there was no birth certificate amongst them. You would need to prove through the courts that you are a relative.'

Bryony sighed. 'I don't think I could face that at the moment.'

'I also feel I should warn you that even if you are her closest relative you could receive nothing, even possibly find yourself out of pocket. The state would be quite in order to use her assets as compensation for various people as they think fit.' The doctor did not mention that the hospital would press for compensation for Hazel whom Christabelle had hit over the head causing irreparable brain damage and was now blind in one eye.

'I'm sorry. I don't think I am able to help you at all. Now, if you will excuse me. I have a tremendous workload at present. We are a still a number of staff short.'

Doctor Ferguson turned on his heel and walked back to the door, unlocking it and disappearing into the building.

Bryony turned distressed eyes to Marcus. 'How can I prove she was my half sister? We should have asked if her funeral had taken place yet or where she was buried.' She left the shelter of Marcus's arm and banged on the door. 'Doctor Ferguson. Doctor. I need to ask you something else.'

The doctor ignored the banging on the door and hurried along the corridor to resume his supervision of the cleaning operation that was taking place.

'What did they want?' asked Marcella as she scrubbed hard at the floor covering in the hallway.

'Couple of chancers. Trying to claim to be relatives of the Bartlett woman. Said she owned a house and wanted to tell her it had been wrecked. As soon as I said she had died they wanted to know what would happen to her estate.'

'Can you give us a statement, Mrs Patel?'

'Do you have any comment for us, Mrs Patel?'

'Did you know your husband had been married before?'

'You're a doctor, do you know how his first wife died?'

'Did you know he had buried her under the floor?'

'Did he kill her, Mrs Patel?'

'Did he kill her so he could marry you?'

The questions were fired at Saffron as she hurried towards the hospital building, her head down and teeth gritted. Elaine Saunders had warned her that the press might want to speak to her, but she had not expected them to be so intrusive, they tried hard to impede her passage and surround her as she made her way to the entrance.

Saffron entered her office in a rush and locked the door behind her. She must speak to Detective Inspector Baker and ask for a meeting with Ranjit. She must talk to him so he could tell her the truth about the allegations. There must be a rational and logical explanation.

Saffron sat across the table from her husband. She had been warned that she must not try to embrace him or touch him in any way and there would be two police officers accompanying her during the meeting. She was struck by his apparent calm and nonchalance.

He gave her a thin smile. 'It is good of you to visit me, although not necessary. No doubt I shall be home within a week,' he raised his voice deliberately, 'and suing the police force for a sizeable sum for detaining me.'

Saffron shook her head as if to dismiss his words. 'I need to know the truth, Ranjit. What happened to your wife, to Nandita?'

'I have no idea. I arrived home and found her sitting in the chair. There was nothing anyone could do for her. It was too late.'

Saffron frowned. 'Ranjit, you're a doctor. You know as well as I do that under those circumstances you have to call the medical authorities. You need to have a death certificate.'

Ranjit shrugged. 'I panicked. I acted foolishly. I did not think anyone would find out.'

'But her family in India? Surely they would wonder why she did not write to them or telephone?'

'Nandita was a bad correspondent. I wrote and told them she was dead and they accepted that.'

'Why were you planning to go to Venezuela?'

'Unfortunately her brother had come looking for me. He wanted more money for his father and a photograph of her grave. I decided if I went away for a while he would soon return home.'

Saffron shook her head slowly. 'You could have taken a months' leave and gone and lived in Birmingham, Manchester, even Scotland and Nandita's brother would not have found you. I want to know why you planned to go to South America. Why did you draw all the money from our joint account?'

'I have always wanted to travel on that continent.'

'Why did you have to take my money?' Saffron spoke bitterly.

'Travel costs money.'

'But you had all that money in a separate account. You told me you were sending most of your salary to India every month. That was why I was paying for the car, and your new suit and things. If you were sending him the amount you had agreed why should he want more?'

'He is a greedy man.'

'The police said you had transferred thousands to an account in Venezuela. Why would you do that if you were planning to return?'

'What I planned to do is no concern of yours.' His voice was cold and hard.

'Ranjit, I am your wife. I have a right to know.'

'Married women do not have rights. They are subject to their husbands.'

'Don't be silly. That's archaic. Even if it was still like that in India it isn't in England.'

'That is your opinion. I suggest you go now. I have satisfied your curiosity and there is nothing more to be said.' Ranjit stood up. 'I am ready to return to my accommodation.'

'Ranjit, you've told me nothing.' Saffron stood up also. 'I feel so foolish when the police ask me questions and I have to say I don't know why or when.'

Ranjit glared at her, his eyes no longer seemed the deep hypnotic pools she had thought, but hard and cold. 'You do not have to answer any questions put to you by the police. A wife cannot testify against her husband. Had you not made such a stupid fuss about me not returning home I would not be in this situation.'

Saffron left the police station deep in thought. She did not believe that her husband had panicked when he found his wife had died. He was a doctor. Doctors did not panic; even when it was a close family member who had died unexpectedly. He had to be afraid of something not to have reported it to the authorities and Saffron felt frightened. The Ranjit Patel she had just left bore no resemblance to the gentle, charming man who had courted her and was held in high esteem at the hospital. She began to hope that he would not be returning home at the end of the week.

Detective Inspector Baker waited until he knew Saffron had left the police station. 'Right, Simon. I think it's time we had a few more words with the eminent doctor. See if he can come up with any explanation for the entry in the drugs register.'

Ranjit was surprised to be called to the interview room again so quickly. When he saw the Inspector waiting for him his eyes narrowed. Unless they were about to tell him he was to be released he did not want to speak to them.

Tony Baker waited until Ranjit was seated and he had read him his rights yet again.

'Detective Inspector Baker and Inspector Simon Lake are interviewing Mr Ranjit Patel at...' he glanced at his watch and added the date and the time.

'Mr Patel, after receiving a report from the toxicology department I have to inform you that your first wife, Nandita Kavira died from a massive dose of diamorphine. Can you give us any explanation for this?'

Ranjit shrugged. 'She was obviously an addict.'

'Do you have any proof of this?'

Ranjit regarded the Inspector scornfully. 'She did not go around announcing the fact.'

'Could you give us the name and address of her local doctor? He may have been prescribing for her.'

'She had no local doctor. She had never registered with one.'

'We can check that, of course, Mr Patel.' Tony Baker looked steadily at Ranjit who did not flinch. 'Were you treating her for any illness?'

'No.'

'I see. So where do you think she was getting a supply of diamorphine from?'

'I have no idea.'

'Mr Patel, I think you know exactly where the diamorphine came from. Inspector Lake has visited the hospital and examined the drugs register. Three days in succession there is a record of a phial of diamorphine being accidently broken. The doctor who signed for this was yourself.'

'If I was on duty when the accident happened then I would have signed for the breakage.'

'I suggest there was no such breakage. I suggest that on three occasions you made a false entry in the drugs register.'

'You have no proof of that. It is assumption on your part.'

'We have no proof at present, but I'm sure by the time we have finished our enquiries we will find some.'

Ranjit shrugged and Tony Baker had a desire to hit the smug man before him. He terminated the recording of the interview.

'I'd like to offer you a piece of advice, Mr Patel. I suggest you make arrangements with the bank in Venezuela and have your account transferred back to England. You could find that to employ a defence lawyer is very expensive.'

'Marjorie, I want to change all the locks,' Saffron announced as soon as she arrived home.

'Change the locks? What for?'

'Ranjit said he could be home by the end of the week. I don't want him back here. I'm frightened of him, Marjorie.'

'I'm sure there's no need for you to be frightened. That Detective said he would be held in custody for an indefinite time whilst they were conducting their enquiries.'

'You didn't see the way he looked at me. I think he blames me for his arrest because I reported him missing.'

'Stupid man! If he had given you a plausible explanation for going away, you would have thought nothing of it. We can change the locks if it makes you feel safer.'

'I'm sorry, Marjorie.'

'What are you sorry for? You've done nothing.'

'I brought him into the house, your house. I should have asked more questions about his first wife, seen her death certificate, found out how much he was repaying her father each month, not just taken his word for everything.' Saffron sank down on the sofa. 'I'm such a fool.'

Marjorie sat down beside her. 'You're not a fool. I never asked your father details about his first marriage. I trusted him. When Jeremy told me he had divorced your mother, I believed him. I didn't ask to see the papers.'

The telephone rang and Saffron stiffened. 'I'll answer,' said Marjorie. 'If it's a reporter I'll tell them they have the wrong number.'

Saffron tried to follow the one sided conversation.

'Yes, she's in, Inspector. If it's important of course you can come round now. Yes, I'll tell her, about half an hour.'

Marjorie sat back on the sofa. 'That was Detective Inspector Baker. He says he needs to speak to you and will be here in about half an hour.'

Saffron sighed. 'I've only just returned from the station. Why didn't he speak to me whilst I was there? I'm going upstairs to have a wash and change my clothes. I feel dirty.'

The Detective arrived with Elaine. He pulled a sheet of paper from his briefcase. 'I'm sorry I missed you earlier. Unfortunately the report from the toxicologist came through whilst I was out of the office.' He waited and Saffron paled, but said nothing. 'A quantity of diamorphine was found in the lady's body. We have interviewed Mr Patel further and he said his wife did not have a local doctor who would have prescribed the drug for her, nor was he treating her for any illness. Inspector Lake has checked the drug register at the hospital and on three occasions when Mr Patel was on duty there is an entry that claims a phial of diamorphine was broken.'

'That can happen, Inspector. The drug is in sealed glass phials. They are specially manufactured to have a weak point where the doctor can break them. If they happen to be accidently dropped and hit that spot they break.'

'Does a breakage happen regularly?'

Saffron shook her head. 'We are very careful. Drugs are far too expensive to waste with carelessness.'

'I'm afraid, Mrs Patel, that the circumstances regarding the first Mrs Patel's death are not in your husband's favour. It does appear that we could be charging your husband with more than unlawful disposal.'

Marjorie's hand instinctively grasped Saffron's. Saffron sat straight and still.

'You mean you are going to charge him with murder?'

Tony Baker nodded. 'I'm very sorry.'

'When I visited him today he reminded me that a wife cannot give evidence against her husband. I wondered why he made that remark.'

'Do you know of anything that could be considered evidence, Mrs Patel?' asked Elaine.

Saffron shook her head. 'Absolutely nothing. As I told you, I had never been to the house and I had never met his wife. He never said anything that could have aroused my suspicions. It was only today when he admitted he was planning to go to South America and wouldn't give me a straight answer to anything that I truly began to doubt him. I have to admit that when he told me he could be home by the end of the week I felt frightened.'

'Saffron asked me to change the locks,' added Marjorie.

'I don't think that will be necessary. Mr Patel will certainly not be allowed bail.' Tony leaned towards the two women. 'I'm afraid we are going to have to give a press release. There is obviously going to be a good deal of media attention and that could be most unpleasant for you. May I suggest you go away for a week or so?'

Saffron passed a shaky hand across her forehead. 'I don't know. Where would I go? The press know where I work so they would still be able to find me.'

'Could you not take a holiday? Get a bit of late sunshine, maybe? They would not pursue you abroad.'

Marjorie nodded. 'I'm sure the hospital would understand. By the time you returned you would be old news.'

Saffron sighed. 'I'm not sure how I would cope with being alone. Would you come with me?'

Marjorie shook her head. 'I can't. You know I promised the Goldsmiths I would look after their dog and feed the fish whilst they went to Australia. They left in the early hours of this morning. It's a bit late in the season, but you should be able to find a booking for somewhere nice.'

Saffron hesitated. 'If I did go away, would you do something for me?'

'Of course I would, Saffie.'

'Would you move into the Goldsmiths' house until I returned? I'd feel much happier. The press won't be interested in finding you and making your life a misery. Once they found the house was deserted they would assume we had both gone away.'

'If that would put your mind at rest of course I would. I'm sure they wouldn't mind; besides, I'd leave everything exactly as I found it.'

Saffron hugged her stepmother. 'Very well, Inspector. I'll have a look and see what late bargains are on offer. I suppose I'll have to let you know where I'm going?'

Tony Baker nodded. 'Just telephone a message in and it will be passed on to me.' He wished the woman's stepmother was going with her. When she finally realised the enormity of her husband's crime she could well need some support. 'If you could also give me the address where you will be staying, Mrs Bartlett.'

Crete: October 2005

Saffron arrived at Heraklion airport and gave a sigh of relief. She had spent the time at Gatwick in a state of panic. She was convinced she would be refused permission to leave the country at the last minute, despite the assurances she had received from Tony Baker.

She stepped onto the tarmac and took a deep breath. Mixed with the smell of diesel fumes was the scent of herbs and the sea. She forced herself onto the small bus that would transport the passengers from the runway to the terminal and looked at the happy, expectant faces around her. These were people who had come away to enjoy a holiday together, not running away from unwanted publicity. If only Marjorie had been able to come with her.

Saffron gave herself a mental shrug. She must do as Marjorie had instructed. Forget all her problems and enjoy the sunshine and new experience. That way she would return revitalised to deal with whatever problems arose at a later date. The big consolation was knowing Ranjit was being held in custody, without any possibility of bail.

She handed over her passport, wishing it was still in the name of Bartlett. She would change that as soon as she returned to England. It was given a cursory glance and she passed through, scrutinizing the signs telling her where she could collect her luggage. Suddenly everything was very foreign to her and she was frightened. She could not understand the writing or the language. How would she manage for a week if she could not make herself understood?

It seemed an interminable time before her case finally appeared on the carousel and she dragged it behind her towards the exit. She had been assured that someone would meet her and take her to the accommodation she had booked, but how would she know them? How would they know her? She moved to one side to allow the passengers following her to go past and looked around. To her incredible relief she saw a man holding a placard with the name 'Mrs Patel' printed on it. Thankfully, she made her way towards him.

'I'm Mrs Patel,' she said. 'Have you come to meet me? I'm staying at the self-catering apartments in Plaka.'

Giovanni nodded, smiled, and held out his hand. 'Welcome to Crete. Do you have all your luggage?'

'Just this suitcase.'

'I will take it for you. Please follow me.' Giovanni took the handle and began to walk away from her.

Panic surged through Saffron. Suppose he was planning to run off with her case? Suppose he planned to kidnap her? Suppose he was going to rape and kill her?

'Please. Stop.' Saffron's throat felt dry with fear. 'Who are you?'

Giovanni turned towards her with a puzzled frown. 'I am Giovanni Pirenzi. I am the manager of the apartments at Plaka. Is there a problem?'

Saffron felt incredibly foolish. 'No, I'm sorry. I've not been to Greece before.'

Giovanni smiled at her. 'Then I hope this will be the first of many more visits. Crete is a beautiful island and there is much to see here. When you arrive at your apartment you will find a small brochure with details of the most interesting places to visit.' He called a greeting to one of the men who was holding up a notice advertising the name of a travel company and counting the number of people gathered around him.

'Does everyone speak English?'

'Most people. Not all as good as me. I studied the language and married an American woman. She corrects me if I make the mistakes.'

Saffron felt reassured and when Giovanni suggested she rode in the front seat of the car beside him she did not demur. She looked out of the window with interest as they drove through the sprawl of suburbs.

'Do not think that all of Crete looks like this. Heraklion has grown big now. Many people come here to work. At one time this was the countryside, now it is just housing. From here we will drive through Malia. Years ago Malia was just one street. Visitors would come to visit the archaeological site and now that village too stretches back into the hills. It is sad that so much has been spoilt, but,' Giovanni shrugged eloquently, 'that is the price we have to pay for progress. The tourists demand the facilities. We depend upon the tourists for our income, so we have to build more.'

Saffron sat in silence as he talked. The brochure had shown pictures of stunning scenery and she wondered how many years ago the photographs had been taken. 'Is there a beach at Plaka?' she asked eventually.

'A beautiful beach. My family have lived there forever. They had a farm when my uncle was a small boy. Gradually the village fell into disrepair. The people moved away as there was no work. We decided visitors would like to stay there. Now many people come for a holiday. You were fortunate. It is towards the end of the season and we had one apartment free.'

The car mounted the rise of the hill and suddenly the sea came into view before the road dipped again. Saffron gave a gasp of surprise.

'I had no idea the sea was so close.'

Giovanni nodded with satisfaction. 'Everyone is always surprised when they realise it is just over the hill. We will turn off

287

soon and then you will see the view properly. Where you stay the beach is five minutes walk away. It is a private beach, so there is no charge for the sun beds and umbrellas.'

'You own the beach?'

'Not exactly,' Giovanni smiled. 'We have to pay the municipality. It is the same with all the hotels. To keep the beach free for their patrons they have to pay a rental sum each year. It is good for the government, not so good for us. Now we turn off. I will stop to allow you to see the view.'

Giovanni drew over into a space at the side of the road. 'This is for the tourists to take their photographs.'

'My camera is in my suitcase,' frowned Saffron.

'Today you look; tomorrow you can take a photograph.'

Saffron gazed out across the expanse of blue water. There was no sign of a beach, but small boats were out on the water and she could see people swimming. Further out there was a small island, a number of large tourist boats tied up beside it.

'It's beautiful.' She felt lost for words.

Giovanni smiled happily. 'You can swim, take a boat or a pedalo, or just lay in the sun. If you like to dive there is a small inlet where it is safe and you can learn. Also, we have tennis and crazy golf. If you wish to go to Spinalonga that can be arranged from Plaka.'

'Spinalonga?'

'The island. It was a leper colony and is now an education centre. Many people go there.'

'Oh.' Saffron felt something stir inside her. Her grandfather had researched leprosy, hoping to find a cure. 'I'd be very interested to go there.'

'You might also like to purchase the book that was written by a sufferer. He describes his life and the conditions as they were when he lived over there.' Giovanni had long given up telling visitors the book had been written by his great uncle as they tended to react as if he might be infectious. He started the car again. 'A few more minutes and you will be at your apartment.'

He drove slowly down the hill, Saffron catching tantalizing glimpses of the sea until he stopped outside a small bungalow. She waited whilst he lifted her suitcase from the car, then produced a key and opened the door.

'This is your apartment. I hope you will enjoy to stay here. If there is any problem please let us know. The taverna and shop is over there. It is not always open, but the times are displayed in your room along with the brochure listing the places of interest.' He lifted her suitcase inside and placed it on a stand. 'I leave you now. Have a good day.' Giovanni handed the key to Saffron and closed the door behind him.

Saffron sat down on the edge of the bed. It was tempting to lay back and close her eyes. She had not realised how tired she was, drained both mentally and physically. With an effort she rose to her feet. She must unpack and then she had to go to the shop. The apartment was self-catering and she would need to stock up on basic supplies. She frowned. Maybe she should find out the times the shop was open before she started her unpacking. She did not want to find herself without tea, coffee, milk or bread.

She checked her watch and remembered to add on the two hour time difference there was from London. The shop declared itself open from eight in the morning until ten, again from twelve until two, then from four until six. It was already nearly five. A quick telephone call to Marjorie to let her know she had arrived safely; then she must go to the shop and make her purchases.

Despite being late afternoon the heat hit her as she walked the short distance to the shop. Maybe she should buy a sun hat. She did not want to be ill. Inside the small shop it was delightfully cool. The young man behind the counter took no notice of her as she browsed amongst the shelves and picked up various items and added them to the plastic basket. She checked off a mental list, milk, coffee, tea, bread, butter, cheese, jam. That would certainly be sufficient for her breakfast for the next few days.

She would decide tomorrow whether she wanted to cater for herself or eat out during the week.

She waited whilst her purchases were rung up on the till.

'Fifteen Euros, please.'

'You speak English,' she exclaimed.

'Of course.' John smiled at her. 'You've just arrived, I guess. Dad said we had a visitor arriving this afternoon. Is there anything else I can get for you or help you with?'

Saffron hesitated. 'Can you tell me if the taverna is open this evening? I haven't had a chance to look at all the information in my apartment.'

John shook his head. 'This is the taverna as well as the shop. It closes at six. Most people either cater for themselves or go into Elounda.'

Saffron bit at her lip. 'How do I get to Elounda?'

'You take your car. It is only a short drive along the coast road.'

'I don't have a car.'

John looked surprised. Very few people stayed in Plaka without hiring a car. 'There is a bus that runs once an hour. The last one is at six fifteen.'

'So how would I get back?'

'There is a taxi service in the main square. It costs about ten Euros.'

'How far away is it? Could I walk?'

John shook his head. 'It would probably take almost an hour. Better to walk in daylight first.'

'Would I be able to have something to eat now? I can always go back and unpack later.'

'Sure. We only do snacks. What would you like? I can do omelette, fried egg and bacon, scrambled eggs, calamari, ham salad, chicken salad.'

Saffron hesitated. She really did not feel very hungry. 'Ham salad would probably be best.'

'With chips?'

Saffron nodded.

'No problem. You could sit outside and have a glass of wine whilst I cook.' He indicated the patio with colourful umbrellas.

'That sounds like a good idea.' Saffron smiled. Suddenly this was beginning to feel like a holiday.

Saffron sipped at her wine and popped an olive into her mouth. She felt disorganised and wished she had arrived earlier in the day. She was eating her evening meal at four in the afternoon, a long evening stretched ahead of her. She reasoned with herself. She would walk down to the beach whilst it was still light, she could always unpack when it was dark; she had the brochures in her apartment to look through and her book to finish. She would plan what she would do tomorrow and have an early night.

To her surprise, Saffron slept well and woke early. She prepared herself a breakfast and looked again at the brochures. First, she would go up to the shop and check on the times of the buses to Elounda. This was supposed to be an inexpensive holiday and she did not want to spend out on taxis unnecessarily. She would then make herself a snack lunch and perhaps have a swim before visiting the town.

She strolled across to the shop, conscious again of the sun beating on her unprotected shoulders and head. A protective sunscreen cream and hat were essential. She should have thought and brought them with her. A woman was behind the counter, talking on her mobile, and Saffron began to examine the goods on display. She wondered if the prices in the town would be cheaper. She needed a book to read, having finished hers the previous evening, but was disappointed in the selection, seeing nothing that attracted her. The book the boy had recommended about the island looked rather large and she thought it might be depressing. She would purchase a copy before she went back to England.

Marianne closed her mobile and smiled. 'Can I help you?' she asked.

Saffron handed her the sunscreen and a floppy hat. 'I really came in to check the times of the buses with you, but I thought I should be sensible and buy this. It's much hotter than I thought it would be at this time of year.' Suddenly Saffron felt foolish. She was talking to the woman as if she were English. It was doubtful that she had understood more than a few words as she had been talking on her 'phone in Greek.

'Very wise of you. We're having a bit of a late heat wave. It happens sometimes. Where were you planning to go on the bus?'

Saffron smiled in relief. 'You speak perfect English.'

'So I should. I'm from America originally.'

'Oh, Mr Pirenzi said his wife was American.'

'That's me.'

'Can I talk to you for a while – if you're not too busy, that is?'

'Sure. Would you like a juice or coffee?'

Saffron hesitated. She had not long had her breakfast. 'I'd really just like water. If I buy one now I can take it with me.'

Marianne nodded and poured herself a coffee. 'Help yourself from the fridge. We'll sit outside. I can see if anyone comes in from there.' She led the way to the patio where Saffron had sat the previous evening and eaten her meal. 'What did you want to talk to me about?'

'Well, places to visit really. I don't drive, so I would have to take a bus or taxi. I thought I would go into Elounda today. I don't speak Greek, and I feel a bit nervous about going too far afield just yet.'

'You'll have no problem. Most young people speak enough English to understand you and communicate back. I don't suggest you ask the elderly. If you get really stuck go into a hotel and ask at the reception desk. The receptionists are only employed if they are proficient in a number of languages.'

'The boy who was in here yesterday told me the buses go once an hour to Elounda. Where do I stand to catch it?'

'That was my son, John.' Marianne smiled. 'Did he also tell

you that they stop at mid-day and commence again three in the afternoon?'

Saffron frowned. 'I didn't realise that. He told me they finished early in the evening. I had planned to visit Knossos. Will I be able to do that by bus?'

'You could, but you would have to go to Aghios Nikolaos to pick up the bus to Heraklion and then catch the local bus to the site. You're talking a good three or four hour trip. The easiest way would be to book a coach tour. That way they would collect you from here and drop you back. They start collecting passengers at eight from the Aghios Nikolaos area, so they wouldn't be here until nearly nine. You'd be at Knossos in time for lunch and they would probably start back about four. If they collected you last they would drop you back first.'

Saffron nodded. 'That sounds more practical than me trying to find my way on my own. How do I book it?'

'I can do that for you. Which day do you want to go?'

Saffron hesitated. 'I've had a look at the brochures and I thought I would go into Elounda today, then maybe on to Aghios Nikolaos tomorrow. I could spend the weekend on the beach, maybe go over to that island and go to Knossos on Monday.'

Marianne shook her head. 'The sites are closed on a Monday and Friday is Ochi Day. Many places will be closed. Why don't you spend tomorrow on the beach and visit Knossos on Saturday? You can always go to Aghios Nikolaos another day. It's a pretty town with a small museum and if you wanted you could take a bus on to the site at Gournia. It's very different from Knossos.'

'Is that where the Code of Laws is?'

'No, that's Gortys. That's a considerable distance from here. You would have to travel up to Heraklion and pick up an organised tour from there. You're talking a good four to five hours travelling time.'

Saffron sighed. 'I'm only here for a week . I'd wanted to see as much of Crete as possible, but it seems very difficult without a car.'

'There are a number of small villages that are worth a visit and you can do that by bus from Aghios Nikolaos or you could hire a taxi.'

'What!' Saffron looked at her in horror. 'That would cost a fortune.'

'If you worked it out it would be little more expensive than paying for coach trips. It means you can spend as long as you like anywhere and it's obviously quicker. Would you like me to find out for you?'

Saffron shook her head. 'No. I have to be sensible. I'd be grateful if you could book the Knossos trip for me. I could always take the bus up to Heraklion another day and visit the museum. Provided I caught the last bus back to Elounda, I can get a taxi from there. I certainly don't think I can manage Gortys. I just won't have the time.'

Marianne picked up her coffee cup and Saffron took it as a sign that she wanted to return to her work.

'Is there a book shop anywhere? I finished my book last night. I've had a look at the ones you have for sale and I've either read them or they seem to be love stories. I'm not into that.'

'If you're going into Elounda there's a very good book shop there. Ian will be bound to have something to interest you. He has an excellent stock. We carry just a few for those people who are desperate at the last minute.' Marianne looked at her watch. 'I don't want to rush you, but the next bus will be here in twenty minutes, otherwise you'll have another hour to wait. If you wait on the road, you will see it turn and come back. Give the driver a wave and he will stop for you.'

Saffron ambled slowly along the waterfront at Elounda. She found a seat and unwrapped the cheese and tomato sandwich she had brought with her. She ate slowly, looking at the view she had of Spinalonga and watching the bustle of small boats advertising their trips to the island. Tourists boarded them eagerly, their cameras around their necks, mothers admonishing children to sit still whilst they applied yet more sun cream, others studying the guidebook they had bought earlier. As one boat left another seemed to arrive to disgorge its chattering passengers and prepare for the next trip.

It seemed to Saffron that the trip to the island was the only reason to visit the village. A large hotel commandeered a man made beach and a large Venetian style church stood prominently beside it. She would wander over there later and see if it was open. A small parade of shops stood opposite the waterfront, but she could not see the bookshop the taverna owner had mentioned. She took a mouthful of water from her bottle, surprised to see how little was left. She would buy another and a piece of fruit to eat.

Saffron walked to the end of the small marina and saw that a path for pedestrians ran round to another small area of shops. She followed it and within a few steps she had found the bookshop. She entered the dim coolness and waited for her eyes to become accustomed after the glare of the sun. A grey haired man looked up over his spectacles.

'The English section is over there,' he smiled.

'How did you know I was English?'

He shrugged. 'Something you just get to know over the years. Are you looking for anything special or just a novel?'

'A novel, but not a love story; an adventure with a spy theme, maybe.'

'Try that section.'

Saffron browsed happily amongst the titles, finally selecting two she felt happy with. She looked at the price. 'They're rather expensive,' she frowned.

'I have to cover the import costs. There's a second hand shelf over there. If you bring these back when you've read them I'll give you three Euros back on each one.'

'I'll have a quick look over there.' Saffron scanned the shelf where Ian had indicated, but once again they all appeared to be romantic novels. 'I'll stick with what I've got,' she smiled. 'I'll bring them back when I've read them and see what else you have then.'

'Where are you staying?'

'The self-catering apartments at Plaka.'

Ian nodded. He was not really interested where his customers stayed, but he felt obliged to make conversation with them. 'They've made that into a very nice place,' he observed.

'I only arrived yesterday so I've not had much chance to explore yet. Do you know if the church is open? I wanted to have a look inside.'

'Probably. There's a good taverna just across from there if you want a meal.'

'I've only just eaten my lunch, but I'll bear it in mind for later.' Saffron picked up her books. 'Is there anything else to see here apart from the church?'

'Spinalonga. You can get a boat over.'

Saffron shook her head. 'I thought I'd do that from Plaka.' The thought of sharing a small boat with the crowds she had seen earlier was abhorrent to her.

'You could walk up the hill to old Elounda. Much of it is just the same as it was a hundred years ago.'

'Do people still live there?'

'Many of the older people have lived there all their lives. The young ones tend to move away, partly for work and partly because they want the modern conveniences. One day it will end up deserted like Plaka was before they developed it.'

'I'll try the church first. It's a bit hot still for walking up hills. Thanks for your help.' Saffron left the shop, the books stowed in her beach bag. She should have waited and bought them later. Now she would have to carry them with her for the rest of the afternoon.

Saffron walked slowly up the steep hill towards the village of old Elounda. As she rounded the corner of the narrow road and the houses began to come into view she drew in her breath. It was like stepping back in time. The small stone houses stood cheek by jowl, on one side of the road they had a small paved area at the front and on the other they opened straight from the road.

Built against the wall where two houses adjoined was a sink unit. A bucket stood beneath the waste pipe. A flimsy roof of corrugated tin was suspended from a post at each end, an oil lamp hanging from a nail on each post. A gas cylinder stood beneath a work bench and two corroded gas rings holding a kettle and three saucepans sat on top. Saffron halted and looked at it in surprise. Was this their kitchen?

She wished she had a camera with her; then her face reddened with embarrassment. How rude of her to stand and stare and even consider taking a photograph. As she stood there an Alsatian dog rushed out through the doorway and barked vociferously at her. A woman drew back a corner of her curtain and dropped it back into place. A tourist was of no interest to her. Saffron backed away nervously and continued to walk slowly, scrutinizing the houses as she went, wondering what life must be like to live in such primitive conditions. A front door was open and she was able to look inside as she passed. The interior of the room was tiny and crammed into it was a large bed, settee, table, chairs and side board. To be able to move from one side of the room to the other you would have needed to move furniture out of your way. She longed to ask if she could enter and look around, but also felt uncomfortable, peering uninvited into peoples' private lives.

The higher up the hill she walked the more spaced out the houses were, but as she drew closer the gaps were due to buildings that had collapsed. One or two looked uninhabitable, but there were lace curtains at the windows and one had a plastic table and chairs outside. Two cups sat on the table with a fly inspecting their recent contents.

Seeing the cups made Saffron realise that she was thirsty. She took up her water bottle and drained the remains. As she did so, she heard a voice calling and looked in that direction. An elderly woman on the other side of the road was beckoning to her and calling something she did not understand. She smiled vaguely back and the woman approached closer and took her elbow in a grimy hand.

'Taverna. Come. Taverna.' She waved her free hand towards a doorway. The interior dark and unwelcoming.

Saffron shook her head. The woman gripped her elbow even harder. 'Taverna. Come.'

With a resigned sigh Saffron realised she would not be released unless she went with the woman. She ducked her head to go through the low stone doorway and the woman indicated to a small wooden chair with a damaged cane seat. Saffron guessed from her hand actions that she was being asked to sit and gingerly she lowered herself, hoping the chair would take her weight.

'Coffee. Cola. Juice. Tea.'

Saffron considered. As her eyes became accustomed to the darkness she could see the cracked cups, the dirty sink and the cooking rings encrusted with spilled food.

'Water?' she asked and held up her empty bottle.

The woman frowned. 'Coffee. Cola. Juice. Tea,' she intoned again.

'Cola,' Saffron said firmly and withdrew one from the crate by the door, noticing as she did so that the floor of the room was of beaten earth. The woman took it from her outstretched hand and passed it to a man whom Saffron had not noticed earlier. Suspended from the belt of his trousers was a bottle opener and with a flick of his wrist he pulled off the cap and handed the bottle back to Saffron. The woman handed her a straw, which to her relief was in a paper wrapper and they both stood and watched her.

Feeling self conscious Saffron unwrapped the straw and placed it into the bottle. She took a tentative sip. She did not like cola very much, but at least it was in a bottle. Had she asked for a fruit juice she dreaded the state of the glass that would have been used.

Sitting on the low chair Saffron angled her body away from the sunlight coming through the doorway and looked around. A large, high bed stood in the far corner and next to that was a fireplace. Four small tables with their chairs stacked on them were pushed to one side and on a fifth stood the most enormous television screen Saffron had ever seen. No doubt the villagers congregated there in the evenings or at weekends to watch a football match or maybe the news.

She had a tremendous longing to talk to these people. Did they actually live in this building? How long had they lived there? She felt something tickle her foot and looked down in apprehension, seeing only a small spider. The woman noticed her look and bent and flicked it away with her hand. Saffron smiled her thanks.

The woman let forth a torrent of Greek and Saffron felt incredibly ignorant as she was unable to understand a word. She felt unreasonably annoyed with her father. Had he not taken her away from her mother she would have been able to communicate with the woman and anyone else on the island. Her mother had always spoken a certain amount of Greek to her and she knew her older sisters had been fluent. She shook her head. Not a single word had come back to her.

Saffron took another mouthful of the cola. She really did not like it. She placed it on the floor and the woman immediately dived forward and lifted it up whilst the old man brought over a footstool. A crocheted cloth was placed over the footstool and the woman put the bottle down in front of Saffron. Saffron stifled the desire to laugh and at the same time felt guilty. They were showing her such hospitality and she was rude enough to think it amusing.

'Thank you,' she said. To her amazement, she had used the Greek word. She felt tears come into her eyes and brushed them away impatiently. She took another mouthful of her drink and replaced it on the table, fumbling for her purse in her bag. She held out a handful of change and the woman's grubby fingers picked through them, selecting what she wanted. She showed the coins to Saffron before handing them to the man who threw them into a box beside the sink.

Saffron picked up the bottle again and rose from the low chair. The woman immediately made hand signals urging her to sit back down. Saffron shook her head, her fingers making a walking motion, then she pointed down the hill. Smiling and waving her hand she backed out of the doorway, the woman still calling after her as she began to walk on down the road.

She walked a short distance out of view of the taverna and leant against a wall. She looked at the nearly full bottle of drink in her hand and wondered if she dared to leave it there by the side of the road. It would be better manners she decided to return the empty bottle. A scuffling behind the wall made her hair stand on end and she stiffened. A scrawny chicken forced its way beneath an ill-fitting wooden door and fluttered half-heartedly across the road.

'I'm not sure I like it up here,' she thought. 'I'll return the bottle and leave.'

She tipped the contents of the cola bottle into the weeds at the side of the road and walked back to the taverna. As she reached the doorway the woman called to her and Saffron shook her head. She was not going inside again to buy another drink that she did not want. The woman darted out and caught at her elbow and Saffron pulled it away roughly. The man appeared and held her sunhat out to her.

Feeling terribly embarrassed Saffron took it and thanked them again in Greek. She placed her empty bottle into the crate, her hat on her head, and waved goodbye as she retraced her steps back down the road.

Down in the square she purchased a bottle of water from the small supermarket, checked her watch, and decided she would catch the next bus into Aghios Nikolaos. There was nothing more to see in this village and the remainder of the afternoon stretched ahead of her.

Aghios Nikolaos was closer than she had realised, the journey taking no more than twenty minutes. She made the mistake of remaining in her seat until they pulled into the bus terminal and she realised she would have to walk back over the hill to return to the town. She walked on the shaded side of the road until she reached the small town square. On both sides of the square were gift shops selling a variety of souvenirs. The shopkeepers urged her to go inside and examine their goods more closely and at first she yielded to their pleas. After she had examined embroidered tablecloths, blouses and shawls, looked at models of the Athenian Guard and cheap jewellery she decided that entering the shops out of curiosity was a waste of her time. She did not intend to buy anything.

Taking a mouthful of her water, she began to walk down the hill on the other side of the square, passing shops selling the same variety of tourist souvenirs. Interspersed with them were shops offering fast film developing, chemists, vases and ornaments, shoes and sandals and a general store. There seemed to be nothing more here than there had been at Elounda, it was just larger.

Disappointed, she reached the bottom of the hill. She stood and looked about her. Across the bridge she had travelled over earlier by bus she could see tavernas with gaily coloured umbrellas, the waiters bustling between the tables, taking and delivering orders. That looked more inviting.

She walked across the bridge and found that once again she was looking at shops selling the same goods as before. Picture postcards stood on stands outside, interspersed with cheap necklaces and worry beads, the smell of the leather goods mingling with the cooking smells from the tavernas. Tucked away in a corner was the information bureau.

Saffron pushed open the door. There was no one in attendance at the desk and she browsed through the pamphlets on display, waiting for someone to come out to attend to her. She looked at the one for Gournia. By the opening times given for the archaeological site she was far too late that day for a visit, but at least it told her the number of the bus she would need to take. Another had a photograph of Aghios Nikolaos and she opened it curiously. It described the area around the lake as having the best tavernas in town, with views of the bottomless pool and a walk along the side where you could see the birds and small animals in cages on the side of the hill. It also mentioned the museum and gave a rough map.

Saffron tapped the pamphlet on the counter impatiently. She could clearly see a man and woman working in the adjoining room and they had looked at her a couple of times and ignored her. She looked again at the map. It appeared simple enough to find the museum from where she was standing. She did not need to ask directions from them. Obviously, the information bureau was only a place to collect information, not to ask for it.

She stood outside with the map in her hand. With the pool behind her, she judged that she needed to go half way up the hill. Again, she walked on the shaded side of the road, but the area seemed a part of the business quarter. There were no shops here, but nameplates outside the entrances showed the occupants of the buildings to be doctors, dentists, and lawyers. Without difficulty, she found the museum and paid her entrance fee to the elderly woman who sat beside the door.

To her surprise she found she was the only visitor. The lighting was dim and most of the labels were in Greek or so faded as to be unreadable. The artefacts were mainly of pottery, repetitious, very few of them were complete and the attempts that had been made at restoration that had been made looked clumsy. Thoroughly disappointed she moved swiftly between the exhibits and within ten minutes found herself back at the exit.

'That was a waste of money,' she thought. 'Now what shall I do?' She leaned against the wall and looked at the map again. It appeared that the road ended there, but she could see that it continued. She would go to the next intersection, walk along that road, and turn back down towards the pool. She would then decide whether to eat at one of the tavernas or return to Elounda for a meal.

Saffron sighed. She wished Marjorie were with her. She would have enjoyed looking at the souvenir shops, deciding where to go next and what to eat. They would have chatted over their meal and the time would have passed rapidly. Feeling lonely and miserable, Saffron continued up the road past the impersonal facades and then halted before a very different shop.

She looked in the window at the display of glass and ceramics. Black marble shelves at different angles showed off the pieces to perfection. Saffron stood and gazed entranced at the colours and shapes. She would have to buy something from here to take back to Marjorie. Saffron frowned, how would she ever transport it back to England in one piece? Maybe she could ask them to pack it very carefully for her and she could put it into her hand luggage.

As she looked at the different items, trying to decide what Marjorie would like best, a white Persian cat strolled into the window. It sat down nonchalantly, licked its front paws carefully, and tucked them discreetly beneath its body. The cat fixed an unblinking stare on Saffron and she could not help smiling.

Saffron pushed open the door and two elderly women looked up from where they were sitting behind a counter. They both smiled in welcome, but made no attempt to come forward and offer to serve her. Saffron looked at them covertly as she moved around the shop. They were both incredibly smart for shop assistants. In fact she had not seen anyone so well dressed since she had been in Crete. Maybe they were wealthy customers who were waiting for their purchases to be wrapped.

She moved slowly, shelf by shelf, examining the statues, glass and pottery items, but not daring to pick them up and handle them. This was the ideal place to find a present for Marjorie to add to her glass collection. An ash tray was useless, neither she nor Marjorie smoked. Champagne glasses would never be used and take up far too much space in the cabinet. A punch bowl, with the cups hanging from it was also impractical. Then she saw a vase that made her catch her breath. It was almost twelve inches tall in apple green glass, shaped like a flower, the petals laid back.

Saffron looked back at the women and realised they were watching her whilst pretending to look at a magazine. As she smiled at them, one rose, walked over and Saffron pointed to the vase.

'How much?' asked Saffron.

The woman turned it upside down and revealed the discreet label underneath. Saffron calculated rapidly. It was expensive, but if she used her credit card she could pay for it next month when her salary was in the bank. She nodded eagerly.

The woman placed it carefully on the counter and spoke to Saffron in Greek. Saffron shook her head. 'I'm sorry, I don't understand.'

The second woman looked up and said something equally unintelligible in a different language. Saffron shook her head again. The woman sighed, raised her voice, and let out a torrent of Greek again. Saffron took a step backwards. If the woman thought she would understand if she shouted at her she was mistaken.

A man appeared from the back room, leaning heavily on a stick. He smiled at Saffron. 'English? he asked. 'Gift? Wrap?'

'Yes, yes please. Can you wrap it very carefully so I can take it to England?'

'England?'

Saffron nodded vigorously. 'England.'

The man fumbled beneath the counter, produced a piece of laminated card and handed it to Saffron. She looked at it curiously.

Crete: October 2005

We wrap and pack goods for export to any
country in the world.
Price dependent upon weight. Full insurance.
Guaranteed delivery.

'How much would it cost to send?' asked Saffron.

Yannis turned to Ourania. 'Have you got the postal charges? It's to go to England, add on five Euros to make sure we cover the cost.'

Ourania ran her finger down a list and pointed to two figures. Yannis nodded. He would ask the higher price, that and the five Euros added would ensure they made a profit. He wrote the price of the vase, the cost of the postage and added the additional Euros, marking them as insurance and handed the scrap of paper to Saffron.

'Cash? Credit?' he asked.

Saffron held out her credit card. Yannis took it from her and handed it to Ourania. No customer would try to walk off with the goods whilst Ourania held their credit card. He added a further five Euros as she was not paying cash. Saffron shrugged. It would be worth every penny to have it delivered safely. She stood and watched as the women went into the back room together and she could hear a discussion taking place between them.

Whilst she waited she looked at the sketches that were mounted high up on the walls. There was something vaguely familiar about them.

The women finally returned with a roll of protective bubble wrap and two wooden boxes. The first box was obviously too small, and by the embarrassed smile one gave the other this had been the subject of their discussion.

The vase was stuffed with the wrap, then each petal was covered, the base being wound around with layer after layer of wrapping until the whole became a shapeless mass. Two more layers were rolled around it and then taped securely before the

305

vase was laid gently into the box and any crevices were stuffed with more of the wrap to ensure a snug fit. A business card was handed to Saffron and another placed inside the box before small brass nails were tapped into the corners to hold the lid in place. Finally, Yannis took a large sheet of brown paper and covered the box. He pushed it across the counter and handed Saffron a pen for her to write the address.

Saffron printed Marjorie's name clearly on both sides of the parcel and handed the pen back. 'Thank you,' she said again in Greek, pleased she had managed to remember the word.

Ourania handed the credit card back to Yannis and he placed it in the machine, finally giving Saffron the slip of paper to sign. He handed her the card and receipts and waited whilst she replaced them in her purse before he held out his hand. The two women followed suit and Saffron was struck by the difference between their hands and the old lady in the village of old Elounda. Hers had been hard and dirty, whilst theirs were soft and clean, with well-manicured nails.

Saffron left the shop feeling well pleased with herself. She felt she could trust them to post the vase on to England and then wished she had been able to ask how long it would take to get there. She looked at her watch. It was too early to eat an evening meal, but if she delayed in Aghios Nikolaos much longer she would miss the bus from Elounda to Plaka. Trying to make a decision, she walked back down the hill to where the tavernas were along the waterfront.

To her delight the menus were written in both Greek and English and many of them had photographs beside each item they were offering. She hesitated. It was foolish to return to her apartment at such an early hour. There would be nothing to do except read a book. She would walk around the pool, look at the animals and birds, check out the menus of the tavernas over there, and spend out on a taxi. After all, a day on the beach tomorrow would cost her very little money.

As darkness fell, the town took on a different aspect. Lights came on at the tavernas, music played and there seemed to be more people everywhere. She had made a mistake going to the self-catering apartments at Plaka. She should have stayed in the town.

Once again, awake early, Saffron walked over to the taverna only to find it closed with a notice saying that it would open at mid-day. Of course, she had been warned that places would be closed, it was Ochi Day, a Public Holiday. She shrugged. She had eaten breakfast, so she would go and spend the morning on the beach as she had planned.

As she returned to her apartment she saw the people who were staying next door for the first time. A couple with two small girls were loading up their car with beach equipment, whilst the girls kept asking when they were leaving. Saffron smiled enviously at them. She wished she could have company for the day.

She changed into her swimming costume, covering it with shorts and a loose blouse, filled her bottle with water from the tap, and made a cheese sandwich, wishing she had some tomatoes to add to it and a piece of fruit. She placed her towel and book into her bag, along with her purse and key and walked down to the beach.

The beach was deserted, the umbrellas still furled up and the sun loungers on their side. She hoped no one would object to her raising the umbrella and making herself comfortable on the lounger. Out on the water she could see a small boat making its way towards the island and watched it curiously. After the way the woman had spoken, she had not expected any trips to be running that early on the Friday.

She settled back comfortably, her head resting on her folded towel, and watched as the boat rounded the island and was lost from view. She opened the book she had purchased the day before, hoping she had chosen wisely. It was difficult to concentrate.

Finally she placed her book to one side and looked out again at the sea. The boat was returning and appeared to be coming in to Plaka.

There were a number of people aboard, but they looked more like local people than tourists. The boat went out of sight as it nosed its way in to the jetty that was the other side of the beach and hidden by a breakwater of large stones. She picked up her book again and tried to read. Two more pages and she found her eyes were closing. She was not tired, but she was already feeling uncomfortably warm. She would go for a swim, that would wake her up properly. She could lay in the sun until her costume was dry, then see if the taverna and shop was open.

The water was refreshing and wonderfully clear. Saffron swam the width of the beach and then ventured further out where she turned on her back and floated lazily. Turning back on to her stomach she saw a small procession of people walking down the hill from the tiny church. She watched until once again they were out of sight behind the stones of the jetty. It was only a matter of minutes before the boat headed back out to sea again, this time staying close to the coast. Saffron screwed up her eyes to see more clearly who was aboard, but the boat was moving too swiftly for her to discern anyone distinctly.

Deciding she was cool enough she turned and swam back to the shore. She dried her hands and face, creamed her shoulders and legs and turned the lounger so her head was still beneath the umbrella. It wouldn't hurt to have a short sleep.

She sensed rather than saw someone approaching and opened a sleepy eye. John adjusted her umbrella slightly and moved on to the next, unfurling it and placing the loungers beneath its shade. Idly Saffron wondered where he had come from. Maybe the family lived above the taverna. There appeared to be another storey. She looked at her watch. She must have been asleep for over an hour. Her mouth felt dry and she was conscious of being too hot. She took a mouthful of her tepid water and debated the wisdom of another swim. That would mean she had to lie in the sun and get dry again. It would be more sensible to visit the taverna now, have something to eat, maybe purchase something she could make a meal from later, and have another swim in an hour's time.

She pulled on her shorts and blouse, collected her belongings together and walked up to the taverna. John was sitting outside on the patio reading a magazine. He looked up as she entered and raised his hand in greeting. For a moment Saffron stood still, revelling in the coolness after the heat outside. She selected a bottle of water from the fridge, opened it immediately and drank greedily.

She walked out to the patio and sat beneath an umbrella at a table opposite John. 'I owe you for this,' she waved the bottle at him. 'I was desperate. I couldn't wait.'

John smiled. 'You should dig a hole and put your water bottle in that. It keeps it cool.'

'I had left it in the shade,' protested Saffron.

He smiled again and she had the feeling that he thought her a simpleton. 'Is that all you wanted?'

Saffron shook her head. 'I thought it would be a good idea if I had some lunch up here. I understand from your mother that most places will be closed today.'

John shrugged. 'They might be. Once people have been to church they usually open up again. The tourists expect everywhere to be open all the time.'

'Is that why the taverna and shop were closed earlier this morning?' asked Saffron. 'Did you all go to church?'

'Not my very old grandmother. It doesn't mean so much to her anyway. She wasn't here during the war.'

Saffron was struggling to overcome her curiosity. 'I'm sorry. I'm very ignorant. Your mother told me it was Ochi Day, but what does that mean? Why is it so special?'

'It was the day when the Greek people said no to the Germans. They would not stand by and be occupied without a fight. We go to church to say thank you for delivering us from them and also remembering the brave men and women who lost their lives.'

Saffron nodded understandingly. 'I saw some people coming back from the church on the hill.'

'That was my family. We always go to the service in Elounda, then visit the island to remember the people who died over there and up to the church to say a special prayer for our relatives who are buried there.'

'Is the church always open?' asked Saffron.

John shook his head. 'Not now. Unfortunately it was robbed in the past so it has to be kept locked. My father has the key if you are really interested to see inside.'

'I would like to see inside a proper Cretan church. I went into the big Venetian one in Elounda, but it is so vast and ornate.'

'I will ask my father to bring the key.' John pulled his mobile 'phone from his pocket.

Saffron looked at him in horror. 'Not now. I mean, there's no rush. He mustn't make a special journey on my behalf.'

'It will be no problem,' John assured her.

Saffron shook her head. 'No. I actually came up to get something to eat. I'm not dressed for visiting a church anyway. I'm in my beach gear.'

'I will ask my father to bring it up and leave it here. When you feel ready you will be able to borrow it.'

Saffron smiled at him gratefully and studied the menu he offered.

Knossos was a delight to Saffron. The coach had arrived no more than five minutes late to collect her and she had sat beside the window as they drove up to the city. Despite the traffic, they were no more than fifteen minutes behind their schedule when they arrived. Throughout their journey the guide had told them, in excellent English, the history of the site, how the Minoan civilization had reached great heights and then been virtually lost until Sir Arthur Evans had excavated at Knossos.

'You will see how he has restored parts of the palace to their former glory. Of course, the murals are reproductions. The originals are in the museum at Heraklion along with many other of the beautiful works of art that he uncovered.' She held up a guidebook. 'I will pass this amongst you and you can see for yourselves a small selection of the items. We will not have time today to visit the museum, but there is another tour tomorrow that drives around Heraklion. It enables you to see the Venetian fort and many of the old buildings. It also allows you three hours inside the museum before the return journey. If anyone is interested please speak to me and I will add your name to the list of passengers. We still have a few places available.'

Saffron had looked through the guidebook eagerly. She would purchase a copy for herself and certainly book the visit for the following day. Now, tired and satisfied, she sat back, looking out of the coach window as the sun went down and reminisced on the site. She would have liked a good deal longer there, to wander alone and examine nooks and crannies. To walk with a guidebook in her hand and find the places for herself that the guide had indicated before moving the group rapidly on. She wanted to look again at the palace where the guide claimed they had a water cistern for the toilet and the King and Queen had their royal apartments. She had been unable to make out the carved double axes on the stone walls as there had been no time to stand and stare. She could imagine herself as a fine lady at the court, fashionably dressed for the time, walking up and down the staircase that was decorated with shields, or sitting and watching the bull leaping.

She had asked if they could go to the caravanserai and the tomb, but to her disappointment the guide had said it was no longer available to the public. Maybe if she returned alone she would be able to find a way that she could sneak in and gain a look. She sighed. There was no way she would be able to return on this holiday. Next year she would persuade Marjorie to accompany her. If she saved really hard she might be able to afford to hire a taxi for a couple of days and they could drive further afield, possibly to the other side of the island even, and spend as long as they wished.

Maybe they could come for two weeks. They would stay in Heraklion. That would enable them to travel to all the places of interest more easily and they would be close to the museum and just a short bus ride from Knossos. The town would be available for them to walk around during the evening and there was certain to be a beach nearby where they could swim and relax if they wished.

'Madam, we are at your apartments.'

The voice made her start. She had been deep in thought with plans for the following year and had no idea how quickly the journey had passed. Also, in the darkness she had no idea where they were. Hurriedly she checked she had her belongings, thanked the guide and the driver, assured them she would be waiting the next day to go to Heraklion, and clambered down the steps.

Saffron waited until the coach had drawn away, then walked to her apartment. It looked dark and unwelcoming. 'Don't be silly,' she said to herself. 'You've had a lovely day. You're tired and hungry now, that's why you feel miserable. Have something to eat and drink, go to bed early and be prepared for another enjoyable day tomorrow.'

The museum in Heraklion did not disappoint her. She wished again that she had been alone and could wander from case to case, spending as long as she wished admiring the decoration on the pottery, marvelling at the carving and re-examining the reproductions of the frescoes. As it was, the guide would gather the party together, talk about an item for some minutes, then wave her hand towards a case and almost before they had all had a chance to look at it she was calling them back to her again. Saffron found it frustrating, but did not dare to leave the group. There were so many other coach parties milling around that she was not at all sure she would be able to find them again, despite the red umbrella the guide shot up into the air when she was ready to move to another part of the room.

They were finally told they had half an hour to themselves. They could either get something to eat or drink in the cafeteria, continue to look at exhibits or visit the souvenir shop. The guide emphasised they must be gathered together outside at the designated time. All the tours were given a time slot, she explained. It saved congestion in the museum and also in the coach park.

'We have negotiated for a good time,' she continued. 'We do not wish to be unreliable and penalised. Please ensure you are ready outside at the time I have said.'

Saffron raced back up the stairs to where the frescoes were displayed and looked at them again. She did not remember having seen all of these reproduced at Knossos. This time she looked at the labels. She was right. Many of them had been discovered on Santorini. Had the guide told them that? She really could not remember. Her head was reeling with information about 'Pre-Palace Ware', 'Kamares Ware' and 'Marine and Floral' designs and she could not remember the order in which they had been produced.

She smiled to herself. Did it matter if she could not remember? She was certainly not planning to act as a guide to the museum or anywhere else. She returned to the ground floor, checked the time on her watch, and shouldered her way through the group of people clustered before the case with a tiny ivory statue displayed. She could appreciate the workmanship involved, but the piece did not appeal to her in its present form. She much preferred the rhyton made from rock crystal, and wished she could spend hours examining the seals and jewellery. She promised herself a visit to the British Museum upon her return to London. She knew they had an excellent display and she would be able to spend as long as she wanted pouring over the display cases.

Conscious of the time, she made her way to the exit and was gratified to find that she was not the last person to arrive back at the coach. The drive around the town was interesting and Saffron, along with some of the other tourists, would have liked to visit the Venetian fort. Having left the waterfront, where the Venetian store houses were pointed out to them, they drove a short distance around the city walls before taking the road that led out of town.

Saffron leant her head against the glass of the window. She had such a headache. No doubt it was due to spending most of the day in air conditioning. She drank some more of her water and closed her eyes. Then she realised, she had eaten nothing since her breakfast that morning. No wonder she had a headache. The taverna would be closed by the time she arrived back and she only had bread, cheese, tomatoes and olives sitting in her apartment. It would be more sensible if she spoke to the guide and asked them to take her on to Elounda or even Aghios Nikolaos and she ate a proper meal.

The guide frowned as she approached her. 'What is wrong?'

'Nothing. I just wanted to ask if it would be possible for you to take me into Aghios Nikolaos or Elounda?'

'You are staying at the apartments.'

'Yes, I know, but the taverna there will be closed and I want to have a proper meal.'

'We are supposed to drop you where we collected you.'

'I am not going to tell anyone, so who will know if I missed my stop?'

The guide turned to the driver and spoke to him. He shrugged. It made absolutely no difference to him where he dropped his passengers. Grudgingly the guide agreed to take Saffron in to Aghios Nikolaos and Saffron realised she would be expecting a large tip for the favour.

Despite drinking more water and eating an appetizing meal, Saffron's headache persisted. She had no inclination to walk around and enjoy the interesting bustle that happened each evening as people decided what they would do for the last hour or so before retiring to their hotel for the night. The shopkeepers calling their wares and urging her to enter their premises only seemed to make her head ache more. She waved down a taxi and sank back gratefully. She really needed a long sleep and tomorrow she would have a relaxing day on the beach.

John squatted down beside Saffron. She was sitting with her legs drawn up, her hands clasped around her knees and her head resting on them. She had been sitting like that for at least the last half an hour whilst he had been photographing some sparrows who were squabbling over a piece of bread.

'Excuse me, are you feeling all right?'

Saffron raised her head.

'You've been sitting in the sun for ages. You ought to be under an umbrella.'

'I only meant to sit here for a short while before I had a swim.'

'The sun is right on the back of your neck. You don't want to make yourself ill.'

'You're right. I should know better.' Still Saffron did not move.

John looked at her in concern. 'Are you sure you're not feeling ill?'

Saffron shook her head. 'No, I was just trying to sort out some problems I have at the moment.'

'You're on holiday. This is a time to forget your problems.'

'I wish I could!' Saffron sighed wearily. 'I think I'll have another swim and this time I'll lie under the umbrella when I return, I promise.'

'Aren't you going anywhere today?'

'I understand the sites are closed. I've been to Aghios Nikolaos and looked at the town. I plan to go over there again tomorrow and take the bus to Gournia.'

'Have you been out to the island? Spinalonga's worth a visit. It used to be a leper colony.'

Saffron looked at the island just across the water from them. She really ought to go out there. Her grandfather had been something to do with leprosy.

She nodded. 'I keep meaning to make arrangements.'

'Why don't you come out with Nick and me this afternoon? I'm just waiting until she's finished up at the taverna with Mum and then we'll go back to the house and pick up the boat. We have to come back this way so we could pick you up from the jetty. You'd be company for Nick. I'm planning to do some underwater photography so she'll be on her own. The swimming out there is good. By the time we get there most of the tourists are leaving and then we have the island to ourselves.'

Saffron hesitated. 'Are you sure your friend won't mind?'

'She'll be only too pleased to have someone to sit and talk to. I've promised Mum that I won't go off on my own to photograph under water so poor old Nick has to suffer. I'd take it as a favour. I feel guilty if I spend too long making her wait for me.'

Saffron sighed. 'I'm not very good company, I'm afraid.'

'Nick will just appreciate not being alone.' John turned and waved. 'She's coming now. Go and grab yourself some clothes for later and a jumper. We'll be back here in about half an hour. By the way, what's your name?'

'Saffie,' she called back and John nodded in acknowledgement.

'Elizabeth. Good to hear from you. How's Eleanor?'

'She's recovering quite well considering. We are going to try her back at school, just two mornings a week to start with and see how she copes. I'm really phoning about Nicola. She ought to come home next week. The High Schools and Universities in other States have found extra places for those who can't attend here due to the damage. She ought to be over here or she could lose her place.'

'Of course she must be there. I shall miss having her around and so will John. She's been a great help. She's welcome here whenever she wants to come over. What's the situation over there?'

'Getting better. I can't say it's back to normal. We're living upstairs whilst the ground floor dries out. We can't really tell how much damage has been done. We've thrown out all the appliances. I've had to go back to washing by hand – can you believe it!'

Marianne laughed. 'You should have lived over here when Grandma was a girl. All the washing was done by hand, a good deal of it in the sea.'

'How is your grandmother?'

'Wonderful. You'd never believe she's ninety-five.'

'Have you heard from Bryony?'

'Not for a few days. I imagine they're still trying to get themselves sorted out. No doubt they're both working all hours at the insurance company.'

Elizabeth hesitated. It was really none of her business. 'I saw Marcus yesterday.'

'Really? How was he?'

'He was shovelling rubble into the back of a lorry.'

'What! Why was he doing that?'

'I don't know, but he's obviously not working on insurance claims.'

'Are you sure it was him?' A puzzled frown creased Marianne's forehead.

'Absolutely certain.'

'Did you speak to him?'

'I couldn't. I was stopped at the lights.'

'I'll have to 'phone her and see what's happening. He might have just been being neighbourly and helping out.'

'That's probably what it was. Is Nicola around? I ought to have a word with her about coming home.'

'She's over on the island with John. I'll ask her to 'phone you

317

as soon as they get back. John's still playing with his underwater camera and I've made him promise he'll always have someone with him. I shall be quite pleased when it's too cold for him to swim and he goes back to photographing his bugs and beetles.'

Elizabeth giggled. 'I'm glad he puts them in your fridge and not mine. Eleanor would probably have a screaming fit and Nicolas would probably eat them!'

'He wouldn't!'

'I've seen him eat some weird things, but I don't think he'd go quite that far,' Elizabeth admitted. Elizabeth settled herself comfortably. Hopefully this could be one of her long chats with Marianne.

Saffron saw the small boat coming towards the jetty and scrambled to her feet. She was feeling unaccountably excited. John helped her aboard.

'This is Nicola. Nick, meet Sophie.'

Saffron did not bother to correct the mistake he made with her name. Often people had thought she was called Sophie and it was less effort and often less embarrassing for them if she accepted it.

'I thought you and Nick could have a swim whilst I go and do some photography. Do you know how to use a snorkel?'

Saffron shook her head. 'I've never had the opportunity.'

'That's a shame. We could have taken you through the canal to see the sunken city. Anyway, Nick can show you. It's easy. When I come back I'll show you round the island,' continued John.

Saffron shrugged. 'Whatever you want I'm happy to go along with.'

It took only a matter of minutes before John tied the boat to the bollard on the main quay. 'This is where they dumped the lepers when they brought them over. That building there is where they stored their food and later it became the disinfection room.

318

That was when they were allowed visitors. I'll tell you more when we go through the arch into the village.'

John stripped off his shorts and Tee shirt and donned a wet suit jacket. He sat at the edge of the water and fixed his flippers firmly on his feet. 'I'm off. Give me about half an hour. I'm going to the rocks at the end.'

Nicola nodded. 'Do you want me to bring the boat to pick you up?'

'Only if I wave both hands in the air.' He winked at Saffron. 'Distress signal. Not had to use it yet, though.' He pulled his goggles over his eyes and adjusted his snorkel before walking backwards into the sea.

Nicola turned to Saffron. 'Shall we swim?' She checked her watch before placing it safely in her bag beside her mobile 'phone. 'I must remember to keep an eye on the time. I always allow for him to be a bit longer than he says, but no more than a few minutes.'

'What would you do if he didn't return?'

'Take the boat up to where he said he was swimming. Once I can see his snorkel I know he's safe enough and I would sit and wait. If I can't see any sign of him I would telephone the shore and raise the alarm.'

'Has that ever happened?'

Nicola shook her head. 'He's very responsible when he dives. He has his certificate to say he is a fully qualified diver. He knows how to use the oxygen tanks and is allowed to teach others.'

'Most of my swimming has been done in a pool.'

'You should ask John to give you a few lessons. It's great.'

Saffron shook her head. 'I haven't got time. I leave on Wednesday.'

'That's a shame. Are you ready?'

They walked into the water and Nicola struck out strongly, then turned and swam back to Saffron, showing her how to breathe through the snorkel whilst her face was under the water. For the next twenty minutes they swam back and forth, Nicola occasionally diving down to the sea bed to investigate something she had seen, encouraging Saffron to join her. Finally Saffron shivered and announced her intention of returning to the shore. Nicola nodded.

'I'll have one more swim, then I'll join you.' She set off at such a fast pace that Saffron thought she was going to swim back to Plaka. Half way to the shore she turned and swam back just as strongly.

Saffron watched her enviously. She wished she had such confidence. Nicola walked back up the beach and flung herself down beside her.

'That was good.' She checked her watch. 'Five more minutes, then John should be on his way back. I'm going to put some dry clothes on. I suggest you do the same. There can be a very cold wind when we go to the other side of the island.'

'Is that why John told me to bring a jumper?'

'I expect so. It can be cold on the boat going back sometimes so it's just as well to have something extra to put on. Here he comes.' Nicola pointed to where John could be seen swimming out towards Plaka before turning and making his way towards them. 'There are rocks around that end and you don't want to bang your legs or feet on them,' explained Nicola. 'They also have sea urchins living there and you certainly don't want to get any spines in your feet. You only need to brush against them and they break off. They're so painful and tend to fester up.'

Saffron smiled politely. She did not really know what a sea urchin was.

They waited whilst John came ashore and placed his camera carefully beside him whilst he stripped off his jacket and began to dry his body.

'What did you shoot?' asked Nicola.

'There wasn't much up there today. I was surprised. It must be due to the current. It was quite strong round the headland.'

He draped his towel around his waist. 'I did find a good patch of coral, though.' He picked up his underwater camera and walked to the boat, emerging a few minutes later dressed in his shorts and Tee shirt, with a different camera slung around his neck. 'Now for the conducted tour.'

John led the way through the arch and up the slope to the main path that ran around the island. 'This is what you would have seen when you first arrived, except the laundry hadn't been built when our uncle arrived. He was sent here from the hospital in Athens in a strait jacket as he was considered a trouble-maker.' John took the path leading to the right. 'We'll start at the square. Then we'll walk through the village and I'll point out everything relevant to you.'

Saffron walked beside him, listening avidly as he described the conditions the lepers had encountered and how they had worked to make the island habitable. She followed him warily inside a couple of the ruined houses that had notices saying they were dangerous structures and should not be entered, and looked at the sagging stairs and crumbling walls.

From the main road he led them round the end of the island, where the cliffs went down sheer to the sea. 'The diving is pretty good round here, but I really need the full suit and the tanks with me. I also like to have a qualified companion. It's not safe to go deep diving alone. The current can be strong and it can be quite difficult to get out of the water due to the rocks. Now on this side of the island was the church they used for burial services.'

John unlocked the door and led the way inside. Both he and Nicola immediately lit a candle and placed them in a bucket of sand. Saffron stood there, wondering if they expected her to do the same.

'They're for our uncle who lived over here,' explained Nicola, whilst John locked the door. She looked at John who gave her an imperceptible nod. 'When he died his widow asked that his body be placed in the tower over here. He has a grave up in the village cemetery, but this is really his resting place.'

Saffron's eyes opened wide in horror. 'Is that legal?'

John shrugged. 'I've no idea, but they'd never be able to sort out his bones from all the others down there. Come on, this way. I'll show you.'

Saffron shook her head. She immediately thought of Nandita Patel buried beneath the floor of her house and could feel the bile rising in her throat. 'I'd rather not, if you don't mind.'

'That's okay if you're the squeamish type. You don't have to come and look. We'll just look at the cemetery.' John pointed to the slabs of concrete that were laying in rows along the ground. 'That was the proper cemetery, but it was too small to accommodate everyone. That was why they used the tower. In that little house,' he waved his hand towards the ruined building, 'lived the carpenter who made the coffins. Hold on a minute.' John bent down and focused his camera on a centipede that was languidly uncoiling itself.

Nicola placed her hand on Saffron's arm and they both stood still. John straightened up. 'It's still sleepy. Put your hand down, Nick.'

Saffron watched as Nicola bent down and allowed John to place the centipede on the back of her hand. He waited until it raised its head and searched the air with its antennae before taking more photographs. He made no attempt to stop it when it decided to leave Nicola's hand and she gave a final shake to help it on its way.

'Don't you mind creepy crawlies?' asked Saffron.

Nicola shrugged. 'I'm used to them. John's forever using them in his photos. I'm just convenient to perch them on.'

John covered the lens of his camera and began to walk on. 'Now we're back to where the tourists land.'

John strode on ahead of them and walked through the tunnel. To Saffron's surprise she was suddenly back in the village square.

John waited for them to catch up with him, then climbed up on a block of stone that the guides used when talking to their group.

'Everywhere was in ruins, like this. Uncle Yannis persuaded them they had to rebuild the houses, make them habitable, or their chances of survival were very slim.' John stood in the late afternoon sunshine and began to relate the history of his great uncle's life.

'How are you both?

'We're fine. How's Grandma?'

'I think she's enjoying herself. You'd think she'd never been away. Were you able to collect any of her belongings from *Green Vistas?*'

'I collected a box. The manager asked me to prove the items belonged to Grandma. Luckily the photo album you gave her years ago was near the top and still had Aunt Ourania's address inside. I had a bit of a fight with her. She wanted Grandma to pay for the weeks she hasn't been there and give a months' notice.'

'Was that in her contract?'

'I don't know, but I absolutely refused. I told her that if Grandma had died she wouldn't have been able to give a months' notice, besides she had already been away three weeks. I told her she could sue me and that silenced her.'

'Good for you. How did you find your house?'

Bryony took a deep breath. 'We're not in our house.' Her voice broke. 'It was completely washed away.'

'What! That's terrible. Where are you?'

'We've rented a trailer.'

'You're in a trailer! You can't live like that. How long will you stay there? Why don't you go to a hotel?'

'Those that are open have raised their prices. They're making money out of the homeless. We couldn't stay there indefinitely.'

'What about the insurance? Surely the house was insured?'

'It was, but the company has gone bankrupt.'

'So what are you going to do?'

'I don't know.' Marianne heard the sob in Bryon's voice that she tried to choke back.

'What about your job?'

'We haven't any proper jobs at the moment. The firm has closed down. We've both managed to find some temporary work.'

'With another firm?'

'Not exactly.'

'What do you mean?' asked Marianne suspiciously. 'Not exactly.'

'I'm working in the evenings at the pizza place and Marcus is working for a builder.'

'What are you doing, Bryony? Waiting tables?'

'I'm washing up.'

'And Marcus?'

'He's helping with the clear up. The building firms have been employed to clear the roads and the sites.'

'You mean he's shovelling rubble. Elizabeth was sure she had seen him. Why didn't you 'phone and tell me?'

'Tell you what?' Bryony spoke mutinously.

'That you had so many problems.'

'I'm not too proud to wash up,' said Bryony defensively.

'That's not the issue. Is Marcus there?'

'Yes.'

'Let me speak to him,' Marianne demanded imperiously and waited whilst Bryony handed her mobile 'phone to her husband.

'Marcus, I can hardly believe what Bryony is telling me. It's too awful for words. I want you to tell me exactly what your position is.'

'How do you mean?'

'Bryony says you're living in a trailer, she has a job washing up and you're shovelling rubble. Is that right?'

'Yes.' Marcus sounded bemused.

'That can't possibly continue. Book yourselves flights out to us. You can come and live with us. There's work available here for you.'

There was a silence from the other end of the phone.

'Marcus. Marcus, are you still there?'

'Yes.'

'Then get those flights booked and let me know when you will arrive. We'll be there to meet you.'

'I can't, Marianne. We haven't got enough money to fly out again.'

'I know the flights are expensive and if that's a problem we can help.' Marianne promised wildly. 'Take down my credit card details. You can always pay me back later.'

'I'm not sure I should. It's a big undertaking.'

Marianne took a deep breath. 'Marcus, you have no house, you are living in a trailer, and you haven't any money. How long are you going to be able to live like that? Please, get a pen and paper and write down the number. Get a flight booked as soon as you can and get over here.'

'I'll speak to Bryony, see what she says.'

'No, Marcus, don't talk about it. Just do it. Here's the number.' She read it out slowly to him and made him read the numbers back to her. 'I expect to hear from you within the next hour. Promise me, Marcus, please. I can't bear to think of you both in that situation.'

'You've done what? Without asking Uncle Yannis? And you've told them to use our credit card.? What on earth were you thinking about?'

'I was thinking about them. When I asked Uncle Yannis before he was quite happy for them to stay here as long as they wanted. I didn't think he'd mind if they came permanently.'

'Don't you think you should have asked him first? It's one thing having your relatives here for a holiday, but inviting them to come and live is different. We've already taken in your grandmother. We've had Nicola all summer. Suppose your mother and then Helena and Greg with the boys want to come? What happens then?'

'They won't come over.' Marianne felt close to tears. It had seemed such a practical idea at the time, but she realised she should have asked Giovanni's uncle first. It was his house. 'I'm sorry, I should have spoken to Uncle Yannis, but it will work out, I know it will.'

Giovanni raised his eyebrows. 'What makes you think that? There's no work for them over here. Marcus doesn't even speak Greek.'

'There is work,' protested Marianne. 'I could do with help up at the shop and taverna. It's been easier this year having Nicola. I have to spend some time looking after my grandmother. I have to wash her hair, and now your mother and Ourania expect me to do theirs instead of visiting the hairdresser. I will never be able to cope on my own once I have to look after both of them when they're old. John will be off to University, then there will be his National Service to be completed. He won't be available to work here next season. Eventually it will be just us, trying to cope with all this on our own and looking after three elderly people. At least Marcus will be able to help you with decorating and repairs and Bryony will be able to help me.'

'That's keeping them occupied, not providing work for them. We can employ staff. There are plenty of local people who want work and they won't expect American salaries.' Giovanni spoke bitterly.

'Why employ strangers when we can have family members who we can trust working for us?'

'Because that would be just for the season. What work will they be able to do during the winter months?'

'Marcus can help you with the repairs and decorating. I'll make it clear to them that they can live here for nothing in return for working and just a small amount of money. How would you feel if I was spending hours washing up each evening to bring some money in just to provide us with food? It will work out, Giovanni. I know it will.'

'And how are they going to pay you back for their fares? Have you thought about that?' Giovanni swung angrily out of the door.

Marianne dropped her head in her hands. Of course she should have asked Uncle Yannis and spoken to Giovanni before she made such a rash promise to her cousin. She would speak to him immediately he returned from the shop and try to make her peace with him.

Yannis listened to Marianne's apology sympathetically.

'It was wrong of me. I should have asked you first. I should have asked Giovanni as well. I did it on the spur of the moment. I just felt I had to do something for them.'

Yannis patted Marianne's hand. 'They're family. Naturally you had to ask them. Of course you should have asked me first, but there's no harm done. If fact, it could be quite fortunate. Marcus can drive Ourania and Marisa to the shop each day.'

'Are you giving up driving, Uncle Yannis?' Marianne looked at him in surprise.

Yannis shook his head. 'Not permanently I hope; but it will mean I can have my hip replacement. I'll not be able to drive for a number of weeks. Giovanni hasn't the time to keep taking them backwards and forwards.'

'Is that why you've put it off for so long?'

'Partly. I don't like the thought of going into hospital, but I was more concerned how you and Giovanni would manage without me.'

'Oh, Uncle Yannis!' Marianne hugged him. 'We would have managed. You should have spoken to us earlier. We could have worked something out.'

'You're a good girl, Marianne. Go and make your peace with Giovanni. He's only put out because you made the offer before he thought of it. Tell him I'm pleased they're coming back. Your grandmother will be delighted, I'm sure.'

Saffron looked out towards Spinalonga whilst she waited for the bus to take her to Aghios Nikolaos. It was her last full day on Crete. She wished she had visited the island earlier as she would like to go again and wander around, remembering all John had told her the previous day. She would certainly buy the book written by the man who had lived out there.

As the bus made its way ponderously along the road a child's scream rent the air. Saffron looked around. At the apartment next to hers the family had been loading their car ready for an excursion whilst the two girls ran around and played catch. Now the woman was kneeling on the ground and one girl was sobbing hysterically whilst her father tried to comfort her. Saffron looked at the bus and back again at the family. She had to go over and ask if they needed help, even if it did mean she missed the bus.

'What's happened? Can I help?'

'We need a doctor. Elise is unconscious.'

'Let me see.' Saffron knelt down beside the limp body. 'I'm a doctor,' she informed them. The child was breathing and her pulse was strong. 'What happened?'

'They were just playing around and she tripped over.'

Saffron lifted the child's eyelids and looked at the pupils, then ran her hands over the child's head, feeling the large lump and something damp and sticky in her hair. She withdrew her hand and saw there was blood on it.

'She needs to go to the hospital. Go over to the taverna and tell whoever is there that we need help.' Swiftly she checked the child's limbs, relieved not to find any obvious broken bone.

The man disentangled himself from his daughter and ran across to the taverna. The small girl began to scream hysterically again. 'What's happened to Elise? Her eyes are shut. Is she dead?'

328

Saffron looked up at her and spoke sharply. 'Stop that silly noise. She's not dead. She's just bumped her head.'

Marianne returned with the child's father and took in the situation at a glance.

'I'll get my car.' She looked at the family. 'I can't fit all of you in.'

'I'll stay here with Mia. I'll drive in behind you. It's better that Elise has her mother with her.'

'I'll come with you,' said Saffron immediately.

Marianne looked at her in surprise.

'I'm a doctor. She should be monitored during the journey. I need a clean towel to put under her head, then her head can be rested on my legs.'

'Give me two minutes.' Marianne ran back to the taverna, picked up her bunch of keys and locked the door before driving her car over as close as she could to the apartment. Saffron slid into the back seat and placed the towel across her knees.

'Lift her very carefully. I don't think there's anything broken, but I can't be sure.'

The journey to Aghios Nikolaos seemed to take for ever as Marianne drove slowly and carefully, trying to avoid the many bumps and pot holes in the road. As they entered the town Marianne placed her hand on her horn and forced her way through the traffic until they finally drew up outside the hospital.

'I'll stay with you,' she assured Elise's mother. 'The doctor will probably speak very good English, but you may need some help if there are forms to complete. Wait in the car and I'll go inside and find someone to help.'

Within a matter of minutes two nurses appeared with a trolley and Elise was gently transferred on to it. Saffron folded up the stained towel and climbed out of the car. She really was not needed any longer, but nor did she feel she could just walk away. She followed the small procession into the hospital and waited by the door. As soon as she could she would speak to Marianne and let her know her intention to leave them and visit Gournia as she had originally planned.

Saffron walked back over the hill at Aghios Nikolaos to the bus station. At a taverna where she stopped for coffee she had asked for information about the bus, having decided a visit to the information bureau would be useless. This time she stopped in the small square and looked at the palm trees and the small monument that stood between them. The waiter had told her how the Germans had tied the local government to the trees and subsequently shot them. The scars of the bullets, still visible on the trunks, made her shudder.

She enjoyed the short bus journey to Gournia, checked the time the buses returned and walked along the path to the site. She stopped and shook her head. From the distance the village looked very similar to the one she had visited in Elounda. From her bag she pulled the pamphlet that she had taken a few days earlier from the information bureau and sat down at the side of the path to see if it was of any help.

A strident voice came to her ears and the sound of muttering and footsteps. Hastily she rose to her feet, pushing the pamphlet back into her bag. The woman in charge of the group stopped a short distance from her and waited whilst the tourists clustered around her.

'The village of Gournia was excavated by Harriet Boyd. Although there is a palace here it does not have the grandeur that you see at Knossos. No murals or frescoes were found here. According to the artefacts discovered and interpreted by Miss Boyd the village was a farming community. As you walk through the narrow streets you can look inside the remains of the houses. The village gives us an insight into how the ordinary Minoan people lived and worked. As we walk up the hill, we will pass the temple where the villagers made libations to the Gods and hoped their prayers would be answered. When we reach the palace area I will talk to you more about the apartments and you will have a chance to ask me any questions you may have.'

Saffron moved forward. 'Excuse me. Would it be possible for me to join your group?'

The guide frowned. There was no reason why Saffron should not, but she did not have to make it easy for her. Visitors often tagged along behind an organised tour and took advantage of the talk she gave.

'You did not book to come on the tour?'

'I was delayed. You had already left by the time I arrived in Aghios Nikolaos.'

'We have come down from Heraklion,' the guide informed her smugly. 'I suppose there is no reason why you should not walk around with us. You will not be able to ride back on the coach.'

'Of course not,' Saffron agreed readily. 'I would just like to listen to the talk you give and have the places of interest pointed out to me.'

The woman gave an imperceptible nod and began to walk up the hill. 'Follow me,' she called and the group of tourists began to move.

Saffron joined them and smiled tentatively at a couple who were walking hand in hand. The girl smiled back at her.

'She's a real tartar. Knows her stuff, but woe betide you if you keep the group waiting. We're a bit late arriving, one of the group needed a toilet, and she's already warned us that we'll not have as long here as was planned.'

Saffron smiled guiltily. 'I'm sorry, I've held you up even more now.'

The young man shrugged. 'The coach driver probably wants to get back to Heraklion before the rush hour traffic is too heavy and she's probably fed up with telling ignorant tourists the same thing over and over again. Where are you staying?'

The remainder of the afternoon passed pleasantly for Saffron. There was enough of the buildings still standing for her to envisage a working village, occupied mainly by farmers and their families. Saffron could almost hear the women gossiping in their doorways whilst the children played in the narrow streets, moving to one side as a laden donkey was driven through. She listened intently to their guide and when they parted company at the coach she held out some Euros. 'I really appreciate being able to come with you,' she said. 'Thank you so much.'

The attitude of the guide softened. People usually expected to join her group of tourists for nothing.

'You can have a lift back as far as Aghios Nikolaos on the coach if it helps,' she offered.

'I'd be terribly grateful. I have a long wait for the next bus.'

The guide counted the tourists aboard, spoke briefly to the driver who nodded.

'We can drop you just outside the town,' she said to Saffron. 'It is only a short walk from there to the bus station.

Saffron walked over to the taverna, relieved to find Marianne sitting outside with a glass of wine. 'How is the little girl?' she asked immediately.

Marianne smiled. 'They're keeping her in under observation, but they think she'll be fine. The doctor put a couple of stitches in her head wound and by the time her father arrived she had regained consciousness. It was very good of you to come in with us this morning. Her mother was most appreciative of the way you took charge. I hope it didn't upset your plans for the day.'

'Not at all. I had decided to visit Gournia and I was half way there.'

'I really am grateful. Would you consider joining us for a meal this evening?'

Saffron was tempted. 'You have your family. They wouldn't want a stranger there.'

'Nonsense. I'm sure your family would welcome me if I had done you a favour whilst in England.'

'I haven't any family.'

'No family? None at all?'

Saffron shook her head. 'Not really. I have my stepmother and I may have a few relations in America, but when I tried to contact them there was no reply.'

'Maybe they've moved?'

Saffron shrugged. 'I only know my grandparents' address and I expect they are dead by now.'

'Did your letter come back?'

'No.'

'Then it probably got lost in the post. You ought to write again.'

'They won't want to know me.'

'Why ever not? My grandmother would be over the moon if her grand daughter contacted her. Do come to supper. I'm closing up now, unless there's anything you need, but I'll come back out at eight for you.' Without waiting for an answer, Marianne picked up her empty glass and keys. 'If I don't go back now no one will get any supper,' she smiled.

'So, Mrs Patel, how are you enjoying your stay in Crete?' asked Giovanni as he handed her a glass of wine. 'My wife has asked me to look after you whilst she puts the finishing touches to our meal.'

'Please call me Saffie, Mr Pirenzi.'

'Sophie, that is a pretty name.' Saffron did not attempt to correct his mistake. It could be embarrassing to John and Nicola to know they had called her incorrectly the previous day. 'And you must call me Giovanni. I know; it is an Italian name. My father is Italian. He was over here during the war and met my mother. It was very romantic. When he returned to Italy they continued to write and as soon as my mother was of age they were married.'

'Her family did not approve?'

Giovanni shrugged. 'They thought she was too young, it was a long way from home, a different country, language and customs. I am pleased to say they were very happy together. And your husband? I assume by his name that he is Indian.'

'My husband and I are separated.'

Saffron took a gulp from her wine. Her eyes filled with tears as she spoke and she looked away, hoping Giovanni would not notice.

'I am sorry. I had no idea.' Giovanni was embarrassed. He wished he had not mentioned the woman's husband. To his relief he saw John approaching.

'Hello, Sophie. Mum told me we had one of our guests coming for the evening, but I didn't realise it was you. She said it was a doctor and I expected some stuffy old man.'

'I may be a bit stuffy, but I'm not an old man,' Saffron rejoined.

'I would never have guessed you were a doctor.'

'Oh? What are doctors supposed to be like?'

John shrugged. 'I don't know really, but I always thought they were rather stand-offish and full of their own importance. You're not. Besides,' he added with a grin,' You were too squeamish to look at the bones in the tower yesterday.'

'I'm in orthopaedics. I've probably seen more bones in my time than you have in the tower.'

'What about skulls? There are lots of those down there.'

Saffron shrugged. 'I'm pleased to hear it. There should be one for every body. How did your photographs turn out from yesterday?'

'Not bad. Would you like to see them?'

'If I could.'

Giovanni nodded to John. If his son was prepared to entertain their guest it would save him from having to make small talk to her. He was still feeling aggrieved by Marianne's offer to her cousin and also the way his uncle had accepted the situation so willingly.

'I would like to introduce you to my aunt and uncle. Uncle Yannis and Aunt Ourania speak very little English. I am sure they both understand more than they let the tourists know.' Giovanni winked at her.

'Oh.' Saffron looked at the couple she had met briefly in the gift shop. 'I had no idea they were your relations.'

Yannis shook her hand. 'Parcel is posted,' he announced proudly.

'And this is my mother.' Giovanni put his arm around the woman. 'Mamma speaks Greek, of course, and also Italian. She does not know the English language.'

Saffron sighed inwardly. This could be a difficult evening.

'John and Nicola you have met I understand. I hear you spent an afternoon on Spinalonga with them. No doubt John told you all the history.'

'He was a wonderful guide. I think I enjoyed that visit even more than Knossos and the museum.'

Giovanni smiled proudly. 'There is one more person you must meet. My wife's grandmother also lives with us. She is very old and has said she does not feel she can join us for a meal this evening, but she would like to meet you. Please, come with me.'

Saffron followed him back into the large room that was both a dining room and lounge, various doors were interspersed along the back wall and she guessed they must lead to bedrooms. Above the fireplace hung a picture and Saffron stopped. There was something so familiar about it. Giovanni noticed her interest.

'Uncle Yannis's mother was a talented artist. We treasure the sketches we have. They are all of the family.' He pointed to one set in an alcove. 'That was my mother when she was a child.'

Saffron looked at it. She could see no resemblance between the small, curly haired girl and the elegant elderly lady who was sitting on the patio talking animatedly to her brother. She looked again at the larger picture. Of course it was familiar. She had seen similar sketches in the gift shop.

Giovanni knocked and opened a door. 'Grandma, I have brought Sophie to meet you.'

Saffron looked at the white haired woman sitting in her chair. She felt completely tongue-tied and wished again that she could speak Greek.

Annita smiled at her and held out her hand. 'I'm pleased to meet you,' she said, her English heavily accentuated with an American drawl. 'I hear you are a doctor and helped out with a rather nasty accident this morning.'

'It was nothing,' Saffron managed to say, completely taken aback. 'I'm not really an accident doctor, but you don't forget your basic training.'

'What do you specialise in?'

'Orthopaedics.'

Annita nodded. When she had worked as a nurse, a doctor was a doctor, capable of dealing with everything that arose. Times had changed.

'I hope you will forgive me for not joining you for the evening meal. Some days I seem more tired than others. I can't think why. I do nothing.'

Saffron smiled back at her. 'That happens to all of us. I managed to feel quite exhausted after lying on the beach for a day.'

'So you come from England? Where do you live? London?'

'Yes, how did you know?'

Annita shrugged. 'Everyone always seems to live in London. I visited it with my husband many years ago.'

'I hope you enjoyed yourself.'

'It is so long ago I hardly remember where we went or what we saw. I hope you have enjoyed your stay over here. Do you plan to return?'

'Oh, yes. I want to bring my stepmother next year. There is so much I haven't been able to see during this visit.'

'She didn't want to come with you this year?'

Saffron reddened. 'I decided to take a holiday at the last minute. She had already made other arrangements and couldn't change them.'

'So you came alone?' Annita sighed. 'It is sad when you have no one to discuss your experiences with.'

Once again Saffron could feel tears coming into her eyes and they were not lost on Giovanni.

'We should return to the dining room. I'm sure our meal is waiting for us and Uncle Yannis will have opened another bottle of wine. Shall I ask Ourania to bring you a glass, Grandma?'

'Just a small one. It helps me sleep.' Saffron was sure she saw the old lady and Giovanni wink at each other. 'It has been so nice to meet you. You must visit us again when you return next year.'

Saffron enjoyed her evening. She felt comfortable with the family, despite having to have some of the conversation translated to her and also her replies to them. Once again she felt annoyed that she had not insisted on keeping up her Greek language skills from when she was a child. She tried to drink sparingly, but her glass was refilled continually and by eleven thirty there seemed to be a large number of empty bottles.

'I must go home,' she declared finally. 'I have to be at the airport by mid-day. I haven't packed yet and I will need to make some purchases from your shop before I leave. I mustn't oversleep.'

Giovanni rose. 'I will take you back to your apartment. It is far too late for you to walk.'

Saffron hesitated. She knew Giovanni had drunk a considerable amount. John grinned, also stood up and spoke to his father in Greek.

'You're over the limit, Dad. If the police decided to do one of their spot checks you'd be prosecuted. I'll take Sophie back on the bike, provided she doesn't mind riding pillion that is.'

Giovanni frowned in annoyance at his son. 'I am perfectly fit to drive.'

'People who have had too much to drink always say that.' He turned to Saffron. 'Are you happy to ride pillion on my bike?'

'I've never ridden on a motor bike,' she admitted.

'You'd never done any snorkelling until yesterday,' John reminded her. 'Come on, I'll take it slowly. You'll be perfectly safe. I've been riding it for years now. Just make sure you tuck your dress well under your legs. I don't want to find I'm dragging you behind me.'

A look of alarm crossed Saffron's face and Nicola smiled at her. 'Take no notice of him. If your dress did get caught up the wheel would probably rip a piece out of it and you'd still be sitting on the bike. I'll come out with you and make sure there's nothing trailing.'

'I really don't mind walking,' protested Saffron.

'You can't possibly walk. There are a load of stupid tourists over here who drive too fast and forget which side of the road to drive on.' John said firmly. 'Let me take a photograph first. Stand there between Mum and Dad.'

Despite feeling tired, Saffron found it difficult to sleep. She dreaded returning to England. She was frightened that Ranjit would have been released and would be there waiting for her. She would telephone the Inspector when her flight landed and make sure he was still in custody. She tossed and turned, finally falling into a deep, but disturbed sleep.

She was on Spinalonga, but it was Ranjit who was there with her. They were standing by the tower that John had pointed out to her. Far below she could see the bones that had been deposited in the tower over the years. She could feel Ranjit's hands on her shoulders, trying to force her to join them, whilst she held on to the side of the opening, resisting him with all her might. She woke, bathed in sweat, her hands scrabbling at the wall beside her bed.

For a while she lay there, taking deep breaths and waiting for her heart to stop racing. It was only a bad dream. Finally she swung her legs over the side and walked into the shower. That would wake her up properly and dispel any lingering memories of the nightmare.

She stood under the water, letting it course its way down her spine and relax her. She began to make a list of her jobs in her head. First, she must go over to the shop and make her purchases. A copy of the book about Spinalonga, some olives for her secretary and a couple of packs of herbs for Marjorie. Then she would find out what time Giovanni was taking her to the airport and she might have time for one last swim before leaving. It would only take her a few minutes to pack. She must also write a card and thank the family formally for her dinner invitation.

She stepped out of the shower and towelled herself dry. There was more to do than she had realised. She hesitated about what to wear. If she was planning a quick trip to the beach she needed only to wear her shorts and a top. She would change into her warmer and more suitable travelling clothes when she returned.

There was only enough coffee and milk for one more drink and she did not want to buy more as she would not be using it. She decided to breakfast at the taverna and save what she had for later. Whilst she was there she could buy a postcard and the other items she wanted. She added a bottle of water to her list and hoped she would have enough Euros. She did not want to change any more money at this late stage.

Saffron walked over to the taverna, pleased to see she was the only customer. Marianne was behind the counter and greeted her with a smile.

'Could I have a breakfast, please? You can never be sure whether the meal on the 'plane is going to be eatable. I'll have a look around. There are a few bits and pieces I want to buy before I leave.'

Marianne nodded. 'Help yourself. One or two eggs?'

'Only one, thanks.'

Saffron browsed amongst the goods for sale. She was tempted by the olive oil that came from their own local olives, but to carry a bottle could be impractical, and she decided the olives and herbs she had first thought of were a better choice. She placed the packs on the counter along with a postcard. To her annoyance there was no sign of the book about the island. She would ask if they had one in stock when she paid the bill for her breakfast.

When Marianne returned with a heaped plate Saffron wondered if she would be able to eat it all and also of the wisdom of swimming after such a meal. She shrugged. By the time she had packed and cleared up her apartment she would have worked most of it off. She would be sensible and only swim a few feet from the shore.

Saffron deposited the last of her possessions into the case and padlocked it, placing the keys safely in her handbag and made a final check to ensure she had her passport and return ticket. She looked around the apartment that she had called home for the past week and felt unaccountably sad. She left the postcard she had written propped up on her pillow, deposited her bag of rubbish in the bin outside, dragged her case across the threshold, locked the door, and continued over to the taverna.

She handed the keys to Marianne. 'Thank you for such an enjoyable week.'

'I am only too pleased you enjoyed your stay here. I do hope you will come again. Giovanni will be here shortly to take you to the airport. He knows the time you are to be there and he will not be late. In the meantime I have been asked to give you something.'

Marianne put her hand beneath the counter and drew out an envelope and a bag. Saffron looked at both items curiously. 'What are they?' she asked.

'You won't know that until you open them.'

Saffron lifted the flap of the envelope and took out a photograph, the one John had taken the previous night just before she left. She looked up at Marianne in delight. 'Oh, how lovely. How kind of him. I will have no excuse to ever forget this holiday now.'

Marianne smiled. 'I should hope not.'

Saffron placed her hand inside the bag and drew out the book she had been unable to purchase earlier. 'You did have one in your stock room,' she exclaimed in pleasure.

Marianne shook her head. 'That is a gift. The parents of the little girl wanted to give you something to say thank you. I suggested they gave you this book as you had said you wanted to buy it today. I can put the others back on the shelf now.'

Saffron laughed. 'You mean you hid them so I couldn't buy one?'

'I would have had to refuse to sell it to you and explain. I wanted it to be a complete surprise. Have a look inside.'

'It is.' Saffron opened the book and looked at the writing on the fly leaf.

For the kind lady who helped me when I hurt
my head. Thank you. Elise.

Saffron felt the tears come into her eyes. 'How kind of them. I really did nothing.'

'You bothered to come to the hospital with us. Most guests would have just continued with their own plans.'

'I ought to see them.' Saffron looked towards the apartment.

'There's no time, Giovanni's here, besides, I think they have already gone in to the hospital.'

'Of course.' Saffron held out her hand. 'Thank you again for such an enjoyable week and especially yesterday evening.'

Saffron opened the book whilst she waited at the airport. It should certainly keep her occupied for the whole of the flight. She looked at the pictures that were in the centre fold and frowned, then smiled. Of course, the man who had written the book was a relative and Giovanni had said his great grandmother was an artist. Obviously she had visited the island and they had used some of her sketches as illustrations.

November 2005

Saffron sat with Marjorie, showing her the photographs she had taken and the guidebooks she had purchased whilst in Crete.

'It really is beautiful over there, Marjorie. I want to go back next year and I'm sure you'll love it.'

Marjorie looked dubious. 'I'm not that young to go dashing around sight seeing like you can.'

'Don't be silly. You're not old. We can stay in the main town and take the organised trips from there. That way you won't have to walk until you get to the site or have to worry about changing buses.'

Marjorie smiled. 'I'll think about it nearer the time. Where did you buy the herbs? I suppose they're in all the shops over there.'

'The mass produced ones are. These come from the shop at Plaka. I was assured they were locally grown and packed. The taverna is called *'ANNA'S'* and these are labelled *'ANNA'S HERBS'*. The woman in the shop told me her Aunt Anna was a herbalist. People used to consult her with all their ailments. She used to make them up for them to sell in the shop and after she died they carried on the tradition.'

'They probably just make up their own labels.'

'Don't be so sceptical, Marjorie. They seemed very nice people. They didn't have to invite me into their home for a meal. You should see their house. It's enormous. Mind you, it would have to be, because the whole family seem to live there. The photo I have is only of the couple who run the apartments. I wasn't at all sure who the other people were, but they were all relatives. There was one very old lady I was introduced to. The boy said she was his great grandmother. I expected her to only speak Greek, but she spoke English with an American accent. It was such a surprise. I would have liked to talk to her longer, but she said she was too tired to join us at the table.'

'If you do return to Crete next year do you plan to visit them?'

'I'd like to. We could go down to Plaka and see whether we could go to Spinalonga from there. Just the two of us, with their son as a guide. You'll have to read the book about their relative who lived over there. I've nearly finished it and it's fascinating.'

Saffron continued to talk enthusiastically about her holiday for most of the evening and Marjorie began to wish she had been able to accompany her step-daughter.

'Mr Martin Burton, I sentence you to two years imprisonment. You and your associates have preyed on vulnerable people, charging them extortionate amounts for unnecessary work on their property. I have taken into account the fact that you are married with young children. Your wife has said she will stand by you as she considers you are a good father and only turned to petty crime to improve their standard of living.'

Martin bowed his head. Thank goodness Lorna had never found out about his dalliances with many of the women he had cheated or she would certainly not be standing by him.

Saffron opened the door when the postman knocked and then handed the parcel to Marjorie. 'A little present for you from Crete.'

'But you brought me the herbs,' protested Marjorie.

'That was just something small until this arrived.' She waited whilst Marjorie unwrapped each layer carefully, finally exposing the vase.

Saffron let out her breath. There was no damage at all to the delicate object.

'It's beautiful, Saffie. Thank you. It must have cost you a fortune.'

Saffron smiled. She would certainly not tell Marjorie the amount she had paid. 'It was such a strange coincidence. I told you I was invited to a meal with the family who run the apartments, but what I didn't tell you was that their relatives run the gift shop. The man remembered me at once and said he had posted my parcel. I couldn't talk to them properly as they don't really speak English. I had to have someone interpret for me the whole time. I wish I'd asked Dad to let me have Greek lessons when we came to England. It didn't seem important at the time.'

'And it does now?'

Saffron shrugged. 'In a way. It seems an opportunity lost. I would have liked to speak to people out there, particularly the old couple in the village I told you about.'

'You could always go to evening classes. You could try out what you've learnt when we go next year. It will make the winter months go more quickly having something to look forward to.'

Saffron sighed. 'I'm not looking forward more than a day at a time at the moment. I just hope I won't have to attend Ranjit's trial. The detective said it wouldn't be necessary. I haven't any evidence to give, but he told me Ranjit's defence lawyer might want me to testify to his good character.'

'If you can't testify against him I don't see how you can testify for him.'

'Nor do I, but I don't understand the way the law works. When I asked Detective Inspector Baker about starting divorce proceedings he suggested I waited until after the trial. He said it could be considered as prejudicial to Ranjit's case.'

Marjorie looked at Saffron in disbelief. 'Prejudicial to his case! Is he expecting get off?'

'I think so. From what the Inspector told me he has pleaded guilty of unlawful disposal, claiming mitigating circumstances.'

'Oh, no! I thought he would be charged him with murder.'

Saffron shrugged. 'Inspector Baker wouldn't tell me what they were charging him with. He told me not to worry about anything, just to leave it in their hands. He's promised to contact me when a trial date has been set.'

'Saffie,' Marjorie swallowed hard, 'if he does get off what do you plan to do?'

'I'm divorcing him just as soon as I can.'

'No, I meant about living here. Do you want to go back to America?'

Saffron looked at her in surprise. 'I hadn't even thought about America. I did think it might be a good idea to move away to a different town and change hospitals; but is there really any point? If he wanted he could find me wherever I went.'

Bryony held her grandmother's hand. 'It's so good to be back here with you. I've brought all your belongings that were salvaged from *Green Vistas*. There's your photo album that Marianne gave you all those years ago. I collected your strong box from the bank, as well as the photos you had of everyone when they were children and growing up. We can spend some time sorting them out properly. I'll ask Ourania for another album and we can mount them. At the moment they are just sitting in a box. You are naughty; you should have done that years ago.'

'There just never seemed to be the time. I did write the names on the back.'

'Just as well. I can't tell the difference between Aunt Elena and Aunt Maria when they were small.'

'Maria. That reminds me. Have you got my address book? I can't remember her address and I ought to tell her where I am.'

'I have it here. There might be some other people you want to write to, or I can write a letter for you and you can sign it. I'm sure Marianne won't mind if I use their computer one evening.'

Bryony handed the address book to her grandmother. As she did so some loose pages fluttered out from the front and fell to the floor. Bryony bent and picked them up.

'What's that?' asked Annita, and held out her hand. She began to look at the pages and drew in her breath. 'I had forgotten about this. I was going to show it to you on your next visit and then there was all that hurricane business and I forgot. Do you think I should write back?'

Bryony took the letter and looked at it curiously, then began to read avidly. She turned to her grandmother, with tears in her eyes. 'Of course you must write back. Saffron! Who would have believed it after all this time?'

'You write back to her. After all, she's your sister and I really don't feel I can concentrate on letter writing. You'll know what to say to welcome her back into the family.'

Annita sat back. How she wished she had returned home earlier. If she had left America after Elias had died she could have spent time with her brother and cousins before they died. It had been a misplaced loyalty and affection on her part. She thought her children and grandchildren needed her. How wrong she had been. The only ones who had thought about her were Bryony who had visited her once a week and Marianne who had telephoned her monthly. All the others had been too busy with their own lives. Helena was always too busy with her own family and Elena spent a good deal of her time with Andrew and Sarah in San Antonio. Andreas lived in New York with Laurie, Maria only wrote if she was in need of money and of Anna there was no word.

'Oh, Elias,' she sighed as she looked at his photograph. 'We had a good life in America, but I should have returned to Crete years ago. This is where I belong. I'm a Cretan at heart.'

Saffron closed the front door behind her and as she turned she almost bumped into the postman.

'I'm so sorry,' she said. 'I didn't realise you were there.'

'No problem.' He handed her four letters and she looked at them quickly. One was for Marjorie and three for her. Bills no doubt. She posted Marjorie's through the letterbox, stuffed her own into her handbag and continued on her way towards the bus stop. She would open them on the bus.

She took her seat and opened her bag, just about to pull out her letters when the bus began to draw away. There was a sudden jolt that nearly made her spill the contents of her bag and a grinding noise from the gears. Then engine died and Saffron looked up in surprise.

The driver stood on the platform. 'Sorry passengers. I've got a problem. You can either wait on the bus until a replacement arrives or get off now. I'm afraid this one is going nowhere but the garage today.'

Saffron pushed the letters back into her handbag and rose to her feet. She could not sit there and wait for an indefinite amount of time for a replacement bus to arrive. If she walked around the corner there was a taxi rank and if she was lucky one would return within a few minutes of her arrival. She hated to be late, particularly when she was due in the operating theatre.

To her annoyance, she found the taxi rank was empty and two people were already waiting and looking at their watches anxiously. She took out her mobile 'phone and left a message for the receptionist at the hospital, explaining her dilemma. There was nothing more she could do except wait patiently.

Finally arriving no more than ten minutes late Saffron hurried towards the operating theatre and prepared herself for her first operation, thankful that it was a routine re-setting of a fracture. By the time the patient was wheeled in, she had completely forgotten that she had arrived late due to the breakdown of the bus and her complete attention was given to the minor operation.

Saffron worked continuously until one thirty, when she peeled off her gloves and threw them to one side. She looked at her list for the afternoon, relieved to find that she had only two patients scheduled, the first one for two fifteen. At least she could have a quick break and some lunch.

She sat at her desk with a cup of coffee and remembered the post that still sat unopened in her handbag. There were ten more minutes before she was due to return to the theatre, she had plenty of time to see who wanted money from her this month.

One was advertising for life insurance and the other her credit card bill. She frowned. Had she really spent that much in Crete? She picked up the third, noticing for the first time that it had a Greek stamp. She opened it curiously. Why would anyone write to her from there? She drew in a sharp breath as she began to read the typewritten words.

Dear Saffron

This is Bryony writing on behalf of your grandmother. She was so delighted to have your letter. I am sorry it has taken so long for a reply to reach you.

The letter was forwarded to her from the hospital to the care home where she was living. She received it just before Hurricane Katrina struck Louisiana. My husband and I took her to safety in Dallas and then over to Crete to live out her last years with her family over there.

When Marcus and I returned to New Orleans we found we had lost everything and OUR cousin, Marianne, asked us to return to Crete and live with them. We collected Grandma's possessions and when I unpacked them with her, I found your letter in her address book. She had forgotten all about it.

Sadly Grandpa died nearly twenty years ago, but I am pleased to say that Grandma is very fit and well, quite remarkable for ninety-five. She would LOVE to see you –

*we would all love to see you. Please telephone me on the
number I have written below.*

Please, please, contact us.

Your sister

Bryony.

Saffron felt her eyes fill with tears and she put her head down on
her desk and sobbed uncontrollably. It was amazing. After all these
years she had found her family. She took a tissue from her bag,
wiped her eyes and blew her nose. She read the letter again. What
was the 'phone number? She would try to telephone when she went
home from work, but first she must call Marjorie and tell her.

Saffron picked up her telephone.

'Marjorie,' her chest felt so tight she could hardly speak. 'I
have the most wonderful news. I've had a letter from my sister.
From Bryony. And guess where they live? In Crete.' Saffron
realised she was crying again. 'I just want to come home and
telephone them. Isn't it marvellous?'

'Saffie! That's amazing. I thought they were in America.'

'So did I. Bryony says they left after Hurricane Katrina. My
grandmother is in Crete with them. They took her with them and
she's *ninety-five!*'

'Goodness me – and when you suggested we went to Crete
next year I wondered if I was too old to go!'

'Of course you're not. Oh, Marjorie, I'm so happy, but I just
can't stop crying.'

Marjorie replaced the receiver thoughtfully. She was pleased
to know that her stepdaughter had found her American family.
Marjorie just hoped that when Saffron met up with her mother
again she did not decide to go to live with her and leave her
stepmother alone.

Saffron checked the time. 'It's just after seven here, so it will be
nine over there. It's not too late to 'phone, is it, Marjorie?'

'I wouldn't think so. I'll go and get on with washing the dishes.'

Saffron had delayed making the telephone call when she had arrived home from the hospital, insisting they ate first. Now the moment of contacting her family had come she was apprehensive. What would they say to each other? She dialled the mobile number and waited, tempted to cut the connection.

'Hello.'

Saffron swallowed. She seemed to have lost her voice.

'Hello?'

'Could I,' Saffron cleared her throat. 'Could I speak to Bryony, please.'

'Speaking. Who's calling?'

'This is Saffron.'

There was silence at the end of the telephone line. Saffron's heart sank. They didn't really want to know her.

'Saffron? Our Saffron?'

'Yes. You wrote to me.'

'Just a minute.'

Saffron could hear Greek being spoken and then the sound of someone blowing their nose and the clink of glasses in the background. She had obviously 'phoned at the wrong time, they must have guests for dinner.

'I'm sorry.' Bryony's voice was tremulous. 'I was just so surprised I didn't know what to do or say for a minute.'

'Have I called at a bad time? Have you got visitors?'

'Not at all. I was sorry to hear about your father.'

'How's mother?'

Again there was silence for a moment. 'I can't really talk about that at the moment.'

'Is she ill?'

'No, no, I don't think so.' There was a distinct hesitancy in Bryony's voice.

Saffron frowned. Surely Bryony would know if their mother had been ill. 'Has she had an accident?'

'I can't talk about it on the 'phone. There are some difficulties, complications. I'd rather tell you in person when you visit us. How soon can you come over?'

'I'm not sure. I've some problems of my own that have to be sorted out over here first, and I have to catch up on my work. I've had to have some time off recently and I'm rather behind with my schedule.'

'You could come for Christmas,' suggested Bryony.

'I can't make a definite date at the moment.'

'We really do want you to come over. You're welcome any time. Grandma would love to see you again.'

'Could you come to England?'

'That's not possible at the moment, and I don't think Grandma could make that journey a second time.'

'Can I speak to her?'

'Certainly you can. I'll pass the 'phone to her.' Once again, Saffron heard a rapid interchange of Greek.

'Hello, Saffron?'

'Grandma! Oh, Grandma, it's so good to speak to you again.' Saffron took a fresh tissue from the box at her side and mopped her streaming eyes. 'How are you?'

'They tell me I'm very well for my age. Now, I need to see you again before it's too late. When are you coming over? Next week?'

Saffron gulped. 'I can't. I'm a doctor and I have a heavy case load. I've already had more than my fair share of time off this year. I promise I will come as soon as I possibly can.'

'Just don't leave it too long. I'll hand you back to Bryony and you can make some arrangements with her.'

Saffron shook her head in despair. 'Bryony? Please explain to Grandma that I can't come over yet. There are a number of reasons – and I'd rather tell you when we're face to face. Just tell Grandma I have medical commitments. I'll explain everything else later.'

'I understand. Hold on a moment.' Saffron heard a chair scrape and footsteps, then Bryony spoke again. 'There are certain things we don't tell Grandma. We don't want to worry or upset her. We really do want you to visit us as soon as you can. In the meantime we must keep in touch. Give me your 'phone number and if you don't call me once a week I shall bombard you with 'phone calls until you have to speak to me. I'm not prepared to lose touch with you again.'

Sorrell settled herself on the steps leading to the National Museum in Athens. She might have more success if she begged there. The money she had for selling the diamonds long gone. She tucked her leg beneath her voluminous skirt pretending to be disabled. She had not eaten properly for days, scavenging half-eaten giros, pizza and sandwiches from rubbish bins. Her hunger was nothing compared with the craving that was eating away inside her. She tried to resist, she had only a very small amount of heroin left over from her last purchase.

She held out her hand as a tourist passed, but he ignored her. Her hair hung lank and dirty around her face as she leaned back against the cold stone. She needed a generous tourist quickly. She was desperate to take the remainder of the drug, but she needed to know that she could afford to buy some more.

Shivering and hungry she closed her eyes. This could not go on. When she had lived in Athens before she had found life an exciting challenge. It had been amusing to go along with Joseph's plans and schemes, living off their wits, but now she was alone and she was too exhausted both mentally and physically to think clearly.

Finally giving in to her craving, she sniffed the powder from her hand, snuffling like a dog to ensure she took in the last grain. Now she would see what the day brought. If she managed to make enough money she would have a decent shot, then a meal.

There might be enough over for her to stay in a cheap boarding house over night and have a bath. She sighed in despair. It was unlikely she would make more than a few Euros. She had no choice. She would have to hand herself over to the American Embassy and ask for their help. It would mean having to confess her past crimes and she would probably end up in prison. At least in prison she would be able to keep herself clean and be fed regularly. They might even be willing to put her on a drug rehabilitation programme and she would be able to kick the disgusting and degrading habit that had been forced on her and ruined her life.

Over the six months she had spent in Athens she had considered that option on a number of occasions. Now she was so desperate that it was no longer an option but a necessity. She would rest a while; then make her way to the Embassy. Her leg began to cramp and she eased herself into a more comfortable position. If she could rid herself of this awful feeling of insects crawling over her body she might manage to sleep for a short while. The Embassy would not be open yet.

She could feel a cockroach on her foot and she tried to flick it away. Now there was one on her leg, creeping and crawling, tickling her with its feelers. She tried to brush away the one on her hand. Now she could feel them in her hair. She banged her head, time and again, against the wall to dislodge them.

They were behind her eyes – she could feel them pushing to get out. How had they got inside her? She wanted to scream, but if she opened her mouth they might enter her that way. Then she felt them, scratching to get a purchase, trying to climb up her throat. She could feel their hard bodies in her mouth and tried to spit them out. Everywhere, she could feel them everywhere. They were suffocating her, creeping around inside her brain causing incredible agony.

The museum guard poked her with his toe. 'Move on. You can't sit there and beg.'

Sorrell made no response and he kicked her harder. Slowly her body keeled over and she lay slumped on the ground. The guard looked at her in exasperation. This was all he needed. A dead body on the steps ten minutes before the museum was due to open and visitors already beginning to form a queue.

March 2006

Saffron mounted the steps to the witness stand with her knees trembling, despite the assurance of Mr Norton, Ranjit's defence lawyer, that she had nothing to worry about. He would not ask her leading questions or try to put words into her mouth.

She confirmed her name and address and waited whilst Mr Norton shuffled his papers, looked up and smiled at her.

'Mrs Patel, I have asked you to come to Court today to give everyone a clearer picture of your husband, Mr Ranjit Patel. He has been accused by the Prosecution of a premeditated murder, an act that he strongly denies. He had no motive for murdering his first wife whom he loved dearly. Now, Mrs Patel, I understand that you and Mr Patel met at the hospital where you both work?'

Throughout his trial Ranjit had sat with his head bowed, now he lifted it and looked at Saffron.

'Yes.' Saffron's voice was a whisper. She felt totally intimidated under her husband's gaze.

'Please speak up, Mrs Patel. You formed a relationship that subsequently led to marriage, am I right?'

'Yes.'

'During the time that Mr Patel courted you, did he make any reference to his first wife?'

'He told me she had died.'

'Did he say under what circumstances the lady had met her death?'

'He said she had returned to India for a family visit and died from cholera.'

'And you had no reason to doubt the validity of that statement?'

'No.'

'You have not been married very long, Mrs Patel. Now, during that time have you ever had a violent disagreement with your husband?'

'Not violent.'

'But you have had disagreements?'

'Yes.'

'At any time, during any of these disagreements, has Mr Patel raised his hand to you? Threatened you in any way physically?'

'No.'

'Thank you, Mrs Patel. You may step down.'

Thankfully Saffron returned to her seat in the court room.

The judge consulted with both lawyers and shook his head. 'We will take a recess and proceedings will recommence at ten tomorrow morning. The case for the Prosecution will be stated in the morning and Mr Norton can present his case for the Defence in the afternoon.'

'All rise.'

The court obeyed as the judge left for his Chambers.

The defence lawyer for Ranjit Patel rose to his feet, cleared his throat and shuffled his papers.

'You have heard the case put before you by the Council for the Prosecution against Mr Ranjit Patel. It is based on circumstantial evidence. There is no proof offered by them to substantiate the accusation that Mr Patel murdered his wife, Nandita Patel.

'Mr Patel has pleaded guilty to the unlawful disposal of human remains. Why, I hear you ask yourselves, should a doctor dispose of his wife's body if he has nothing to hide? Why not call another medical man and get a death certificate? I will tell you why Mr Patel did not do this.

'As you all know, Mr Patel is an eminent heart surgeon. He was liked and respected by his colleagues and they all speak highly of his operating skills. He has made no secret of the fact that he comes from a humble background. His father had a grocery store and was a poor man. Mr Patel had a burning desire to become a surgeon and there was no way his family could possibly afford to send him to England to study and gain the qualifications he needed.

'A wealthy landowner, a neighbour of the Patel family, heard about the problem. He agreed to finance the further education of the young man and a contract was drawn up between them. Mr Kavira agreed to pay for Mr Ranjit Patel to come to England and all his tuition fees on the understanding that upon his qualification he would commence repayment of the money until the debt was cleared.

'In addition Mr Patel was to marry Mr Kavira's younger daughter, Nandita. Mr Patel was quite amenable to the arrangement, and after he had qualified as a heart surgeon, he returned to his home in India and married the young lady, subsequently bringing her back to England with him. Mr Kavira also gave him the money to purchase a small property in a London suburb, again on the understanding that the expenditure would be repaid to him at a future date.

'Sadly the marriage foundered. Nandita Patel, as she was then, did not like England. Despite the couple being very much in love she could not adjust to the different way of life over here. Her husband was working long hours and she was alone and unhappy for most of the day and often some of the weekends. She sought consolation in drugs. For some time she managed to keep this hidden from her husband and when he finally found out he urged her to go for treatment. She refused.

'Mr Patel was in a dilemma. He loved his wife, but abhorred her habit. He could not force her to seek help. He cut down on his working hours so he was able to spend more time at the family home. To please her he began a renovation project on their kitchen, something he had promised when they had first moved in.

'Imagine, if you can, how he felt when he returned home after a stressful day in the operating theatre, to find his wife slumped in the chair, dead. He had a position of respect at the hospital and felt that to have his wife confirmed as a drug addict would taint his reputation. He could not risk asking for the attendance of a medical practitioner to certify the cause of her death. By pure coincidence, at this time he had some of the floorboards lifted in the kitchen. He panicked. There was a cavity beneath the floor. He wrapped his wife's body in polythene and placed it in the hole, packing it round with concrete.

'Mr Patel wrote to his relatives in India and fabricated a story about his wife having been hit by a bus and killed. There was no reason why they should not believe him. Tragic accidents happen every day of the week. If anyone in England asked after her he said she had returned to India and died from cholera. Again there was no reason why he should be disbelieved.

'These were not the actions of a cold-blooded, scheming, killer as the Prosecution would have you believe. If Mr Patel fell into that category, surely he would have left the country immediately and disappeared. He did not do so. He continued to live at the house for some considerable length of time before deciding it was impractical. He did not need a house, reminding him every day of the wife he had loved and cherished. His simple needs could be fulfilled by a small flat. He sold the house and moved.'

Saffron inadvertently let out a gasp of disbelief. Ranjit had told her their marriage had been far from happy.

'In the course of his work at the hospital he met a female doctor and struck up a relationship with her. With her he felt he could move on, have a second happy marriage and family life. They spent an idyllic week in Paris. He was invited to attend a conference and his wife enjoyed visiting places of interest in and around the city during the day. They extended their time over

358

there so Mr Patel could enjoy some of these visits with her over the weekend.

'Imagine his consternation when he arrived back at the hospital for work only to find that his first wife's brother was searching for him. He decided his only option was to go away for a few days. He did not feel able to tell his wife, it would be too traumatic for her. He did not want to inflict that kind of pain on her. Quietly he packed his clothes and left the house he shared with his wife and mother-in-law, planning to spend a few days anonymously in another town.

'Had he not seen a copy of the newspaper that reported that a body had been found beneath a house he would have returned within a week, made an excuse to his wife about his absence, and pleaded sickness for not performing his duties at the hospital. Once again, Mr Patel panicked. He decided he must leave England and subsequently booked a flight to Venezuela. He knew he would only be able to stay for thirty days without a visa. He did not apply to the Foreign Office for one, so he evidently proposed to return.

'Why should he transfer a large sum of money to a bank over there if he was planning to return, I hear you ask yourselves. He had no idea how much it would cost to live over there. He would simply move the money back to England when he returned. Your next question, no doubt, is how did he manage to have such a sum accumulated. He had been repaying Mr Kavira a minimal amount each month, planning to pay him one final instalment and clearing the debt forever.

'Why should he park his car at Gatwick airport if he knew his flight left from Heathrow? Mr Patel was under great strain. He booked himself into a small hotel for the night in the vicinity of Heathrow Airport and deposited his luggage. The previous week he and his wife had left the car at Gatwick car park and without thinking he returned there. It was not until after he had paid the fee that he realised his mistake. Rather than drive to the other airport he left his car where it was and returned to London by tube.

'You have heard the testimony given by his present wife. He made no secret of the fact that he was a widower when he commenced their association. Never once did he raise his hand to her or exhibit any form of violence towards her person. Mr Patel is not a violent man.

'The police have searched the drugs record at the hospital and found that on three occasions Mr Patel signed to record breakages of phials of diamorphine. These accidents happen. There are other entries signed by other doctors. It was just coincidence that three breakages happened in quick succession and at times when he happened to be on duty.

'You can see how remorseful my client is. I put it to you, members of the jury, that Mr Patel is innocent of murder. He acted foolishly, he admits that, and will take his punishment accordingly. He is no murderer. There was no evil intent behind his actions. He is a surgeon. He saves lives, he does not take them.'

Mopping his brow, Mr Norton resumed his seat. He did not believe Ranjit Patel's plausible explanation for the events, but he had been well paid to defend him and now it rested with the jury.

Detective Inspector Baker looked in despair at the Council for the Prosecution. He knew they had no proof that Ranjit had falsified the drugs register or administered the lethal dose of diamorphine to his wife. He just hoped the jury would take the circumstantial evidence into account and it would sow seeds of doubt in their minds. It was not the action of a normal man, particularly a doctor, to hide a body beneath his kitchen floor.

Saffron clenched her hands together and sat rigidly in her chair next to Marjorie. If they did not find Ranjit guilty of murder, would they at least sentence him to a term of imprisonment for unlawful disposal of human remains? She certainly did not want him to return home to their house that night and have to pretend relief that he had not been convicted of any crime.

Eventually the court was dismissed by the judge. The jury was still out and it was hoped they would have decided upon their verdict by the next morning.

The jury filed into the courtroom. Saffron desperately tried to read their faces for any sign of the verdict, but they averted their eyes from the public. She clutched at Marjorie's hand and was somewhat reassured by the squeeze she received.

'Members of the jury, have you reached a verdict?'

'We have, my lord.'

'And is this the verdict agreed by all of you?'

'Yes, my lord.'

The foreman of the jury handed a slip of paper to the clerk who passed it to the judge. The judge read it and frowned. He cleared his throat.

'Mr Ranjit Patel, the jury finds you not guilty of murder.'

Saffron gasped.

'You have admitted to the crime of unlawful disposal of human remains and as such I sentence you to five years detention. You will serve your time in an Open Prison as I do not consider that you are a danger to the public.'

Ranjit smiled complacently as he was led away, firmly handcuffed between two warders.

The press cameras clicked as Saffron and Marjorie left the court.

'Can you give us a statement, Mrs Patel?'

'How do you feel about the sentence your husband has been given?

'Were you expecting him to be convicted of murder?'

'How much do you want for your story?'

'Will you give us an exclusive? We'll make it worth your while.'

Horrified, Saffron elbowed her way through towards the kerb, Marjorie clinging to her arm.

'Mrs Patel. Mrs Patel. Please, I'm not the press. I am Mr Kavira.'

Saffron hesitated, then Marjorie propelled her onwards. Tariq Kavira caught up with them and stopped in front of her.

'Please, Mrs Patel. I just want to say how very sorry I am. I should like to apologise on behalf of my family.'

Saffron regarded him steadily. 'I don't think your family can be blamed for Ranjit's actions.'

'My father should not have broken the agreement with him.'

'You mean Ranjit doesn't owe him money?'

Tariq shook his head. 'Unfortunately he does owe him a great deal of money. The original agreement was for Ranjit to marry Sanya, my older sister. A wealthy suitor asked for her hand and my father agreed. He did not tell Ranjit. He altered the wording in the arrangement and Ranjit was forced to marry Nandita.'

'Surely he could have refused? The arrangement could not have been altered without his permission.'

'His family put pressure on him, and,' Tariq spread his hands, 'Ranjit was given an ultimatum. Repay your debt immediately or marry Nandita and repay it over a number of years. He had no option.'

Saffron looked at the man before her in horror and he refused to meet her gaze.

'I am truly sorry that you became involved, Mrs Patel.' Tariq turned and began to hurry along the street towards the tube station.

Marcus was enjoying himself. Over the past two months he had ferried Ourania, Marisa and Bryony to the shop in Aghios Nikolaos and had become accustomed to driving in Crete, dealing with the erratic driving he encountered each day.

Ourania and Marisa would spend the morning together, then after lunch Bryony would take Ourania's place whilst she visited her husband in hospital. Although Yannis had delayed his operation, due mainly to fear, he now appreciated being free from the excruciating pain he had suffered in his hip during the past year.

Marcus knew that now Yannis was able to drive again he would no longer be called upon to undertake the journey, but Giovanni had already mentioned a number of jobs that would need to be completed on the apartments before the season started. He knew he would enjoy undertaking the repairs and decoration, no longer spending his days driving from one appointment to another to try to sell insurance or settle claims. Despite his previous misgivings, he decided the move to Crete had been a success. It was certainly worth it to see Bryony looking so happy.

April 2006

Saffron entered the visitors' room nervously and looked to see where Ranjit was sitting. He looked at her arrogantly as she sat down opposite.

'And to what do I owe the honour of a visit from my wife?' he asked.

Saffron clenched her hands together tightly. 'I've come to tell you that I have started divorce proceedings. My lawyer has said you will be served with the papers within the next two weeks.'

Ranjit gave a thin smile. 'I do not intend to sign them.'

'Under the circumstances it will make no difference whether you sign or not. The divorce will go ahead. The jury may have believed that load of rubbish your defence lawyer presented to them, but I don't. Goodbye, Ranjit.' With her head held high, she walked across the room and requested the prison officer to let her out.

Martin watched her in surprise.

'Who's she?' asked Lorna. 'Do you know her?'

Martin shrugged. 'Never seen her before in my life,' he lied. 'Just wondered why anyone would bother to come for such a short visit. Now, tell me about the children. How's Tommy doing at school?'

Martin sidled up to Ranjit in the exercise yard. 'That was a short visit you had.'

Ranjit shrugged. 'It was a marriage of convenience on my part. I'm really not interested in her visiting me.'

'She's your wife?'

'What business is it of yours?'

'None. Just making conversation.'

Martin sat in his cell thoughtfully. He had taken little notice of Ranjit Patel before today, sharing in the jokes the other prisoners had made about placing your wife under the kitchen floor. Now he began to take the action as a personal affront to Saffron. He knew he had treated her badly, but that was no reason for someone else to do so.

The men had plenty of freedom to fraternise and Martin began to ask how they truly felt about Ranjit Patel. It seemed they all thought he had got away with murder and should have been in a high security prison.

'Might turn on one of us,' grinned Joe, a burly man, who had just started his sentence for receiving stolen goods.

'Could be a good idea to do something about it,' suggested Martin.

'Yeah? What are you suggesting?'

'Bit of a beating. Show him we know how to stand up for ourselves.'

Joe nodded slowly. 'We could arrange for a group of us to give him a going over. No one involved who's due for release soon. Don't want to wreck their chances. How much longer are you in for?'

'Eighteen months. So what if I get an extra six?'

'I'll sound out some of my mates. We've got to look out for each other after all.'

Ranjit took to standing alone whilst the other prisoners played football or chatted in small groups during their exercise time under the watchful eye of the guards. That his companions seemed to shun his company did not perturb him. Martin sidled over to where Ranjit was standing.

'Your wife coming to visit you again tomorrow?' he asked.

'I'm not expecting her.' Ranjit looked around warily as he realised more men were closing in around him.

Martin's fist shot out and he hit Ranjit squarely on the chin. 'She's worth more than murderous scum like you.'

Ranjit lay on the ground and Martin kicked him hard in the ribs. 'Stand up and fight like a man.'

Still Ranjit lay there and the other inmates added their kicks and blows. Martin and Joe began to move away, but Martin was seized by the prison officer who had blown his whistle to attract the attention of the other guards.

'You'll be charged with assault. I saw what happened. It was an unprovoked attack.'

Martin looked at the man lying on the ground, the other inmates continuing to beat him as the prison officers tried to rescue him.

'I really fancied her,' he said and winked at Joe as the officer led him away.

Detective Inspector Baker read the faxed report that he received from the prison. He would have to visit the woman. It would not be right for her to hear the news of her husband's death through the media. Personally, he was not sorry, feeling it was just desserts for the man.

Saffron answered the door with a worried frown. 'I wasn't expecting to see you again,' she remarked.

Tony Baker shook her hand. 'I felt we should call. May we come in?'

Saffron opened the door wider and led Tony and Elaine through to the lounge. Marjorie switched off the television. She would have to watch the news later as they had company.

The Detective looked ill at ease as he sat on the settee and waited until Saffron was seated also.

'I had a communication today from the prison where your husband was being held.'

Saffron looked at him in horror. 'He's not being released, is he?'

'No, I can assure you that will not happen. I wanted to speak to you personally, rather than you hear it first on the news.'

'What?' Saffron's throat felt dry with fear. What had Ranjit done now?

'During exercise time some of the other prisoners decided to pick a fight with your husband. I'm sorry to have to tell you that he has died as a result of his injuries.'

'Dead? Ranjit's dead?'

Tony Baker nodded. 'Obviously there will be media coverage. The reason he was in prison will be dragged up and re-examined by the press. I'm afraid they will probably be hounding you again for a few days.'

'But why would they want to pick a fight with Ranjit?'

'These things can happen in a prison. The inmates decide justice has not been done and take matters into their own hands.'

'But surely, the guards, they could have prevented it.'

'According to the report one man started the fight and the others joined in. Again, this is something that happens. Prison life is obviously mundane. Any small incident will be seized upon as a diversion.'

Saffron shook her head. 'I don't believe it.'

'There will be some formalities to go through, Mrs Patel. Obviously funeral arrangements will have to be made after the post mortem.'

'Post mortem?'

'The authorities have to ascertain the cause of his death. It may have been due to a blow that caused a head or internal injury or something as natural as a heart attack.'

'And if it was a heart attack?'

'His assailants will probably be accused of causing it'.

Saffron let out her breath. 'So how long will it be before I receive a death certificate?'

'No more than a few days. Is that a problem?'

Saffron frowned. 'Ranjit was not a Christian. I have no idea what kind of a funeral he would have wanted.'

'I believe most Indian religions prefer cremation.' Elaine spoke for the first time. 'I know Mr Kavira asked for his sister's remains to be cremated and he intended to take them back to India.'

'But what am I expected to do with the ashes?'

'The disposal of the ashes is always according to the wishes of the family.'

'Exactly. I am not his family. His family is in India. They should be notified. It should be what they want.' Saffron turned anguished eyes on the Inspector. 'I have no idea where they are.'

Elaine looked at Tony and he nodded.

'We may be able to help you there. When Mr Kavira returned to India we asked for his address. We have it on file.'

'May I have it?'

Tony pursed his lips. 'Can I give you a piece of advice, Mrs Patel? I think you should consult a solicitor and ask them to write to the family. It would be better if you were not involved personally.'

'Why not?' Saffron was genuinely puzzled.

'Mr Patel, as far as we can ascertain, did not have a current Will. As his wife, you are his next of kin and as such are entitled to inherit his estate. I believe Mr Patel owed a considerable sum to his father-in-law. If that money has been repaid there is no problem, but should the debt still be outstanding the family could place a claim against your inheritance.'

Saffron compressed her lips. 'The debt should be repaid if there is sufficient money. All I would expect is the money he withdrew from our joint account. That is rightfully mine. Anything more would be recompense for the other bills he accrued and I paid on his behalf.'

'Exactly. That is why I think you should place any communication with the family into the hands of a solicitor. You are not in a position to demand to see their accounts. They could tell you any figure they decided upon and you would not be able to disprove them. If necessary a solicitor can take out an injunction and subpoena all Mr Kavira's financial records. I am not suggesting that they would be dishonest, but I do feel you should safeguard yourself.'

Saffron frowned. 'Would I be able to use the same solicitor as I'm employing for my divorce?'

Tony looked at her sympathetically. 'Mrs Patel, you do not need a divorce. You are now a widow.'

'Oh!' Saffron shook her head. 'I haven't quite realised that yet. Of course I don't need a divorce; but what happens in the meantime? To – to Ranjit's body, I mean.'

'Arrangements can be made for it to stay in the morgue until you know the family's wishes. I don't want to rush you, Mrs Patel, as I realise this must have come as a great shock to you, but if you could consult a solicitor tomorrow and ask them to contact us I would very much appreciate it.'

Saffron nodded sombrely. 'I'll do that, Inspector. And thank you for taking the time to come and tell me.'

Saffron saw the Inspector and Elaine out of the house and sank back down on the settee.

'Oh, Saffie. How awful. You must feel terrible.'

Saffron rubbed her hand across her forehead. 'Do you know something, Marjorie? All I feel is the most tremendous relief. I'm free. I don't have to go through the ordeal of a divorce and I can finally make some plans to go to Crete and find my family again.'

May 2006

Saffron telephoned Bryony when she arrived home from the hospital. Over the ensuing months they had spoken regularly over the telephone. Their conversations had been stilted, neither of them able to feel relaxed and they had both avoided any mention of the personal subjects they wished to discuss face to face.

'Would it be convenient if I came over this month?'

'Of course. We'd be only too delighted.'

'I'd like Marjorie to come with me.'

'That's fine. What about your husband?'

'No, he won't be coming.'

'Provided you don't mind sharing a room with Marjorie, that's no problem.'

'Share a room?'

Bryony gave a gurgling laugh. 'Amazingly we are beginning to run out of space.'

'I thought we would stay in a hotel in Heraklion.'

'We wouldn't hear of it. You're family. You'll come and stay with us.' Bryony spoke firmly.

'I'm sure you won't want us under your feet the whole time, besides, I have promised Marjorie some sight seeing.'

'That's no problem. You won't be under our feet, I promise you. We have the car and can take you to far more places than you could ever visit on your own.'

'I don't know,' Saffron hesitated.

'We won't take no for an answer. Book your flight and let me know when you're arriving. We'll be there to meet you. I'm so excited. It's beautiful weather over here in May. Remember to bring your summer clothes and just something warmer for the evening. Do you swim? The swimming here is fantastic.'

Finally Saffron replaced the receiver and turned to Marjorie. 'She wouldn't hear of us staying in a hotel. She said we would have to share a room, but we were prepared to do that in a hotel. I do hope we actually like each other when we meet or it could turn into a nightmare two weeks.'

Saffron and Marjorie walked into the airport terminal at Heraklion. Once through passport control and having collected their luggage, Saffron hesitated.

'Do you think we'll recognise each other after all these years?'

'Maybe you should have made a placard with your name.'

'I wonder if they have thought of doing that.' Saffron looked around, then clutched Marjorie's arm. 'Yes, look, there's Bryony.'

She pointed to the small, plump woman standing next to a tall man who was holding aloft a piece of paper with Saffron's name printed on it. Despite the strands of grey that streaked Bryony's hair, she still had the slightly surprised look about her that Saffron remembered as a child. Now the moment had come Saffron felt frightened and tongue-tied.

'Go on,' Marjorie urged her. 'She obviously hasn't recognised you yet.'

Saffron walked towards the couple and placed her suitcase on the ground. 'Hello, Bryony.'

Bryony threw her arms around her half sister, hugging her so tightly that Saffron felt the breath leaving her body.

'This is wonderful. I'm so happy. So pleased you have finally come to see us. We've been waiting *hours* for you. I insisted we arrived early. I couldn't bear to think of you arriving and no one being here to meet you.'

Finally released Saffron drew a deep breath, she realised she had tears running down her cheeks and she brushed them away impatiently. 'This is Marjorie,' she managed to say.

Bryony shook Marjorie's extended hand. 'I'm so pleased to meet you. May I call you Marjorie? After all, you are my stepmother as well. Jeremy adopted Sorrell and me when he married mother. This is my husband, Marcus.' Bryony waved her hand in his direction. 'Marcus will take your luggage out to the car for you. Have you got everything?'

Saffron nodded. 'We only have one case each.'

They drove away from the airport and into the suburbs of Heraklion. It was an entirely different direction from the one Saffron had taken the previous year when she had visited.

'We're not going straight home,' Bryony informed them. 'I have some English friends who have a villa on the outskirts. I've arranged to go there and we can sit in their garden and talk before you get thrown into the family. I know once we arrive home everyone will want to talk to you and we won't have a minute to ourselves.'

Saffron nodded. She really had no option but to comply with Bryony's wishes.

Vanessa greeted them and led the way into her secluded garden at the rear of the house. A pale green umbrella was open over the table and matching chairs. A small dog emerged from the shade and barked at them. Saffron hesitated.

'He won't hurt,' Vanessa assured them. 'Once he's given you a sniff he'll settle down again. I'll bring you all a drink. What would you like? Fruit juice, wine or a cup of tea?'

'Tea, please.'

'And fruit juice for us,' added Bryony. 'Marcus and I are teetotal, unlike the rest of the family, so feel free to enjoy a glass of wine whenever you wish.'

Saffron sat down. Suddenly she felt drained. She wished they were on the beach and she could close her eyes in the sunshine.

Vanessa returned bearing a tray with plates of biscuits, olives, and fruit juice. 'Kettle's just about to boil,' she announced as she placed cups on the table along with the other items. 'I did offer to get lunch for you, but Bryony insisted you would have eaten on the 'plane and she didn't want to spoil your appetite for your evening meal. Won't be a second.' She disappeared back into the kitchen as the shrill whistle of the kettle could be heard.

'I don't recommend olives with tea,' smiled Bryony as she popped one into her mouth, cleaned off the flesh, and spat the stone into her hand. 'Somehow they just don't mix.'

Vanessa returned with a teapot and milk. 'I'll leave you to it,' she smiled. 'You know where everything is, Bryony, if you want refills.'

Marjorie looked at the table before her. 'If it were not for this beautiful sunshine I would think we were still in England,' she remarked. 'I hadn't expected a pot of tea and biscuits.'

'I thought it could be a good idea if we came here first and had a chat. There was so much I couldn't tell you over the telephone. All I ask is that you don't tell Grandma any of this. She would be so distressed. The rest of the family know, but we never discuss it. Grandma speaks Greek and English, so it's very hard to have a private conversation if she is around – and she isn't deaf, so you have to be careful.'

Saffron smiled and took a biscuit from the plate. Lunch on the 'plane had not been particularly satisfying and she knew they would probably be eating late.

'You asked about mother first, of course,' continued Bryony. 'She died over ten years ago.' She held up her hand as Saffron was about to interrupt. 'Let me tell you from the beginning. There was an almighty row between mother and Jeremy at Thanksgiving and that was when he left, taking you with him. Within a few days Sorrell and I were sent back to boarding school and I never saw mother again. Sorrell told me mother was expecting another baby and that it wasn't Jeremy's. She'd gone off to Florida with her new man and we were told when she had settled out there she would send for us. She never did. Whenever I asked Grandma, she said mother had just moved, or it wasn't a convenient time to visit.

Eventually I just stopped asking. I decided mother didn't want us. I felt so abandoned. Grandma and Grandpa were very good and kind to us, but they didn't really want two young girls around. They were both so engrossed in Grandpa's research. I felt I had lost my family.' Bryony's voice broke at the painful recollections.

'The only place I really felt secure was at school and I asked to stay on an extra year. I had a good friend there, Sabena, and she used to ask me to her home some weekends. That was where I first met Marcus.' Bryony smiled at her husband. 'He's Sabena's older brother. I thought he was gorgeous right from the start and would try to wangle an invitation to stay in the hope that he would be home.'

Saffron looked at Bryony's husband. She could not imagine him being gorgeous, even as a young man. His long, mournful face reminded her of a Bloodhound.

Bryony waved her hand. 'Anyway, that's getting away from the point. Sorrell left home to go travelling. I only ever saw her once after that. She turned up at my apartment, shortly before Marcus and I were married, and asked if she could stay for a couple of nights as her apartment had been flooded by a burst water tank. When I returned home from work she had gone. I was rather upset with her, I'll not go into that, but I made no attempt to find her. I did hear that some years ago she was working as a prostitute to support her drug habit. I have no idea where she is now.'

Bryony selected another olive and Saffron waited until she had disposed of the stone. 'Anyway, after Marcus and I were married I continued to visit Grandma and Grandpa. Occasionally I would meet up with my Aunt Elena and I always made a point of visiting if Uncle Andreas and Laurie came down from New York. Grandpa died, well, just faded away, really, but Grandma decided to stay on in the house for a number of years. After her second hip replacement she realised she could no longer manage alone and moved to a Care Home.

'Unexpectedly, I had a 'phone call. It was from a girl called Christabelle. She had no idea I was her half sister, she thought I was one of her mother's friends. She was calling to say that mother was dead. She said mother had been murdered and there was a man being held in custody. She wouldn't discuss any details with us, she said it was too traumatic for her and we understood how she must be feeling.'

Saffron's eyes opened wide in horror.

'We visited her and tried very hard to draw her into the family. Mother had never told her about any of us and she thought she was alone in the world. We didn't tell Grandma. We were rather worried about the effect the news could have on her. Christabelle said she wanted to get to know people gradually. We kept trying to make arrangements to meet and she would always have an excuse. She was out of town on a modelling assignment, she had an appointment with her agents, all sorts of reasons.'

Bryony pulled an out of date magazine from her bag, folded it to a certain page, and handed it to Saffron. 'She was very beautiful and became very famous.'

Saffron looked at the advertisement and nodded.

'I expect you heard the news about her?'

Saffron frowned. 'What news? When?'

'Last year. The beginning of August, when she was arrested.'

'I do.' Marjorie spoke for the first time.

'Then you can tell Saffron the gist of it later. I only know what was reported by the media at the time. Christabelle was arrested and was going to be charged with murdering our mother and a number of other people. After psychiatric tests she was declared insane. They gave it some flower name. What was it Marcus?'

'Narcissistic Personality Disorder.'

Saffron licked her dry lips. 'What happened to her?'

'She was placed in a prison mental hospital. We went to visit her after the hurricane and the doctor in charge said she had met with an accident during the storm and died.' Bryony spread her hands. 'Do you understand why we have never told Grandma any of this?'

'Of course. It's quite terrible.' Saffron shook her head.

'You realise now why I wanted to tell you in person and not over the phone?'

'I appreciate it, Bryony. You could have just told me our mother had died and left it at that. When I've had time to think about it I'll probably want to ask you for some more details, but I'll make quite certain Grandma isn't around when I do.'

Bryony sat back and selected another olive. 'More tea?' she asked and drained her glass of orange juice.

Marjorie held out her cup and pointed to Saffron's. 'Yours will be cold by now.'

Marcus rose. 'I'll get rid of this and you can have a fresh cup.' He smiled at Saffron and she suddenly realised why Bryony had thought he was gorgeous. His whole face changed, the smile lighting up his eyes and his mournful expression disappearing.

'I've been talking all the time,' apologised Bryony. 'Now you must tell me about yourself and all you have been doing over the years. You're a doctor, obviously the only one in the family who inherited the medical brains.'

Saffron took a deep breath and began to tell Bryony about Ranjit.

Bryony reached out and squeezed Saffron's hand. 'You poor thing. How dreadful for you. No wonder you didn't want to talk about it on the telephone. What will you tell Grandma?'

'I hadn't actually thought about it.' Saffron frowned. 'I think it would probably be best to say that he was set upon by a gang of ruffians and died as a result.' She shrugged. 'It's true, really.

She doesn't have to know he was in prison at the time and the reason why.'

'I think you're right,' Bryony nodded emphatically. 'We'll keep our dark family secrets to ourselves.' She looked at her watch. 'We ought to go. I want to get home before the others return from the shop. That way you can meet the family in two halves, rather than all of them at once. The bathroom is through there if either of you want it. We've about an hour's drive in the car. I'll let Vanessa know we're leaving.'

Saffron sat back in the car and closed her eyes. Her head was reeling with the information Bryony had given her. Maybe it had been a bad idea to write to her grandmother and try to find her family.

'We're nearly there.'

Saffron opened her eyes. Had she actually fallen asleep? She looked out of the car window.

'I know where I am. These are the apartments where I stayed last year, Marjorie.'

'You stayed here?' Bryony swivelled round from the front seat and looked at Saffron in amazement.

Saffron nodded. 'I found it a bit difficult to visit some of the places I'd planned, but I loved it, and the people were so kind and welcoming.'

'Did you buy Uncle Yannis's book?'

'Of course. I started reading it on the way home on the 'plane, but I never managed to finish it. What with Ranjit's trial and catching up on my work I just never got round to it again.'

Bryony's eyes danced with amusement. 'If you had you would have realised you had already met some of your relations.'

'We're home,' Marcus announced as he swung the car into the driveway to Yannis's house.

to be continued...

Authors Note

I do hope readers have enjoyed the sixth book in the saga of the Cretan family.

Now I have to take a short break to allow time to move on. The family ages, John has to do his National Service and Nicola has to decide on a career for herself.

Will John and Nicola decide their lives should be spent together? Does John achieve his ambition to become a photographer? Are Bryony and Marcus happy living in Crete? Does the business thrive or fail due to the recession? Will Saffron visit regularly? Will she finally find the right man and have a happy marriage?

There are so many questions to answer in book seven.

Of course, I do not plan to stop writing. I have just started MANOLIS. Remember him? The fisherman who fell in love with Flora. What does he do during the war years? Does he hide or help the Resistance? Where does he get the money to buy Yiorgo's house?

Hopefully his life will become an 'open book' and available in November 2010.

First book

The compelling story of Yannis, who comes from the village of Plaka on the island of Crete. He attends school in the town of Aghios Nikolaos and gains a scholarship to the Gymnasium in Heraklion.

Whilst in Heraklion, he is diagnosed with leprosy, shattering his dreams of becoming an archaeologist. He is admitted to the local hospital for treatment and subsequently transferred to the hospital in Athens. The conditions in the hospital are appalling: overcrowding, lack of amenities, poor food, and only basic medication. The inmates finally rebel, resulting in their exile to Spinalonga, a leper colony just across the water from Yannis's home village.

The book tells the heart-rending account of his life on the small island, his struggle for survival, his loves and losses, along with that of his family on the mainland from 1918 to 1979.

Beryl Darby

ANNA

The second book in a continuing saga

Second book

In this, the second book in a continuing saga, Anna is left to care for her invalid mother and her sister's children when the Germans invade Crete. A battalion of Italian soldiers is billeted in the village to prevent a seat of resistance being formed on Spinalonga, the leper village opposite the village.

There are resistance workers in the area.

How will she protect strong-willed Marisa from the Italian soldiers, and impulsive Yannis from joining the resistance?

Unwillingly she becomes involved with the resistance and has to draw on all her resources and ingenuity to fool the Italians, finally risking her life to save the man she loves.

Beryl Darby

GIOVANNI

The third book in a continuing saga of a Cretan family

Third book

Yannis has become a successful businessman with a number of hotels. He has taken his resourceful nephew, Giovanni, into partnership. Giovanni is full of ideas to improve the business. He has only one failing – he is susceptible to a pretty face.

His younger brother, Joseph, is resentful of Giovanni's success and determined to avenge himself. With the help of a beautiful woman, he schemes and plans to bring about his brother's disgrace. His final act of revenge has dire results for all involved.

Marianne, Annita's granddaughter, visits Athens with her friend and meets relatives who were previously unknown to her. Elizabeth finds the city romantic in many ways. Later they both visit Crete, which has unexpected consequences for Marianne.

Yannis's loyalty to his extended family saves all of them from shame and humiliation.

Fourth book

Joseph has moved to Rhodes. He lives and works in a warehouse that is a centre for drug distribution and is responsible for taking the money to Turkey each week. He becomes over ambitious and has plans to become a wealthy man.

Sorrell is searching for Joseph to wreak her revenge. She accepts the offer of help from a millionaire hotelier and enjoys a life of idleness and luxury before she finds herself in the clutches of a ruthless criminal. She is both used and abused. Fearing for her life she finally has to ask Joseph for help and protection.

Events take an unexpected turn and a number of people find they are under the scrutiny of the police. Both Joseph and Sorrell are able to evade the law, but they are unable to evade their ultimate fate at the hands of their associates.

Beryl Darby

CHRISTABELLE

The fifth book in a continuing saga of a Cretan family

Fifth book

Christabelle is beautiful and highly successful in her chosen career as a model. She has also inherited her talent for acting from her unknown father. Everyone is charmed by her; but there is an evil side to her nature. Anyone who upsets Christabelle regrets it. She takes her revenge to extremes, becoming more confident in her actions each time. She is convinced she is invincible.

As she travels across Europe a trail of fatal accidents follow her. It finally takes subterfuge and John's talent for photography for justice to be done.